TEST OUTCAST

First published in Great Britain by
PELHAM BOOKS LTD
52 *Bedford Square*
*London, W.C.*1
1970

7207 0381 6

Set and printed in Great Britain by
Tonbridge Printers Ltd, Peach Hall Works, Tonbridge, Kent
in Baskerville eleven on thirteen point on paper supplied by
P. F. Bingham Ltd, and bound by James Burn
at Esher, Surrey

CONTENTS

ILLUSTRATIONS

ACKNOWLEDGEMENTS

The Author's thanks are due to the following whose photographs are reproduced in this book: *Press Association:* 1, 16, 17. *W. A. C. Fownes:* 3, 4, 11, 14. *Central Press Photos:* 8. *Sport & General:* 9, 12, 15, 18. *Southern Newspapers Ltd.:* 10, 13.

1 *Growing Up in Barbados*

Wine, Women and Song! I know they go well together but the combination sounds out of place at the start of a cricketing book. At least, it may seem like that to many people but not to me. Every time I hear the expression I am reminded of the greatest moment in my cricketing life – the day in 1961 when Hampshire held off a challenge from Yorkshire to win the Championship title. Our success shocked the cricketing world, and no wonder!

It was Hampshire's first Championship in their 98-year-old history, and the magnitude of our performance was rather like dear old Fulham walking off with the European Cup.

When we had made sure of the championship by beating Derbyshire in the last but one match of the season our skipper, the old Etonian Colin Ingleby-Mackenzie uttered those now famous remarks on wine, women and song.

He was being interviewed for a television news programme by a commentator who knew little of Colin's reputation as a leg-puller.

'What has been the recipe for your success?' he asked Colin.

Keeping a straight face but with a gleam in his eye, Colin answered, 'Wine, Women and Song!'

The interviewer accepted it as a genuine reply and asked Colin if he had laid down any special rules for his team during the long summer months of battle. 'Only that they should be in bed by breakfast time.'

Colin was joking, of course, but plenty of people were prepared to take his statement seriously. Ever since then Hampshire players have had to live with his words, one way or another.

I could not have cared less what Colin said that night, especially after wading into the champagne. That day, as I say, was the most memorable of my life. It meant so much to me and I had come a long way to realise such a moment of glory.

Almost 4,000 miles away, from the 166 square miles of Barbados in the Caribbean, that magnificent little island which has produced so many cricketers, among them the almost legendary triumvirate of Walcott, Weekes and Worrell; those menacing fast bowlers Hall and Griffith, and the incomparable Gary Sobers.

To play for Hampshire I had turned down the chance of a long test career in a West Indies side which was to become one of the most entertaining and popular ever known under the shrewd captaincy of that wonderful person, the late Sir Frank Worrell.

I have always regretted not being able to play for the country of my birth since I turned my back on test cricket at the ripe old age of 21. Yet Hampshire's victory in the Championship more than made up for the disappointment.

I suppose I was born to be a cricketer from the day I entered this world on April 25, 1930 on a sugar plantation 10 miles outside Bridgetown – a plantation the MCC team pass every time they set foot on the island, travelling from the Airport to their hotel in the centre of the capital.

Apparently there have always been Marshalls on the island, looking after the sugar crop. How or why we went there I have never been able to discover.

Recently a member of the family tried to discover our

origin. He got as far back as 1750 and there were Marshalls on the island then. I suppose that as Marshall is a Scottish name we came from north of the border, but whether we left the Highlands of our own free will or were cast away I have never found out.

I consider myself lucky to have been born in Barbados. For no person who has cricket in his blood could possibly wish for a better start in life. The conditions are ideal, everybody is cricket-mad and the opportunities are there for a youngster who has more than average ability.

I was the last of a family of five children, consisting of four boys and one girl, who were born on various plantations throughout the island.

My father was a planter all his life. My eldest brother is still planting in Barbados and the rest of the family also live in the Caribbean.

Although he was below average himself as a player, my father was mad about the game and gave me every encouragement to take up the sport. Here I believe I was fortunate in being last of the line. I had more freedom and opportunity as a youngster to learn the art of the game than my brothers who, at an early age, had to turn their minds away from sport and concentrate on the needs of the plantation. I never had such worries.

As a boy I always seemed to have either a bat or a ball in my hand and on a cricket-crazy island such as Barbados I was never short of volunteers to give me a game.

In fact, we went through an evening ritual of playing cricket on a vast lawn rear of the house. My family were also keen players of tennis but as my appetite – and that of my elder brother, Norman, who also played for the West Indies – for the game of cricket increased, tennis was pushed to one side.

Indeed, eventually the tennis courts on the lawn were transformed into three cricket pitches. I doubt if you could have found better wickets in any other part of the globe. They were beauties, without a blade of grass in sight. They were lovingly watered and then rolled while still wet to produce fast, true strips on which batsmen could flourish. We used the first one night, another the next night and so on. Work on the plantation finished at four o'clock every afternoon and within a few minutes the stumps would be up and a match in progress. Workers would join in with my family and at times there were as many as thirty of us playing on this lawn.

Being the youngest I suppose I was treated a little more sympathetically than the others because they always allowed me to go in first. That was where indulgence ended. If I was out, there was no question of giving me another chance.

I remember an occasion when I was about nine or ten, I padded up first, went in and was bowled first ball. I was so angry I threw the bat away, turned and kicked over the wicket before running, howling into the house some ninety or a hundred yards away. If I thought this would get me another chance I was mistaken.

Bad sportsmanship was something my father would never tolerate. He summoned me and gave me the sternest of rebukes. 'Play the game and expect no favours,' he said.

I knew from that day that if I wanted to bat I would have to survive by my own ability.

I made up for that show of petulance later that same year. Again I went in first and my brothers and the other workers treated me gently at first. They bowled accurately but there was little fire or venom in their deliveries but after I had been batting half an hour, they became irritated and began putting a lot more effort into their attack. The deliveries came down faster and shorter but I was 'king' that night. The harder and faster they bowled, the more I thumped them back. I stayed all evening and it was dark before they finally called off the attempt to get my wicket.

During the day-time, nothing was allowed to interfere with

the work of getting the fields ready for the planting of the sugar cane on which the island depended for its existence. Nevertheless, I still managed to get in some cricket. An odd job boy was employed around the plantation buildings. He was about six or seven years my senior and a useful cricketer. What odd jobs he was supposed to undertake I never knew because we seemed to spend most of the time playing cricket together. Looking back from this distance in time, I am more convinced than ever that my father employed this boy to provide me with a cricketing playmate and not as one of the plantation staff.

This cricket on the lawn gave me my basic training in the game. Under such ideal conditions nobody could really fail to gain a sound knowledge of the fundamentals in the art of batting. It also meant that I led a very outdoor life. I could swim almost as soon as I could walk. Although I hated running I was nimble on my feet. Such open air life obviously helps a person to become a natural athlete which explains why teams from the West Indies, South Africa and Australia always appear to be more natural and graceful in their movements than English-born cricketers whose formative years as players are limited by cold damp winter months when little practice is possible and certainly not out-of-doors.

Although I met with the best of conditions on that plantation lawn, I was also fortunate to have the time and opportunities to experience other types of wickets which helped me considerably when I came to play in English conditions.

When my father realised that I had a little more ability than the average youngster he put down a concrete wicket on the edge of the lawn. This was as true as any pitch in the world can be and I am sure it gave me confidence to play my shots. We used a variety of balls—a proper cricket ball, a rubber ball and a tennis ball. Keeping a rubber ball or a tennis ball on the ground when making a stroke is a very difficult thing to do and I used to spend hours perfecting the art.

In addition, between two buildings in the yard which were about forty yards apart, we put down a strip of matting on a tarmac surface. I spent hours playing on it with the odd-job helper and again this taught me to play straight.

The ball turned quite appreciably on the matting and this gave me a distinct advantage over other young players because they had little opportunity to practise batting on a turning wicket.

These tussles with the odd job boy were always strictly fair. There was never any question of my batting all day while he delivered the ammunition for me to fire away. I did my proper share of bowling. When I was out, I was out (father's early strictures had been duly noted!) and then it was my turn to try and get him out. So I had to bowl properly.

In those days I did a little of everything as a bowler. I started by trying to bowl quick which I think every youngster should do. Only in that way is a boy likely to learn to develop a natural action and rhythm. Once he has mastered this, he can specialise. If a player wants to be an off-spin bowler I think it is wrong to make him start bowling off-spin from the very beginning.

With the aid of the matting wicket I tried my hand at spinners. In those days I favoured the leg break and grew quite proficient at it. I could pitch on a length and turn it but I never mastered the ability to bowl the googly. A leg-spinner without a googly is like a boat without a rudder – no good at all.

Eventually I became an off-spinner which was to help me gain a place both in the school and the local club sides in Barbados but I had to give this up about six years ago because of an arthritic condition in the joint of the second finger of my right hand. I have been unable to curl that finger round a ball ever since.

Another advantage I enjoyed over English youngsters was the opportunity of playing against grown men, some of whom had played for Barbados, others of International experience, before I had entered my teens. This was because of the set-up of cricket on the Island.

When playing for my school I was given the chance of taking part in the system of club cricket in Barbados.

The set-up there is very much like the one in Australia. We had a number of clubs which were split into divisions. The first division contained the best players on the island, including the Barbados players when they were not engaged in a first class match.

It meant that if a youngster was good enough ten or fifteen years ago to play for his club in the first division he could, quite possibly, find himself batting against Wes Hall or Charlie Griffith. If he was a bowler, he might well have seen somebody like Seymour Nurse or Conrad Hunte in his sights down at the batting crease. Such experiences either made or broke the youngster – if he was good enough to survive them Barbados had another 'find' for the future.

I was only 12 years old when my school thought I was good enough to play in their first team which played in the second division of the league. We were playing Empire, one of the oldest established clubs on the island and the opposition consisted of grown-up men. To give you an idea of the standard, players such as Martindale, Weekes and Worrell played club cricket for Empire.

I shall always remember being driven to town from home that morning, a little boy of twelve going to play cricket against grown-up men in his first competitive game at Bank Hall, the home of the Empire club. At that stage it possessed the fastest wicket on the island and probably one of the fastest in the world. In my hands I clutched a new pair of boots given to me by my father, and a brand new pair of shorts.

I soon discovered that I was the only player on either side not in full length trousers!

My start was not crowned by glory. I was out for a duck. These matches were played on two Saturday afternoons and I had to wait another seven days before the second innings and a chance to make up for my first innings failure.

I did a little better but not much. I was out for four, although I stayed around at the wicket for almost half an hour. I had the ability to survive, even to play straight, but I did not have the strength to get the ball off the square.

That happened to be the second-to-last match of the season. I did not play in the last game and I can still recollect the feeling of bitter disappointment I experienced at the news that I had been dropped.

Still, time was the great healer and the following year I was given a further chance. I suppose I was still three or four years ahead of my time because most of the others who made up the school first eleven were in their late teens.

In that first match when I made my inglorious start in senior competitive cricket, I had batted at No. 8. The following season I was moved to No. 5 and then, because of a chance remark, I became an opener. I have stayed there ever since until Hampshire signed Barry Richards two seasons ago and I thought it better to revert to the middle order.

Half-way through that second season playing for the school we ran into a crisis over the opening position. We were not getting the starts we needed to build a foundation to our innings, which was hardly surprising, considering the strength of the opposition we came across. Three or four players who were tried as opening batsmen did not make a success of the position and we came to one period when nobody wanted to go in first.

Although the ball does not swing for any length of time in the West Indian conditions it moves about a little for the first five or six overs. These players kept asking: 'why should we go in when the ball is moving and the rest of you have the advantage of magnificent conditions?'

The swinging ball never worried me, so I volunteered for the role.

Fortunately, I did quite well and from that moment I always considered myself an opening batsman and I have never really wanted to bat anywhere else. Although I did not know it at the time, my chances of opening regularly over the next three or four years were to be severely limited because of the war.

Organised cricket in the West Indies almost came to a stop but not, as in England because of the bombing and the war effort. Our reason was much more basic. We ran out of cricket balls!

2 *First Class Debut at Fifteen!*

I was lost without cricket. During those wartime days I went anywhere just to get a game, to feel a bat in my hand. Much of the time I spent at the club ground where I could always find somebody willing to bowl at me. Being a schoolboy I was able to get to the ground in the early afternoon and have long sessions in the nets before the 'workers' arrived.

My interest in first-class cricket was heightened during those early war years. Although major competitive cricket had been severely restricted there was still some taking part. Each season Barbados would play two matches against Trinidad. One season the matches would be in Barbados, the next year our island team would travel to Trinidad.

The islands were only 200 miles apart and the rivalry between the two sides has always been intense. By this time brother Norman, who is six years older than me, was playing regularly for Barbados. My father had taken me to see one match between Barbados and Trinidad early in 1939 and I had seen my brother play a couple of times in the 1940's.

Like any other cricket-mad youngster, I marvelled at the skill of the greatest batsmen in action and attempted to pick up tips which I could adapt to my own game.

Each December the Barbados Cricket Association invited possible candidates for the island side to practice sessions and games held at their headquarters at the Kensington Oval.

Much to my surprise and delight I was asked to go along in December, 1945. I was still only 15. I could hardly believe it. In fact, when I was first told the news I thought it was a joke but the invitation was serious enough. Even so, the full implications that the Barbados cricket selectors thought I might be good enough one day to play for the Island, took some while to sink in. Naturally, I thought those days were still three or four years away. Little was I to know what would happen.

About 30 cricketers from this island were invited to participate in these sessions and I felt quite pleased with my performance in the practice games. In one innings I made 72 and in the next I scored 80.

On the strength of those two knocks I found myself selected in the island squad to go to Trinidad in January 1946 for the only two first-class games to be played in the Caribbean.

I expected to go along purely as a passenger. I reasoned that the Barbados Cricket Association were giving me a chance to sample the atmosphere of big time cricket which could serve me well in the future.

I am sure this is all they had in mind when they announced the 14 names but things did not work out that way. On the way over Frank Worrell developed 'flu and Roy Edwin Marshall was tossed into first-class cricket while still a schoolboy of 15!

I was overwhelmed by my selection. To think that I was to play alongside International players. Such things happened in fiction and in dreams but rarely in reality.

The Barbados side abounded with talented players. We had George Carew, already a West Indies Test player, Everton Weekes who was just beginning to make his presence felt, although he was not fully established at the time; Clyde Walcott and his brother, Keith; a fast bowler named E. A. V. Williams who toured England with the West Indies in 1939.

My brother Norman was with me and the side was skippered by Tom Pierce, now President of the West Indies Board of Control.

Trinidad were able to produce just as impressive a list of names, including the two Stollmeyers, Gerry Gomez, Prior Jones, Kenny Trestrail, Lance Pierre and Wilfred Ferguson, a leg-spinner who toured Australia.

The match was played on matting at the Queen's Park Oval in Port of Spain, the largest cricket ground in the West Indies and one of the most beautiful, set against a background of the mountain chain which runs along one side of the island.

Matting is one of the easiest surfaces to bat on, if you have the experience. At the same time it does encourage spin and, feeling as nervous as I did, I stood no chance.

To help convey how I felt, let me say it was like a 15-year-old English schoolboy being called up for his county debut in a match involving Yorkshire and Surrey, each of them having half a dozen players with Test experience.

I batted at No. 8. At least I was fortunate to go in when my brother Norman was at the wicket. The sight of him gave me some encouragement, although he told me afterwards he has never seen anybody so nervous in all his life. Against me was the fact that Trinidad had a leg spinner on at both ends on this matting wicket. Talk about leading a lamb to the slaughter!

To add to my confusion I had been coached in the dressing room by my team mates and George Carew, in particular, on how to combat the fast bowlers. The new ball had become due while I was waiting for my turn and they were all convinced Trinidad would take it straight away in an attempt to polish off our tail.

Instead, Trinidad delayed taking it. No sooner had I got in than I gave a chance against Ferguson's leg spin off the second or third ball I faced. I was hopelessly beaten and the ball flew to slip. Fortunately he muffed the chance.

I did manage to get one run from Ferguson off the edge. I sneaked another single off the other leg spinner which took me back to Ferguson's end where I promptly gave another catch. This time slip made no mistake.

My performance must have looked worse to the onlookers because brother Norman – trying to be kind and in an attempt to give me confidence – started lashing out to show that the leg spinners could be hit. I finished with two runs and he ended up with about 80. That was my only innings. On those wickets and with batsmen of the Walcott, Weekes class around, it was not often that we had a chance of a second innings.

For the second time in my life I had made a mess of a debut. First as a 12-year-old in the school side and now as a 15-year-old playing for Barbados.

Naturally, I was not surprised when I was left out of the side for the return game the following week. Instead of playing, I was given the opportunity of watching one of the finest partnerships anybody could wish to see. Frank Worrell had recovered from 'flu and took my place and, with Walcott, he proceeded to tear the Trinidad attack into shreds. Seldom can bowlers have suffered such indignities. The pair compiled the then highest stand in the history of first-class cricket with their unfinished partnership of 574. Walcott made 314 and Worrell 255.

Their batting was magnificent to watch. Seeing the way that they went for their strokes, the technique they used in reaching the ball, steering it through the gaps and displaying all the other facets of batting did me more good than actually playing out in the middle. I sat enthralled from the first to the last moment of their partnership.

Thanks to these two, Barbados, at one stage looked like gaining their first victory over Trinidad in Port of Spain for many, many years. We failed because of another fine innings, this time by Gerry Gomez who scored an undefeated double century in Trinidad's second innings.

I didn't spend *all* the match watching from the boundary. One of our players was taken ill and I was on the field throughout the entire Trinidad's second innings. When the final hour came we needed just two more wickets to win the match but failed to take them.

It was a great disappointment to us all, especially as one wicket was that of Lance Pierre. To give a clue as to his ability with the bat he managed only two first-class runs throughout the whole tour when the West Indies came to England in 1950. Both of those were off the inside edge, one against Kent and one against Yorkshire. The other wicket belonged to a batsman who was even more of a 'rabbit' than Lance!

A further disappointment awaited me on the trip. We were due to finish with a one day match at Point-a-Pierre. This would have been an ideal match to have blooded me for first-class cricket. Unfortunately for me, I got sun-stroke when fielding during the Trinidad second innings and spent the match in bed.

That is the story of my entry into first-class cricket in 1946. Another three years passed before I was to get a second chance. Meanwhile I had to come down to earth and go back to my school-time cricket with the Lodge School to further my education in the demands of the game.

They were three of the most miserable years of my life. With the Lodge School I played in the first division in the leagues against senior players and did well. Well enough, in my opinion, to have warranted another chance in the Barbados side before 1949.

The Barbados selectors obviously didn't think so and I shall always remember the words of brother Norman at that time.

He told me 'If you are good enough, you'll get your

chance. Maybe not as quickly as you want or if you were being pushed into the side by somebody with influence. But you'll get there in the end.'

I must admit that I had one ulterior motive in making runs for my Lodge School side or for the Wanderers Club side which I had joined.

With two or three of the other lads I used to go into Bridgetown on a Saturday evening to the cinema. I had passed my driving test and it was always much easier to persuade my father to let me have the car if I made forty or fifty runs. If I was out for a duck I knew there was not the slightest chance of getting the car. That meant a ten mile walk there and back!

Going to the pictures was a comparative luxury in those days. During the war when petrol was rationed I was virtually confined to the plantation because my father could not afford the petrol from his weekly allowance to go into town.

Looking back now, I suppose I would have been very fortunate to have made the Barbados side in the late forties. After all, there was great competition for places and, with the three W's around, there wasn't great scope for other batsmen.

In fact, it was only when some of our best players went to India with the West Indies team that I got my second opportunity in 1949. John Goddard was captaining the West Indies side and took with him Weekes, Walcott and Carew.

During my three years in the 'wilderness' I had been invited to the December trials of the Barbados Cricket Association but at that period football was taking up a lot of my time at school. When these trials were held I was usually out of form.

I left school when I was 18 and got a job in town as a salesman with an import company and this left me much more time to concentrate on cricket. The following season the Wanderers Club won the first division championship for the first time in twenty-five years.

This probably had a lot to do with Barbados inviting me

for trials again in December 1948. This time I was successful and I made the side to play against Trinidad in January, 1949.

I still had to work, even though I was playing cricket, spending two hours in the office up until ten o'clock before going to the ground for the match. This did nothing to calm my nerves but, fortunately in a way, we lost the toss and had to field.

At least it gave me a chance of getting the feel of the game before I had to bat and I received considerable help from my captain, Tom Pierce. Obviously he could tell I was nervous and although I was an off-spin bowler of no special ability, he brought me on as first change while the Trinidad opening pair were still together.

I'd like to think it was a tactical move but I am sure that Tom was just being kind to me, getting me into the game and doing his best to make me feel at home.

Surprisingly the move worked and I was able to split the opening pair of Simpson Guillen and Ganteaume – who was later to play for the West Indies. My first couple of overs were rubbish, a succession of half volleys but then I began to pitch a length. On those wickets it is possible to spin the ball so much that instead of breaking back from the off, the off-spinner can go the other way. I managed to produce one and Guillen gave a chance to second slip trying to drive. The catch was missed but in my next over, the ball must have hit something outside the off-stump and it turned, beat him completely and took middle. I had taken my first wicket in first-class cricket and most of my nervousness melted away after that.

Trinidad collapsed and, despite a century partnership lower down the order, they were all out 40 minutes before close that night.

By this time I was an established opening batsman. Charlie Taylor, who was never far short of Test class, and I managed to survive the remainder of play. The next day we took part in a stand which almost reached 300 before we were separated. Charlie scored 160 while I made 149. So, in my second first-class match, I had made a century.

That was my only innings in the first game and in the second match I managed to score another century, making 110 in the first innings, followed by 57 in the second.

On the strength of those three performances I was tipped as a possibility for the third opening batsman position in the West Indies party to tour England in 1950. If I could repeat that form in the two matches we were due to play against British Guiana – as it was then called – during January of that year I had hopes of a place.

Two of the opening positions were already virtually booked by Jeff Stollmeyer from Trinidad and Alan Rae of Jamaica. There were two other candidates for the third opening batsman position. One was Andy Ganteaume from Trinidad who toured England in 1957 and Bruce Pairaudeau who was a schoolboy wonder from Guiana and who would be playing in the same match as myself. While we were playing Guiana in two matches, Trinidad were similarly engaged against Jamaica. The party to tour England was to be announced immediately the games were finished.

I got away to a flying start. John Goddard helped by winning the toss so that Barbados had the first use of a beautiful wicket and I never put a foot wrong. How poor old Bruce must have suffered in the field watching me make 191 in about four hours without committing any serious mistakes.

Yet the previous evening I had made myself almost sick with worry. The trouble was caused by Barclay Gaskin, who toured several countries as manager of West Indies teams, and is now one of the leading administrators in the game in the West Indies.

Barclay was a very fine in-swing bowler, a type of bowler

we rarely saw over there in those days and who had been the terror of many Barbados sides.

He had played for the West Indies the previous year and the prospect of having to face up to him troubled me all evening. Finally I pulled myself together with the thought that if he got me out that was that and there was nothing I could do about it. He did get my wicket, but by that time I had almost made sure of my sea passage to England.

Barbados scored just over 600 runs and there was time only for one innings each. Bruce, my main rival failed twice when it came to his turn and if there were any doubts about who should have the third opening batting position, I think I must have swept them away in the second match.

This time the conditions were more difficult. We had some rain overnight and there was a damp patch on a length at one end where the water had trickled through the covers.

That made things awkward. Unfortunately I was stuck down that end for most of the morning but I managed to survive which must have impressed the selectors, especially as they had English conditions very much in their minds. Mind you, it wasn't that I wanted to stay down that end. The fact was that Clyde Walcott, who had joined me earlier in the morning, preferred to stay at the other end. I just wasn't good enough or crafty enough to get away from that damp patch!

Clyde landed in trouble when he returned to the pavilion for lunch. Our captain John Goddard took him aside and told him that as he was the more experienced player he should have taken charge of the damp patch to protect me, a youngster who was playing only his fifth first class match. Possibly Clyde should have done but, in a way, I was thankful for the opportunity of being able to show the selectors that I was able to play a turning ball.

I made forty-odd and that must have clinched my place in the tour party because, when British Guiana batted, Bruce made a gallant last bid to oust me by scoring 160. Although I didn't know it at the time, his effort came too late.

After my innings I had an anxious two-day wait before the team was announced but John Goddard gave me a broad hint that I would be a member of the tour party.

I was sitting down on the verandah above the pavilion at Kensington Oval watching the rest of our side bat when John came and joined me. Casually he remarked, 'You know it's funny when you think of it. Here we are enjoying this wonderful sunshine, yet in another month or so we'll be shivering in the cold in England.'

I didn't think anything of it at the time but later the significance of the words 'we'll' hit me. Taken literally it meant that John, who was captain of the West Indies side, must have known the make-up of the party and was giving me a gentle hint that I would be going with him.

Although John's remark helped to relieve my anxiety I still didn't count my chickens until the actual invitation came and I saw my name in black and white in the Barbados daily paper.

I was off to England! My dream had come true and it was a journey which was to change my way of life completely.

3 *I Hit a 'Ton' off Hampshire!*

Before we had reached the halfway stage of that 1950 tour programme of England I was to play an innings that was to shape the course of my career as a first class cricketer. I made 135 in fairly good time against Hampshire at Southampton.

That innings was my first century of the tour – in fact my first score of any note since my arrival in England. Watching every stroke from leg slip was the then Hampshire captain, Desmond Eagar, who is now secretary of the club.

Nothing was said to me at the time, apart from the usual polite congratulations when I reached three figures. In fact, two more years were to pass before Hampshire acted on the promise I had shown in that match.

I went on to make 1,117 runs on the tour, although I did not play in any of the four test matches. The cricket record books show I averaged 39.89 which I thought was highly satisfactory considering I was making my first tour and in strange conditions. I was 19 when the tour started and the second youngest member of the party.

Yet, considering all the things that happened to me at the start of the tour, I'm surprised I made any runs.

Things really began to run against me as soon as I boarded our boat in Bridgetown. I was to share a cabin with Ken Trestrail from Trinidad who turned out to be a very bad sailor. So bad, in fact, that he was sea sick before we left Bridgetown – when the ship was still in dry dock!

From that moment Ken hardly left his cabin. The crossing was rough for most of the time. The ship was tossed about wickedly and as I felt sorry for Ken, I stayed down in the cabin with him which was the worst thing I could have done. I lacked exercise and fresh air, something I had always taken for granted and hearing Ken moaning and groaning on his bunk made me feel ill.

So I was hardly in a fit state to cope with a comment from the tour manager, Jack Kidney, which has always stuck in my memory.

He came into the cabin one day to pay us our weekly £5 spending money. Ken was flat out on his bunk, not having moved all the trip and I was feeling almost as bad.

We had both been wondering what was in store for us in England and Ken asked the manager what he thought of our prospects and how he considered we would fare as individuals. Jack Kidney had a good idea of what to expect, having managed the 1939 West Indies side in England.

Jack replied, 'Well, Frank Worrell and Everton Weekes have been playing in the Lancashire Leagues. They have had experience of English conditions. Both are great batsmen and they will do well.

'Alan Rae is over there already and he'll do well. Jeff Stollmeyer and Gerry Gomez toured in 1939, so they know what is needed. They'll be all right.

'Bob Christiani and Clyde Walcott are very fine batsmen and will be able to look after themselves. As for you Ken, you've had plenty of experience on matting wickets where the ball turns and you should be able to cope.'

Jack had gone through the batting list with one exception – me. Slowly he turned to me, looked me up and down as I lay full length on the bunk and eventually said, 'Well, there has always got to be one failure in the side.'

He was probably joking, although he kept a straight face. Even so it struck me as an unfortunate remark to make to a 19-year-old – and a rather naïve 19-year-old at that, having been brought up on a plantation and led a rather sheltered life. An unthinking comment like that can shatter the confidence of immature players. Fortunately, I was able to dismiss it from my mind but it does illustrate the responsibility tour officials bear when they have charge of inexperienced players.

I'm afraid my first impression of England was not very favourable. We sighted Southampton on an overcast April day with light drizzle. A far cry indeed from the weather we had left behind.

Yet one thing did strike me, how green England was! The grass and other foliage of Barbados seemed yellowish by comparison.

During my first week in London I felt like a little boy lost in the giant maze of this cosmopolitan city. I was very much the country bumpkin come to town.

Then came the first competitive match of the tour against Col. Stevens' XI at Eastbourne. We fielded what was expected to be our test side, while the rest of us played for Col. Stevens' team.

I was to play only the first day. I had Trestrail to thank for that. He had caught measles on the way over. After the first day at Eastbourne – a match, incidentally, which was interrupted by *snow* – I broke out in spots.

Immediately I was confined to bed and later moved to hospital while the team finished the match and completed valuable practice, training with a string of one-day matches.

By the time the party moved to Worcester for the first county match I was back with them – but without any sort of practice or form behind me.

We fielded our strongest side at Worcester and I was also left out of the following match at Bradford because I had not had sufficient practice. While the rest of the boys were in the middle, I was busy in the nets trying to catch up with them.

Finally I was given my chance to make my mark in England. I was named for the third match against a county side, versus Surrey at the Oval. Not that I profited by my inclusion. Continuing my long streak of miserable 'firsts', I was out cheaply, picked up by M. R. Barton off the bowling of Alec Bedser.

Barton was not the only person picking up things in that match. I had played too soon after my illness. The weather was still cold although we were into May and I went down with acute bronchitis.

I had been chosen for the next match against Cambridge University at Fenners but was left behind in London, confined to my bed. My spirits were not improved when I glanced at the scoreboard in the papers each morning and saw that Cambridge University had made over 500 to which we replied by making 704 for three.

Nor indeed, when the boys came back to the hotel and told me. 'You'd have loved that wicket, man. It was just like Kensington Oval at home.'

I was still recovering when the team played Oxford University, was selected as 12th man for the next match against Glamorgan at Cardiff Arms Park over Whitsun and finally made the side for the match against Somerset at Taunton.

I was overjoyed when I heard the news. But my mood soon changed when I got off the coach on our arrival at Taunton on the Tuesday evening to be met by manager Kidney and skipper Goddard. Both looked serious.

They told me 'We'd like a word with you in private as soon as you have booked into your room.'

I wondered what I had done wrong. I thought of everything as I checked in at the hotel and sorted out my kit. I could not think of one foot which I had put out of place. Their news was far worse than even I had feared.

When I went to them they told me, 'We're very sorry to

have to break this news to you, Roy, but your father died last night as a result of a heart attack.'

I was stunned. My father had suffered two or three attacks over the years and I knew he was not 100 per cent but I had never thought in terms of death.

The manager and the captain both asked me if I wanted to continue in the Somerset match. I told them :

'I would like to do what my father would want me to do. I am sure that if he could advise me, he would want me to play.'

That night I could not sleep. I lay there – in a foreign land – powerless to do anything. Obviously I could not get home in time for the funeral. I was out on the streets of Taunton before six o'clock the next morning just wandering around aimlessly. I looked into shop windows without noticing the goods on display. I gazed at people without really seeing them. I felt utterly forlorn and longed to be with my family. Instead as people bustled off to work I had to return to the hotel for breakfast.

Although I was near to tears I managed to score 30 in one innings. I felt a little better in the next match against Lancashire when I made 47. Then the first Test was upon us.

I knew I stood no chance of being selected, having played only three matches in the first five weeks of the season. Yet I was named as 12th man because of my fielding. Many people may not believe it, looking at me today, but in those days I was quite a sprightly lad in the covers.

We lost the Test on a dry, dusty wicket. Manchester, for once, had been without rain for about a fortnight and England's spinners Eric Hollies, Jim Laker and Bob Berry were too good for us. Had the match come later in the summer I think we would have won because it would have been ideal for Valentine and Ramadhin. At the time they were too inexperienced.

I suppose, following our defeat at Manchester, there might

The Author

The day I joined Hampshire. Greeted at Southampton Central Station by Desmond Eagar (left) and Gerry Hill, then the senior professional

Congratulations from the skipper, Colin Ingleby-Mackenzie after Hampshire win the county title in 1961

And now for the celebrations! (*l. to r.*) The Skipper, Leo Harrison, Danny Livingstone, Derek Shackleton, Alan Wassell, Mike Barnard and 'Butch' White

have been a slight chance of my making the side for the second Test match at Lord's but I never really had the opportunity to impress anybody with my form.

One of the problems of playing in the West Indies side in those days was that with so many wonderful batsmen around it was seldom that we needed a second innings! If you failed in the first innings that was usually your lot.

Immediately after the First Test, we played at Trent Bridge on a magnificent wicket, just the type, in fact, which I needed to strike some sort of form. I made 47 in the first innings and shared a partnership of 130 with Everton Weekes in an hour before I was run out. Everton went on to make two hundred and we did not need to bat again.

The only other match before the Second Test was against Sussex at Hove where I was down to bat at number five. I didn't even get in! Stollmeyer and Rae turned their last practice session before the Test into a run riot by putting on around 350 for the first wicket.

By the time we had won the Second Test we were entering July and I had scored just over 100 runs. From that moment however, things began to go my way, in more ways than one, as it turned out.

We travelled to Southampton where Everton Weekes and I shared a stand of 139. I succeeded in matching Everton almost stroke for stroke and even today people still stop me and say my knock of 135 was one of the finest innings they have seen on the Southampton ground. I'm thankful that they remember it, especially as Weekes went on to make yet another double century.

Nevertheless I would not count it high on the list of my top twenty first-class hundreds. To be fair it was a beautiful Southampton wicket, just the right touch and the ball sped over the outfield. I know more than half my runs came in boundaries.

In those days too, the Hampshire bowling attack was not

particularly strong. Derek Shackleton worried me and kept me in check, but few of the others carried much penetrative power.

In fact, I got myself out or rather Everton did for me! Once Everton got going he wanted all the bowling. I was lucky if I received one ball in three overs and I became completely fed up at doing nothing.

In the end I played a disgusting shot against Shack. I tried to hit him over square leg which was a silly thing to do and lost my middle stump.

Still, things went my way completely after that. I made 188 against Leicestershire in a match in which Weekes and Worrell both scored double centuries. Altogether I completed three centuries and also hit 99.

My third 'ton' was against Surrey at the Oval, an innings which I thought might just squeeze me into the Test side for the Fourth and final match against England which was to be played on the same ground.

I knew I did not stand a chance of disturbing Stollmeyer and Rae. Then came Weekes, Walcott and Worrell. The only possible place open for me was at number six in place of Bob Christiani who had not been quite so successful as the others.

Instead, the selectors decided to keep a winning side after beating England in the Second and Third Test matches. I was out in the cold.

Some people may think that, as an opening batsman, I was expecting rather too much to get into the Test side at number six but I had batted everywhere on that tour.

I became the fill-in boy. If one of the openers Stollmeyer or Rae wanted a rest, I took their place. If one of the three W's rested then I stood in again. I batted in every position in the batting order.

This did not help me really because I am a person who likes to be able to plan. I can't stand waiting around for my turn. All the chopping and changing proved a little unsettling.

I found another difficulty when opening. Stollmeyer would never face the first ball. On the other hand Rae always wanted to take first strike.

It suited them well when they batted together but it meant that when I opened I had to adapt myself to the particular likes and dislikes of the batsman at the other end.

4 *The Age of Indiscretion*

Although my tour of England was a success cricket-wise, I made one vital mistake. I never learned when to keep my mouth tightly closed.

I've always been one to speak my mind. If a thing needs saying I've always come out with it. I have never believed in hiding behind a false word, false praise, false promises. Such an attitude, in my judgement, can only lead to more trouble in the long run. Stating this, of course, may be all right now that I have had lots of experience and I have already said goodbye to my fortieth birthday. But back in 1950 I was only just turned twenty.

I realise now that I would have been wiser to have kept my opinions to myself, especially when I was dealing with older and more experienced colleagues. I am afraid that I upset one or two of them and it didn't help matters that they came from the rival island of Trinidad.

Intense rivalry has always existed between Barbadians and Trinidadians. In fact, the West Indies was not a team in those days. The party was made up of a group of people who each represented their islands and could not forget their background, even when they were labelled together under one title.

This led to several internal disputes and petty jealousies. I am sure this did not help matters when the team were fighting an uphill battle in a match. Although I do believe that the 1950 side to England played more together than any of their predecessors.

It took that wonderful man, Sir Frank Worrell, to persuade the individual members to forget their differences and play as a complete team during the late 50's and early 60's.

I don't know how he did it, but he was such a magnificent person that everybody in the side looked up to him. Probably it was not so much a case of forgetting their differences and playing for the West Indies as of playing for Sir Frank himself.

Certainly our team was not as united as those who played under Sir Frank, nor do I think the same understanding exists today in West Indies tour teams. Although Gary Sobers is probably the greatest cricketer the world has produced I do not believe he possesses the flair of Sir Frank in being able to blend a group of individuals into a team.

My first really heated words of the 'fifty' tour came when I clashed with Gerry Gomez, following our second meeting that summer with Yorkshire, this time at Sheffield. We chose one of our strongest batting sides and I opened with Jeff Stollmeyer. To follow were the three 'W's'. I had scored about 20–24 when Norman Yardley came on to bowl his fiddling little in-swingers and I tried to hit him back over his head. I've no real time for this type of bowler, especially when he uses his delivery in such a negative way as Norman often did.

Unfortunately I missed completely and was bowled. The sight must have looked ugly from the boundary and dressing room. My dismissal did not mean all that much at that stage but when Weekes, Worrell and Walcott also failed we found ourselves being headed by Yorkshire on first innings. That night, back at the hotel, we were all feeling sorry for ourselves and, inevitably, an inquest started on the day's play.

Gomez was the first to have his say and he picked on me. He criticised my attitude and the stroke I had made, inferring that I was the cause of the West Indies collapse.

I told him 'I know it was a silly stroke. I don't need telling when I've played badly, but you can't blame me for the failures of the others.'

The argument developed from there. I suppose I made it worse when I told him 'If anybody else bowls medium-paced inswingers at me I'll hit them over their heads where they deserve to be hit.'

That didn't make things any easier. Gerry was a medium paced inswinger. From there the row became a little personalised with me telling him that next time he bowled to me I would hit him back over his head!

That was the one serious verbal clash I had with Gerry. My quarrels with Jeff Stollmeyer never reached such proportions, but they were far more frequent. I am afraid Jeff and I did not see eye to eye on many things.

Stollmeyer was vice-captain on this tour. Whereas John Goddard, the captain, was a very easy-going and a likeable sort of chap Stollmeyer was something of a perfectionist.

He then seemed to have a way of rubbing some people up the wrong way. Some of the players took exception when Stollmeyer said something contentious.

Instead of keeping my thoughts to myself as I should have done as the 'babe' of the team, I voiced my dislike of his views.

Stollmeyer, I believe, always thought that he should have been the captain of the side. Judged purely on ability, he was a better player than John Goddard and he would probably have made a successful captain on the field. But he did not help his cause by his apparent reaction to Goddard's status.

A lot of this feeling could be traced back to 1948 when England visited the West Indies. Before the tour started the West Indies named three captains for the Test matches.

George Headley was to captain in two Tests with one each going to Stollmeyer and Goddard.

This was purely and simply to ease inter-island rivalry and avoid the type of demonstrations which MCC discovered on the last tour of Pakistan when people in Lahore objected to Hanif Mohammed from Karachi and Hanif's supporters in Karachi demonstrated against Saeed and held up play in that ill-fated Third Test for almost an hour.

At it turned out George Headley was unfit for one match and John Goddard actually skippered in two games. He was the more successful captain result-wise and he did a good job in India in 1949.

Stollmeyer probably reckoned that this was an unfair way of choosing a captain but once Goddard took over the leadership he proved an extremely popular man with the players, and the results went his way – at least until we got to Australia in 1951–52.

That tour was a disaster from the West Indies point of view. Although the visit to England had generally been happy, with only occasional disruptions caused by inter-island disputes, these became more open with our lack of success 'down under'.

If they were not apparent to the public at the matches, they could be seen off the field with some of the Barbadian and the Trinidadian factions not mixing freely together.

After a particular disastrous match against South Australia, one of the correspondents travelling with the team cabled back to the West Indies that our downfall had been caused by racial feelings between the white and the black West Indians in the party. I am certain he grossly overstated his case but his views showed that some sort of jealousy did exist between various groups in those days.

Being a white West Indian myself, the son of a planter and living a fairly sheltered life, I suppose I did grow up with slight racialist feelings. It was never anything that was said or done but just that I was brought up in a white man's world and white men, at the time, probably ruled the day-to-day life in Barbados.

As a result of my fair skin I was able to enjoy membership of special clubs, make use of special privileges which are not enjoyed by the coloured people. I was brought up in an atmosphere which gave the impression that the white man was superior.

I lost all such feelings and impressions when going on tour – and the man I have to thank most for this was Frank Worrell. When I started touring I was only nineteen and Frank was six or seven years older. He had already travelled fairly extensively and knew the way of the world. He held no such views. To him every man was entitled to equal consideration, whatever the colour of his skin. Being around with Frank and seeing how he treated everybody, you could not help but come to the same conclusion.

He probably influenced me more than anybody else on those tours, particularly when I went to India with George Duckworth's Commonwealth side for five months in 1952–53. Frank and Sonny Ramadhin were also on that trip and the three of us shared a room for most of the time. Naturally, I got to know these fellows very well. One moment I had this slight racialist feeling in me. The next it had gone and I am happy to say that it has never returned.

This is why I had so much sympathy in 1968 for Basil D'Oliveira and the South African problem. I believe the South Africans are wrong and I am sure that the Springbok cricketers playing over here in county cricket would all voice the same opinion, if they were given the freedom to do so.

They have mixed freely with coloured cricketers on private tours, International Cavalier matches and in county cricket and, to the best of my knowledge, there has been no awkwardness. The majority of white South African cricketers would, I am sure, welcome coloured cricketers into first-class cricket in their own country.

They would be only too willing to play the West Indies, Indians and Pakistanis in their own country. The South Africans have a wonderful side at the present time. They are proud of their team and their ability and they would be keen to match their own skills against those from countries other than England and Australia.

This is why I believe the South African government made a grave error of judgement in not allowing D'Oliveira into the country in 1968. The opportunity was there to welcome a South African born coloured back to his native land without damaging their own internal policy.

Playing cricket with coloured cricketers helped me to get rid of silly prejudices. It would surely help South Africans towards a better understanding of other nations problems if their government were to accept the sportsmen and sportswomen of all countries, white and coloured.

5 *Winning My First Test Cap*

Australia was a big let-down for the West Indies in 1951–52. We lost the Test series 4–1, made little headway against the State sides and flopped as a team. Personally I enjoyed the trip. Australia is one of the greatest tours of all and I was so impressed that before I joined Hampshire I thought seriously of moving to Australia to live.

We arrived there in various parties. Some went straight from the West Indies and six of us travelled from England where we had been playing in the Lancashire League. We had established a strong reputation following victory in England in 1950 but the Aussies are no respecters of fame. We left there a well-beaten side. Frankly, the Australian bowling of Miller, Lindwall, Johnson, Johnston and Ring was far too good for us. Of those, I suppose Doug Ring was the weakest link in the attack. Even so, he was probably the best leg-spinner in the world at the time.

Our batting failed. Too much was expected of the three W's but in 10 Test innings Weekes made only 254 runs, 70 of those in one innings and Walcott made only 87 runs in six innings before he was hampered by a back injury.

In addition, our bowling was not strong enough. We had no really fast bowlers in those years. We relied too much on Valentine and Ramadhin. Although 'Val' bowled splendidly,

Ramadhin was not the force everybody expected. He could not turn his leg break on the hard Australian wickets and in the end the Australian batsmen gave up worrying about it. They played him purely as an off-spinner.

On the way over I was determined in my own mind that I would score so many runs that the tour selectors would be forced to include me in the Test side. Moreover I decided I was not going to care how long it took me. It did not quite work out the way I had planned.

Yet when I put my policy into operation in the very first match it worked well. We had agreed to play a testimonial match for Bill Ferguson, a wonderful figure and friend of many touring sides in Australia.

The West Indies were to field their accepted Test side, with the rest of us making up the opposition along with Bill O'Reilly, Alan McGilvray and others. We were well beaten. Frank Worrell hammered an undefeated 130 before the West Indies declared at 251 for five.

I opened for the Combined team, determined to make a good impression and I carried my bat, making 56 out of our total of 120. The only other person to reach double figures was our manager, Cyril Merry, who opened with me.

Throughout the opening sparring sessions in the two-day matches against the country elevens I did as well as anybody and in the only first-class match before the First Test I was second highest scorer in our first innings against Queensland with 42. Bob Christiani went one better.

But I suppose I was still too immature as a batsman to make a real success of the plan I had outlined for myself on the boat passage. I was still prone to make a bad shot when circumstances demanded a head-down approach. People who have watched me in England since those days have said that I possess the ability to score a boundary against deliveries most other batsmen would be pleased merely to stop. That may be true in some cases but when these 'impossible shots' do not come off, I must look an ugly sight at the crease.

My early form was good enough to win me my first test cap in the First team at Brisbane. The rest of our batsmen were still struggling for runs after the short acclimatisation period. In addition, our fast bowlers had not struck form and it was decided to play the extra batsman with Gomez and Worrell opening the bowling attack. I was the extra batsman, probably getting the position over Ken Rickards of Jamaica on the strength of some off-spin bowling in the match against Queensland in which, at one stage, I had figures of 4 for 15 – eventually stretched to 4 for 70.

I batted at No. 8 and on both occasions I was out to bad shots. In the first innings with the West Indies struggling against some fine fast bowling from Ray Lindwall, I attempted to lift Johnson out of the ground after I had made twenty eight. I hit right across the line of flight and was bowled. Next morning I woke up to see my exit described in the Australian newspapers as a 'stroke which was as crude as it was untimely'.

Only a fine innings by Lindwall who made 61 enabled the Australians to gain a ten-run lead on first innings. We did much better in the second innings but again I marred what had been a fairly competent innings by a piece of rashness.

I came out worse in a tactical battle against Keith Miller. In the first innings when I had been going quite well against the spinners, the Australian captain, Lindsay Hassett, brought back Miller. Almost immediately he sent down a bouncer which I just managed to fend off. The ball popped into the air and, luckily for me, fell just short of a fielder.

Whether it was the sight of the ball going up into the air or the fact that Keith thought he could frighten me because I was wearing glasses I don't know, but in the next over five or six of the deliveries were short and rearing up chest or head high – a bombardment which caused the Australian umpire to step in and warn Keith not to do it again.

When Keith came back for a second spell during my second innings I was determined to show him that I was boss. I felt I had to take a stand at this early stage of the tour. I wanted to show him he couldn't scare me. That I could dictate to the bowlers.

My first effort ended in failure. Keith bowled me an off-cutter. I swung, failed to middle it and skied a catch to mid-off. It was a long walk back and I was greeted by a silent dressing room. The rest of the boys were obviously as disgusted with the stroke as I was.

Only one man had a good word for me, Sir Don Bradman, who was watching the game from the dressing room. He said in his funny little squeaky Australian voice 'Nice innings, Roy'.

'Not too bad but a bloody awful shot,' I muttered.

'Never mind. Those runs will come in useful.'

That remark demonstrated the 'Don's' remarkable ability to sum up the state of the wicket and read the match, because Australia struggled in the second innings to make the 236 runs they wanted before getting home by three wickets.

Those two bad shots were almost certainly responsible for my omission from the Second test match in Sydney, although between these tests I had become the first member of our tour party to make a first-class century on the tour. I hit 114 off the New South Wales attack in our second innings when we were set 380 to win, a target we failed to reach by only 24 runs.

By the time the Second Test arrived nobody else in the party had got anywhere near to matching my score but I was left out so that we could play an extra bowler, Prior Jones. We were well beaten by seven wickets.

We had made a disastrous start to the tour. Of the first-class matches we had lost both the tests, drawn against Victoria and been beaten by Queensland and New South Wales.

Worse was to follow, when we went to Adelaide to play South Australia who were then the weakest of the State sides. Our spirit was low, there was a certain amount of bickering in the side and I was given a lecture by manager Merry.

With about half-an-hour remaining on the third day we were left to score 321 with the wicket taking spin and morale at an all-time low. I opened with Rickards and he was out before the close with only three runs scored.

The following morning, the last day of the match, manager Merry and John Goddard, our captain, called a team meeting to give us all a lecture and to try and work out why everything had gone so badly, not only in that match but on the whole of the tour.

As the meeting broke up I began walking from the room but the manager called me back and told me: 'Some of the boys have been talking about you. They say you can't fight in tricky situations. They say you can't get your head down. Go out there today and show them that they are wrong!'

I knew we couldn't get the runs, so I went out that morning determined to resist as long as possible. Runs were of secondary interest. Survival was all that mattered and I stayed there for more than 2½ hours before I was ninth out, having scored only thirty runs. That was almost a third of our total. We were all out for 93 and my score was 12 more than the next highest in an innings in which Frank Worrell was out first ball for the second time in the match to give him a 'King' pair.

I've never liked employing a completely negative approach to batting. We lost that day easily and the only other time I have adopted such a method when there has been so much time to spare, was in India on the Commonwealth tour of 1953–54 when I batted almost four hours for another thirty runs.

I had gone out there that day in India to prove a point. Our batting was so bad on that trip that Gupte, a magnificent leg-spin bowler, only had to pick up the ball and wickets would start falling.

We lost that match, too, and I never think this playing for time policy really pays off.

I had proved my point against South Australia. I had shown I could control myself when the situation called for it and this was to take me into the side for the Third Test on that same Adelaide wicket.

When the team left to play Western Australia in Perth in the final match before the Test I had been left behind in Adelaide to get some rest. At that stage I had played in every match on the tour, apart from the Second Test. I took the decision to leave me out of the Perth game as a healthy hint that I would be back in the test side and so it proved.

We started the game tired and dispirited, like men with little hope. Our morale had not been improved by some poor fielding in a match against Western Australia. We were also forced to field a weakened side. Walcott was suffering from a back injury and both Weekes and Worrell had only just recovered from injury. The Australians also had problems. Their skipper Lindsay Hassett, was not 100 per cent fit. The Australian selectors knew this two or three days before the match started but had decided against sending for an extra batsman. When Hassett was ruled out on the day of the match, they were forced to take the field a batsman short, with a long tail to come.

I came into the side to open the innings with Stollmeyer in place of Alan Rae who had never struck form on the tour. He constantly found difficulty against the extra pace which the Australian opening attack could extract from the wicket.

The match was all over in three days – and we were the winners! Australia were out for 82 in the first innings. We managed only 105 of which I made 14. They replied with 255 and this left us needing 233 to win on the Christmas morning. Nobody gave us a chance.

That assessment was based on our form of the tour, our low score in the first innings, the fact that Walcott was missing and that I had pulled a hamstring fielding during the Australian second innings.

I could hardly run and there was great discussion about whether I should go in first with a runner or whether I should go lower down. In the end it was decided that we would probably have a better chance of winning if I could, at least, stay there to see off the new ball attack rather than expose our main batsmen to Lindwall, Johnston and Miller when they were fresh.

Fortunately the moved worked. Stollmeyer and myself had almost an hour to survive on Christmas Eve but we made such good headway that by the close that night we had scored 54 without any alarms.

On Christmas day we took the score to 72 before I was out, caught behind, attempting to cut a ball from Ring. Stollmeyer and myself had batted 102 minutes together and our partnership was easily the best of the series by any side. It was just the foundation we needed to give everybody else confidence and we won with four wickets to spare to get back into the series and make sure there was nothing wrong with the Christmas celebrations that year.

The hamstring injury finished my cricket in Australia that tour. I couldn't play in the Fourth Test that followed immediately which we lost by one wicket and did not have enough time to find my form again to challenge for a place in the Fifth Test. By that time the series had been lost and the team was once more split into two factions. I am sure this was the reason why Goddard dropped himself from the Fifth Test.

Admittedly he was not 100 per cent fit, but he was fit enough to have played for his captaincy. I have no means of knowing what went on at the selection meeting but the Trinidad players in the party were not entirely happy with the way things had been going. The vice-captain Stollmeyer was from Trinidad, so was Gomez, the next senior player and a schoolboy chum of Stollmeyer. The manager was also from the same island. Unfortunately the change of captaincy did not bring any improvement in our form and we lost by 202 runs. And we left Australia a well beaten and bitterly disillusioned side.

We still faced four matches in New Zealand and I managed to make 100 in the second match against Otago, despite the blustery cold winds which ripped through Dunedin, the most southerly of their major towns.

For that century I had Worrell to thank. We batted last and had plenty of time to get the runs on the final day. I opened and by lunchtime I had made 82 with only another 18 more runs needed for victory. Worrell was my partner. Going out after lunch he said to me 'Would you like a century, Roy?'

'Of course, Frank. Nothing would suit me better,' I told him.

'Well, I'd better make sure I don't score any runs,' he said. And he didn't but he almost forgot himself once. One of the New Zealand bowlers sent him down a waist high full toss. Instinctively Frank shaped to clobber it for six, was halfway through his stroke before he remembered his promise, checked his bat and almost popped up a catch.

I got my century thanks solely to Worrell's kindness. That was the kind of man he was. He realised full well that a 'ton' would get me into the next test side and it did.

We won easily enough and I stayed in the team for the last test, this time batting at No. 3 behind Rae and Stollmeyer. They put on a huge stand but I was out for a duck in the only innings we had. And, although I didn't know it at the time, that was to be the end of my test career at the age of 21 . . .

6 *I Join Hampshire*

Towards the end of the 1950 tour of England I had been approached to play cricket for Lowerhouse in the Lancashire League. I spent two seasons with them, not all that successfully but the experience helped to give me a thorough background in the demands of the game.

I was just 21 when I first played for them and I suppose I was easy prey for some of the hard and crafty characters you find in the league.

These people knew all the tricks of the trade and, although I had every confidence in my cricketing ability, I still did not have much confidence in myself away from the field. The league atmosphere helped me to grow up.

Not that I was particularly impressed by the standard of play, which did not compare with our first division cricket back home. For a start many of the wickets were bad and ours at Lowerhouse was numbered among them. In addition, they also had some funny rules. Ours was not a small ground by any means, yet to hit a six a batsman had to place the ball *outside* the ground. Over the boundary was not good enough!

The umpiring was not too hot, either. You could be half way down the track when hit on the pads and still the decision would go against you.

One occasion remains in my mind, not so much for the

incident itself but for a remark made to me afterwards. I was playing against Phadkar, the Indian Test bowler. He could swing the ball and I was still in single figures when I played forward, was rapped on the front foot and still given out leg-before.

Naturally I was very disappointed but there is nothing you can do about these things. A little while afterwards I was taking a stroll around the ground when one of the Lowerhouse committeemen approached me. He was a jolly, friendly little man and he said to me 'Do you mind if I give you a bit of advice, Roy?'

'Not at all,' I said, knowing he would give me the advice whatever I said.

'I think I know your trouble. You're playing with your bat and pad too close together!'

'Thank you,' I said. 'That's the biggest compliment I have ever been paid in my life.'

At the end of the Australian-New Zealand tour I had sailed back to England with three or four of the boys for my second season in Lancashire League. On the boat was Ray Lindwall who was going to England for his first season of League cricket with Nelson. We became very friendly and continued our friendship in England, which was perhaps just as well . . .

In the League I seldom bowled off-spin. I tried to bowl quickly or at least as fast as possible and I was attempting to bounce them around the ears of the batsmen when we played against Nelson.

When it came to our innings all the Nelson batsmen tried to get Ray to bowl bouncers at me but he never did, although why I never knew. I was just thankful for our friendship!

In the League they have this system of collections for bowlers who take six wickets in an innings for less than five runs each and batsmen who score 50 or more.

On this particular day Ray was ripping through our side

and taking Nelson to an easy Victory. I had managed to survive mainly because whenever I came up against Lindwall he would give me one on my pads and I would tickle it around the corner to long leg for a single and scuttle up the other end out of the firing line!

I was at the bowlers' end when Ray took the eighth wicket, his sixth of the match and I was still 14 runs short of my half century. As the new batsman walked in, I turned to Ray and said:

'Have a heart, Ray. You've made sure of your collection. I want to live, how about letting me get mine?'

'Okay,' he said simply. He could have taken the new arrival without any trouble but for the rest of the over he bowled off the wicket and the batsman survived. In the next over I slogged and got the 14 runs I needed.

Strangely, by bowling off the wicket in that precious over Lindwall lost his rhythm completely and did not get it back. This new batsman survived and so did I and we managed to hold out for a draw in a match Nelson should have won with plenty of time to spare.

Soon after this match I was invited to join Hampshire although I nearly didn't get there.

When the first approach came I was feeling fed up with league cricket and was considering going to Australia to live. Then, out of the blue I received a letter from Desmond Eagar, the Hampshire secretary-captain, saying 'I know this is probably a long shot and you can rip up this letter if it is, but would you be interested in playing for Hampshire . . .'

I jumped at the chance and arranged to go to Southampton for talks late in July. I didn't get there. In fact, I nearly didn't get anywhere.

I was driving down in the early hours of the morning when I went over a rise in the road just outside Newcastle-under-Lyme and straight into the side of an articulated lorry that was turning right into an all-night café.

There was nothing I could do but hit it and from that moment I've always been thankful for being 6ft. tall.

I was so shocked at seeing the lorry that I sat bolt upright in my seat. When the crunch came my forehead hit the roof which was protected by felt padding instead of going through the windscreen when the impact came and I was thrown forward.

I staggered out of the car and I felt all right. I declined a visit to hospital when the police arrived.

'Are you sure?' they asked me. 'You don't look so good.'

At that I put my hand up to my forehead to wipe away what I thought was the cold sweat on my brow, only to discover that I had scraped away all the skin and my hand was covered in blood. It didn't really hurt and must have looked far worse than it actually was. Anyway, it was back home to Lancashire that night and I didn't meet Hampshire officials until shortly before I sailed home to West Indies for our cricket season out there.

I was very tempted to sign straight away but as India were visiting the West Indies in season 1952–53 I thought I would have one more crack at making the test side. I didn't get in the first one.

That almost decided me, especially when my old friend and rival Bruce Pairaudeau from British Guiana got into the side, batted at No. 6 and scored a century.

I couldn't see much hope for myself but I had one final chance of impressing the selectors that season in the match between Barbados and India. I was going well until I reached 25 and then I was involved in a muddle over a run with Clyde Walcott which put paid to my hopes.

I shall always remain convinced that a run was there, yet I should have known better than to have shouted for it. I was striking against the last but one ball of the over and I drove it into the covers to the left hand of a fielder at extra cover. It meant that he had to run round to pick up with his right hand which would have been ample time for me to get up the other end and Clyde to get home as well. I called immediately and set off but Clyde was not thinking of a run at that stage in the over. He was thinking of the over to come. He sent me back late and I was too far up the wicket and did not make it.

That was my only innings of the match and I did not make the side for the Second Test. I was named as twelfth man but that did not satisfy me. Halfway through the game I pulled out the contract Hampshire had sent me some months earlier and signed for a career in England.

I knew I was turning my back on a test career with the West Indies but I was eager to play cricket six days a week. At that moment in time I know I did not have much chance of disturbing Rae and Stollmeyer as the Regular West Indies opening batsmen. In addition, I had to take into consideration the bickering between myself and Stollmeyer who was playing, more and more, a leading role in the affairs of West Indian cricket as well as captaining the best side.

There was one further point. In those days the West Indies didn't have such a full fixture list as they have nowadays. First-class cricket itself was very limited because there was no Shell tournament as they have between the islands today. I knew no other life than cricket and I was hungry to play it at the highest standard I could find, as often as I could.

Money and financial security did not enter into it. My contract for Hampshire guaranteed me £800 a year. And that was all. I had agreed that if they found me a job, then my wage would be deducted from the £800.

So I signed and committed myself to another two years in the wilderness while I fulfilled the M.C.C. regulations on the qualifications for overseas players. A far cry, indeed, from the advantages and wages overseas players enjoy today.

7 *Four Letter Words—and a Plea*

I thought I knew a fair amount about the game when I started in County cricket, but I was in for some shocks. Not even my two years qualifying prepared me completely for the strange demands of three-day matches.

The only thing qualifying did was to give me a false reputation as far as the Hampshire crowd was concerned. I acquired it in my first season with the club in 1953 when the Australians came to Southampton. That was one of the few first-class matches in which I was allowed to play and apparently many spectators in Hampshire have not forgotten the occasion.

The wicket was spiteful which is unusual for matches between counties and touring sides. Almost from the first over, the ball turned and lifted. The Australians were lucky to have the best of the wicket on the first morning when they were able to make a start towards a respectable score. Even so they owed most to a wonderful innings by Neil Harvey whose century that day was worth 300 runs on a good track.

Hampshire were always in trouble and we faced an impossible task in the last innings when the wicket was really vicious. A batsman would be lucky if he survived 15 minutes in those conditions against an attack of the standard the Australians possessed.

When I walked out to the wicket I decided I would have no alternative but to hit out. If the ball was pitched up I would have a swing. If it was short I would hook or just try to get out of the way. I approached the task of batting as I would have done on a wet wicket in the West Indies where the ball rises so quickly it is virtually impossible to play a defensive stroke.

That is how I set off against the bowling of Ron Archer. I kept swinging and luck was on my side. The ball flew everywhere and I managed to survive 85 minutes, during which I scored 71 runs, including five 6s. That set a fast scoring standard Hampshire fans have often appeared to think I should have matched repeatedly in later years.

Barry Richards built up a similar reputation when he came to Hampshire from South Africa in 1968 and had such a brilliant season. He took over from me as opening batsman and finished the second highest run getter of the summer. Yet it is almost impossible to maintain such a standard season after season, but Barry's performances will always be measured by that great first impression he made.

In addition to that 71 I had also made that 135 for the West Indies against Hampshire in my first match inside the county. People were obviously judging me on these two performances, but then came the big let-down in 1954 when Pakistan came to Hampshire.

The first innings score-line read: Marshal l.b.w. Fazal Mahmood 0. The second innings read exactly the same. I had collected my first 'pair', the only time so far that I have bagged them in my life.

Some of the clashes between England and the West Indies – particularly those in the Caribbean – have not been noted exactly for the friendliness between the two teams. After my first experiences of county cricket I am not particularly surprised.

I think the thing that shocked me more than anything

else was the amount of swearing I heard on the field. I've learned to ignore the language hurled about, but don't let anyone fool you that cricket is always a gentlemanly pursuit.

The bowler v. batsmen versions are the worst. Often when a batsman plays and misses, the bowler will shout angrily down the wicket 'You lucky so and so'. If the batsman connects and sends the ball to the boundary, he is always likely to receive a torrent of abuse from the bowler 'Do that again and I'll knock your blank head off!' is one of the polite threats.

We played the game hard in the West Indies. We were out to win but narrow escapes, dropped chances and big hits were never followed by abusive and unfriendly remarks.

I suppose that playing for a living has a lot to do with this. Victory means more money. Championship points mean bonuses. All this adds up to a better standard of living, and success for an individual can mean selection for the Test side which brings even higher rewards.

The most outstanding incident I can recall involved myself and Wilf Wooller, the present Glamorgan secretary.

Wilf was always a great talker. When batting you could hear him chattering on from the short leg position, having a go at this, that or the other, nattering to wicket keeper Haydn Davies between deliveries as the bowler was going back to his mark and even when the bowler was running up. His flow of conversation could be very distracting to a batsman trying to concentrate.

This particular incident happened when we were playing them at Neath in 1958 on a really bad wet wicket from which the ball was lifting awkwardly.

We shot out Glamorgan for 72 in the first innings. Only the left-hander Alan Watkins, with the superb knock of 42, reached double figures. Wilf was using the new ball when we batted and with only two scored he dismissed Jimmy Gray, caught by Peter Walker.

Soon after I played at one from Wilf and missed the ball which just cleared the top of the stumps. Wilf who at the time, was both skipper of Glamorgan and an England selector, strode down the wicket and said 'You lucky so and so . . .'

The remark somehow stung me into replying: 'Who the hell do you think you are, calling me a so and so and anyway, you need luck to bat on a wicket such as this.' In my anger I forgot he was on the England selection committee and an influential figure on the England cricket scene.

Wilf glared back and my batting partner Henry Horton hurried up the wicket and pleaded 'Don't fall for it, Roy. They're trying to get you rattled.'

The next ball was a long hop which I smashed clear over the pavilion. This time I heard 'Well, that's a better shot anyway.'

Two overs later Wooller was crouching at short leg when I was taking strike. I received one delivery which lifted sharply. I managed to get my bat up in time to prevent the ball crashing into my face and it dropped just clear of the cluster of legside fielders.

Immediately Wilf threw up his arms in disgust and, I suppose understandably, made some pungent comments about Glamorgan's bad and my good luck. I waited until he drew breath and before he could resume, I rounded on him and, also understandably I think, replied with some outspoken and rather heated remarks of my own.

That cleared the air. In fact, Wilf and I seemed to get on better after that. Anyway Hampshire had the last laugh. We won by an innings and two runs. The whole match lasted only seven hours.

The English players have grown accustomed to hearing such exchanges. They have grown up with it from the time they entered the game. It is part of their way of life: but I'm afraid these remarks can be easily misunderstood when they are uttered against overseas sides, both in England and abroad.

The strangers are apt to be shocked by the type of abuse which the English county players treat as a matter of course. The overseas players do not always realise that in 99 per cent of these cases no personal feeling of animosity is intended. The bowler or fielder is just letting off steam – and a few four letter words are his way of doing it.

I know from talking to players from overseas that many of them are irritated by the way English fielders fling up their arms in anguish whenever a ball narrowly misses the stumps or drops tantalisingly short of a fielder. These theatrical gestures by bowlers and fielders have been the cause of a lot of the unpleasantness which has become noticeable at Test match level in recent years.

I think it is time the M.C.C. gave a lead by issuing a stern warning that such behaviour will not be tolerated. I would like to see MCC tour parties issued with specific directives to watch their manners on the field *as well as off it,* when they gather for the traditional eve-of-tour dinner at Lord's.

I know that when M.C.C. are visiting countries where politics can easily interfere with sport, the players are given *gentle* reminders on how they should conduct themselves and what sort of subjects should be avoided in discussions at receptions, etc. This talk needs to be widened in scope to include a salutary warning that British swear words and physical gestures of annoyance may not be acceptable when heard or seen by players of other countries.

Let me stress here that I am not advocating a clean up of the language exchange in our own domestic programme. Heaven forbid! The county scene would be a far duller place without a few Anglo-Saxon expressions. I do say English player need to curb their language when playing against overseas sides.

I still don't think we realise how much MCC teams are

respected abroad, especially in the developing countries where first-class cricket is not played six days a week, and to which touring sides go only once every six or seven years or so.

I know, particularly from my earlier experiences in the West Indies, that if an English county cricketer went over there he would be treated with great respect and everything he did would be copied.

This brings me to another surprise I experienced when I first came to England. As a youngster I had always made heroes out of cricketers – my own countrymen and leading English cricketers.

I had admired them from afar and for a great length of time but when I actually met them and played against them I felt strangely let down. They were not immortals. Most of them cursed and were as bad tempered as the next man!

One aspect that did shock me was the distinction between amateurs and professionals which has now, happily, been removed by labelling us all together under one roof as 'cricketers'.

I thought the old attitude was totally wrong, the absurd class distinction in which the player trying to earn his living from the game was liable to be looked down upon by the 'amateur' ranks who had things made easier for them particularly as a result of having a University background.

I started playing cricket because I loved the game and the only way that I could continue playing it regularly to satisfy my appetite for batting was to become a professional. I was proud to do so.

No one today ought to be ashamed of being a *professional* cricketer. If someone is ill he does not call for an amateur physician to attend him. If someone needs legal advice, he doesn't seek out the barrack-room lawyer. He approaches the professional practitioners and nobody looks down on them.

Fortunately in my early days with Hampshire, we did not

suffer from the two class system. Desmond Eagar was the only regular amateur on the staff and our professionals were not upset – like those in many other counties particularly the south – by amateur players coming along in the summer holidays and wanting a game. They were often found a place in the side, although they did not always possess half the talent of the professional player they displaced. The change in the regulations which made us all equal was a very welcome move.

A certain amount of class distinction is still evident in cricket today particular when it comes to the appointment of the England captain. In recent years there has been a growing tendency to look towards the 'professional' type, as the appointment of Brian Close in 1966 and 1967 and Ray Illingworth in 1969 illustrates. Generally, however, a player who has been to one of the Universities still stands a better chance of becoming England's captain. Tradition dies hard.

Wickets in England, too, were a disappointment to me although I had been warned about them when I first came here with the West Indies in 1950.

I shall never forget one on which I played in 1955 – the season I qualified for Hampshire. That was at Weston-Super-Mare where Derek Shackleton took eight for four. I had never seen anything like it in my life. How people expected cricket to be played properly in these conditions is beyond me.

At that period English batting was going through a very defensive phase. A great deal of leg theory bowling was making it difficult for batsmen to score runs. Almost every county side seemed to have one bowler who could specialise in this negative art and I always thought Cliff Gladwin of Derbyshire was the most defensive bowler of all.

Perhaps I ought not to have been so surprised after one experience in 1954 during my second year of qualifying when Hampshire played the Army in a two-day match.

When Vic Cannings set his field, he placed a slip, gully, extra cover and the rest of the fielders on the leg side. I couldn't get over it and after a couple of overs watching this from the gully I asked the wicket keeper which way Vic was swinging the ball.

'He is bowling out-swing of course. He can't bowl in-swingers' said the wicket keeper.

This surprised me even more until I realised that Vic was starting off bowling outside the line of the leg-stump, so that the out-swing was taking the ball into the batsman on his leg-stump. It was virtually impossible for the batsman to play the ball on the off-side and with the leg side packed with fielders it was almost impossible for him to score runs there. And this was against the Army although, in those days their side did contain a fair sprinkling of first-class players who were doing their national service.

Despite my new and sometimes surprising environment – I was very satisfied with my start in county cricket, scoring over 2,000 runs in that first year which was more than Hampshire expected from me.

At the start of the season Desmond Eagar had told me that if I did some bowling he would be satisfied if I scored about 1,200 runs. If I was not going to do any bowling he would consider 1,500 runs a fair return while I was still feeling my way. In fact, I scored 2,000 odd and also did a fair amount of bowling.

The fact that English batting was so defensive helped me considerably. When I went out to start an innings, I would find the field close up round the bat, with three men behind square on the leg-side, all in for the catch, slips and gully but seldom did anyone think of having a mid-off or a mid-on, third man or long leg.

I have always been a reasonably good driver of the ball and the cut has also brought me a fair proportion of my runs. Such fields that I often hit a 20 or 30 runs before the fielding captain would think to himself 'Hello, we've got someone different here' and start re-arranging the field in an attempt to check the flow of runs.

So, in a way, my first year was made easier for me than it should have been. My one real difficulty was standing up to the strain of playing cricket for six days a week and all that it entailed. The travelling involved between matches meant that on some occasions we had to leave one ground at six in the evening and travel in the region of 200 miles to get the next match which started the following day.

I had never been accustomed to these pressures and with the best will in the world it is difficult to retain enthusiasm over a four-month period and produce a peak performance every time.

During 1968 when we had the first real influx of star overseas cricketers, they all voiced similar feelings to me. In their own countries they probably played no more than six or eight first-class matches a year. All other times they played local league or club cricket which allowed them to relax between first-class matches, recover from the tensions of the last match and be fresh and eager for the next first-class game.

The English county cricket is the hardest, most demanding circuit of all. It is made even more difficult by the high degree of tactical thinking that goes on in the game, notably by captains and bowlers.

I doubt whether any bowler in the world can sum up the strengths and weaknesses of a batsman as quickly as those in England. As a newcomer in the early 1950's I was astonished at the amount of discussion which went on in the dressing room or the bar after a match, when bowlers would argue among themselves as to the best way either to dismiss a batsman or to contain him. This is especially true when a new batsman comes on the English scene. Before he has played half a dozen innings, the whole county network seems to have a detailed picture of where he is going to look for his runs, an itemised list of his favourite scoring strokes and a detailed analysis of his weak points.

The strains and stresses of playing continuous cricket and the swift summing-up of my technique were to tell against me. In that first season I made three centuries but I was out as soon as I had reached three figures. I needed to summon all my reserves of stamina and concentration to reach 100 so that by the time I completed it I had nothing left inside me to help me build up on that score.

In the second season I found runs harder to get because bowlers and captains had their own dossiers on me. When I took guard I found there was a mid-off waiting for me. I found that there was a third man and a long-leg and, whereas in 1955 my favourite shots had brought me fours or twos, I discovered in 1956 that they were bringing me only singles.

The English wickets also forced me to change my grip. When I first arrived in this country I used a grip in which the back of my left hand used to face mid-off and the full face of the bat went through quite a long way on the line of the ball. I used to try and drive a ball that was not quite a half-volley and every time it 'stopped', mid-off would then have a dolly catch or the bowler an easy caught and bowled.

I countered this by turning my left hand so far around the bat that the back of it was facing point. This prevented the line of the bat going too far along the line of the ball. Although it meant that I mis-timed the ball, they were smothered mis-times because the bat was turning over the ball and stopped it popping up for a catch. I've used that grip ever since.

I've always been in favour of experimenting. Yet when I talk to youngsters who have had only two or three seasons in the game and suggest they might be able to correct some of their faults by altering their grip or stance, many of them tell

Off to work – with Jimmy Gray, a splendidly unselfish partner

The team which won the Championship in 1961

Practice with the family – and the dog – in readiness for more serious business. . . .

. . . Crouching, for example, with the Hampshire slip fielders

me it can't be done. When I look at their record and see that, perhaps, they are only averaging around 20 with the bat, I am surprised that they don't at least try another method. The true professional, surely, is the person who has studied *all* aspects of his job.

Despite the problems which scientific field placings created for me I was satisfied with my form for the county in 1955, especially as we finished third in the table which was then the highest place Hampshire had ever attained.

Perhaps the outstanding memory of that season was when we met Yorkshire at Bradford early on in the season. We won which was the first time Hampshire had achieved that distinction in Yorkshire for about 20 years. I was pleased with my own contribution in that victory. Not only with the bat but also with the ball because I took nine of the Yorkshire wickets.

8 *Crazy Gambles and Great Wins*

Nobody gave Hampshire much chance of winning the county championship in 1961. Not even in the last few weeks of the season when it had become a three-team race between Yorkshire, Middlesex and ourselves. Everybody expected us to crack under the pressure, much in the way that Gloucestershire did in 1969 after holding what looked an unassailable lead in the middle of July.

Why did we win it? In a sentence, because everybody clicked for us that summer. We grew in confidence as a team until, by the start of August, we were convinced we were good enough to beat anybody.

All our batsmen lived up to their reputation and ability. Jimmy Gray, Henry Horton and myself each scored more than 2,000 runs. As we were the first three in order, I don't think any captain could have wished for a better or more solid foundation on which to launch a bid for victory.

Numbers four, five and six could bat with greater freedom, they did not have the worry of propping up the side and were able to score their runs in fairly quick time. They took their opportunities well. Danny Livingstone and Peter Sainsbury each scored more than 1,500 runs and Colin Ingleby-Mackenzie weighed in with 1,300.

I suppose, too, the bowling that season was better than ever. Derek Shackleton took 158 wickets for an average of 9.56. Off spinner Mervyn Burden started in the side and stayed for half the season. Alan Wassell, slow left arm, took over the second half of the season. Between them they took 116 wickets. When we needed a third seamer Malcolm Heath gave us wonderful support and, above all, we had 'Butch' White rolling in like a runaway train. He took 117 wickets and they cost him less than nine apiece. 'Butch' was a fairly new addition to the side and a vitally important one. For the first time in my years with Hampshire we possessed a genuine fast bowler, capable of digging out two or three batsmen at the start and then coming back to finish off the tail in double quick time.

The most important single factor in our successes of 1961 was the captaincy of Colin Ingleby-Mackenzie – although at times he made me and two or three more of the senior players groan with despair at some of the tactics he adopted and some of the risk he took when going for victory.

Indeed, there were moments that summer when Colin made me livid. Yet such was his charm and his cheerfulness that it was impossible to remain angry with him for long. He created a wonderful team spirit throughout that summer. Colin was well liked by everyone in the dressing room and by 99% of the people who came into contact with him. He could mix with Lords, Dukes and Earls – and frequently did with the greatest of ease. You could take him into a public bar in the roughest area of the country and he would be equally at home.

Perhaps his greatest asset was his capacity to get on so splendidly with members of the opposing sides and the great majority of rival captains. One or two did object to the way he approached the game but the rest appreciated that they could guarantee having a real match with Hampshire. They knew Colin would take every risk he could do to achieve a result in Hampshire's favour and, by doing so, this always let in the opposition with a chance.

Colin, as I mentioned at the start of the book, was the man who gave us the title as champions of wine, women and song as well as cricket. He was the person who claimed he gave no special instructions to the team, apart from insisting that everyone must be in bed by breakfast time!

Three or four years earlier he had captained a side on a private tour to the West Indies. The team did not perform as well as they might have done in some of their earlier matches and, on the eve of the most important match, one of the tour officials approached Colin.

'We must put up a good show tomorrow' he said. 'We can't afford to let this game slip. I think it might be a good idea if the team were in bed by 11 o'clock.'

'I can't see any point in that,' replied Colin quickly. 'The match is due to start at 11.30.'

This was very much Colin's approach to the game. He enjoyed his cricket and he enjoyed his living as well. His first love was horse racing and he brought a touch of the gambling fever into his tactical thinking on the cricket field and this is where he and I often disagreed.

I don't mind taking a gamble to achieve victory but to me some of the decisions he made were more like committing suicide! In 1961 his hunches paid off. If he backed horses the same way, he must have made a fortune that year.

Typical of his audacity as a skipper that summer was in the match against Gloucestershire at Portsmouth. Rain interrupted play three times on the first day and washed out the entire second day.

Gloucestershire batted first and were all out for 176, leaving us just three overs at the end of the first day during which we scored about 24 runs. After the first hour on the third day Jimmy Gray and myself had taken the score to 96 without loss when Colin declared just when we looked certain to take four points for first innings lead, which was the maximum both Jimmy and myself thought we could take from the game.

Neither of us could believe it when we saw Colin waving us in from the pavilion door. I was furious at his apparent madness but there was nothing I could do about it. Gloucestershire were presented with an 80-run lead and built that up to 198 before Arthur Milton declared, leaving us 137 minutes in which to score the runs – at a rate of 88 an hour.

We had no alternative but to go for them if we were going to get anything from the match after gaily tossing away first innings points. We made it, with just two minutes to spare – the most remarkable victory of the summer.

For a long time the odds seemed to be in Gloucestershire's favour. With 22 minutes left we had lost seven wickets and still needed 38 runs but 'Butch' White threw his bat at everything while scoring an undefeated 33.

This made Colin grin even wider than usual as he chided those of us who had ridiculed his decision.

Looking back, we did some crazy things that summer. Colin was the sort of person who seemed to be able to take late nights in his stride without it really affecting him on the field the next day. Colin never worried about what hour he or his team mates went to bed and there were times when our performances were probably affected by not getting as much sleep as perhaps we should have done.

One example of the crazy things we did was in August that year, just as we were entering the final run towards the championship title. We were playing at Derby over a weekend and in the past Derbyshire had often proved our bogey side. We started well on the Saturday and made 350 for 8 declared. Henry Horton scored 141 before he was run out and I contributed 72 before lunch.

Through his love of horse-racing Colin naturally made many friends in the racing world and on the Sunday of that match he had arranged for three or four of us to play in a charity fixture at Newmarket. The four consisted of Colin, Derek Shackleton, our match winning bowler, Leo Harrison, our wicket keeper and myself who, I suppose, was looked upon as the side's leading run scorer. In fact, four of the key members of the side, if you will accept my apologies for putting my name in that category.

We drove down from Derby on the Saturday evening and Colin's generous hosts supplied us with champagne from the moment we arrived. The festivities carried on throughout Saturday night, most of Sunday when cricket was secondary to the drinking, and again deep into Sunday night.

I suppose that week-end I snatched only about three or four hours sleep before we drove back to Derby. We arrived at the ground shortly before play was due to start with almighty hangovers and knowing that we faced a day in the field.

I am not sure how I managed to keep going through it. Shack's performance in the circumstances was little short of miraculous. In all, in that innings, he sent down 36 overs and took six for 90 while bowling Derbyshire out – which meant that I had to bat again that Monday evening.

Our lead was 98 and we needed runs quickly but with Harold Rhodes and Les Jackson bowling very briskly in a light which had started to fade and with my own eyes threatening to close at any second, I am afraid I didn't score as fast as I should have done.

In fact Michael Melford, describing my innings for the *Daily Telegraph,* wrote the following morning: 'The champagne sparkle of Saturday had left Marshall's batting!' If only he had known . . .

Our foolishness might easily have cost Hampshire the Championship but we still managed to win, thanks to an heroic showing by Shackleton and a brave final fling by 'Butch'. We left Derbyshire to score 263 in 208 minutes and their innings had only just started when Shack twisted a knee.

Despite the pain he bowled as tight as ever he has done off only three paces and kept Derbyshire's run chase in check. Nevertheless a splendid 91 by Laurie Johnson, who was my cricket captain at Lodge School in Barbados for a while, put Derbyshire in with a chance of making victory but when they still needed 71 in the last 35 minutes, they put up the shutters.

We had been unable to use 'Butch' White because he was handicapped by a groin injury but Colin kept him on the field and just when it looked as though Derbyshire's last pair might hold out, Colin tossed 'Butch' the ball. 'Can you manage one last shot at them,' asked the skipper. 'Butch's' answer came with his second delivery which dismissed Bob Berry and we gained 14 points.

Another famous – or should it be infamous – late night incident occurred when we were returning to Hampshire after an away match. We called in at one of Colin's friends for a 'nightcap' and the discussion inevitably turned to cricket. Soon an argument developed between Colin and myself over captaincy. Neither of us would budge from our points of view and with the aid of a little cognac, time slipped by unnoticed until dawn was beginning to break, when we finally made our way home in a rainstorm.

That morning the pitch was quite wet when Colin lost the toss and he had to field. Colin peered through bleary eyes at the rest of the team as we led him out and went across to 'Butch' White to discuss the setting of the field. As he did so he failed to notice a pile of sawdust, tripped and fell flat on his face.

I don't believe cricket can be played on late nights. One or two a season are all right but I find that a succession of them upsets my play. Mind you, there are individuals like Colin who thrive on late nights. Moreover, those who look askance at cricketers who do not go to bed before midnight, tend to overlook that fact that matches don't start until 11.30 in the morning. So that even if a cricketer doesn't get to bed until one o'clock in the morning, he can still get eight hours sleep and have a hearty breakfast before the day's play commences.

Sometimes early nights don't help either as I discovered in our 1961 Championship winning year when we played Surrey at the Oval early in the season in a mid-week match.

We were in the field on the first day and this was a beautiful Oval wicket. Surrey went well and we took a lot of hammer both from John Edrich and Ken Barrington who scored a century apiece before Surrey declared at 356 for 4, leaving themselves half an hour in which to try and get a Hampshire wicket.

Throughout the partnership between Edrich and Barrington I had gazed longingly at the wicket and thought to myself 'There's a huge score for you, tomorrow Roy, if only you behave sensibly.' During that last half an hour of batting I played with extreme caution while making 12 runs.

I sipped a couple of drinks that night in the bar before going back to the hotel for an early dinner and was in bed just after nine o'clock. I woke at five o'clock the next morning still dreaming of that wicket and what I was going to do. By breakfast time I had made a double century.

When I resumed my innings I took a single to fine leg and in the next over edged one into the safe hands of Kenny Barrington at slip off Peter Loader. I had made 13 and we were bowled out that day for 190.

Owing to the experimental law the Surrey captain, Peter May, was unable to enforce the follow on, so they batted again, scoring 141 for two before declaring and setting us to make 308 to win in 320 minutes.

On that Thursday, evening Tony Lock had a benefit dance in Croydon to which we were all invited and it was nearly five o'clock in the morning before I got back to my hotel.

On the last morning we soon lost Jimmy Gray but then I joined with Henry Horton in adding 180 for the second wicket in 135 minutes. We obtained the runs with an hour to spare and I scored 153 of them in just over three and a half hours, which was one of my best performances that summer.

An early night had meant failure. A late night had brought success and we claimed an extraordinary victory over unfortunate Surrey who had lost only six wickets in the match while making 497 runs.

We were involved in several other remarkable finishes that year, not the least being our four wickets' victory over Essex at Cowes.

Essex recovered well from a bad start and totalled 321 for 9 declared. During their innings I slipped while running in the field and strained a hamstring muscle. The strain was so painful that I could hardly walk. I had my thigh heavily bandaged and there was no question of my opening the innings. I eventually batted No. 7 and immediately I came in, the Essex captain, Trevor Bailey, brought back leg-spinner Robin Hobbs to expose my lack of mobility. Trying to play leg spin with both feet together is suicidal and so it proved. We were all out for 231, giving Essex a 90 run lead. They scored another 150 for 5 before Trevor again declared, leaving us to score 241 to win in 215 minutes. The declaration was generous enough considering the form of our batsmen that year but Bailey gambled on the fact that I was injured and he wanted to leave himself as much time as possible in which to bowl us out.

We travelled to Cowes from the mainland by boat every day which took an hour, and what Bailey did not know was that on the journey I had taken off the bandage and found that I could move my leg quite freely, although it was still painful.

I told the skipper but it was decided not to risk me in my usual position. We made a disastrous start, losing four wickets for 35 before Colin went in soon after lunch and played a remarkable innings. Danny Livingstone helped him put on

86 runs and Alan Wassell joined him in making 50 more, but we had lost six wickets and still needed another 72 runs when I decided to go out to bat – much to the surprise of everybody, including my own team mates. Indeed, when Wassell was out both Shack and I started walking to the wicket, before Shack realised I was going in.

Before I went out I said to Danny Livingstone in the dressing room that as soon as Bailey saw me coming out he would bring back Robin Hobbs. Hobbs would pitch one up, trying to get my feet in a tangle and I would hit him for four.

This is exactly what happened and I can still see the look of amazement on Robin's face when he found I could use my feet. He tried to counter this by dropping them shorter and this was exactly what I wanted. Colin and I saw Hampshire home by four wickets – the skipper scoring 132 not out in 140 minutes.

We had thirty minutes in which to score the last 14 runs needed, and I remember walking down the wicket to Colin and saying, 'Look, don't do anything stupid now. If you get out at this stage, there isn't much batting to come and the pressure will be on us again.'

'All right,' he said. 'I'll be careful,' and proceeded to score 18 runs off the next six balls!

In another amazing match of that amazing season 'Butch' White swept us to victory over Sussex by taking four wickets in five deliveries including a hat-trick – a feat he was to perform the following season as well.

The game, played at Portsmouth in early August happened to be for my benefit and I skippered the side in place of Colin who was injured.

The first innings fight had been a hard one. Sussex scored 141 and we replied with 179 on a wicket that helped the seam bowler.

On the second afternoon Sussex began their second innings

well with Alan Oakman, Richard Langridge and Ken Suttle making useful scores and the position was beginning to look decidedly unpromising for us towards the close with Sussex 141 ahead and only four wickets down.

'Butch' had already put in a long stint when I threw the ball to him again. 'Come on, Butch. Just let it go for one final over,' I urged.

With his first delivery, a military medium pace, Jim Parks played on to his wicket. With his next the 'night watchman' Ian Thomson was caught behind, and suddenly 'Butch' had switched on full steam and was bowling flat out.

Don Smith, who had been dressed and started to stroll to the Lord Mayor's tent for after-game drinks, hurriedly changed back to take Thomson's place and he was bowled to give 'Butch' his hat-trick. Still 'Butch' had not finished.

Graham Cooper was the next batsman and got an edge to the first ball he received. It went wide of second slip where Jimmy Gray dived and did extremely well to get his right hand to it but he just failed to hold it. Back came 'Butch' with a bouncer and Cooper, trying to hook, gave a catch to Henry Horton. From 179 for four Sussex had slumped to 179 for eight.

Worse was to follow for Sussex on the third morning. Ted Dexter, who had watched his side collapse from the bowler's end on the previous evening, made up his mind that he would take care of dangerman White. Ted is such a fine player of fast bowling that I knew he could still regain the initiative for his side.

Sure enough, he proceeded to play some magnificent shots against 'Butch'. Real stinging blows that all deserved four runs but I had spread the field round the boundary to prevent him scoring. Not wanting his tail enders to face 'Butch', he declined the singles offered.

That was where Ted made his mistake. We had another bowler called Shackleton who was a useful performer and he stepped in to take the last two wickets without cost. The last six Sussex wickets fell for only one run and that was a leg bye.

Not surprisingly, Ted was annoyed at all that had happened and he tried to bowl at a fairly nippy pace when we went in to make the runs for victory. He bowled one bouncer to me outside the off stump which I flashed at and missed. It didn't miss by much and wicketkeeper and slips all threw up their hands in annoyance.

I turned round to them and said 'Pity I didn't get a top edge to that. It might have gone for six.'

The next ball from Ted was another bouncer. I flashed again, somehow managed to middle it and it went for six *over third man*! It was one of my most unusual and most memorable shots. I think I was more surprised than anybody, except perhaps Les Lenham who was fielding at third man and watched the ball soar over his head into the crowd.

So we gambolled and gambled our way to the last but one match of the season at Bournemouth. Once more Derbyshire were our opponents – victory would give us the championship. A draw or defeat meant the prospect of facing second-in-the-table Yorkshire in a match to decide the destiny of the title. And none of the Hampshire team fancied that!

This time Colin's tactics exasperated several of the senior players, especially when Derbyshire went out after lunch on the second day to continue their first innings chase to match our total of 306. For a period of one hour between lunch and tea Colin kept the all spin attack of Peter Sainsbury and Alan Wassell while Laurie Johnson and Bill Oates added 100 runs.

Few of us could understand why he persisted with the slower bowlers. Admittedly the occasional ball was going up in the air but not to hand and Colin probably thought one of them would give a catch before long.

Not for the first occasion I thought Colin had given away 20 or 30 runs in a day which made our task harder, but everything worked out. We went on to win that match against Derbyshire without trouble. In another match Colin's bowling changes in one day consisted of bowling Shack and Vic Cannings between the start and lunch, Peter Sainsbury and Mervyn Burden between lunch and tea and Shack and Cannings from tea to the close. Truly, the gods looked kindly upon Colin that summer. Together they saw us safely home, although many had predicted we would crack under the pressures and allow Middlesex and Yorkshire to go on to fight out the title between them.

The reason we didn't can be traced back to 1958 – Colin's first year of captaincy – when we led the County Championship from mid-June to the final run in late August after going from May 21 to August 26 with only one defeat.

That season the tension was too much for us. We were still a fairly young side and I don't think we possessed sufficient confidence in our ability. We were top of the table but could not really understand why we were top. An uncomfortable feeling existed among us that we did not belong there. I suppose it was an inferiority complex because Hampshire had never previously been a tremendous force in the Championship.

We should have taken the title then and there but, like Gloucestershire in 1969, we were frightened of winning and we lost. By 1961 we had learned to withstand pressure. We had been through it all before in 1958 and knew how to live with tension. Nine of the regular side in 1961 had played regularly in 1958.

Things started to go wrong in 1958 when we played Derbyshire at Burton on a wet wicket and lost by 103 runs, being bowled out for 23 and 55. Altogether 39 wickets fell on that second day. And I consider we were lucky not to have been beaten by a wider margin!

I made four but before I scored, I made two very poor shots against Harold Rhodes and I don't know to this day why I wasn't bowled. Somebody else edged on through slips and should have been caught but scored four runs. Another batsman thought he heard a 'No ball' called, took a mighty swing and hit a boundary. He would never have done that if he had realised the shout had come from the crowd and not the umpire. That was 12 runs we were lucky to get, so that our 23 runs might easily have been 11!

Not only was 1961 a happy season for me because of the Championship victory, it was my benefit season and I scored 2,607 runs, my best aggregate in County cricket.

Normally I hope I am not considered a mercenary character but a cricketer's life is not particularly rewarding financially and a benefit provides the one opportunity of making money to cater for the future.

So before the season started I made up my mind to score as many runs as possible. I would not throw my wicket away once I had reached a 'ton'. I knew that the more runs I made, the more money I would get, and I shall always be grateful to the kind people of Hampshire for supporting me as magnificently as they did.

My figure reached £5,865.

With this policy in mind I suppose it was no coincidence that I scored my first double century in my career – and it could not have come at a better time.

We had returned to Bournemouth after a disastrous tour up North during which we failed to take a point off Yorkshire and Lancashire. Somerset provided the opposition and we were soon struggling again, being bowled out for 137 on a turning wicket, Brian Langford, the Somerset off spinner, came on after only seven overs of the new ball, and took six wickets.

Somerset gained a 102 run first innings lead and we started a second time on a wicket which was wearing badly. We certainly did not fancy our chances and I did not fancy mine in particular.

In the previous match against Lancashire I had batted badly, making nine and nought. In the first innings of this match I scored only five. I felt my form had deserted me and was far from confident when I started my second innings.

I remember Ken Palmer bowling to me and I got an inside edge which just shaved the leg stump and went through for four. I had groped for the delivery. I wasn't batting like a man in form but for some unaccountable reason everything clicked after that escape and I went on to make 212 out of our total of 363, the next highest score being 47 by Danny Livingstone.

Taking the conditions into consideration I would reckon that was one of the best performances of my career. After that early error against Ken Palmer I could do no wrong as Jimmy Gray and I put on 155 for the first wicket, 116 of them coming from my bat. Danny helped me add 112 in 84 minutes for the fourth wicket. I batted for 260 minutes and I see the record books show I hit seven sixes and 21 fours.

Naturally, the score gave me immense pleasure but, most important of all, it gave Hampshire a chance of winning a match we had looked likely to lose. And win it we did – which set us off on a run of five successive victories which put us boldly on the championship trail.

Yes, 1961 proved the highlight of my career, the most memorable summer of all time as far as I am concerned. I thank all those who made it possible.

9 *Colin and Company*

The County Championship has thrown up many more glamorous sides than Hampshire. Certainly there have been far more successful counties. I knew, too, that I would probably have been paid more by several others but I am certain I could not have joined a *better* bunch of men.

I have enjoyed my cricket immensely with Hampshire C.C.C. I have them to thank for so many, many happy hours and I am grateful in particular to Jimmy Gray who opened with me through the majority of my seasons and gave me such tremendous and unselfish support.

He helped me settle down in the county. He encouraged me, both on and off the field and I would not have been so successful in the number of runs I have scored without his advice.

During the 1961 season we shared six century opening partnerships, three more in the nineties and three more in the seventies. Together we hold the record opening partnership for the county of 249 and we took part in 33 partnerships of over 100 in our time together.

Perhaps the biggest contribution Jimmy made towards my well being with Hampshire was the fact that he – the established player in the side – changed his style and game to suit me. I did not have to adapt my game to his demands.

In 1955 when I had my first Championship season with Hampshire, Jimmy went through a miserable summer and could never get going. Although I did not realise it at the time, I was largely responsible for his failure that summer.

You see, he suddenly found himself batting with somebody who was scoring twice as fast as he was. Somebody who wanted all the bowling when in form. Once I got going I would take a single off the fifth or sixth ball of the over in order to take the strike. Jimmy never grumbled. He just concentrated on adapting his game to fit the changed circumstances.

He was a very thoughtful player, meticulous in his appearance, and in his habits. Whereas I am basically an untidy fellow who leaves his clothes strewn about a hotel room, Jimmy would always put his shirts in one drawer, his handkerchiefs in another, etc.

I would not trust very many cricketers to give me an accurate and detailed description of how I got out but I could rely implicitly on Jimmy's judgement.

Whenever I was dismissed while he was at the wicket I would wait for him and ask him what happened. He would tell me in concise terms: 'You played a bad shot,' or 'You left a gate,' or 'You followed the ball,' or 'You played absolutely correctly but the ball did a bit and you stood no chance.'

This sort of information is even more important when you are going through a bad patch. Jimmy helped solve a number of my problems this way. I think I was able to solve a number of his as well, but it was only with Jimmy that I could do this. I batted with Henry Horton a considerable number of times but I could never ask him what I had done wrong. He was too absorbed in his own game to be able to tell me.

Sharing a hotel room with Jimmy on our away matches obviously helped as well. Often after play all the Hampshire players would meet in the bar and discuss the day's events.

Jimmy and I would carry this conversation further before settling down to a night's sleep. We would analyse particular aspects of the cricket and discuss ways and means of improving our batting techniques.

I recall a clear instance of this in 1958 when we played Gloucestershire at Bristol. For years batsmen had complained about the wicket, saying it was too slow and almost impossible to play strokes. Even the Gloucestershire players moaned about it and many of them blamed this for Tom Graveney's in-and-out career in the 1950's. Certainly, he became a more consistent batsman when he moved to Worcestershire.

On this particular occasion we were in trouble. Gloucestershire had made 201, bowled us out for 89 and scored another 120 in their second innings. We were left to score 233 for victory and nobody thought it was really on.

Before falling asleep on the second night Jimmy and I sat up in our beds discussing the peculiarities of the Bristol wicket which certainly played odd tricks from time to time. Many batsmen got themselves out by walking to the wicket convinced they were not going to stay very long. A lot of cricket is in the mind.

Jimmy and I thought about this, admitted to each other that the odd delivery was going to be awkward but decided that in between these occasional awkward balls there would be many opportunities for scoring runs. If we got a nasty one, there was nothing we could do about it. But between times there was no reason to hold back our strokes.

By the time we had finished our discussion we had satisfied ourselves that the right policy was to play our natural game. This we did, put on 70 for the first wicket before Jimmy was out and I went on to make a century. We won the match with five wickets to spare.

Even now I am not quite sure how I originally came to open with Jimmy. A certain amount of uncertainty has always surrounded the decision.

When I joined Hampshire, I told Desmond Eagar that opening was my favourite position and that was the job I wanted if it were possible. The county already had a regular pair of openers in Jimmy and Neville Rogers and would have preferred me lower down. They told me so, but they appreciated that I was not too happy at the thought of not going in first.

Before the 1955 season opened we were due to play our usual pre-season friendly match against Sussex. Neville and Jimmy were down as the opening batsmen.

Driving over to Sussex on the morning of the match I went in my own car and took Jimmy with me. Neville went in Desmond Eagar's car.

On the way they stopped at a café for coffee and were not at Hove when the match was due to start. We had no alternative but to bat and I opened with Jimmy. I batted steadily and I stayed in that position.

Whether the others had stopped at the café to make themselves late so that I could go in first I have never discovered, but I have always been thankful that circumstances worked out the way they did.

Apart from Jimmy, I suppose I saw more of Henry Horton than any other Hampshire batsmen. We were fairly successful together but we never established the same understanding.

As I said earlier Henry would become completely enveloped in his own batting, concentrating so hard that he rarely had any time left to think of the batsman at the other end. Consequently he was not a good runner between the wickets. He was a late caller because he came out of his concentration too late and this resulted in many narrow escapes.

Yet you could not wish to have a more dependable cricketer in your side than Henry. His peculiar stance made it appear as though he was resting on an invisible shooting stick as he waited for each delivery.

If somebody came to me now and said 'If you could have

one man from all those you have seen in the past to complete your side who would you choose,' I would have no hesitation in asking for Henry.

You could not find a more reliable batsman or a greater fighter. He saved Hampshire time and time again by his refusal to quit when the chips were down and the odds stacked heavily against him.

Another wonderful servant for the side over the years has been Peter Sainsbury, a player in the Jimmy Gray mould in that he thinks deeply about the game. I have a lot of admiration for him.

Peter, who made his county debut back in 1954, is not a batsman endowed with a lot of natural ability. I think he would be the first to admit that he is not as talented as perhaps half the players in the County Championship today. Yet he has been as effective as those with greater gifts by extracting the maximum from the ability he has been able to summon.

I don't think I have seen a better fielder than Peter, day in and day out. He is accepted throughout cricket as one of the best short leg fielders in this country – if not the best.

Because he fields there 90 per cent of the time people accept him only as a first-class short leg. In fact, he is an outstanding fielder in any position whether it be at slip, cover or out in the deep. How many cricketers can you think of with such all-round fielding ability.

He took over from another superb short leg fielder in Desmond Eagar, a captain who could lead by example when he demanded a high standard of catching.

Desmond was never satisfied with himself and could never get close enough to the batsman. At the start he would stand closer than the majority of short legs – and if the ball pitched in front of him, he would mark the spot and move up. If it still pitched in front of him, he would go nearer and nearer. I have seen him take some incredible catches to his left hand, pure reaction catches but once they were in his hand they rarely dropped out.

Desmond, incidentally sported an Oxford Harlequin cap when I first joined Hampshire. He always wore it in the South of England but never in the North except on one occasion. This was against Yorkshire. When a couple of little boys saw him in the cap, they commented 'There goes Gordon Richards.' Desmond survived a couple of balls, and as he returned to the pavilion, the same couple added, 'First past the post again!' In getting changed his first move was to put on his cap. The ritual never ceased to amuse us as he undressed from his civvies down to the nude and then put on his cricket gear, all the time with that cap firmly settled on his head.

Fielding played an important role in our Championship success in 1961 and much of it was inspired by the example of Peter Sainsbury and, indeed, Danny Livingstone, who has an extremely safe pair of hands.

We must have saved a number of runs in the field that year which was vitally important when Colin dangled tempting carrots in the way of opposition batsmen by his sporting declarations. We took a number of wickets by run outs. Not returns to the wicket-keeper but direct throws at the wicket.

Somerset discovered our accuracy in our second match of the season on a dreadful wicket at Frome.

In a low scoring match they needed only 172 to win. I say only but it was a formidable target on a wicket taking spin. Somerset started well by scoring 29 in good time but then they made their first error of judgement in going for a single – Colin Ingleby-Mackenzie, who was not the best of fielders, picked up smartly at mid-on and ran out Miles Lawrence with a direct throw.

Although we were generally in command, we feared two men in that Somerset side. Harold Stephenson and Brian Langford who were both capable of slogging the spinners.

Harold did not last long. He played a delivery wide of Colin and called for a single. As he raced down the wicket he shouted 'Lightning can't strike in the same place twice,' but it did, and Harold was run out.

They were two very important run outs. As we feared, Langford struck some lusty blows and Somerset were only 18 runs short when their last wicket fell.

I suppose Carlton Forbes could justifiably consider himself unlucky against us that season. We ran him out twice.

The first time was a vitally important occasion. We had two splendid matches against Nottinghamshire that season and in the first game at Southampton they made a brave bid to score 196 runs for victory in 125 minutes.

I did not play because of injury and had spent the day on Brockenhurst Golf Club. However, I returned to the county ground in time to see the closing stages. Notts needed another 16 runs with two wickets left when Forbes backed himself to beat a return from Peter Sainsbury. He would have done so if somebody had had to take the return and whip off the bails but Peter knocked the stumps over.

That was 180 for nine and another direct hit, this time by Denis Baldry, dismissed the last man Mike Morgan at the same score, and we won by 15 runs with three minutes to spare.

In the return match at Trent Bridge just over a month later we scored 358 for six declared and Nottinghamshire were heading towards a possible first innings lead when Carlton – or 'Cha-cha' as he is known – was run out in an unfortunate way.

He hit the ball extremely hard and went for two runs. Danny made a fine stop and his return broke the wicket with Carlton just home on his second run. The ball glanced off the wicket and Carlton went for a third but I managed to pick it up and ran Carlton out at the bowler's end with another direct throw. We won that match as well.

Mentioning Forbes, a big friendly fellow from Jamaica, reminds me of a story involving Fred Trueman which demonstrates how cricketers treat the black v white issue which seems to bother everybody else in the world except cricketers. If only politicians could find a similar language to use when discussing racialism, the problem would quickly disappear.

Yorkshire were playing Nottinghamshire at Trent Bridge and the weather had not been too kind. As the Yorkshire team arrived at the ground the light was very bad with dark thunderous clouds covering the whole of the sky. Fred, as he usually did, made straight for the opposition dressing room, poked his head round the door and said to the Nottinghamshire lads, 'It doesn't look as though we'll get much play today. It's a bloody Carlton out there.'

But to return to Hampshire's fielding I have already referred to Danny Livingstone's catching ability. He seldom missed much and one incident in that vitally important last-but-one match of the 1961 season against Derbyshire illustrates the faith we had in him.

Derbyshire stood no chance of winning the match and we needed only one more wicket on the last evening to clinch victory and the Championship.

We were held up by some stubborn resistance from Bob Taylor who was attacking the spin bowlers. Two or three times he struck Peter Sainsbury over long on.

Once more he swung the bat at Sainsbury and this time the ball soared in the direction of long on where Livingstone was fielding.

Bob had given it a mighty crack and by the time that ball had started its descent we were already on the way to the dressing room where the bubbly was opened and waiting for us. We had not the slightest doubt that Danny would take the catch and he was left on an almost deserted stretch of outfield to hold it while we raced off without a backward glance.

The first time I saw Danny in Hampshire was in a pre-season practice match against Somerset before the 1959 season and I marvelled at his ability as a left-handed batsman. I did not think it was possible for one player to look so good. Although Danny has performed well for Hampshire since then I don't think he has quite succeeded in showing his true ability. Nevertheless, he has achieved many notable feats for the county including a century in each innings against Kent at Canterbury in 1964 and he holds the ninth wicket record for Hampshire – sharing 230 with Alan Castell against Surrey at Southampton in 1962.

From 1955 until 1961 we had a fairly settled side which must have helped us in our Championship cause. Eight of the 1955 side were still going strong in 1961. One of the newcomers was Danny. The other was 'Butch' White and he made a tremendous difference.

For a long time 'Butch' played under the cloud of having twice been called for throwing against Sussex in 1960. This was complete rubbish. 'Butch' could never throw with his action.

The trouble started in the previous match at Portsmouth when we were trying to blast our way through the Nottinghamshire second innings, after gaining a first innings lead of 122 runs.

During that last afternoon 'Butch' bowled several bouncers with Paul Gibb umpiring from square leg. Nothing was said at the time.

From Portsmouth we went to Hove to play Sussex and Gibb was again one of the umpires.

All went along peacefully until Graham Cooper came in to bat. For some reason I have not discovered, Cooper is like a red rag to a bull as far as 'Butch' is concerned – at least at the wicket. It is just one of many private individual battles which go on in cricket.

As soon as Graham came in 'Butch' bowled a bouncer and

immediately there was a shout of 'no ball' from Gibb at square leg. None of us could understand it. We thought we must have had three men behind square on the leg side or something like that. Certainly, we never thought in the terms of throwing.

'Butch' bowled the next delivery without any trouble and as he walked back he said to me, 'What was all that about just now?'

'I'm not quite sure,' I told him. 'I think he's called you for throwing. Bowl another bouncer and see what happens.'

'Butch' did and Gibb again called him for throwing. Those two calls were a great shock to us all because we could not see how 'Butch' could possibly fall foul of the throwing regulation. It was a physical impossibility.

'Butch' should have been a regular player for England in the early sixties. Some people may criticise my captaincy, but I am sure that if I had been leading Hampshire at the time, 'Butch' would have been a regular in England's Test side.

'Butch' is a great character, very much in the Trueman mould. He can be relied upon for a funny remark to lift the tension in the dressing room, likes his pint of beer, gives everything he has got at all times and is very aggressive as a bowler.

Everything was right for him when he came on the scene. Trueman and Brian Statham, although not over the hill by a long way, were coming towards the end of their Test career when 'Butch' started to make an impression.

No other genuine fast bowler was around at the time and 'Butch' should have been the natural successor. Instead he played in only two Tests against Pakistan in Pakistan on the 1961–62 tour.

Under Colin Ingleby-Mackenzie's captaincy we were sometimes a little slack and 'Butch' came under this influence. If I had been in command I believe I would have been able to steer and push 'Butch' into greater effort early in his career and he would have made an even bigger impression than he did.

Not many batsmen could have annoyed bowlers so consistently as Colin. He was an extraordinarily difficult person when it came to setting a field for him. Bowlers did not know how or where to bowl to him and nothing upset them more than to see what they considered 'unearned' runs coming from his bat.

They could bowl a delivery to Colin outside the off stump and he would miss it by three inches. They would put the next ball in exactly the same place and he would connect with a mighty wallop.

When he did middle there was no telling where the ball would go. With what looked to be the same cross-batted swipe he could either send it sizzling through the covers before a fielder had a chance to move, or high over square leg.

One of his most dazzling performances came in 1958 against Kent at Southampton over the Whit weekend. An innings of sheer magical unorthodox strokes, sharpened by a tinge of anger.

Kent batted very slowly on a good wicket on the Saturday and made 266 for five. Rain delayed the start on the Monday until 1 o'clock and Colin Cowdrey decided to bat on – a move which was almost unheard of in those days and which annoyed us intensely.

We collapsed badly when we batted and only the last pair saved the follow on. In the end we were set to score 305 to win in four and a half hours – not a generous task by any means, the target being 26 runs higher than the previous highest total in the match.

I know I was seething when I walked to the crease and the only thought I had in my mind was 'I'll make sure I'm not beaten by these so and sos.' David Blake, who was deputising for Leo Harrison, opened with me and started getting a few runs. By lunchtime we had taken the score to over 50 and I began thinking in terms of going for victory, instead of merely avoiding defeat.

To have a chance it was essential that Colin should bring his agricultural swipes to the wicket next and he promoted himself in the order when David was out.

Kent hardly knew what struck them. Colin hit everybody out of sight as he raced to his century in 98 minutes. Together we put on 204 runs in 109 minutes. Both of us were determined to make Kent pay for their shabby batting policy on the second day and we won with 10 minutes left and with five wickets to spare.

Colin went even faster against Somerset that same year on the Bournemouth wicket – after one of his later nights. The position was just right for a slog when he went in. Jimmy Gray and myself had scored 144 before lunch and everybody had made a few.

Henry Horton was at the wicket when Colin arrived and how Somerset suffered! With Colin charging and swinging at everything and Henry attempting to do the same, our score increased by 161 runs in 66 minutes. Colin took only 61 minutes over his century. That was some hitting.

Colin's great love of the turf and gambling often clashed with his cricket but he would not let cricket interfere with his thirst for knowledge of the winners of the big races.

I remember once when we were playing at Lord's and were in the field on the afternoon of the 1,000 Guineas. Colin had wagered a few pounds and naturally wanted to know as soon as possible whether he had won.

His solution was to find a small transistor radio which he gave to umpire Harry Baldwin, himself a bit of a character, and stationed himself at square leg so that he could hear the race uninterrupted. Only Colin would have dared to do that at Lord's.

On another occasion Colin's racing thirst caused a misunderstanding. We were playing at Bristol over the weekend and Colin went down to breakfast to join Henry Horton. As Colin, head buried in the racing pages, sat down at the table Henry looked up from the cricket scoreboard in his own paper and said 'Leicester had a good day yesterday skipper.'

'Yes,' replied Colin, 'He's not a bad jockey, that fellow.'

None of our high times in the late fifties and early sixties would have been possible without Derek Shackleton. Throughout his career Derek carried a secret with him. *He was almost blind in his left eye.*

His failing sight in that eye was discovered by the school optician when he was about 13 or 14. Derek kept the secret to himself by conveniently forgetting to give the optician's report to his parents. I never knew about it until Derek retired from the game.

Many people thought of Derek as a defensive bowler but he was much more than that. He must have been to have taken so many wickets in his career.

In fact, he was a very deceptive bowler, looking at him from the boundary. He bowled with a very easy, economical action. He just seemed to flow up to the crease without apparently putting much effort behind the delivery. The delivery itself looked innocent enough.

I am sure this must have lured many batsmen into a false sense of security when he first started bowling in county cricket. Yet he could do most things with the ball. He kept it just short enough of a length to prevent batsmen slogging him and he was capable of moving it either way.

Few batsmen ever really got hold of him although there were two for whom Shack held no terrors whatsoever. Time and again Fred Trueman tucked into Shack and pasted him around the park with his bold, cross batted swipes. The other is the present Essex captain Brian Taylor whose left handed big hitting always presented problems for Shack. Brian, one of the hardest hitters in the game, had the knack of picking

Shack up beautifully and carting him over mid wicket or long on.

No chapter on Hampshire would be complete without a word on Leo Harrison, a better wicket-keeper than many people gave him credit for. Alert, nimble and full of life Leo helped us considerably in 1961 by bringing his experience to bear on the lower order batsmen. He was a very knowledgeable man to have around when the chips were down – as they most certainly were on occasions during that spectacular summer.

10 *Fear of Fast Bowling*

Nobody likes fast bowling. Some people just play it better than others. I am not ashamed to admit that there have been many occasions in my life when I have been frightened as I went out to face a fast bowler for the first time in a match.

I have had two battles to overcome. First the one in the dressing room trying to calm myself as I pulled on my flannels and shirt, laced up my boots and strapped on my pads. That was to overcome my thoughts. The second battle was overcoming the fast bowler himself.

Many people may wonder why I became an opening batsman when I had this fear inside me. The plain truth is that I just cannot bear hanging around. I get even more nervous if I have to sit in the dressing room and watch other batsmen going through agonies at the crease while I am waiting for my turn to come.

In a way, opening the innings was forced upon me, although it is true I did volunteer for the job myself when playing for the Foundation School in Barbados. As I said earlier in the book, nobody wanted to open at this particular time and I opened my big mouth as I was apt to do at that stage in my life.

When, at the age of about 14, I moved to the Lodge School

in Barbados they put me down to number three or four in the order. When I first started attracting the attention of the Barbados selectors, they remembered that I had shown promise as an opening batsman and I went back to that position for the school side.

Barbados used me as an opening batsman but on tour with the West Indies I played all over the shop. I have already related the story of how I became Hampshire's opening batsman in 1955 but, despite getting over 2,000 runs that season, I am sure that Hampshire did not think it was my best position.

In the second season they asked me to consider dropping down the order to number three or four and I agreed, albeit reluctantly.

I think I only played in that position for three matches and in two of them I found myself facing the new ball when it was only two or three overs old.

In the end I told Hampshire: 'If I am going to face the new ball anyway, then I might as well face it right from the start.' They put me back to number one and there I stayed until Barry Richards joined us from South Africa.

When Barry arrived in 1968 I met him off the boat and asked him where he preferred to bat. He told me, 'I don't mind. I'll bat wherever Hampshire think best.'

At that time I was opening with Barry Reed and although we might not have been the best opening pair in county cricket, we had our fair share of success. The committee decided to leave it that way with Barry Richards batting at number four.

We kept this going for the first few matches of the season but Richards did not get the runs he thought he should be getting and I could sense that he was keen to open.

Although not originally an opener, Barry had been opening for Natal in the season before he joined us. At the time, South Africa were short of recognised Test class opening batsmen, and for the sake of his career, and because I was not getting any runs, we decided to change round.

Suggestions were made that Barry should open with me but we decided against that. Anybody is likely to get out against the new ball and it was felt that if Barry and I should fall early it might cause the rest of the side to panic.

So the change around took place and worked wonders immediately, with Richards scoring a century in each innings against Northamptonshire. He never looked back that season and I doubt if he will ever look back again.

Perhaps I was being a little selfish in wanting to open but like most batsmen I never feel at ease until I get one off the mark. Few things are worse in cricket for a recognised batsman than to return to the dressing room with a nought after his name and I think I stand a better chance of avoiding the dreaded 'duck' when going in first.

For a start there are more opportunities to score. The bowler generally requires two or three deliveries – sometimes a couple of overs – to get into his stride and to find his rhythm. So that means you are quite likely to receive a loose delivery or two in the early moments of the innings.

Secondly a fast bowler always starts with an attacking field. Every member of the inner ring of fieldsmen is crouching close to the wicket hoping for a catch and perhaps only two fielders are patrolling an area away from the wicket. It is generally easy to get a run somewhere, off the opening overs. If the ball is swinging, there is the added chance that you will get a run off the edge.

I did count up once and found that I had played more than 50 innings in first-class cricket before I was out for my first duck and that came against Victoria in Melbourne towards the end of my visit to Australia in 1951–52. Since then, of course, I have bagged a pair and been out for ducks more times than I care to recall but, even today, I feel it is so important to get that first run.

A true professional at his craft and a model of accuracy – Derek Shackleton

The moment all batsmen relish!

Now where's that one gone? Colin Ingleby-Mackenzie seems to be saying

And I'm wondering, too!

If I can survive the new ball I am in a far better position to dictate to the bowlers for the rest of my innings. I will probably have 20 or 30 runs behind me by the time the first change is made. In the old days that usually meant a spinner coming on but nowadays it is usually a medium paced bowler who replaces the fast bowler.

Whoever it is, he is only just starting when I have been going for 45 minutes or so. That gives me a feeling of 'one-upmanship', if you like, and I reckon that the bowler is probably more worried about me than I am about him.

I always felt, for instance, that Tony Lock – great bowler though he was – never really fancied coming on to bowl against me when I had been in for a little while. If he didn't fancy it, then surely he could not bowl at his best!

On the other hand, how different it might have been if Tony had been bowling for a spell when I first walked to the wicket. I doubt whether I would have lasted very long.

One of the disadvantages of batting lower down the order is that the incoming batsman faces a bowler who has just taken a wicket. Obviously that bowler is feeling on top of the world and is thirsting for more blood. The newcomer has to fight his way into a position where he can dictate.

The advantages to opening which I have outlined, more than make up for that sinking feeling I have known when going out to face a genuine fast bowler who is sending down a hard object at you at speeds of upwards of 80 mph.

I have never told anybody before of my fear of facing a top class fast bowler. For years I shared a room on tour with Jimmy Gray and not once did he ever mention to me that sometimes he was frightened, although I am sure he must have been on occasions. Of course, some people appear not to have any nerves. They are the lucky ones.

The Hampshire players may not have noticed anything different in my approach when I was due to face somebody really fast. Yet if anybody had studied me over the years, they would notice on these occasions that I would be quieter than usual. I would dislike anybody talking to me, anybody laughing or making a funny crack. If I have snapped at anybody just before going out to bat then they now know the reason why.

Freddie Trueman could upset me in this way. He was always in the visitors' dressing room before the start of a match to try out his latest line of stories. On one occasion in Bradford he burst in, full of life, just at the time when I was trying to settle myself and overcome this fear, not only the fear of failure but the fear of physical danger.

I remember thinking to myself: 'Why doesn't he get the hell out of here. What right has he got to come in here cracking jokes at this moment when, in a few minutes' time out there in the middle, he will be trying to knock my head off?' I don't mind laughing and joking after the game but I certainly don't want it before the game starts.

People have asked me: 'Who would you sooner face, a fast bowler or a slow bowler?' My answer has always been that against a fast bowler you encounter two fears. The fear of getting out and the fear of being injured. Against a medium paced bowler or a spin bowler there is only one worry to occupy your mind: that of being dismissed.

Whether I was scared or experienced the normal apprehension any batsman feels before going to the crease depended upon several things. First of all, the pace and the reputation of the fast bowler on the opposing side, plus the pace of the wicket. I have come across some genuine quick bowlers and never worried about them in many matches because I knew they were unlikely to get any assistance from the wicket. On the other hand, I have met bowlers of fast medium pace and been worried because they were operating on a track that was to give them every assistance and, therefore, they could prove dangerous.

Yet there have been half a dozen bowlers through my

career who have brought my heart into my mouth on their reputation alone, whatever the conditions underfoot. Starting with Ray Lindwall and Keith Miller back in Australia in 1951–52. I had never seen anything like them before.

They were faster than anything we had ever seen, which explains the West Indies' failure during that series. A bouncer was a genuine part of their armoury.

Now and again in the West Indies we had bowlers who would get mad for a delivery or two but they could never keep up the pace and even on our fast wickets we saw very few bouncers.

Lindwall and Miller used the short pitched delivery which reared up chest high as a deliberate part of their tactics. Such balls were designed to make you apprehensive and force you to fend off the ball with a chance of it popping up a catch. They used it in the same way as they would bowl an out-swinger, a slower ball or a faster ball, all part of their tactical campaign against us.

Lindwall never appeared to bowl flat out, although he was very quick. You always felt that he was holding something back to produce an even faster delivery just now and again. Of all the bowlers I have met I think his run-up was the most rhythmic and controlled I have seen. I would go anywhere to see him. Lindwall in full flow was one of the great sights of cricket – as long as he wasn't bowling at me!

Miller was far different. He bowled off a shorter run and you could never really tell what he was going to do next. He could bowl a real fast one, a gentle medium-pace, an off-cutter and, now and again, toss in a slow googly. I think it took a lot of nerve to face these two. I can appreciate how both Sir Len Hutton and Cyril Washbrook must have felt in the late 40's and early 50's when they had to take everything from this fine pair, knowing that there was no bowler in the England side at that time who was capable of dishing it back.

Not that there was much joy in getting away from Miller

and Lindwall only to face Fred Trueman and Brian Statham who were then climbing towards the peak of their careers.

Freddie was one of the fastest bowlers I have come across, *in his day,* but to be at his best everything had to be right for him. He had to feel on top of the world himself and he had to be sure that the wicket suited him. Brian, on the other hand, lacked Freddie's extra zip but bowled his heart out, whether the wicket suited him or not.

Then Tyson came on the scene. Frank could never bowl slow. I first came across him just before he went on the tour to Australia in 1954–55 when we played against each other in a Torquay festival match. I still recall the feeling of shock which came over me as I settled down to face my first delivery from him. Apart from my partner and the umpire at the other end, everyone else seemed to be almost out of sight, including Frank, who was running in almost from the boundary line.

The match meant nothing, except as entertainment for spectators in an area starved of first-class cricket. Yet even in those circumstances, Frank could not bowl slowly and it was the same in the nets. Frank was almost as fast then as he was out in the middle.

In 1956 we went to Rushden and played them on a slow wicket and Frank was not any real trouble and I managed to score a century. But someone who must have had a strange sense of humour, had arranged for a return match to be played at Portsmouth which was then the fastest wicket in the country.

None of our players was looking forward to this match and I knew it would take a brave effort to resist Frank on that day.

In those days I had a theory about playing fast bowlers on fast wickets. I thought that if I threw my bat at the ball then even if I got an edge the ball would fly away so quickly that the fielders would never stand a chance of catching it.

That, in fact, is how I played Frank at Portsmouth. The ball went everywhere and Frank grew angrier and angrier at each run I scored. Finally, after I had flashed at another one that flew just over slips head and went to the boundary for four, Frank turned around to the Northants captain, Dennis Brookes and said 'All right, let's have all the fielders out and we'll play baseball.'

You can often tell what type of delivery to expect from a fast bowler but I had no idea what Frank was going to deliver next. I had never seen him that angry before and I was trying to make up my mind whether it would be a bouncer *or a beamer*. In any event I was expecting one to come around my head.

Instead Frank bowled me a half-volley and I took a tremendous swing at it. I caught it right in the middle of the bat and it flew through the covers before anybody could move. That was the last ball of the over and Dennis Brookes turned to Frank and said 'Take your sweater now.' I was so relieved that when I got up the other end I was out first ball! I had fought a battle with Frank – and myself – and won. Yet I was never able to enjoy the fruits of my victory.

Those are the five fellows who have caused me most anxiety about their speed.

When I say scared I don't mean to say that I went out to the wicket shivering and shaking, but I thought about it in the dressing room and I was conscious of the damage they could do. I hope it didn't show. Even today I feel the same way when I come up against John Snow or Alan Ward, but being scared doesn't mean that you are going to run away.

Fortunately I have not suffered greatly in the way of physical injury, apart from the bruised and battered fingers and knuckles which all cricketers get from time to time. The worst was in 1957 at Canterbury when I was hit by Fred Ridgway – a bowler who never scared me in the slightest. In fact, I was so sure of myself against Fred that I played him off the front foot, something I would never attempt when tackling Tyson. This probably caused the trouble. I was on the front foot when Fred dropped one short. I went to hook and it glanced up and caught me just below my left eye. I was taken to hospital where I needed six stitches in the wound.

By the time I returned to the ground we were in danger of following on and I had to bat again. Ridgway was bowling when I went in and the sight of my puffed eye with stitches and dressing was enough to make Fred give me another bouncer immediately. It missed me which was not surprising because by that time I was flat on my back! Still I got up and managed to make 50.

The next match was at Portsmouth against Surrey who had Peter Loader in their side. In those days his action, at times, was not all it should have been. Knowing Loader's pace and the nature of the wicket, Desmond Eagar asked me if I wanted to play. I insisted on going out. If I had not played in that match I am sure my confidence would have been shaken for a long time. As it was I had one of my best games, scoring 50 in the first innings and a century in the second innings.

When I was about 70 in the second innings Peter produced a real sizzler that caught me on the temple only an inch or so away from those six stitches. I was so angry that I did not even feel the blow at the time but I am sure that if Peter had come near me – even to apologise – I would have crowned him with the bat!

I know that after those two blows the whole of my face felt tender. So tender that after the game I could not even pick up my daughter and give her a cuddle which must have seemed strange to her. She was then only three years old.

Some fast bowlers do not appear to show any sympathy towards a batsman when they hit them. My fellow countryman, Charlie Griffith was one of them. A batsman could be doubled up at the other end and Charlie's face would not seem to show the slightest concern.

Yet his partner, Wes Hall, was just the opposite. I played against Wes in Jamaica when I toured with the Cavaliers in 1965 and in this match he twice hit me on the chest.

Each time I had played at him with the bat fairly high up. I did not rub the spot because I wanted Wes to think I had taken each one on my gloves and was not worried.

Later that night my chest felt painful and while a group of us were having a drink in a hotel room, Wes walked in. I said to him :

'What the hell were you doing today. Trying to kill me?'

'Why man, I didn't even touch you,' replied Wes.

'Yes you did. Twice you caught me on the chest.'

'Man,' said Wes. 'You know I wouldn't try to hit you.'

I am sure that Wes genuinely meant it. Mind you, our association went back a long way, to the time I used to pay him half-a-crown a session to bowl at me. Imagine anybody paying somebody of Wes's pace to bowl at him ! I rank him, along with Tyson, as the fastest I have faced.

My 'lessons' from Wes took place in 1957 when I went on the Duke of Norfolk's tour to the West Indies. I had gone to Barbados a fortnight earlier and I went down to the Wanderers Club in the afternoons for practice. The groundsman told me he knew of a young fast bowler, who had just left school, who would give me the practice I needed. I said 'fine, bring him along.'

The next day this gangling youth appeared and bowled at me for half an hour. At the end we went back to the pavilion where I bought him a 'coke' and gave him half-a-crown for his trouble. This happened two or three afternoons and it was not until some time later that I learned the person concerned was the one and only Wes Hall.

To play fast bowling properly – or any bowling come to

that – I like to consider what I am going to do *before* I walk out to the wicket.

I don't mean where to score runs or how I am going to strike out, but my first basic movement. It is essential for me to know the pace of the bowler and the pace of the wicket. From this I can then decide whether I should make the back foot my initial movement or whether I can risk going on the front foot. These basic movements were the ones I employed before the introduction of the new lbw experimental law, introduced for the 1970 Championship season.

As I said earlier I always played Fred Ridgway of Kent off the front foot. I was always on the back foot against Tyson. I decided on this tactic before I went to the wicket. I believe it is impossible to wait until the ball is actually coming towards you to decide which way to go.

Even Gary Sobers is the same. Study Sobers closely at the crease and you will find that his first movement is always slightly back on his left foot. This takes the weight initially, which is why he is such a fine player of the short ball.

Where Sobers is so fortunate is that he has the reflexes to take him on the front foot immediately he needs to be there. It looks to many people as though he has been on the front foot all the time, so perfect is his execution of the stroke. In fact, he has moved backwards initially.

Most players are superstitious. I don't like batting in a cap. I once had a run of failures and I tried wearing one while I was at the crease. That did not make any difference, so I threw the cap away and started making runs again. Since then I have avoided a cap as far as possible. I don't mind so much when I have made a few runs and I am set but I will not start my innings with one unless the sun is absolutely blinding me.

11 *Best of their Breed*

I've always been more proud of the runs I scored against Brian Statham than those I took off Freddie Trueman.

Freddie was faster but he was more erratic and with my policy of trying to combat force with force, I found it easier to get runs against Fred. A few of them were what bowlers called 'unearned runs' because they came off the edge, but each one counted in the scorebook.

You seldom had this kind of opportunity against Statham. He bowled straight at the wicket. You could not afford to take a chance because you knew that if you missed, it was the end for you.

Brian never swung a ball in his life – at least intentionally. He moved it off the seam and I am sure that he didn't know which way it was going, and neither did the batsman. This is why I always regarded it a greater challenge to face Brian than Trueman.

These were the fastest around in my early days of county cricket. Yet I am sure that if you had asked other batsmen playing regularly in the 50's whom they most feared as a bowler I am sure that many of them would have come up with a name to surprise a lot of outsiders. The player they would probably have plumped for was Les Jackson of Derbyshire who deserved to have played more than just two Test matches – against New Zealand in 1949 and Australia in 1961.

He certainly worried me as much as anyone, perhaps because Hampshire never seemed to do well against Derbyshire. I should think they got the better of us eight times out of ten and Les was mainly responsible.

He was a shade slower than the other two but his bouncer was an excellent delivery, better than those delivered by many genuine fast bowlers.

As with Tyson, my first movement against Les was on to the back foot which was often asking for trouble. Les could hit the seam and make the ball nip back onto the batsman. Being on the back foot against this type of delivery was close to committing suicide.

Obviously the way to play Les was off the front foot but I did not know many batsmen who could manage this or even be prepared to have a go. He could be the most difficult of bowlers to master.

In one match, after Les had skittled us out yet again, I was standing next to umpire Arthur Fagg at square leg and praising Les's craft. 'He really is a magnificent bowler Arthur, I've never been able to fathom him out. How can you play him?'

Arthur, who opened for Kent and played for England, had faced Les and he agreed with me. Then he added: 'There was one thing I discovered when I batted against him. If he held his first and second finger wide apart when he bowled, he would never bowl a bouncer.

'If he held his fingers close together this did not mean that a bouncer would be coming but it was a fair indication.'

Next time Les bowled against us I studied him closely and Arthur Fagg was right. Not once did Les bowl his bouncer when he had his fingers apart.

Even so I did not have the courage of my convictions to test this out in the middle but I passed on the information to

Peter Sainsbury who, as I have said, is a great thinker on the game.

Peter decided to put this to the test. Whenever Les had his first two fingers wide apart then Peter would go on the front foot and this helped him considerably whenever we played Derbyshire.

I have said that I was proud to make runs against Brian Statham. Over the years England have produced a number of bowlers off whom I have been thrilled to make runs because of their high degree of skill.

Any batsman who scored against Shack must have felt very pleased with himself. I have never played against him in serious combat for any length of time but just by facing him in the nets I developed a great admiration for his ability.

We use a variety of cricket balls in the nets. Some so aged and battered that they have no seam left and are covered in dirt from months of hard service. Nobody could possibly do anything with them, apart from bowl straight – except Shack.

Shack would come along, pick up the same ball and never bowl one straight. They would all do something. Shack just had this gift. All perfectly natural right down to his action. He was always perfectly balanced and so light on his feet, he hardly made a mark on the wicket in his delivery stride.

Every time he bowled the seam would be pointing down towards the batsman. This meant that it swung in the air and when it pitched it moved off the seam.

In my early days I fielded quite a lot at slip and in the end I managed to pick Shack. I could tell whether he was going to bowl an outswinger or an inswinger. So could wicket-keeper Leo Harrison and Jimmy Gray who fielded at slip.

But this only came after years and years of close study, with Shack sending down endless overs. I am sure opposition batsmen never picked him, never detected the slight change in his action.

I have seen Shack start the ball outside the line of the leg stump and make it drift to the middle. The batsmen would shape to hit him over square leg and would suddenly have to check their stroke at the last minute. When he was younger and a little quicker these batsmen would never get the bat down in time to stop the ball hitting the wicket.

After Shack, the best medium paced bowler I have faced was Tommy Cartwright of Warwickshire.

When I first knew him in the early fifties Tom was just an inswing bowler.

Then he suddenly developed into an all-round swing bowler who could move the ball both ways through the air. Again, like Shack, he could make sure the seam was pointing at the batsman and move the ball off the wicket.

Yet I don't think he was quite as subtle as Shack. I was able to read Cartwright and I knew which way he was attempting to swing the ball. His action was not as perfect as Shack's and therefore, when he changed his style for each type of delivery it was more noticeable. Mind you, reading a bowler is one thing. Playing him is an entirely different problem because there is no telling how much it is going to swing.

Both these fine bowlers have now left the first-class game but there could be another Shack around in county cricket. His son is a good bowler of similar type.

He has taken a lot of wickets in school cricket and shows great promise. He is now studying at Millfield and, at the moment, I think he has possibly outgrown his strength. He is a very tall lad but when his frame fills out he should be just right.

In this medium paced category Alec Bedser was a very great bowler. He was quicker than Shack or Tom Cartwright but not fast enough to be classed in the Statham group.

His stock delivery was the inswinger which moved considerably. For his shock delivery, he would use the leg cutter hidden in his great big hands. He never actually palmed the ball but he placed it well in his fingers which gave advance warning when the leg cutter was about to appear. He could be read but he was still one of the most difficult to play against.

These were good bowlers on all types of wickets, deadly on the bad ones. The greatest bad wicket bowler I have ever come across is Derek Underwood. Certainly he is the best of my time and probably the best of all time.

He is almost fast enough to be included as a medium paced bowler but Derek dislikes the term. He claims he is a genuine spinner of the ball and I would agree with him.

This is the combination which makes him so successful. He does turn the ball with his spin, yet he is too quick to get at. He bowls a ball which comes straight on with his arm without very much change in his action. On a bad wicket against a right handed batsman he is almost impossible to play.

To me he has got everything, yet I know one former England captain and chairman of selectors who did not fancy him at one stage.

We were playing Kent at Canterbury in 1964. I had been dismissed and was taking a stroll round the ground when I was joined by 'Gubby' Allen.

He asked me if I had seen any young bowlers I could recommend. At the time the M.C.C. were looking for a young side to play the visiting Australians in a match at Lord's.

Derek was then only in his second season but I pointed to him bowling and I said 'There's a fine bowler for you.'

Gubby didn't agree with me. 'What has he got,' he said. 'On a good wicket he's got nothing.'

I told him 'He bowls a good length, he can turn the ball and he varies his pace. What more do you need on a good wicket.'

I don't agree with the people who claim that Derek is only a good bowler in this country and it would be a waste of time to take him to Australia in the 1970–71 winter.

On the last M.C.C. tour of Australia, Fred Titmus and David Allen took a few wickets between them in the Test match at Sydney and helped to take England to victory. If they could bowl out Australia on a wicket giving them some assistance, then this fellow can do it twice as quickly. A wicket that will suit Fred Titmus, will suit Underwood down to the ground.

On the subject of off spinners, Jim Laker was the best I have encountered. He seemed the most natural of the lot. Bowling never appeared a strain with Jim and he could put the ball exactly where he wanted it *and* spin it.

Since Laker, off spinning in England has been dominated by four bowlers, Fred Titmus, Ray Illingworth, John Mortimore and David Allen.

I have a great respect for all of them yet I split them into two categories. They are all classed as off spinners but of different types.

If I were captain and could choose an off spinner for a bad wicket then I would go for David Allen or Ray Illingworth. If the wicket was going to be good then I would select from Titmus and Mortimore.

Obviously the England selectors have agreed with me over the years. There has been little to choose between these four in County cricket but, expecting sounder wickets for Test matches, the selectors have gone for Titmus.

He is a great fiddler out of batsmen. So, too, is Mortimore who never stops thinking about the batsmen and ways and means of beating them. Obviously Allen and Illingworth think about batsmen to a great extent but I doubt whether there is anybody who knows so much about the strengths and weaknesses of the batsmen they come across as Titmus and Mortimore.

For genuine leg spinners in County cricket one has to turn to the overseas invaders. Harry Latchman of Middlesex comes from the West Indies. Mushtaq (Northamptonshire) and Intikhab (Surrey) are from Pakistan. All three are good at their craft.

In 1969 Latchman lost a little of his control and I have heard several people say that Mushtaq can be erratic, although he has always bowled well against us, and Intikhab is considered by most cricketers as the best of his type in the world.

The best leg spinner I have met was Gupte from India. After I played against him for the Commonwealth side in 1954 I never worried about leg spinners again. As good as he was, I believe he could have been an even better bowler if he had a little more faith in himself.

Frank Worrell was on the same tour and he told me that, in all his many duels with Gupte, he had received only one googly. That had been fairly early on in the battle and Frank had clipped it for four.

The next time I was batting with Frank on that tour against Gupte I watched and not one googly went down to Frank. During that partnership I never had one from Gupte, either.

Yet when Frank was out, Gupte bowled me a googly. I played it as a leg break, missed and it just went over my stumps. Thereafter Gupte bowled me several, probably more than he should have done, knowing I couldn't read which way the ball was going.

After that first googly of his against Frank had gone for four Gupte obviously decided Frank could read him and never tried again. I am sure this sort of attitude caused Ramadhin to decline as a Test bowler quicker than he should have done.

After 'murdering' England in 1950 and again in the first Test in 1957, Ramadhin faded once Peter May got hold of him and Colin Cowdrey padded him about at Edgbaston.

Going through leg spinners, Richie Benaud was as successful as any. Yet his googly was fairly easy to spot. His great asset was his deep knowledge of cricket. He was always trying to outwit batsmen.

I had a conversation with Richie and Sonny during a Commonwealth tour of New Zealand. Sonny was complaining 'I can't bowl against so and so because he can read me.'

Richie replied 'Nearly every batsman I play against can read my googly from my leg break but they still have to play me.' This variance in attitude made all the difference to their results on the field. Richie may not have had so much natural ability as Gupte and Ramadhin but it did not stop him from pegging away and *thinking* batsmen out.

Now I would like to add a few impressions on the batsmen who have impressed me most.

The Australians have produced some brilliant stroke makers, yet the one I admired most of all during the West Indies tour in 1951–52 was their skipper at the time, Lindsay Hassett.

I stood enthralled during one of his innings – a performance many of the spectators found tedious. Indeed some left the ground grumbling at its slow character. The knock in question came in the Second Test at Sydney and I was on the field as substitute during the time Lindsay made a century.

Certainly he took a long time – somewhere in the region of five hours – to make his runs but I could scarcely take my eyes off him. Not because of his strokes but his footwork. No choreographer could have dreamed up a more remarkable display for a batsman. I thought Lindsay was first class.

Of those in England, Hutton was obviously a superb player. One innings, in particular, stood out in 1950 when he played against the West Indies at Sheffield. I was fielding at cover and I don't think I can recall another occasion when the ball whistled through me or around me so often. Stopping them was a painful business and my hands were really sore at the end of the day. Alf Valentine could do nothing to stop him. Hutton had all the strokes and it was a tragedy that he was rarely able to give full rein to them in Test cricket because so much rested on his batting at the time. Often if Len failed, England did, too.

I came on the scene too late to see the best of Denis Compton but I caught glimpses of what he had been as a batsman on a visit to South Africa I made with him.

He must have been an exceptionally fine player of off spin bowling. Not only could he sweep soundly but he hit them through the off side field with the greatest of ease. His placing of the ball in one match against 'Toey' Tayfield when I toured with him had to be seen to be believed.

One man in my time in England stood head and shoulders above the rest, in my book. He was Peter May. He was elegant, yet he hit the ball with tremendous power, unlike many of the class batsmen who prefer to stroke it. He was good against fast bowlers, equally at home against spinners. His weakness, if he had one, was not being able to hook against the bouncer. His strength was in recognising this weakness and leaving all bouncers alone.

Tom Graveney is high up on my list of batsmen I like to watch. Like most wines, he became better as he matured and it was not until late in his career that he made a complete success of Test cricket.

I think the England selectors were wrong to use Tom as an opening batsman as they did during the fifties when trying to replace Hutton and Washbrook. To use a batsman with Graveney's style as an opener, picking the bat up as high as he did was just asking for trouble against fast bowlers such as Lindwall and Miller who could produce such devastating yorkers.

At times the batting of Colin Cowdrey is a most beautiful spectacle. On other occasions he looks a complete novice. He is a batsman who clearly possesses every stroke but, for some strange reason, he often seems incapable of using them.

Colin likes the ball to go to the boundary without really

having to hit it. A batsman can only do this on certain days in his life. When his timing is absolutely spot on and the outfield is in excellent condition.

I suppose Colin and I will never agree on one aspect. That is our outlook when first arriving at the wicket. I read an article by Colin in one schoolboy annual in which he said that a batsman should be content just to stay at the wicket for the first half a dozen overs of his innings. This would give him time to adjust himself to the surroundings, to the bowler, to the pace of the wicket, to the feel of the bat in his hand. This is completely contrary to my own thinking on the game. If I saw an opportunity to hit the first ball for four or six, then I would have a go.

Two other batsmen who, I felt, suffered at times through being too bound up in theory were Ken Barrington and Ted Dexter. Before Ken became the defensive player with his two-eyed stance, I saw him play one innings in which he looked even better than May.

I have watched Ken slam 'Butch' White out of sight and I have also had to endure one of the most boring sights in cricket – Ken batting against Derek Shackleton.

Not only did Ken believe that Shack could not be hit, he appeared to think it was impossible to score off Shack. Whenever we saw Ken coming in while Shack was bowling, we knew we were in for a rest in the field.

Dexter was a magnificent hard wicket player but one who did not use his ability to the best advantage. I batted with him once in Jamaica when we shared a century partnership of which I managed to make no more than a dozen runs. He was striking the ball so hard and straight that it became dangerous for me to back up. I had to stay in the crease at the bowler's end to avoid being hit.

After one of these Cavalier trips with Denis Compton, Ted returned with the idea that he must play the sweep shot. No matter how hard he tried, he could never do it successfully. Dexter's bat was too straight to play the sweep. To be successful with such a shot a batsman must bring his bat down from the direction of third man which Ted never did. He was so strong he had no need to play the sweep. He could lift the left armer over his head, through the covers or anywhere he chose. That was the measure of his eye and his timing.

12 *England's Test Prospects*

England's immediate Test future has not been so bright for a number of years. I cannot see many sides being a match for them over the next half a dozen years or so despite the shortage of young class batsmen around in county cricket today.

To be successful internationally, a country must possess a well balanced and varied attack of the highest quality. The Australians proved this when they had Lindwall and Miller on the scene, backed up by some useful spinners.

The greatest days of the West Indies came when they had Wes Hall and Charlie Griffith in harness, supported by Gary Sobers and Lance Gibbs.

Until the middle of the 1970's and possibly later I am sure England will be able to boast of an attack of similar standard. I can't remember of a time when I have seen so many bowlers of such rich promise under the age of 25.

This does not take into account the people who are already recognised England regulars such as John Snow and David Brown, who have a few more years ahead of them in international cricket.

In some respects these two are very much like Statham and Trueman in that they must be good for each other when working as a team.

Brown is very much in the Statham mould in that he attacks the stumps, which is a great thing in a fast bowler. He too, is very much a trier who gives his last ounce of energy whatever time of the day he is called into the attack.

Several other county batsmen have mentioned to me that they believe Brown sprays the ball about too much. Possibly he does on occasions when the wicket is not helping him and he is trying too hard to get something out of it.

On the other hand, I have no complaint about his direction when I have watched him – except possibly when he is bowling us out!

He has always bowled straight against Hampshire. He does not do a lot with the ball but that does not matter too much. A batsman can't really afford to relax his concentration when facing Brown.

He is very much a Test match bowler in that he rises to the atmosphere of the big occasion. Snow is vastly different. He is a very temperamental bowler and he needs to be angry or have a pitch which gives him some assistance before he is seen at his best.

When the circumstances are right and he is in the mood he is the most hostile and effective fast bowler in the country. He often manages to hit the seam and he can bowl what appears to be a fast leg cutter, a delivery which pitches on middle and straightens up a little to take the off stump. A batsman has little chance against this type of delivery.

He does not swing the ball so much these days – not as much as he did two or three years ago and no batsman should worry about his swing. What he does possess, similar perhaps to Neil Adcock of South Africa, is the ability to make a ball rise just short of a length.

He is awkward to look at because of his very strong arm action. He rarely puts much body into his bowling. His arm is sufficient. His strength can be seen in the field. He throws the ball in like a rocket with a low trajectory.

Quickly establishing himself is Alan Ward who is living up to the Derbyshire tradition of producing good fast bowlers in the line of George Pope, Bill Copson, Les Jackson, etc.

To me Ward is very much like Tyson and Hall. He is a bowler who cannot bowl slowly. He relies on sheer pace. Obviously the odd ball must move off the seam but I don't think he tries to move it and, to my knowledge, does not swing it in the air.

The first time I saw him was towards the back end of the 1968 season when we played at Derby.

We all went to the ground the first morning thinking Harold Rhodes was the bowler we would have to worry about. So it came as a surprise to see wicketkeeper Bob Taylor standing even deeper to this chap Ward – somebody we had never heard of.

Without a doubt Ward is the fastest bowler in the country day in and day out. On the very occasional day Snow will reach a similar pace but this is not very often. On other days Snow is no more than medium.

Obviously Ward is going to be around for a long time. He has had a tremendous rise in the game, making his Test debut against New Zealand in 1969 within 12 months of establishing himself in the Derbyshire side. Some people may say he has gone ahead too quickly and that he still has a lot to learn. If he is short of knowledge about the intricacies of the game then Test cricket will soon show him the way.

Ward still has two or three years to go before he reaches his mid twenties. Another in that category and one I rate as a genuine quickie is Chris Old of Yorkshire. He is another bowler with great potential.

Yorkshire are bringing him on carefully. They use him only in short spells of four or five overs. In that way he remains hostile all the time he is in the attack and does not burn himself out while he is still learning his trade.

I should not be surprised if Old is not elevated to the

Test ranks within the next couple of seasons. If he maintains the promise he has shown in the last two seasons, England will possess the fastest attack since Tyson and Trueman were together.

A shade less in pace than these two but still fast enough to make batsmen sit up and take notice is Geoff Arnold of Surrey.

Geoff does not rely so much on sheer pace. He is still accurate and nippy off the wicket but he moves the ball as well. He has a natural outswinger and he has the added attraction of being able to bat a little when he sets his mind to it.

Providing his batting does not slip under the strain of doing so much bowling, he will make an ideal third bowler in an England attack when they have to play three quickies. His batting could slip him in ahead of some rivals.

Geoff's problem is fitness. He has had trouble at some stage or other for the last three seasons but this is natural in a youngster bowling fast. He suddenly has to strain muscles he never used before and probably never knew he had.

These injury problems should sort themselves out about this stage of his career – he is now 25 – when his muscles have grown accustomed to the extra demand made on them and he has become hardened to the game of cricket.

Injuries have upset the career of Ken Shuttleworth who is another bowler of great promise in his mid twenties. He has the ability and the pace. He had a bad run in 1969 and this setback will show whether he has the determination to fight back and show his real qualities.

The last of the bowlers in the 'fast medium to fast' bracket whom I think will make it is Hampshire's own Bob Cottam. Naturally I have seen more of him than the others. As his captain I know what he can do and each season I grow more impressed by his talents.

At one stage I thought he might be a good bowler only in

English conditions. After his tour with the M.C.C. to Ceylon and Pakistan in the winter of 1968–69 I am now convinced he would be more than useful overseas.

Bob has the ability to adapt himself to the conditions under which he is playing. He studies the game closely and he is not afraid to experiment as he goes along.

He started his career purely as a medium to fast bowler but in 1968 when we encountered many wet wickets Bob cut down his run and bowled off cutters. I should think he took 75 per cent of his wickets with off cutters that summer.

In 1969 the summer was drier and the wickets were generally better. His off cutter was not as successful so Bob switched back to his longer run and still took over 100 wickets, most of them with fast medium seam.

Bob has a natural outswinger. He has learned to bowl an inswinger which he does not control properly at the moment but this will improve with practice. As well as the off cutter which he can deliver well, he is experimenting with a leg cutter. One of the reasons why he was not so successful at the start of the 1969 season was because he experimented too much. This is not altogether a bad thing – except that it makes it more difficult for a captain to set a field – and should hold him in good stead for the future.

Some spectators may possibly get the wrong impression of Bob by his reactions on the field. He is a very excitable young man when he scores a success and a very angry young man when he misses a wicket by a mere whisker, but he is not a bad tempered chap. I know he throws his arms up in the air a lot and shows great disappointment when a leg before appeal is turned down. This is a direct result of his keenness.

In August 1970 the England selectors are going to have a problem whittling down this list of fast bowlers to the four they require for the winter tour of Australia and the bid to win back the Ashes.

As an opening batsman who has played against them and,

I think, knows what is required of a fast bowler, I'll give you my four.

Certainly Ward would be the first choice and with him I would have Snow, probably these two forming the opening attack.

By the time the selectors get around to their meeting I would have expected Old to have developed enough to be worth one of the places and the fourth place is likely to rest between Cottam and Arnold.

I have a sneaking suspicion the selectors, if confronted with this choice, would go for Arnold. I, personally, would take Cottam because I think he has more strings to his bow. In addition Bob has bowled a tremendous number of overs in the last two seasons without showing the slightest sign of injury. He could be useful on the hard conditions in Australia – both as a shock bowler and a stock bowler.

When talking about young England bowlers it must be remembered that Underwood is still under 25 and he will be a force for several years.

Coming down rapidly in pace to off spin there is only one around at the moment, Pat Pocock, who seems to be out of favour with the selectors. I am certain it is only a temporary phase.

He was about 17 when I first saw him playing for Surrey against Hampshire and immediately thought he was a fine discovery.

Pat is a genuine spinner of the ball. He has change of pace and he has control. What more does an off spinner want than these three things? In addition he is a good competitor who, like Cottam, is not frightened to try something new to disturb a batsman's concentration. I don't see how he can possibly fail to become a regular member of England's team.

He has one handicap in that he is not exactly fleet footed in the field, rather like Derek Underwood who is another somewhat cumbersome mover for a young man.

A bowler I have a sneaking regard for is Ray East, the Essex left arm spinner. I would class him as a potential match winner and I have a great deal of respect for his bowling.

Whether he gets the opportunity to prove himself at Test level is another matter and may well depend on how the selectors view Underwood's usefulness abroad. With Underwood taking the left arm spinner's role at the moment, East will be extremely fortunate to oust him from the side.

The absence of Cowdrey and Milburn through injury in 1969 and the sacking of Graveney, left a lot to be desired in England's batting in the Tests against West Indies and New Zealand.

A rather miserable picture was painted of England's prospects in the future because of this, and I would agree there do not seem many youngsters around capable of taking over the batting positions.

One position in England will be well served for the next four of five years is that of opening batsmen; Geoff Boycott is a class player. I think he will get even better once he realises he is a human being like the rest of us and, like any human being, is bound to have his failures.

He has got to accept the fact that he is going to be dismissed cheaply now and again. Every cricketer has had a bad patch at some time or the other, even Geoff's idol Len Hutton. Once he accepts this and does not allow it to disturb his thoughts, he will be an even better player.

Like Hutton he has many shots. He has displayed them so many times against Hampshire and against other counties when playing in the Gillette Cup. Like Hutton, he is a little shy of using them in Test matches. He becomes so determined to make runs he forgets them.

John Edrich seems certain to be his partner for some time to come. I would not place Edrich near the class of Boycott as a batsman. He has limited ability but he thinks hard about the game and uses every ounce of ability he has got. He has turned himself into a run machine.

The great qualities of both Edrich and Boycott are concentration and a sound defence. They both play extremely straight. Many people may not think so watching Edrich because he misses an awful lot but this is because he plays along the line of his off stump. Many other batsmen play along the line of the ball as I do. This means we get far more edges whereas Edrich is missing the ball completely. Neither Edrich nor Boycott allows anything to disturb them.

I still think there is great hope for Keith Fletcher. I thought he would have played for England more times than he has done judging by his potential when I first saw him on a Cavaliers' tour of the West Indies.

I expected that he would be a natural for England as I watched him on those hard Caribbean wickets. He has not lived up to his promise so far as I believe the fault lies with the Essex wickets rather than with Fletcher himself.

For a number of years Essex had some notorious green wickets, especially when Trevor Bailey was playing. As a result I think Fletcher lost some of his ability to play at the ball. He then started to play with his pad first and bat second.

He probably had to change to this style to survive on those Essex wickets and I think this did him a great deal of harm. However the wickets are improving. Chelmsford was one of the best in the country in 1969 and there is still time for Fletcher to return to his natural way of playing and make the grade.

John Hampshire is another who would have done better if he had been brought up overseas. Against John is his age – he will have reached his 30th birthday in 1971 – whereas Fletcher is three years younger.

Finding batsmen under the age of 25 who look capable of coming through is a different matter. I have studied the record books and looked at players up and down the country and can't find a youngster who, I could say with any certainty, is a future England player.

Nevertheless there are three who might easily come into that category within the next couple of seasons. So here are the Marshall 'long shots'.

First on my list is David Lloyd, the left handed opening batsman from Lancashire. Next is Barry Dudlestone who was awarded his county cap by Leicestershire in 1969. The third is Peter Graves, the aggressive right hander from Sussex.

I have selected these three because they have one thing in common. They all play with a straight bat. I mentioned this quality about Edrich and Boycott and offer no apologies for bringing it up again.

If batsmen want to be successful they must play straight defensively. It does not matter whether you are an attacking batsman or not. To be able to attack or even survive at the wicket you need to play straight to keep the ball out of the wicket. Whether it is a forward defensive shot or a backward defensive stroke, it must be played with a straight bat.

This is what first attracted me to Lloyd. It was the same thing I noticed with Dudlestone. Although Graves is far more of an attacking bat than the other two, his basic defensive stroke is straight.

One other player could possibly make it. He is Graham Roope of Surrey who had a fine season in 1969. I did not see Roope in 1969 but he looked promising the previous season and several other players told me he had improved considerably. If his bowling improves, he might develop into an all rounder and fill the gap in the England side, left by the retirement of Trevor Bailey.

England has no problem as far as wicketkeeping is concerned. Alan Knott obviously has the position to himself until age catches up with him.

If Alan should suffer a loss of form temporarily England

have a ready-made replacement in Bob Taylor of Derbyshire. He must be the second wicketkeeper on the tour to Australia and it surprised me he was not selected to go to South Africa in 1968 – the tour that was cancelled by the South Africans' refusal to accept D'Oliveira.

13 Cares of Captaincy

Finishing runners-up in 1969, the first season of the Player's Sunday League and fifth in the County Championship – even without Derek Shackleton – gave me considerable pleasure as Hampshire's captain.

It has been the high spot of my four year reign since I took over from Colin Ingleby-Mackenzie. But being a county captain is not always such fun.

Please don't misunderstand me. I have considered it a great honour to lead Hampshire and the players in the side. At the same time captaincy can be an exacting task and a very lonely one.

Brian Close has often remarked that leading Yorkshire has left him drained of energy when it came to concentrating on his own performance. I can understand his feelings. There is far more to skippering a side in first class cricket than going out to toss a coin and then deciding whether to bat or bowl. That, in itself, is a trying enough task. One mistake there and the match can he lost.

A captain is far more than just a dictator of policy on the cricket field. He is supposed to be the master of many other things off the field as well. He is more like a soccer club manager.

This is particularly true when the team are playing away

from home. Sometimes I have been away a fortnight at a time and in complete charge of 12 or 13 players.

It is my responsibility to make sure the players know where they are going, which hotel they are staying in and to look after the travel arrangements

I have to check the room bookings on arrival and examine the hotel bills on departure. Then there is the question of having a word with a player who is maybe off form, or talking to a player I have left out and explaining why.

No two players are the same. Each has to be dealt with in a different manner. If a player has temporarily lost form I try to find out whether any off the field reason is responsible.

Being away from home for a while he might be worrying about his wife and children or his parents, especially if they are unwell when he left them. The captain has to decide, in certain circumstances, whether the player should be allowed to return home.

On the field I get so involved that I find I bowl every delivery with the bowler. That is not all. As well as thinking of the present I have to think two, three or maybe four hours in advance.

Of course, I have a set plan when I go on to the field but, as we all know, the best laid plans can be so easily upset. Improvisation and minor adjustments are often necessary.

I found that leading the side and opening the innings was quite a strain. There was no time to relax. No time to adjust my thinking from the moment I left the field to walking out again with bat in hand. That was why it was quite a relief when Barry Richards joined us and I was able to drop down the order.

Nowadays I have much more time to relax. When we come off the field I generally watch the opening deliveries. Then I go away to a corner of the dressing room and do not want to see the game until the number three batsman has gone in.

Another aspect of the captain's life which does worry me

is the loneliness which can occur. Sometimes members of the side just do not want to be with the captain in the evenings.

Maybe the day has gone badly and they think I have been at fault in my captaincy. The bowlers may feel I have not used them as they wanted to be used. A batsman may consider he batted lower or higher in the order than he should have done. All these things can have an effect on the captain's life off the field, especially after a day's play.

Some people like to be by themselves. I like to be in company and to join in discussions over a drink. Being a sensitive person I admit to being a little disheartened when I find myself dining alone on an away trip.

Although I have enjoyed my role as captain I believe I was given the job when I was too old. It has been the tradition of so many counties to award the task to the senior professional when the captain retires. This is not necessarily a good thing.

I was 36 when I took over. That is an age when I should have been coming to the end of my time as a captain, not starting as one.

By the time a player is in his middle thirties he has seen the best of the game and, with the greatest will in the world, it is difficult for him to retain the same enthusiasm he felt as a young player, and to be alive to the fresh demands each season brings.

I also believe the middle twenties is too young to become a captain. A player of this age has only just finished learning his trade. It is only then that he can really look forward to enjoying the delights of the game. To be saddled with the responsibilities of captaincy at that age could mean a player going through his entire cricket career without really enjoying the game of cricket.

Peter May is a great example. He had become captain of England by the time he was 25. Within five or six years he had had enough and retired. I'm inclined to think that if

Time for relaxation with Gary Sobers and members of the 1963 West Indies team

Barry Richards, the gifted young South African batsman, receives a 'Man of the Match' award from Harold Gimblett, the former Somerset and England player

Left: Putting Power into Hampshire's attack – Bob Cottam. *Right:* Danny Livingstone from St John's, Antigua who, with Alan Castell, shares a Hampshire ninth wicket record of 230

Left: Peter Sainsbury whose all-round skills have served Hampshire so well. *Right:* Pace and determination – 'Butch' White

May had escaped the captaincy until he was nearer 30 he might have been in the game for another six years or so. Think what an asset that would have been both for Surrey and England!

I have one further observation to make on this question of captaincy. I think one person can captain a side for too long. He can get set in his ways and his thinking can become stereotyped. Clearly this is not good for him nor, indeed, is it for those who serve under him. Ten years being in charge is far too long. This is especially true today when the standard of captaincy is higher than ever before.

People often complain that cricket has become dull and defensive. I do not agree. The standard is better than it has ever been. What has become more difficult – and this leads to cries of defensive cricket – is the rate of scoring.

When I first entered county cricket most counties had amateur players as captains and I agree that the cricket was often more adventurous.

The amateur captain knew the basic requirements. He would set his field according to the type of bowler he had under his command. This no longer happens. Nowadays fields are set according to the capabilities of the batsmen.

Cricket used to be played according to the old theory 'feed a batsman's strong points and you will get him out eventually'. Not today. The first task is to find the batsman's weaknesses and then play on it to stop him scoring runs.

Take the Warwickshire players, as a case in point. They seem to be a breed of 'lappers', employing the sweep shot whenever they can against the off spinner or left arm slow bowler.

Mike Smith and Tom Cartwright are two experienced batsmen using the sweep shot and the captain of the fielding side needs to have a man on the boundary behind square leg. John Jamieson is another who likes to sweep. In his case the field has to be moved in front of square.

It is only a minor adjustment in the field, but one which has an important bearing on the run rate. I doubt if such care was taken over field placings 20 years ago.

This is why I rate Brian Close and Ray Illingworth as two of the finest captains in the game today. They are always thinking, making minor adjustments and attempting to outwit the batsmen. It is never easy to bat when either of them is directing fielding operations.

Close is lucky in being such a fearless character himself that he is prepared to stand right on top of batsmen and is willing to take knocks in exchange for wickets.

I have seen him struck blows which would have felled many other players or left them flat on the deck where they had taken cover. At times I have been surprised to see that Close is still upright after taking a terrible crack on the arms, legs or body. And even more astonished when I have heard him shouting at a field 'Why the bloody hell didn't you catch the rebound.'

I have always enjoyed playing against Yorkshire. Most touring sides would say the same. I go into the match expecting nowt and getting nowt in return. That was the way I was brought up to play the game.

Too many sides in the south expect to be given something during a match. It is an attitude I dislike. I remember playing against Somerset a few years ago in a rain-ruined match. There was time only for Hampshire to complete their first innings in the first two days.

On the last day Somerset batted on much longer than we thought they should have done to make sure of first innings lead. Then, when we batted a second time, Somerset tossed the ball in the air, tempting us to go for runs and a declaration.

I spent about three hours over 80 runs that afternoon. I refused to hit full tosses and gentle long hops served up by non-regular bowlers.

Possibly I was wrong. Perhaps I have not got the right attitude but I believe spectators pay to see bowlers try to get me out and pay to see me hit the good delivery to the boundary.

On the question of field placings I have found the Australians are particularly good at sizing up the strengths and weaknesses of batsmen. It came as quite a shock to us in the West Indies during our tour 'Down Under' in 1950–51.

In the West Indies – and in England during the previous summer – we generally found that once we had scored 30 runs or so we were on top. Then was the time to strike out more freely but not so in Australia. By the time we had 30 runs out there the fielding captain and the bowler had summed us up. They knew our strong points and placed fields to cover our shots. They found out our weaknesses – and bowled to exploit them.

This is what happens in County cricket today. Whenever a batsman comes to the wicket I generally know enough about him to attempt to stop his more prolific run-scoring strokes. If I don't, then somebody in the side usually does.

We know whether he likes to drive the ball. Whether he is an off side or on side player. Whether he likes to run the ball through the slips. We make sure he does not get many opportunities to employ his favourite strokes. If a batsman has to search elsewhere for runs, he is liable to make mistakes.

My own unfulfilled ambition in cricket is to take Hampshire to the Championship. I realise that time is running out for me but it could still happen. During the four years I have been in charge we have improved our position each summer. If only we had a genuine slow bowler I believe we might have won the Championship in the last two or three years.

Things could possibly be a little harder in 1970 but we have some very useful players coming through.

They have already started to make their mark. Richard Gilliat had a splendid summer in 1969 and there is no reason why he should not become even stronger.

There are others such as Trevor Jesty, Richard Lewis and David Turner. And, with a bit of luck, we may soon have the off spinner we have been seeking.

He is a West Indian by the name of Worrell. His first name is Larry and he is in his middle twenties, so he has many years ahead of him if he can make the grade.

We spotted him in the Army and he will be qualifying for us in 1970. He is a genuine spinner of the ball and he looked very useful on the occasion I watched him play.

It is, perhaps, surprising that he has not been snapped up before by another county. The explanation could be that Army life has kept him on the move and he has never been in one place long enough to make an impression.

14 *A Strange Affair*

If one particular episode of my cricketing life has saddened me it was the strange affair of the 1969 summer when the umpires awarded a match to Glamorgan because there was nobody from the Hampshire side on the ground when they called 'play'.

This episode left a bad taste in the mouth not only because I was involved but because it made a farce of the game of cricket.

Cricket has taken far too many knocks over the years from people only too ready to run it down and this particular occasion provided them with just the sort of ammunition they like to use.

Fortunately everything has been ironed out and the right decisions made in the end. The points awarded to Glamorgan were deducted by the M.C.C. which must have pleased everybody including Glamorgan who went on to win the County championship. Nobody can now say they took it on a false result.

We played Glamorgan at Bournemouth in the middle of June. There had been some interference from rain in the first two days. There was little hope of either side achieving an outright result.

Just after one o'clock on the last day we were about 90 runs on with one wicket down when it started to drizzle.

The drizzle continued well after lunch. By this time there seemed little chance of any cricket being played in such conditions.

Some of the lads whiled away the time by playing cards, a traditional pastime of cricketers in such circumstances. One or two were having a bath. As we were the batting side they did not expect to be playing any more that day.

With the drizzle still falling at 3.30 p.m. it was obvious neither side could get a result, even if the rain stopped immediately and the ground dried. We had not got enough runs to make a declaration.

About this time, with the ground almost deserted, Tony Lewis, the Glamorgan captain and the two umpires, Peter Wight, the former Somerset batsman and Lloyd Budd, who was having his first summer on the first class list, came into our dressing room.

Peter Wight and Tony came across to where I was in the back section of the room and said, 'What do you think of the situation?'

'I don't mind,' I told them. 'I'm quite happy with whatever decision you decide to take.'

Tony said, 'Well there are still a few people in the bar. Shall we tell them it's off?'

'Yes, you can tell them that,' I said.

Let me say here that the decision to call off a match in these circumstances has nothing to do with the captains. It is up to the umpires to decide but the general practice is to consult with the two captains to find out if either one of them wishes to wait and see if play is possible.

If the captains are in agreement, the umpires usually go along with the decision. In this case, as no result could be possible, neither Tony Lewis or myself wanted to hold on for what could only be an hour's cricket maximum with no more points to be obtained and no spectators to watch the cricket.

Anyway, the outcome of this conversation was that we should take tea as soon as possible, and that was the end of the match – or so I believed. This is where the misunderstanding could have occurred.

I thought the match had been called off. So, I am sure, did the Glamorgan side. But the umpires apparently got the impression that all we had decided upon was an early tea.

We had tea at 3.45 p.m. and at about five minutes past four I went into the Glamorgan dressing room to say goodbye as I always do at the finish of a match.

Our first match against Glamorgan at Neath had been affected by rain and I remember saying something about 'Let's hope we have better luck with the weather next time we meet,' as I shook hands with Tony and thanked him for the game. Most of their players including Lewis were changed or partly changed.

All the Hampshire side packed their cricketing bags in the cars – it was still raining quite heavily – said their cheerios to the Glamorgan team and left the ground.

One or two of the team passed one of the umpires on the way to the cars – carrying their cricket bags – and said cheerio to him.

Not long after our departure the rain apparently eased. Umpires Wight and Budd made an inspection of the wicket and decided play could start, although there was only about an hour to go.

The Glamorgan side hurriedly changed back to flannels and some of them even put on their whites over their civvies and took the field. The umpires waited the two minutes for the Hampshire batsmen to get to the wicket. When nobody arrived they called 'play' and then awarded the match to Glamorgan.

It was awarded to them under Law 17 governing the conduct of the game. This states:

'The Umpires shall allow such intervals as have been

agreed upon, 10 minutes between each innings and not more than two minutes for each fresh batsman to come in. At the start of each innings and of each day's play and at the end of any interval the Umpire at the Bowler's end shall call "play", when the side refusing to play shall lose the match.'

Note One of this law states: 'The umpires shall not award a match under this law unless (1) "Play" has been called in such a manner that both sides can clearly understand that play is to start (2) a appeal has been made and, (3) they are satisfied that a side will not or cannot continue play.'

The first I knew about it was at 5.30 p.m. that evening just as I was settling down at home. And this is an important aspect to remember.

The Hampshire side had no reason to rush away from the ground. We had no away fixture the following day and the only travelling involved was the short trip from Bournemouth to Southampton where most of our players live. In fact we had three days off.

The news of the umpires' decision was broken to me by Desmond Eagar, the Hampshire secretary who called round at my house. I was astounded by what he told me.

Indeed, it took some time for what had exactly taken place to sink in and I went round to Bob Cottam, who lives nearby. I asked him if he could recall any conversation which might have led him to think the match might not have been called off.

Bob said he had heard most of the conversation between Peter Wight, Tony Lewis and myself and was certain the match was called off. This he repeated when he attended the hearing at Lord's.

Then I phoned Peter Sainsbury.

'Guess what Peter, a funny thing happened at the cricket today,' I said.

'Go on,' he replied. 'Make me laugh.'

When I told him, he was as stunned as I had been.

I went back home and wrote out my report to M.C.C. At the finish I asked that before the decision of the umpires had been confirmed by the Test and County Cricket Board I would like a personal hearing with the two umpires and Tony Lewis to state my case.

Obviously some misunderstanding had taken place and I wanted to hear their side of the story and the authorities mine. The next we heard was that Doug Insole and S. C. Griffith, secretary of the Test and County Cricket Board, had confirmed the umpires' decision.

Hampshire immediately appealed against the decision. A committee meeting was called at Lord's in July which I attended, together with Tony Lewis and the two umpires, and our secretary Desmond Eagar.

The decision was reversed, and the match was left drawn.

I believe the whole incident could have been avoided if more common sense had been used.

The Hampshire side were in good company in thinking the match was abandoned as the press who were reporting the match also thought so and most of them left the ground. Indeed only the correspondents of *The Times* and *Daily Telegraph,* both of whom were writing their stories on the conclusion of the match, were the only two pressmen who were left. Even the Glamorgan scorer had filled in his report to the T.C.C.B. as is the usual custom, and it was sent to Lord's with match drawn given as the result. How so many people could believe that the match was called off and the umpires think that it was not will always remain a mystery to me.

15 *Why Not Four-Day Games?*

One-day league cricket is here to stay. And I think we, in Hampshire, can take a certain amount of the credit for bringing about this tremendously exciting version of our traditional game.

Backed by the enthusiastic support of our former chairman Cecil Paris, now chairman of the T.C.C.B. – Hampshire led the first campaign to have a one-day league operating at the weekends when the majority of the public were free to come and watch.

The experiment proved so successful in 1969 that many grounds reported record attendances. Counties received a much-needed cash boost, and, equally important, people were talking cricket again.

Now I expect to see one day cricket extended and the number of matches played in the three day championship game reduced.

I know this will offend many of the traditionalists. I agree with them that the John Player's Sunday League is not 'cricket'. But it is *entertainment*. The county authorities now know they can sell this League to the public and if professional cricket is to survive it must offer the goods which the public want.

Switching to the three day game to one day cricket brought

many extra problems for me as a captain but I still enjoyed playing it and so did the majority of cricketers who found it stimulating to play before large and enthusiastic crowds.

There is a suggestion now that the County Championship will be reduced to 16 four-day matches played in mid-week with two one-day Leagues operating on Saturday and Sunday. This would give each County side a chance to play at home at least one day over the weekend.

Personally I would like to see *four-day* championship matches. Many people argue this would make the game even slower. I disagree.

I would retain the present bonus system for runs and wickets to ensure against slow play. At the same time four-day cricket would reduce the number of boring draws which either send spectators to sleep or drive them from the grounds.

The extra day, too, would provide an opportunity for more time to be made up in case of weather interference. And it would do away with many of the false finishes and declarations which are part of the cricket scene today.

The one aspect of the suggestion which does not completely appeal to me is the proposal to play each county twice in one-day matches. Either in the same League or in two entirely different competitions.

I would rather see the opportunity taken up by increasing the size of the present competition to include Minor Counties, taking first-class cricketers to areas where first-class cricket is not played at the moment.

County cricketers playing at Truro, Durham, Carlisle, Norwich, Lincoln and other such areas would surely go down well and their presence would help promote the game locally.

Eventually I would like to see two divisions of the one day league with a promotion and relegation system introduced as in football. I doubt, however, whether this would ever come about because I cannot foresee first-class counties being prepared to vote for a system which might result in one or more of them playing in the second division.

Yet this is one of the changes which could be made without affecting the actual playing side of the game. For too long cricket has suffered from experiments, new regulations, etc.

Few of them have actually improved the game. In fact, most have produced the opposite effect. I believe cricket today is at last on the right road to recovery.

It is a pity, in a way, that a bonus points system had to be introduced in order to make the players score faster. That said, I must admit I like the present set up of one point scored for every 25 runs above 150 scored in the first 85 overs and one point for every two wickets taken inside the same limit.

Batsmen now know they must get on with the game. The system has promoted extra interest among the spectators. At the same time it occasionally allowed the middle order batsmen to build an innings if they so desired.

Not so the changes which took place in 1966 and 1967.

In 1966, my first year as captain, we played under the ridiculous system in which county sides were limited to 65 overs in their first innings in 12 of the championship matches they played during the summer.

I say it was ridiculous despite the fact that in 11 of those matches Hampshire were successful in coming out on top when going for first innings points.

We succeeded because we had a bowling side fully capable of exploiting the situation. Playing such cricket meant the use of medium to fast seam bowling designed more to keep the opposition in check than to take wickets.

What better line-up could a side have than Derek Shackleton, 'Butch' White and Bob Cottam. Shack could keep one end going almost throughout the first innings. 'Butch' and Bob shared the other end between them.

This still left all three relatively fresh to attack at full pace when it came to the second innings.

I was responsible for such a policy – one which relegated the unfortunate spin bowler almost to the role of spectator. I say now that it did a tremendous amount of harm to the game of cricket but what else could I do when this was exactly the type of game the regulation required.

As I said the spinner was virtually unemployed. Moreover, the middle order batsmen – especially the youngster attempting to establish himself – was given no time to settle in before he was required to hit out.

This regulation had a harmful effect on the players. The system introduced the following season – six points for first innings, only eight for outright victory – had a harmful effect on the spectators.

What better example of the boredom this type of cricket produced than Hampshire's match against Middlesex at Lord's in July of 1967 when no decision was reached on first innings after three *full* days of play?

The match was condemned by every newspaperman who went to cover the game. They were right to do so. Many of the spectators present complained – personally or by letter – to the Middlesex and Hampshire secretaries. Again they were right to do so.

The cricket, for the most part, was bad but I am not blaming anybody in particular. It was a direct result of the regulations in force at the time, combined with a near-perfect batting wicket.

Under the system, first innings points became very important. The regulation encouraged sides to bat on into the second day if possible in order to build up a huge score so that first innings points were safe and also attempt to gain outright victory by an innings.

This is exactly what happened in this match played over a weekend.

By the end of the Saturday we had scored 354 for four, a scoring rate which is above average even today with the bonus points at stake. The wicket was so good that I thought Middlesex were capable of matching the total, so I decided to bat on when the game resumed on Sunday afternoon.

We did not waste any time. I delayed my declaration for 65 minutes in which were scored 67 runs for the loss of three wickets before calling the team. We had made 421 for seven declared. Batting on into the second day was a common feature of the cricket in the 1967 season.

We were in a handy position. Middlesex faced the possibility of an innings defeat. Their only alternative was to try and match our score for first innings points. Nobody can blame them for that.

They started badly. By the end of Sunday they were 126 for four. By the end of the match they were still 70 runs behind on 371 for seven.

As I said, this no decision game provoked a stream of complaints. Most of the blame was heaped on the shoulders of the Middlesex batsmen for their slow batting on the final day. Some of it came our way.

We were attacked because of our slow batting on the first afternoon and evening. We had started with a rush when I made 153 in 203 minutes and then slowed down but that has always been the way of Hampshire's batting.

I was regarded as the team's fastest scoring batsman. When I came off – as I did in this match – we made our early runs quickly. Other counties have their quick scoring batsmen lower in the order. They start slowly and then accelerate.

If Hampshire were to be blamed at all, it was for not finishing off the Middlesex first innings. But it was not for the want of trying.

With runs to play with I set attacking fields throughout the final day. I always had fielders in close catching positions, whether it was the fast bowlers, or the slow bowling of Peter Sainsbury in operation.

It was just that the wicket was too good to play cricket under the regulations existing at the time. If there had not been so many points at stake for first innings I doubt very much whether I would have batted on into the second day.

It was a tragedy that these two regulations should ever have come into existence. Cricket suffered but, in a way, cricket was to blame for their introduction.

Both were designed to make cricket a more exciting spectacle. The game had lost some of its sparkle and appeal and largely because many county authorities had allowed their wickets to deteriorate.

From the time soon after I started in first class cricket in this country, the standard of wickets declined. And they went on getting poorer until the M.C.C. took action three seasons ago, brought in an Inspector of Wickets and took action to ban grounds which did not come up to standard.

In an age when results often mean more than the way the game is played, several counties produced wickets designed to suit their own particular type of top bowlers or ones which could guarantee a result in three days.

It meant that bowlers were given artificial surfaces, pitches which made it easy for them to take wickets without learning the arts of their craft. In some cases bowlers just had to turn their arm over and the wicket would do the rest.

Batsmen, instead of being able to score freely and hit cleanly, were made to fight for survival. Scoring became secondary to survival at the crease. Counties found this policy profitable. Of all the counties to have won the Championship since I entered county cricket, only in Hampshire's case in 1961 was the home of the title winners favourable to batting. This made it necessary to get results through declarations.

This is why the game suffered and why new regulations

had to be brought in to help speed up the game. This has led to another change which will come into force during the 1970 summer. The introduction of the experimental leg before rule designed to cut down the extent of the pad play which has crept into the game.

With the many bad wickets around 10 or 12 years ago batsmen were forced to use their pads as the first line of defence instead of the bat. That makes for pretty dull cricket.

Now batsmen who deliberately pad away a delivery which pitches between wicket and wicket can be given out leg before.

I am looking forward to playing under this experiment. It provides a new challenge but I am surprised that the umpires said they could cope with it in addition to all their other duties.

They have only a split second now between glancing down to see whether a fast bowler is over-stepping and where the ball pitches before being able to give a batsman out.

This will mean they will need to look up a fraction of a second quicker between watching for the no ball from the fast bowler and picking up the flight in time to judge whether the delivery has pitched between wicket to wicket.

How they are going to find time to fit all this in and still legislate whether a fast bowler is running on the wicket I shall never know.

That is not the end of their problem. They still have to make up their mind whether the batsman was aiming to play the delivery with his pads or whether he intended to strike the ball. I have seen some of the experts in pad play in action such as Colin Cowdrey, Dennis Amiss and Brian Bolus. At times I have not been able to tell their intentions.

This experiment might not have been necessary had wickets been kept at an acceptable standard. Fortunately they are improving. Nevertheless there is still a lot of work to be done on many wickets in the country before the game starts with everything to its advantage. Some groundsmen talk of trying to produce a wicket which holds an equal balance between bat and ball. I say they should make the best possible wicket they can. Then it is up to the cricketers to sort out the balance by their own individual skills.

The way things have gone in the last two seasons makes me believe that the game has turned the corner and is striding along healthily. That is not to say there could not be improvements in some places.

For instance, I believe that where clubs own their own county grounds they should do everything to develop their headquarters so that cash is coming in all the year round.

Take our own ground at Southampton, for example. This is used only fifteen days each year for first-class cricket.

What an appalling waste of the county's most valuable single asset! I am convinced so much more could be done by expanding the scope of the cricket club. Instead of just being Hampshire's county cricket club, why not make it the Hampshire's Sporting Club?

I would like to see a much larger and better equipped cricket school in use both in the summer and winter months; squash courts, tennis courts, even a bowling green. We should establish a social or dining club to be used six or seven nights a week all the year round. Warwickshire have given a lead by having dining suites which can be hired out for weddings, parties, etc.

I know capital has to be found both to embark on such building projects and to provide the necessary equipment, but I'm sure it would be a winner.

I would also like to see the setting up of a scheme whereby young cricketers could study for a trade outside the game while they are still under training for first class cricket.

When I joined Hampshire I was interested in studying to be an accountant so that I would have a qualification and trade when my cricketing days were over.

Unfortunately, I was advised that it would not be worthwhile to spend all my spare time studying. Even for a person without any other interests, it takes three or four years to reach the qualified level.

Now I regret my decision. It would not have mattered if I had spent 15 years studying. I would still have a trade on which to fall back. At the moment I am qualified for nothing – except playing cricket.

This is where I think the counties themselves and the M.C.C. should help. They should provide the necessary money for young players to attend courses at evening school or some other training establishment.

I realise it might be difficult to persuade some starry-eyed youngsters that they need to have an outside trade. When they join the groundstaff from school they dream only of playing in Test matches and being successful cricketers.

The lesson is not brought home to them until a few years later when they have been given their chance and failed. Then come the dreaded words 'Sorry son, but you are not being re-engaged.'

The Football League are understandably proud of the vocational training scheme they run which allows for cash grants to apprentice footballers to study another career. Cricket could perform a similar service.

I have one other grouse about the game and this involves the M.C.C. and the Test and County Cricket Board over the question of the captains' meeting.

In the Autumn and Spring county captains are invited to Lord's. In the Autumn we discuss the lessons learned from the season we have just played and discuss what can be done in the future.

By the time we are called together for the Spring meeting all the important decisions have been reached during the various committee meetings on the long winter evenings.

We are given very little say on what goes on or on what

should be done. Yet we are the people more directly involved than anybody else.

I am sure that if the captains – as one body – had been given an opportunity to express their views *before* major decisions were taken by the Test and County Cricket Board, some of the mistakes of recent years would have been avoided.

I know that the views we express at our meetings are put before the T.C.C.B. but quite often vital decisions are made before we have had the opportunity to discuss them.

16 *Wanted by England!*

I was born fifteen years too soon! That is how it strikes me when I see players such as Gary Sobers, Lance Gibbs, Asif Iqbal, Barry Richards, Mushtaq and Majid playing in county cricket.

I cannot help but feel a little envious of them. They have the best of both worlds. They can play first-class cricket in England in the summer and are free to return to their own countries in winter to take part in Tests.

Yet because of the qualification rules then existing in the County Championship my Test career finished when I was only 21, back in New Zealand almost 20 years ago.

That was the last time I was able to represent my country and play in the top flight of cricket.

The chance was there to represent the West Indies in other Test series but that would have meant turning my back on Hampshire and giving up everything I had set my heart on. On another occasion I was asked if I would like to play for England. Those thoughts were soon shattered.

Early in 1957 when the West Indies were due to visit England I received a letter right out of the blue from the secretary of the West Indies Board of Control asking me if I would allow my name to go forward for consideration for the tour.

I believe Hampshire were also approached by the Board. I was thrilled to think I was still considered good enough to attract the attention of the selectors. Unfortunately I had to turn them down.

Under the qualification law, as it then stood, it would have meant breaking my contract with Hampshire to play for West Indies in 1957, and I would have had to spend another two years qualifying before I became eligible to play Championship Cricket again.

I could not face the thought of another two years in the wilderness. I had a duty to Hampshire who had shown faith in me in the first place. I would be letting them down.

Above all, I had to consider my wife, a Manchester girl and keen follower of cricket. It would have been unfair on her.

It did not take me long to say 'no'. Hampshire were very good about it. They made no move to influence my decision one way or the other.

That was the one official invitation I received to make a come-back to West Indian Test cricket. The second invitation was unofficial, some five years later.

It happened during the match between Hampshire and the Australians. Frank Worrell was there covering the match for a newspaper, and during one of the intervals he approached me.

'Let's have a drink tonight. I've something I'd like to ask you,' he said.

Later that evening he asked me 'Now that you have had your benefit and your career is mainly behind you, why not come back to the West Indies to play Test cricket?'

Frank was considering me for the one weak place in the great West Indies side of the early sixties. They were lacking an opening batsman to partner Conrad Hunte.

The thought was tempting. Again I turned it down. Although it was an unofficial invitation Frank had sufficient influence at the time to have got me in the side for the 1963 tour of England if he wanted me.

This time it would have meant a definite 'goodbye' to Hampshire and the end of my first-class career in England.

By the time I had played for the West Indies in 1963 and spent another two years qualifying again, Hampshire would not have required me.

Once more I decided that my future was in this country where I had a young family. Regretfully I told Frank 'Sorry, but it just isn't on.'

Strangely, it was only two months before Frank spoke to me that I got another invitation – this time to come under consideration for England.

After my heavy scoring performances during my benefit year in 1961 I was invited to play for the M.C.C. against Surrey at Lord's at the start of the 1962 season.

The late Walter Robins was then chairman of the England selectors, charged with the task of finding a side to tour Australia in 1962–63.

Before the start of that M.C.C. match he called me out of the dressing room at Lord's and said 'Are you interested in playing Test cricket?'

'Well, that is a thing I would like to think about,' I told him. 'I'd be delighted to play, although it has been a long time since I played a five-day match.'

He told me, 'If you are interested, let me know. We can then approach the West Indies for clearance because I have the tour to Australia in mind.'

He set me thinking most of the day. Being approached by the Chairman of Selectors must have meant I stood a good chance. Pakistan were the visitors that summer which would have made it a little easier for me to make my mark and I also thought of the Test fee.

I did not have to think about it very long. At tea I was

called out of the dressing room again by Mr Robins. He told me 'I'm sorry. I've made some inquiries and apparently you cannot play for England. A decision on this was made some years ago and I had forgotten about it.'

He then read me the actual minute of an M.C.C. Advisory Meeting on the question of players eligible to play for England.

The M.C.C. Advisory County Cricket Committee had made a ruling that anybody who had played Test cricket for one country could not be chosen for England.

This was designed for just such issues as involved me. By that time I had been in England for five years and I was qualified under the rule of the Imperial Cricket Conference – as it was then called – to play for England.

Perhaps now people will understand why I am a little envious of the present day overseas cricketers. If only the present day qualification rule had been in being in the early 1950's, I might well have had the chance of a long Test career.

Despite this I have managed to see almost all of the world by being a member of private tour parties. Some have taken me back to the West Indies, including one tour of Jamaica when I experienced the worst earthquake which had hit the island.

We were attending a cocktail party when the whole place felt as though it were turning upside down. It seemed to last for 30 seconds although it must have been shorter.

It was an astonishing sight, especially to see the water in the swimming pool suddenly swish up and come over the side.

If it was a frightening experience for me, it was even more so far Colin Ingleby-Mackenzie. As usual he was late. He was still in his bath having a nice old soak when the earthquake struck. The next thing he knew was a tidal wave from his bathtub hurling water all over the room.

Perhaps the funniest experience of all was when I joined

a tour organised by the late Ron Roberts, a wonderful friend of cricket.

At one stage we were due to play three one-day games in Corfu on a wicket set in a square in the middle of the town.

The first match was soon over. The locals were no match for us and were easily beaten. On the second day we decided to bat first to make sure the game lasted.

We hit out rather gaily until we decided we had enough runs and promptly declared. What a fuss that caused! They had never heard of declarations. They wondered what had happened when the two batsmen suddenly walked off. With none of us able to speak Greek it was some time before we were able to convince the opposing captain it was all in the rules.

More confusion followed during the last match. Again we batted first to make sure the game ran a decent length of time. When we had scored enough runs we had all agreed to give our wickets away to avoid the confusion of the previous day. I was batting low down the order and taking part in a stand with Wes Hall when the fielding captain suddenly walked across and said 'I declare' and led his team off!

We had two or three narrow escapes on that tour. In Rhodesia somebody set fire to the office of Sir Roy Welensky which was next door to our hotel and we had to be evacuated in the middle of the night.

Then, flying to Karachi, one of the four engines on our 'plane cut out when we still had two hours to go. We made it safely but what we did not know until after we landed was that one of the other three engines was working only on half speed.

We were in Karachi only for a few hours before flying off again. This time we were all set to take off on the end of the runway when one of the engines caught fire.

It meant an hour's delay while everything was checked.

The airport officials would not let us get off the plane. Perhaps it was just as well. There were at least half a dozen of us who would never have been persuaded back on that aircraft!

Despite the upsets, the disappointments and the various 'ducks' I have collected over the years, I would never change my life if I had the chance of living it over again.

Cricket has been good to me and for me. I met my wife Shirley at a cricket match at Old Trafford in 1953. We have three girls Shelley (15), Debbie (13) and Joanne (11). Without their support and understanding I could never have lasted in the game as long as I have done.

I love golf and tennis. I watch Southampton regularly in the First Division, but to me, cricket is a game out on its own.

In no other game do you find a person both fighting for his side and himself. A batsman is scoring runs to help his team. Yet, when he faces the bowler, he is out there completely on his own. Nobody can possibly help him.

That is the appeal of cricket. Being able to do something individually, yet helping others at the same time. Long may it continue!

Index

Numbers in *italic* refer to the illustrations

GIOVANNA

Marino Famiglia Book One

VICTORIA ARROW

Digital ISBN: 978-0-473-67747-3
Paperback ISBN: 978-0-473-67745-9

Cover Design: germancreative

DEDICATION

For my love, SSP.

My inspiration, my sanity, and the best person I know.

PLAYLIST

GAY 4 ME by G Flip and Lauren Sanderson
Supalonely by Benee
Chasing Cars by Snow Patrol
Holy Water by Noah Davis
Before He Cheats by Carrie Underwood
she calls me daddy by KING MALA
Just Like A Prayer by Madonna
Alejandro by Lady Gaga
Why'd you only call me when you're high? by Arctic Monkeys
Iris by The Goo Goo Dolls

TRIGGER WARNINGS

The Marino Famiglia Series is dark mafia romance. Naturally, the books contain a fair amount of sex and violence. Please be aware of this before you start reading. Everyone has their own limits.

Specific trigger warnings for *Giovanna*: sexual assault (historic and talked about but not described), torture, explicit sex scenes (1 MF and multiple FF), profanity, general violence and death.

If you have experienced sexual assault and need support here are a few resources. I couldn't list services for all countries, but I am sure the below online options could refer you to your local help centre.

Australia: 1800RESPECT (1800 737 732) | 1800respect.org.au
United States: RAINN 1 (800) 656-4673 | rainn.org
United Kingdom: Rape Crisis 0808 500 2222 | 247sexualabusesupport.org.uk
Canada: Salal National Toll-free: 1-877-392-7583 | wavaw.ca/get-support
New Zealand: Freephone 0800 044 334 or text 4334 | Email support@safetotalk.nz

CONTENTS

PROLOGUE
SANDY

The door to my office swings open and I lift my head from my hands snatching my discarded reading glasses from the stack of papers in front of me, shoving them up my crooked nose. My bones creak like the unoiled hinges of doors long shut and I am weary.

"Ah, it's just you," I relax immediately at the sight of my oldest friend striding towards my desk.

If age is catching up with his body as quickly as it is with mine, it doesn't show. He's the same sinewy, rigid man I've always known. His shadowed and gaunt face a mask seven decades in the making.

He's wound up tight as an elastic band stretched to its extreme, poised to snap at any moment like the protruding tendons in his neck.

It is no small miracle that the cold and calculating old fuck is still hovering around and not six feet under having suffered a stress-induced heart attack. Or with a bullet in his brain. If he was shot we would have a mammoth task figuring out which of his many foes pulled the trigger.

He's a scheming arsehole, but he's a scheming arsehole who is yet to let me down in the 60-something years we've known each other.

There isn't an important moment in my life he hasn't been part of; from our first day of school to leaving Italy together as young men. He is the godfather to my children and me to his. We've laughed and cried together. We've built a dynasty and now its survival depends on the next generation.

"You look like you haven't slept in a week, mate," Paul Rossi could never be accused of blowing smoke up anyone's arse, even mine. I can always rely on him to give it to me straight, even if it isn't flattering. He is perhaps the only person brave enough to openly criticise me these days.

When loyalty is the most valuable currency, almost anything else can be excused.

"Fuckin' dog's breakfast, mate. Bikies are getting their hands on some serious hardware. Not a good look for us when guns are going off on every street corner."

"Bet it's the bloody Arabs. They're opening up new channels all over the shop." Rossi hates the Arabs and would blame them for a hair in his dinner, but in this case, he is probably right.

Once upon a time we had a monopoly on the importation/exportation business in Sydney and held a significant share of the market nationwide. The Marino *Famiglia* were the only ones who could get what was needed into Australia and across state lines.

Now competition is fierce. If it isn't the Arabs trying to move in on our territories, it's the Vietnamese or the Turks. The Bikie gangs have demonstrated that they're loyal only to a bargain and convenience, happy to forget decades of peaceful business with our *Famiglia*, with Sydney's Mafia.

Following the troubles we had in the early 2000s that saw an unprecedented amount of bloodshed, I have worked hard to reign over the Marino *Famiglia*, and this city, mostly by commanding respect, but I fear my successor will have to resort to good old-fashioned fear more and more often.

It's dangerous when folk think they have options, choices. Whether they want to or feel they have to, to get shit done in this city people need to know they have to go to the Marino *Famiglia*.

"Your fuckwit of a son needs to piss off back to Melbourne, Paul," I grumble, pinching the bridge of my nose.

"Preaching to the choir, mate. He's putting a lot of hard graft into this 'reconciliation' charade. As if I don't know what the sly fucker is up to. Didn't come down in the last shower, son."

He has been complaining for months about having to play nice while his prodigal son Stefan pretends to want to have a relationship with his daddy.

Paul is like those animals you see in nature documentaries. The ones that eat their own young. If he has a paternal bone in his body, I have not encountered it and I suspect neither have his kids.

"The kids on the way back yet?" I change the subject. It is what he has come to talk to me about anyway, I'll bet.

"Our guys should be arriving about now at the flat. We should be able to hear the protests from my youngest all the way from London shortly," Paul looks at his watch. Bemused as ever at the thought of his daughter's attempts to defy him.

Like my Massimo, Francesca is Paul's second-time-round offspring. We both ended up impregnating our younger second wives 24 years ago and produced a pair of Mafia brats spoiled by their mothers and their older half-siblings. They've been gallivanting around Europe, but now it is time to drag them back down under for a dose of reality. They might be the bambinos of the family, but they have their roles to play. Especially that beauty Francesca.

"She's had eight years away to do what she wants, mate. It's time for her to grow up." He nods in agreement. We are on the same page about our children as well as most things.

A shrill ring interrupts us and Paul digs into the pocket of his pants for his phone, putting it on speakerphone. "Francesca, how nice to hear from you. I thought you had forgotten your old man's number," he answers dryly.

"It's a two-way street, *Dad.* Haven't seen any missed calls from you. Anyway, can you explain why two of your goons have forced their way into my flat and are telling me they're taking me home? *This* is my home."

She has picked up a hybrid English/Australian accent in the years since we sent her to live with her mother's parents when she was 16. She squawked and protested about being sent there. Now, it seems she doesn't want to come home.

"Australia is your home and it is time for you and Massimo to come back," Paul speaks as though he is discussing something as mundane as the weather. The rage from his daughter is practically emanating from his mobile phone.

"No! Not happening! You dumped me here eight years ago. *Eight years ago*, Dad. You've had zero interest in seeing me since then and now you want to drag me back into your mob games? You're dreaming!"

I raise my eyebrows at Paul and he just shakes his head slightly, unfazed.

"That's enough, Francesca. You will get on that plane or Sandy will have Massimo put you on it."

"Massimo doesn't want to come home either! We have a life here. What do you want from me?! What could I possibly have that you need after all this time? I know you don't miss me because that would require you to be capable of human emotions!"

Massimo may have told her that he doesn't want to come home, but he will do exactly as he is told. Just like he did when I sent him over there to babysit her and break up her relationship with that posh idiot two years ago.

His deep voice mumbles placating nonsense in the background as he tries to soothe her. My soft-hearted son will hate seeing her so distressed. They love each other more than anyone else in the world. It's a pity he's gay, it would have been easy to marry them off to each other otherwise.

"I'm very busy. You are coming home; whether that is with your dignity intact or not is entirely up to you. Your mother is looking forward to seeing you." Paul hovers his finger above the 'end call' button long enough to hear one last scream of frustration from Francesca before cutting her off.

"If your boy can get her on the plane without sustaining any injuries I'll buy him a beer," Paul rolls his eyes.

CHAPTER ONE
GIOVANNA

Rich tomatoey smells tempt me as I jog past the kitchen calling "hey" to Peta's bent-over form. She is on her hands and knees, her head deep in a maple wood cupboard, but I make out her muffled "Hiya, love" in response.

I'll be down later to sample whatever it is she is cooking.

The woman cooks like an Italian nonna, but she hasn't got a drop of Italian blood in her. She's a true blue Aussie. Being married to my father for 26 years should count for something though. A fuckin' medal for having the patience of a saint for a start.

I head upstairs and down the wide central hallway that acts as a spine for our private living quarters. The first floor of our home can be like Sydney Central Railway Station with all of my father's men coming and going, but the second floor is for our family.

Only a select few get to set foot in Dad's home office. Those important enough to be part of discussions and those who won't live long enough to share their experience with anyone.

Calling it a 'home office' doesn't do the room justice. In the middle of the second floor, it takes pride of place. We have corporate offices in town, but this office is where the real decisions get made. It is the symbolic centre of the Marino *Famiglia. Cosa Nostra.*

Like the rest of the house, the ceilings in the office are high. Shelves line most of the walls, from floor to ceiling, full of books that Dad collects but never reads. He likes to appear well-read, but he isn't.

There is a big central fireplace at the back of the room which, again, is there only for aesthetics given we live in Australia and 20 degrees celsius is considered chilly.

His desk is huge and ostentatiously carved and the chairs for those who come to see him are heavy antiques. A whisky bar with crystal decanters and glasses stands next to a plush leather sofa in the corner. Everything screams prestige and power. Even the ever-changing rug in front of his desk that everyone knows obscures more than one dark stain.

My footsteps are hurried and I'm hoping that this meeting will be a quick one. Today has been a bloody nightmare and fitting in a catch-up with Dad and two of my brothers has fucked up my plans.

"Dad," I acknowledge him and sit down in one of the three antique chairs in front of his desk.

Naturally, I'm the first one here. Matteo will be here next, almost exactly on time, and then we will all sit waiting for his royal highness Elio to grace us with his presence.

Dad looks up from his computer and I'm struck by how much he has aged in the past few years. He's 70 and his once impressive thick black hair, always combed back, is now almost entirely grey. His big nose, broken several times over the years, seems to have grown larger and ruddier, while the rest of him has shrunk. Once he had a few inches on my tall 5'10 frame, but now we look about the same height. All three of my brothers tower above us both.

"Giovanna," he states plainly. "Ah, and Matteo right on time," he adds.

Matteo squeezes my shoulder before taking the chair to my left. He drops into it heavily with a sigh, the world appearing to rest on his shoulders. I observe him carefully, wishing (not for the first time) that I could shoulder some of the load he's had to bear in his 33 years of life.

"What are the odds on *SportsBet* that Elio will be late?" Matty drawls, needling our father. We all hate lateness, but Dad is infamous for his intolerance of it. Dad just grunts in response and goes back to reading his computer screen.

Ten minutes later, Elio breezes in with all the confidence of a man who knows he need not hurry because people will wait for him. With a wide smile that is well known to make panties drop in any room, and dressed the part in

an Armani suit, my brother looks every bit the heir to an enormous fortune and the throne of Sydney's mafia.

"Dad, how's it going?" he sticks on the charm offensive immediately, winking at Matty and me.

"Sit." Dad is not in the mood. "Right, kids. Shit is about to change."

The three of us shoot glances at each other. I don't know about them, but I thought this was going to be a pretty casual discussion. Apparently not. I can't help but sit up straighter in my chair.

"You might have noticed, I'm old and not getting any younger. Anyway, the doc reckons I'm going to have a heart attack or stroke if I don't get my blood pressure down. I've got Atrial Fibrillation - whatever the fuck that is...Oh, don't look at me like that I'm not fuckin' dying!"

He glares at the three of us as if we are solely responsible for his high blood pressure and not a lifetime of cigarettes, rich food, and running the mafia.

"Peta's in a flap," he says with a frown laced with guilt. "Given me the hard word..."

If I wasn't worried about Dad's health and trying to figure out how much he is downplaying this fibrillation thing, I'd laugh at how this feared mafia don listens to no one but his wife.

He clears his throat and continues. "It's time for me to hand things over. Time for you lot to step up and to be frank, this shit with Stefan is doing my head in and the sooner it's your problem the better." He pauses and I imagine my face looks as shocked as my brothers'.

"We've always talked about Elio leading the *Famiglia* after me and that is still the plan on the surface..."

Elio bristles next to me and habitually runs his hand over his closely buzzed head. Anxious about whatever is to come next.

"But, we haven't had as much time as I hoped to transition you into things, son, so behind the scenes and in a lot of practical ways Giovanna will be in charge -"

Elio explodes. "THE FUCK! When was this decided?" He glares at me as if this has happened by my design. In actual fact, I'm as dumbfounded as he is.

Long ago I accepted that due to my XX chromosomes, and the bits in my pants, I would never be my father's heir. Women don't lead the mafia. We cook, clean, and become mamas and then nonnas.

"Elio! You're bloody lucky you get to be anything at all! Your sister is far more capable and if she was my son there wouldn't even be a conversation to be had!" Dad roars slamming his palms on his desk.

Neither Matty nor I have said anything, but he lifts an eyebrow at me ever so slightly as if to say "What the fuck is going on?"

We can communicate with few words, me and Matty. We are the thinkers, the brooding, unsmiling, serious mafia kids. Elio and Massimo are the charmers. They smile and have the gift of the gab. Our polar opposites.

Elio runs a hand over his buzzed dark almost black hair again. He keeps it very short which accentuates his sharp cheekbones and dark brown eyes. All three of us have them, the high, well-defined cheekbones and deep chocolate eyes, but they make Elio look like a god. That is how women treat him anyway. And some men.

"How would this even work?" Elio is uncharacteristically short and quiet.

Dad waves his arm as if to indicate that the details are simple. "You schmooze, charm, and communicate to the world. Your sister makes all the decisions and tells you what to say. It's just playing to your strengths."

My brother is nodding now. Taking it all in. He seems to be hating the idea less and less. "So, G does all the work and I go to meetings and parties?" He grins at me.

"In a nutshell, yes." Dad shrugs.

"Sold!" Elio goes to get up, but Dad motions for him to sit back down.

"Tomorrow I will be moving upstairs to the top floor. This office will become Giovanna's as will the master suite. Elio you can keep your wing. I wouldn't want the women of Sydney to get lost trying to find your bedroom. But you get my corporate office in the Marino Building; people need to see you are the boss there. Matty, are you still happy in the pool house?"

Matty nods. He gutted it years ago when he got out of prison and renovated it into his own suite, private gym included. It has almost no interior walls because after four years locked up my brother has an aversion to small

spaces. In any interior space, his eyes dart to the windows and doors as if to map out all possible escape routes.

"...and Massimo will have the East Wing."

"Massimo? He's coming home?" I finally speak, the words bursting from my mouth in an excited splutter.

I'm not the most expressive of people and I do love all three of my brothers, but I was 14 when Massimo was born and I fell in love so hard with that chunky little fatty. I've missed him far more than anyone realises while he has been doing his O.E.

"Yes, your baby brother should be landing in Sydney in just a few hours. And, Elio... he's bringing your wife home," the wicked grin on Dad's face shows just how much he is enjoying dropping this bomb on his playboy son.

Sandy Marino has always had a flair for the dramatic and he is taking this opportunity to indulge in it.

"Sorry, Dad, I could have sworn you just said '*my wife*'?" Elio is hiding behind sarcasm, but a vein in his neck is pulsating with a ferocity that betrays the panic he is feeling.

"Oh, you heard right, mate. Massimo has been looking after your wife for two years, keeping her out of trouble."

Elio is sweating now. "I was under the impression that Massimo was partying it up with Paul Rossi's daughter, not engaged in a secret wife-protecting mission," he hisses.

"He was doing both. Francesca Rossi will be your wife."

"Absolutely fuckin' not." Elio is on his feet now, pacing. "She's a child for fucksake!"

Matty and I both snort at the same time knowing full well that our brother hasn't had a girlfriend over the age or BMI of 25 in a long time.

The irony isn't lost on Dad either. "She is 24, Elio. Practically geriatric by your standards."

"Wait, what about David?" I suddenly have the thought that Francesca probably doesn't want to come home. Shame leaves a bitter taste in my mouth as I think about how she was just sent away. It took me years to get her some kind of justice, but David is still drawing breath and that just isn't right.

Dad ignores my question and sends me a look that screams 'Shut the fuck up, Giovanna' and like the good daughter I am, I let it slide.

Elio is quiet, but he is thinking so hard we can almost hear the cogs turning. Matty and I watch knowing there is little sense in getting involved. Dad will get his way, Elio just needs room to protest and tantrum first.

I weigh up my own irritation at the situation in the meantime. Having just announced that tomorrow he will hand over the running of the *Famiglia* and our business interests to us, it is dawning on me that there is a whole lot of shit going down that we have no idea about.

Has he got a wife he is going to spring on me next? He knows better than to try giving me a husband. Am I sitting here bemused at my brother's misfortune yet to discover that I'm next? No, thank you.

I haven't been in a proper relationship for a few years now. More than a few years. They're hard to maintain in our line of work. Aussie women just don't get our life and putting time and effort into integrating them is futile because they inevitably eventually decide they don't want to be in a relationship with someone who regularly comes home in the middle of the night covered in blood.

The easiest thing would be to date within the wider *Famiglia*, but it isn't exactly swimming with single lesbians.

Online dating is a no-go too. What the fuck would I write in a Tinder bio?

Giovanna, 38
Mafia Underboss
When I'm not breaking the law and/or fingers,
I enjoy working out, good whiskey, and eating pussy.

Maybe I *should* let Dad find me a wife. At least I'd get laid regularly. Well, in theory.

Elio is pleading with our bemused father now. "Why do I need to get married anyway? We aren't in the 1950s."

Another snort slips out and I nearly choke on my own spit. "Reminding you that despite being the eldest Marino child I can't outright succeed Dad because I'm female…"

Dad sighs and leans back in his chair, cleaning his glasses. "You are getting married because you need to be taken seriously and running around shagging anything in a skirt isn't going to cut it anymore."

"To be fair though, Dad," Matty speaks up for the first time. "Being married isn't going to put a stop to that behaviour. Elio can't even spell monogamy."

"Get fucked. I'm the only one in this family who got a fuckin' education," Elio snarls at him.

"Well, you aren't exactly acting like a screaming endorsement for university education, son," Dad exhales. "Look, all of you. This isn't a joke. You all know that Stefan Rossi isn't getting under our feet because he misses his dad. He's here to destabilise knowing that I'm going to step down soon. The grumbles I'm hearing are that Elio will be a playboy prince and cause instability. Marrying Francesca Rossi gives you, Elio, the chance to put that all in the past."

"What bearing does who I fuck have on my ability to lead the *Famiglia*?" Elio tries to snap, but he is tiring of the conversation.

"If you need me to explain to you the importance of managing perceptions at this point, I have failed as a father to prepare you for this role."

"It's just bullshit. You trying to tell me that the bosses back in Italy aren't swimming in pussy?"

"Enough!" Dad raises his voice and as if he has brought down a gavel, we all know the conversation is over.

"You two, out!" He points to my brothers. "Gio, we need to discuss some practicalities."

Matty gives my shoulder another squeeze on his way past while Elio's slamming and swearing can be heard as makes his way through the house. He will be at the bottom of a bottle with a model's lips around his cock before Dad and I are done with our conversation.

CHAPTER TWO
FRANCESCA

12 Years Old

Sunblock melts down my face and I cough and splutter as a wave of water hits me. Blinking, I push wet hair from my eyes.

Massimo's goofy face appears as he bobs up and down on a pool noodle, roaring with laughter. He has the biggest smile of anyone I know, but he is excited to get braces next year to sort out his crooked teeth. I don't think they're bad, but he hates them. I'll probably get braces too.

"Massi!" I squeal and get up from my perch on the side of the pool to launch myself at him. I land right on top of him and we begin play-fighting under the water. He is stronger than me now which is annoying. It's like once he turned 12 he left me behind.

"Oi! You two! Cut it out!" We surface at the sound of Massimo's big sister bellowing at us from the other side of the pool. She is a lot older than him; a proper grown-up. That's why she looks after us sometimes. Her voice is deep and husky, but she usually doesn't raise it. I think she is annoyed because we were making lots of noise and she has friends over.

"We were just playing, Gio!" Massimo calls out to her and she rolls her eyes in return. She has an arm around one of her friends and the other one lays next to her sunbathing. I can't stop watching them; that's why Massimo splashed me earlier. He was trying to get my attention and I was away with the fairies, as Massi's dad would say.

Grabbing a pool noodle of my own, I float closer to the side of the pool Giovanna and her friends are lying next to. Curiosity burns in my chest and I have to see what they are doing and hear what they are saying.

Giovanna has a hand, the one that isn't draped over the shoulders of the woman in the hot pink bikini, resting on the bum of a woman in a black bikini. As I get closer I can see that her thumb is softly rubbing small circles on the bare skin next to her bikini bottoms.

My heart starts beating really fast and I'm not sure why. My tummy sometimes feels funny when Gio talks to me, but this is even worse. What if I have a heart attack?

Massimo throws a tennis ball at me and I tear myself away from Giovanna and her friends to fetch it and throw it back. I dip under the cool surface hoping that it will calm me down, take the heat out of my cheeks, and slow my racing heart. It doesn't.

Now I'm staring again. Discreetly. Well, I hope I'm not being obvious. Hot Pink Bikini has her hand on Gio's stomach now.

Gio goes to the gym a lot; that's how she is so muscly. Mum says it isn't good for a woman to be that muscly, but I like it. I mean, it looks good on Gio. I don't think I would want to be that muscly though.

My breath catches in my throat as I watch Gio take her hand off Black Bikini's bum and reach over to grab Hot Pink Bikini's chin. She pulls her towards her and kisses her hard. I can see their tongues sliding all over each other and it feels like someone punched me in the gut. I suddenly hate that woman in the hot pink bikini and I can't explain why.

Massimo is focused on something in the far corner of the pool, oblivious to what I am witnessing.

I can't look away for long even though watching them kiss makes me want to squirm. Like I swallowed a bucket of writhing eels.

It's not just my tummy that feels strange. I squeeze my thighs together to try to stop the tingling between my legs. It isn't a sensation I'm used to and I can't decide if I like it or not.

The woman in the black bikini suddenly seems to realise what is happening behind her and sits up. I wonder if she is going to be angry that they are kissing, but she just crawls over, climbs on Gio's lap, and takes a turn kissing her.

Hot tears well in my eyes and I feel so embarrassed. I don't know why I'm crying. I want to throw up, but I also still have funny fluttering butterflies in my tummy and between my legs. I submerge myself again to wash away my stupid tears.

"Ewwww gross!" Massimo's croaky voice calls out as I resurface and kick away from Giovanna and her friends. "Can you not make a porno when I have a friend over!" He shouts at his big sister.

Giovanna laughs. It is good to see her smile. She is the most serious person I know and I worry that she is sad sometimes.

"I think your friend is curious actually," the woman in the hot pink bikini replies to him and then laughing at me adds, "Aren't you?"

I scowl at her. She is embarrassing me in front of Gio and making me look like a baby and I hate it.

"Let's go inside, Massi," I mutter to him as I grab my towel and quickly wrap it around my bony body. With no boobs and bum, I may as well be a little boy. Most of my friends wear training bras now, but there is no point for me.

Turning to check Massimo is following me - he is - I see that the three women have continued kissing. I'm so confused about what watching them has done to me, but I do know that for some reason I am wondering what it would be like to be the one on Gio's lap and that terrifies me.

CHAPTER THREE
FRANCESCA

My bedroom looks exactly the same. It is like a time capsule taking me back eight years to 16-year-old Francesca. Have my parents even been in here at all while I was away? Or did they just close the door and pretend it wasn't there like they did with me? The portal to parenthood sealed off and left to gather dust.

The pale pink walls with gold motifs stencilled in the corners look brash now, but I was so proud of my handiwork when I begged my mum to let me decorate my room when I was about fifteen.

On my desk, eight-year-old magazines sit next to a high school history textbook. It truly is a bedroom frozen in time. Even my well-loved, worn-down teddy bear sits atop the pillows on my bed.

The long flight from London gave me time to simmer down, but I was still furious to find myself back in Australia with my callous parents. A week later and I'm just about climbing the walls, claustrophobic in their massive oppressive mansion. It feels even less like home than it did when I trudged through the front door with my suitcases.

The independence I had in London feels like a distant dream. The freedom of our little flat. Happy and settled for the first time.

After moving out of Nana and Pop's house two years ago, Massimo and I found a flat and I worked at a local gym. I liked my job, loved our home, and

felt free. If we wanted to go to Berlin for the weekend, we did. Paris for a long lunch? Why not! We could be spontaneous and compulsive.

Back here it is as if I never left. They treat me as the 16-year-old girl they packed up because they couldn't stomach dealing with what happened to her. But I am not that girl anymore. Well, I thought I wasn't, but I can feel myself being pulled back into the controlling machinery of the *Famiglia.* It's like battling an undercurrent.

There is a brisk knock at the door and without waiting for an answer, my parents crowd into my bedroom.

"By all means come in," I mutter sarcastically. They pretend not to hear me.

"How's the jetlag, sweetie?" my mum queries tentatively.

She looks at me like I am an unexploded bomb that might go off at any time.

While I haven't seen Dad in eight years, my mother came out to visit me four times. I was living with her parents after all. The conclusion of each visit seemed to be a source of great relief for her. I can see her now. The way she clutched her suitcase and hurtled down the path towards the black cab that would take her to the airport. Her duty complete until the next guilt-triggered visit.

"Fine, it's been a week. When are you going to tell me why I had to be dragged home?" I refuse to look at my parents and instead focus my attention on my fingernails, picking at my cuticles.

Dad clears his throat and hesitates and I immediately realise that there *is* a specific reason they've brought me here. I can't for the life of me think what it is. I am worthless to them. I am my father's extra child who wasn't meant to be. A means for my teenage mother to bind herself to him. So surplus to requirements that they could dump me on the other side of the world for a third of my life without batting an eyelid.

"Well, actually there is a reason we brought you home. Why Uncle Sandy wanted you back here." This has got to be bad. If my selfish, arsehole of a father can't bring himself to spit it out, I know things are dire. "You're going to get married, Francesca."

"MARRIED?" I gasp. "What is this? The bloody middle ages? How many goats is my husband giving you for my hand in marriage, Dad?!" I'm on my feet and spitting tacks. I knew it was going to be bad, but this is something else.

"Take a breath, Francesca," he dares to scold me.

"Take a breath? You are selling me like cattle! This isn't normal, Dad! Actually, I am pretty sure this is illegal in Australia." As if something illegal ever stopped Dad and Sandy before. "Go on, tell me. Who am I supposed to be marrying?"

"Elio," Mum says softly. Her abundance of bangles and rings clink as she carefully runs her fingers through her messy-chic-to-perfection white-blonde hair.

She is irritatingly attractive and because she also had me when she was just 19, the boys at school talked about her incessantly referring to her as a 'MILF' from the moment their internet browsing taught them what it means.

"Elio?" I wasn't expecting that. "Massimo's brother?" I am in shock. I thought I was going to be married off to some third cousin twice removed and dragged to Italy to live life barefoot and pregnant in the kitchen. Being handed to the heir of the Sydney mafia is the last thing I would've guessed.

"You should be honoured -" Before she has even finished the sentence I'm clamouring down her throat.

"-Honoured!? You're shitting me, right? Isn't he like twenty years older than me anyway?" I've never denied I'm prone to exaggeration.

"Twelve years," Mum interjects. If she doesn't stop fiddling with her hair I'm going to lose my mind. She holds her fingers stiff as if the acrylic talons she gets painted weekly are so delicate they might fall off at the lightest touch.

I throw myself back onto my fuschia paisley bedspread and cover my face with my hands. *Fuck this.* Fuck this so much. I'm so shocked that I can't even cry.

Mum strokes my forehead pretending that we have a normal and affectionate mother/daughter relationship. "You always wanted to be a mum, sweetie. Elio can give you everything you ever wanted. You won't ever have to work."

She isn't wrong. Whenever we were asked at school what we wanted to be when we grew up, I always said I wanted to be a mum. But, I kinda always

assumed I would get to choose who to marry and reproduce with. And what if I want to work? I'll not pretend I'm a career woman, but I like the social aspect of working.

Dad is getting antsy now. A twitching muscle in his hollow cheek tells me he is annoyed that I haven't simply accepted his announcement and toddled off to choose a wedding dress.

Mafia men are all the same. They issue instructions and their wives, daughters, sisters, and mothers do as we are told.

I bet Elio is just as bad. I shudder at the thought of what he will expect from me. A maid, a cook, and a whore, I suppose.

Dad starts to walk out the door. "You have four hours to get used to the idea, Francesca. Because we leave at 6 pm for your engagement party at the Marino's house."

I have no words so I just scream through gritted teeth. It takes all my self-control not to flail around on my bed like a toddler mid-tantrum.

Mum goes to leave as well, but I grab her by the wrist. "Mum...will he be there?" I ask quietly.

"Elio? Of course, he will!"

"No, not Elio..."

Discomfort descends over her and I am pretty sure I can see her blood curdle in all of that guilt. She knows. "Ah, I don't know. He moved to Melbourne a couple of years after you left, but he has been around again recently."

"Unbelievable. You drag me home just so you can show me again how little I matter. How my own parents can't manage to find half a shit to give about me."

She is shaking and her eyes won't meet mine. At least I know she isn't a sociopath. She knows what she has done and carries it. I can't say the same for my father. "You know how things work in our world." She whispers.

CHAPTER FOUR
FRANCESCA

When I say I learned to fix myself, I am telling the truth. I pieced myself back together and papered over the cracks until they set hard. Nana and Pop were pretty oblivious to the pain I was in when I arrived. They were glad to have their Australian grandchild come live with them, but more so because they felt it mitigated the embarrassment of their daughter running away overseas at 17, I suspect.

For six years they put a roof over my head and mostly kept me out of trouble, but I was left alone to deal with my trauma and rebuild myself until the only person I ever truly loved showed up on my doorstep.

My Massimo was all grown up and ready to party when he wheeled his suitcase into Nana and Pop's home and brought the light back into my life. My best friend and the only person who has never let me down. Even through years of messaging and video calls from afar, he was my constant.

I sometimes wonder now if Massimo is my soulmate. There is nothing remotely sexual about our relationship and he is God's gift to gay men, but we are bound together in a way that is difficult to put into words. No words I have ever managed have seemed adequate anyway.

Massimo saved me from settling into a life of monotony and duty by showing up when he did. He gave me the confidence to admit I wasn't in love with the well-to-do Englishman I was engaged to marry and reminded me that I was 22 and young enough to live for the pure enjoyment of it. Ironic

considering now it looks like he only bought me two years of freedom leaving me available to be indentured to his own oldest brother.

On the straight and narrow path to becoming Mrs. Gareth Godfrey-White, I had settled into an existence that was sequestered from anything dangerous. Gareth was a nice guy, a safe guy, and he would have provided for me and our future children with ease. Holidays in the Maldives and living in country estates. He played *polo* for goodness sake.

It was easy and a means to motherhood that wasn't entirely unbearable. But, Massimo went and stuck his ginormous foot in and snapped me out of my trance. Single again, I went along for the ride as Massimo danced us through every club in London and many across the continent.

My darling friend with his wide dimpled smile and tragic good looks led us on a two-year excursion consisting mainly of prosecco, dancing, and adventure. We *lived* and blew through a shit load of his Dad's money ensuring we enjoyed ourselves as much as possible.

Perhaps now life is coming to collect the fee for two years of freedom and happiness with my favourite person. I should feel grateful for all I experienced and accept this next phase in my life as inevitable. In any case, I don't have much choice.

~

In the absence of any escape plans, I find myself trawling through Mum's wardrobe looking for something to wear to my engagement party. A party at which I will speak to my fiancé for the first time in over eight years.

He probably doesn't even know who I am. I can't remember Elio ever properly interacting with me and Massi. Avoided us like the plague more than anything. He used to spend most of his time drunk or trying to get laid. Not that he had to try particularly hard. He was as attractive and charming as Massimo is. I wonder if he still is.

If I have to attend this tragic charade, I am determined to look devastatingly beautiful because everything is easier when you are confident in how you look. I'm aware this is a worldview I picked up from Mum, but even I can't disagree with her on this one.

But if I'm completely and truly honest, my determination to look my best has more to do with the prospect of seeing the person who has featured in almost all of my dreams and been the inspiration for every private piece of pleasure snatched between my sheets for eight long years.

The dress I choose is a dark navy blue sleeveless bodycon dress. It is high-necked and reaches just below the knees so appears modest despite hugging so tightly to every curve of my body that I will have to forgo underwear.

Thank goodness my mother is a self-obsessed mafia wife who at only 43 years old is in such great shape that she looks like she could be my sister. Her clothes and shoes fit me perfectly and I choose a pair of brand-new black strappy stilettos to pair with my dress.

Checking my angles in front of the mirror, I tussle the roots of my hair to make my carefully styled loose waves look sexily messy. Chestnut brown roots gradually become blonde tips halfway down my back with some more blonde at the front framing my face.

I'm not the Francesca who was hushed up and ushered out of the country all those years ago. Lightening my hair into the perfect summery balayage was one way of reinventing myself and leaving behind the nervous and broken dark-haired girl. Part of me is looking forward to the inevitable shock from people who haven't seen me in the years since and who won't recognise me.

I'm a cocktail of dread and excitement. Loathing that I am to be traded like property, but excited to be back from exile. Most of all I am filled with raw desperation to see the member of the Marino family who has consumed my thoughts and fantasies for as long as I can remember.

Because Giovanna is the one person under the age of 50 in Australia who doesn't use social media, I haven't been able to stalk her from afar. My only glimpses of what her life has looked like have been through her cameos on her brothers' social media.

But, tonight, finally, I'll get to see if she is still the grumpy but gorgeous woman who made me feel crazy, safe, confused, obsessed, and devastated all at once.

What will she make of me now that I'm a grown woman? I want to capture that moment when she first sees me. Will there be recognition? Attraction? Or worse of all, disinterested?

"Leaving in five minutes, Francesca!" My father's compassionless voice grates on me as it carries up the stairs. I resist the temptation to reply that I am not coming. Instead, I finish off my makeup with the only correct choice of lipstick for an occasion such as this: blood red.

For all my confidence in my appearance, and my parents' reassuring approval of it, as the driver pulls up outside the Marino house I am hit with a bout of nerves. I'm suddenly nauseous and shaky and want to book a flight back to London.

Deep breaths and repeated reminders to myself that I just need to find Massimo and everything will be fine, calm me a little.

"Come on then," Dad's impatience interrupts my attempts at self-soothing. At least Mum has the decency to look apologetic, to Paul Rossi I don't think I have ever registered as anything better than a somewhat useful nuisance.

Heads turn as soon as we enter the vast open-plan living area the Marinos use for entertaining. With no walls to separate the areas, furniture serves to differentiate between the kitchen, dining, and lounge. The space is already full of people; some I vaguely recognise, most I don't.

They call it the 'Big Room'. Or at least they did last time I was here. The name is an understatement though. The multipurpose living area takes up almost the entire first floor of the house. It is an entertainer's dream, but it is also so open that there is nowhere to hide.

Marino *Famiglia* soldiers traipse in and out of the Big Room constantly throughout the day and night, but they know not to venture beyond into the family's living quarters. They enjoy Peta's famous cooking at the huge wooden table with bench seating and often have a few beers in the evening out by the pool.

The house is part family home and part *Famiglia* home.

My heels click on the polished wood flooring and I am taken back to the obstacle courses Massimo and I used to set up in the Big Room when we were children. We would wear socks so we could slip and slide on the polished floor.

The entire back of the room is glass windows and French doors that open out onto the back garden complete with a pool and outdoor entertainment area. More strangers mingle out there, wine glasses or beer bottles in hand.

Outside the air is warm and close and inside it borders on oppressive. I resolve to try to get Massimo to jump in the pool with me at the end of the night. Just like we did when we were kids.

"Francesca, *bella*!" My father's voice is magically filled with affection now that he has an audience. Retrieving a glass of prosecco from a waiter, I trail after my parents putting as much haughty sass in the sway of my hips as I can.

An older Uncle Sandy stands next to Dad and Auntie Peta next to him, she still looks as fabulous as ever. I give Peta a big smile and she wraps me in the first genuine hug I've had since arriving in Australia. Massimo gets his warmth from her.

Uncle Sandy clasps both my hands as he presses a kiss onto each of my cheeks. "*Bella, bella, bella*! Elio is a lucky man, Francesca. You have grown into a beautiful woman."

Trying to hide my cringe at the reminder that I am here to be given to a man twelve years older than me, I give Sandy my most dazzling smile. Mum nods approvingly at me and it makes me want to stop smiling immediately and do anything to rebel, anything.

"Did you miss me?" A warm breath tickles my neck and I turn to find Massimo looking dashing in a perfectly fitted dark navy blue suit.

"More than you could imagine. Why can't I marry you?" I whisper wistfully back to him as he wraps me in a big hug.

"I would do it if I could, you know that right?" He's suddenly serious. "I'd happily pretend to be straight with you for life, but I'm just the youngest son."

I squeeze his hand and nod. I know he would and we would probably have the happiest sexless marriage there ever was.

As we stay wrapped in our embrace, trading whispers, I hear Sandy call out to Elio and a bolt of panic shocks me. I don't think I'll ever be ready for this.

"Elio, come say hello to your bride," his voice drips with the kind of self-satisfaction one can only have when they have the power to play God in the lives of others.

"I'm really not interested, Pop. Thanks for the party, but I'm not getting married." Elio sounds as shitty as I feel. I'm comforted knowing he hasn't been desperately wanking over photos of me and is as reluctant as I am to enter this marriage.

Massimo lets me go and Dad tugs me forwards by the wrist as Mum gives my lower back a push. I half stumble and find myself standing in front of my future husband.

He is just as tall as Massimo, about 6-foot-4, and equally as handsome. However, where Massimo has perfectly styled caramel hair swept into messy tufts, Elio still has the same dark buzz cut he had when I last saw him. His eyes are dark brown and framed by thick lashes and his bone structure can only be described as perfectly chiselled.

Elio is so good-looking that under different circumstances I certainly wouldn't kick him out of bed, that is if I wasn't being made to marry him.

I look up at his scowling face and shrug. "Hi," I say.

He snorts and looks me up and down, assessing me head to toe. Then, completely deadpan, he looks over at his father and sneers, "Okay fine, she'll do."

"I beg your pardon," I keep my voice quiet and attempt to make it menacing.

He smirks in response. "Take it as a compliment."

"Do you think I want to marry *you*?" a shrill, forced laugh escapes me and I poke his chest with my index finger. "Do you think I am happy that I have been plucked from the other side of the world to chase around after you?" The volume of my voice is rising and I can see the anxiety radiating off my parents and Sandy. "Have you considered that maybe I might want to marry someone else?"

Elio takes my chin in his thumb and forefinger and tilts my face up to look at his. "I don't care, princess. I really don't give a shit." He presses his lips ever so lightly and briefly to my temple and then turns on his heel and marches away.

After a second of processing the utter disaster that is this potential marriage, I turn and hurry in the opposite direction. Massimo follows me outside and wisely allows me to down my glass of prosecco and take some deep breaths before he attempts to speak with me.

"Well, that went better than I expected!" He says brightly and he is being dead set serious. "I expected at least a little bloodshed."

"The night is still young, Massi. Don't give me any ideas."

We hide outside for as long as we can get away with and then are dragged around to say hello to relatives and friends who have either pretended I don't exist for eight years or who I have never met. I am in my own personal hell.

I am aware of Elio flitting around like the social butterfly he is, though I would rather die than be caught staring at him. He certainly hasn't let something trivial like the fact that it is his engagement party stop him from flirting up a storm with practically every woman in the place. Even the nonnas aren't safe from his charms.

"Have some self-respect," I mutter to myself, but Massimo hears.

"Who, Elio?" He nods in his brother's direction.

"No, I know how highly he regards himself. I mean those women. Look at them throwing themselves at a man at his engagement party."

The look Massimo gives me is sympathetic, but it also says 'You better get used to it, honey'.

Sipping from perhaps my fourth prosecco, I am now drunk and give significantly fewer shits than I did when we arrived a couple of hours ago. Massimo and I are catching up with his other, much less arrogant, brother Matteo and I'm enjoying myself finally.

Matteo appears grumpy like Giovanna, but he has always been sweet to me. He is three years younger than Elio at 33 and just slightly shorter. He has the same buzz cut and there is no doubt whatsoever that they are brothers. The only real difference is in how their personalities are expressed on their faces. Where Elio is enigmatic and charming, Matteo is dark and brooding. Both draw the attention of a room when they walk in.

Massimo mentioned that Matty spent a lot of the time I was away in prison and I can tell that something haunts him. He is more broken than I am, I think. Curiosity pricked, I am tempted to ask questions about it, but his shuttered expression suggests he doesn't talk about his time behind bars.

Matty gives me a reassuring smile and I realise that Elio would be my last choice of the four siblings.

That sobering thought is interrupted by the arrival of the final Marino sibling. The one who would be my first choice. The one who I have been desperately in love with since I was twelve years old. Giovanna.

CHAPTER FIVE
GIOVANNA

26 Years Old

"Little Miss Rossi? What are you sulking about?" I venture to ask the glowering 12-year-old sitting cross-legged on the floor in her damp swimsuit.

Massimo sits next to her, distracted by his iPod and disinterested in whatever emotional crisis his best mate is experiencing. The pair of them should have already showered and be in their pyjamas by now, but apparently, their ears are painted on.

"I'm fine," she mumbles, elongating the end of the word sarcastically. These kids were so much easier to look after before they discovered eye rolling and developed attitude problems.

"Hmmm," I crouch down so that my eyes are more level with her morose angelic ones. "I don't believe you. What's going on?"

"Nothing!" She shouts and pulls her scrawny legs into her chest, wrapping her arms around them.

"Do you think I'm an idiot?" My question causes her to lift her head in confusion. After a beat, she shakes her head sadly.

"But you must think I'm an idiot if you expect me to see your tear-stained face and believe there is nothing wrong!"

She remains silent.

The sobs she thought wouldn't escape the bathroom walls were clearly audible and I know something is up. The poor kid doesn't have anyone to give a shit about her, well apart from Massimo. Her parents are the very definition of useless.

I just can't pretend that I don't know she is so upset.

"Okay, so you won't tell me what's wrong..." I cast around for ideas. "Okay, okay. How about you choose a song on Massi's iPod that like...reflects how you're feeling? Yeah?"

Her light brown eyes peek over her knobbly knees. She's contemplating it.

"Go on! Gimme a song, Cheska!"

Massimo scoots closer to Francesca and offers her his iPod and after a moment of wordless communication, she sighs and grabs it from his hand.

Massi wriggles his eyebrows at me comically as the clicking sound of Francesca scrolling through his playlists fills the space. She is concentrating and I am just beginning to wonder how long this process is going to take when she attaches the iPod to the aux cord and the opening bars of *Chasing Cars* play through the lounge speakers.

It is certainly an emotive song.

Francesca makes herself into a ball again and listens to the music passively without looking at Massi or me. Fuck. Maybe this is just making the situation worse. I just wanted her to express herself.

"It's not really about the lyrics," she says just loud enough to be heard over the music. "It just sounds sad."

She shrugs and I crouch in front of her again, reaching out a hand to ruffle her damp, chlorine-dreadlocked hair. "It's alright to be sad sometimes though, right? And you have Massi to cheer you up!"

She nods and gives me a small smile that breaks my heart a little.

"Right. After this song, you two need to shower and get into PJs. I'm gonna make us some grub."

I hurry over to the kitchen not wanting to make the kid any more messed up by inserting my own emotions into the situation, but fuck, sometimes I want to slap her bloody parents. She needs some love and attention from her family, badly.

Maybe the song thing was dumb. I'm none the wiser about what has made her upset and now she has one of the world's most depressing songs to accompany her as she plunges into even deeper despair.

Massimo has an arm around her shoulders now and he is forcing her to sway along to the melody. I'm too far away to hear what they are whispering about, but when I pick up a distinctly high-pitched giggle I exhale in relief.

She's okay. She'll be okay. It's probably just prepubescent angst.

Prepubescent angst that I shouldn't be dealing with. I'm young only 26 for fucksake and they aren't my kids.

Not my circus, not my monkeys.

But I know that is a lie. I'll never leave them to fend for themselves like we older kids had to do. I care about the moody little fuckers too much.

Sometimes I wonder if those weeks I spent in hiding with them, and Matteo and Elio, over a decade ago caused me to kind of imprint on them. I was all they had and my only focus was keeping them all alive until we could go back home.

Whatever it is, I'm locked in for life. I'd die for any of my siblings and little Francesca.

"If your mum asks, I gave you some veggies, okay?" I point at Massimo and refuse to give him his homemade pizza until he promises.

They are finally showered and in their jammies. It's a goddamn miracle.

Placing an identical pizza down in front of a much calmer Francesca, I give her a wink. "And for you, little darlin'"

Her eyes follow me as I move around the kitchen. She has to be the nosiest little kid I've ever met. Always curious and watching and asking questions. She's sweet though. The pair of them are cute.

"Have your friends gone home?" Right on cue, Francesca starts her questioning.

"Yes. Now eat up. Look how skinny you are." I see a flash of embarrassment on her face and I feel bad. I don't want to give the kid a complex. We don't need more tears tonight.

"They aren't her *friends*, Cheska. Didn't you see them kissing?" Massimo joins in with his two cents and this conversation is one that I want to wrap up as soon as possible.

"Yes, I saw!" Francesca hisses at him. I probably shouldn't have allowed things to happen as they did in front of the kids. We got a bit carried away, but it was only kissing and these two are heading into puberty not preschool.

I determinedly ignore them as they discuss my love life and whether or not the two women by the pool are both my girlfriends. They aren't. Neither of them is my girlfriend. We just have fun together sometimes.

Shovelling my dinner of chicken breast and green veggies in my mouth, I mentally plan my workout for after I have settled the kids in front of the TV. In a life where I often don't have control, I relish the power I feel through my routines, training, and developing my physique. Everything comes down to discipline and measured actions. I like that.

And women like my muscles. So there's that.

"Do you ever kiss boys?" Francesca's question cuts through my workout planning and I nearly snort broccoli out through my nose.

"Nope. Never." Fuck that. Technically some kid kissed me at kindergarten, but I decked him and had to sit in time-out for the rest of the afternoon.

She nods slowly, clearly processing the information. "How do you know if you want to kiss boys or girls?"

Jesus Christ. I basically raise these kids for their arsehole parents, but I am not equipped for these questions. "Um. You kinda just know. If you feel like kissing someone… then you know."

"I only want to kiss boys." Massimo just comes right out of the closet and he doesn't even realise it. It's not like we hadn't all figured it out years ago though. Despite his Catholicism, Dad made peace with the fact that half his kids are gay a long time ago.

Francesca is also unsurprised by Massi's lacklustre announcement, but then there is nothing these two don't know about each other.

"I guess, I will have to wait and see," she sighs dramatically. The poor girl is so worried her little forehead is all wrinkled.

"Don't stress about it," I ruffle her hair and she smiles shyly.

Not for the first time, I wonder if she might be a bit gay too. She isn't your classic tomboy-budding-lesbian. She is very girly actually. But, the way she watches me when I have women around is beyond curious. It is a little hungry.

Elio calls her my *cucciolotta* because she follows me around like a little puppy.

"I think you should choose one girlfriend," she takes a bite of her pizza and stares at me intently with her big brown doe eyes.

I suppress a laugh. "Why's that?"

She considers her answer carefully, tapping an index finger on her pursed lips before saying, "Well, one might be sad when she sees you kiss the other one. It's just not very nice."

Honestly, the shit these two kids come out with each day. "Hmmm, I see what you mean. I'll think about it."

I don't attempt to explain to her that they don't want to be my girlfriend. Disney hasn't prepared them for the world of non-monogamous relationships and casual sex.

I kind of hope Francesca retains her innocent idea of monogamous love. The world needs more romantics.

CHAPTER SIX
GIOVANNA

Naturally, while I've spent the day trying to track where Sydney's bikie gangs are getting their sudden influx of weapons, my darling brother, the new Don of Sydney, has been swanning around getting pissed at his engagement party.

After sneaking upstairs for a shower and to change into a suit, I am now reluctantly slipping into the celebration late. I wonder if Massimo's little sidekick is as pissed off as Elio about their pending union. She was such a funny little kid, I can't imagine what she is like as a grown woman.

"Gio!" Massimo waves me over.

Matty stands next to him talking to a woman who has her back to me. She wears a dress so tight it could be shrink-wrapped and has the most incredible ass I have ever seen. Her long hair falls in messy waves that nearly reach her perfect peachy bum and her limbs are slim and delicate. I find myself eager to see the face that belongs to the goddess-like body.

"I've missed you, *mio caro*," I focus my attention on my baby brother, giving him a big hug. "Never leave me like that again!"

Massimo laughs and lifts me off my feet in a bear hug. "I missed you too."

When he puts me back down and I've straightened out my shirt and blazer, I look up to find the shrink-wrapped woman's eyes on me. They're big and brown and staring wide at me in shock. Her plump angelic mouth has dropped open into an O shape and she is frozen.

Distracted momentarily by how impossibly soft her pillowy lips look coated in deep red lipstick, I'm about to ask her if she's okay when she suddenly whispers, "Giovanna."

"Yes?"

My confusion must be apparent because Massimo clears his throat and says, "It's Francesca, G."

Now my mouth has fallen open. "You grew up!" I exclaim and she laughs.

It is the most fucking beautiful sound I've ever heard. This can't be the gawky, scrawny kid I knew. She always had those expressive eyes, but she had a mouthful of braces and hadn't grown into her limbs the last time I saw her. Her hair was always a plain brown too, but now it flows perfectly from dark roots to blonde ends and the blonde around her face is stunning in contrast with her olive skin and dark features.

"Yeah, I guess I did. You mostly look the same though." The sweetness is still there. I see it in her eyes and in the kindness in her voice. She hasn't lost it, despite everything.

"A few more wrinkles and a bit softer around the edges, but mostly the same."

She runs her eyes over me as if scanning for the softness I speak of and I swear I see heat in her gaze.

Don't flatter yourself, G.

"So you're marrying our brother?" I don't want to ask, but I do, and then I immediately regret it when she cringes as if the reminder is painful.

"So they tell me. I'd rather marry any one of you three though so feel free to rescue me," she says darkly looking from me to Massimo and Matty.

The idea of offering to rescue her and stepping up the flirting is beyond tempting, but we need Elio married off and settled down. As much as I might now hate the idea, I need to encourage the marriage. Getting distracted by her beauty is not an option.

I give her a kind smile. "He's not that bad. I'm told he's quite handsome. Don't see it myself though."

Laughing, she points a delicate, manicured finger over my shoulder and remarks, "So handsome that women throw themselves at his feet, apparently."

She rolls her eyes at Elio regaling a group of women with a story not far away. They all hang off his every word. "If I actually wanted to marry him I would care, but I don't." She sighs and I don't like the sadness I see despite the efforts she makes to hide it.

"He's being a complete cunt." When Matty-of-few-words-Marino contributes to a conversation he packs a punch. It brings a smile to Francesca's face though. Her teeth are perfectly straight and bright white against her fire engine red lipstick. The braces definitely worked a treat.

She's exquisite. By far the most beautiful woman in the room. Something I need to stop noticing because she is soon to be my brother's wife.

Excusing myself to go get a beer, I make my way over to Elio's harem. Glassy-eyed and almost panting, a woman with white blonde hair has her hand clutching onto one of Elio's biceps. I recognise her from the social scene we all mix in and detest how desperately she wants to secure herself a mafia husband. She is just another Aussie girl with zero clue about the realities of dealing with Italian men.

"Hello brother," I don't bother pretending to be happy to be there. I'm famous for how infrequent my smiles are anyway.

Elio raises his glass to me. "Sister."

"You're a lucky man, Elio." The harem is following our conversation like it is a tennis match.

"In what regard?" He tilts his head and narrows his eyes. Maybe not tennis, but we are playing some kind of game here.

"Your future wife. She's insanely hot. Who knew the gawky kid would grow up to be such a beauty."

The women's faces darken at my comments, but there's an arctic-like temperature drop when Elio replies. "Can't disagree with you there, sis. I'm not totally opposed to the forced marriage anymore."

He doesn't give a shit about the women who would give their left arm to be in his bed tonight. How his comments affect them is their problem, not his.

"Have you considered spending any time with your fiancee? You know, seeing as it is your engagement party?" He picks up on my icy tone and grins. We are in a standoff. Thanks to Dad's complex succession plan it isn't clear which of us has proper rank in this situation. We are going to have to find a way

to navigate these tensions, but I would prefer not to do it in front of an audience of the future cast of *Real Housewives of Sydney.*

He shrugs. "Yeah, I'll get to her at some point. It's not like she's going anywhere."

Matty is spot on. Our brother is being a complete arsehole and not able to stomach his petulance any longer, I leave him with his adoring crowd.

Making short work of the remainder of my beer, I stop by the kitchen bench to grab another. I'm flicking it open when out of the corner of my eye I spot an unwelcome figure. The heat turns up on a specific pot of my rage that has been simmering for several years just below the surface.

Perpetually slightly sweaty and with uncommonly long fingernails, the man weaving through the crowd with purpose inspires discomfort wherever he goes. His ill-fitting suits are regarded with horror by his contemporaries for whom a tailored Italian suit is practically a religious vestment.

David Rossi. Paul Rossi's brother and once one of Dad's innermost circle, David has been living in Melbourne for the past six years. I crack my knuckles and relive the day that I finally got to feel his bones break under my fists.

What the fuck is he doing here at her engagement party? There's insensitivity and then there's just blatant disrespect.

He elbows past a waiter carrying a tray of prosecco flutes and hones in on his target, moving towards Francesca.

I have to get to her first. She had no one to protect her when it happened. I was two years late and have been plagued with guilt ever since. Even if she hadn't arrived here tonight looking like a goddamn angel, I would do anything to prevent David from hurting her any further.

Racing him to his target, my gaze never leaves his blotchy face with its saggy jowls. I hate this man more than anyone else. He shouldn't still be walking the planet, let alone attending our family events.

"David, incoming," beating the piece of shit there, I murmur into Massimo's ear and his head shoots up to search for him.

Reaching out to tug Francesca under his arm, Massimo quietly gives her a heads-up. "You're going to be okay, Cheska. We're right here."

Her expressive eyes stare into mine from under Massimo's huge arm and the fear, anger, and revulsion I see in them breaks my heart. Before I realise what

I'm doing, I reach out and squeeze her hand. My protective instincts are on high alert.

"Welcome home, Francesca," David stands in front of us, his beer gut proudly protruding before him.

The balls on this piece of shit. Though he knows we will want to avoid making a scene so perhaps it is cowardice that he has chosen tonight to reappear.

Francesca somehow manages to look regal while also like she is about hiss like an angry cat. She tilts her head back so she can look down her nose at him, but her hand shakes in mine.

I step forward putting myself between Francesca and her piece of shit uncle. "I presume you've caught up with the news of Dad's retirement. So listen up. We will not tolerate the bullshit our father did. I suggest you get your ass outta here before I run out of reluctance to create a scene." My voice is low, but I spit each word with as much venom as I can muster.

He sneers. "Throwing your weight around already. Don't forget that you're only backroom, girly. Elio is the one in the hot seat. Now excuse me; I want to catch up with my niece."

"Show some fuckin' respect." Matty growls. His quiet anger is often more menacing than the more explosive rage of others. His chocolate brown eyes blacken and his cheeks hollow slightly as his jaw clenches.

Francesca remains silent. A picture of disdain and poise. Only her eyes betray the burning hatred she feels. Her strength and beauty hits me in the gut like a tonne of bricks and trickles of guilt drip through me for all the less-than-sisterly thoughts I'm having about her.

Wryly I think back to Bible studies at the Catholic school Dad sent us to. *Thou shalt not covet his brother's wife.* Whoops. But hey, that's the least of my problems. According to the Bible, I'm well and truly already going to burn in hell.

A large tanned hand slaps down on David's shoulder. It is a heavy whack and it unsettles him. Never one to be found far from trouble when it's brewing, Elio has joined our little gathering.

He leans down and speaks over David's shoulder. "What the fuck are you doing here?"

Okay, so just when we think our brother is a complete lost cause, we are reminded that he is actually on our side.

Francesca is surprised and she visibly softens. She too is backtracking a bit on her earlier assessment of Elio, it seems.

David seethes, blotchy redness ascends his neck and settles in his cheeks. The power he wielded for decades under my father's protection is all but gone and the next generation is more than willing to prosecute historic crimes.

"Last chance, sexpest," a droplet of my spit hits his face as I step into his space. "Leave now or be removed." David flinches and his hand moves as if to wipe his face, but he resists the urge and remains ramrod straight with a hideous sneer directed at us all.

"I'm sure we'll catch up later, Francesca," he leaves the threat hanging in the air as he slinks away. Matty and Massimo follow him to make sure he is off the property entirely.

A single tear rolls down Francesca's cheek and her voice quivers. "Thank you," she looks at Elio and me and then with a weak smile adds, "I'm fine, honestly. It's just nice to have people stand up for me."

As much as I want to stay and be the one to support her, I gently pat her back and assure her it is no problem at all before leaving her with Elio. He needs to build a relationship with her. He should be her hero.

CHAPTER SEVEN
FRANCESCA

Elio and I are barely alone for a minute after the Marino siblings boot David out of the party before he makes an excuse and hurries off to return to his harem. It seems he can't get away from me fast enough.

Awkwardly busying myself with inspecting my entirely unremarkable prosecco flute to avoid feeling like people are observing my aloneness, I am jolted out of my thoughts when a lean man with a sharp nose and cold, dark eyes slides in front of me.

"Congratulations Francesca," his voice is polished and clipped. "You are happy about your engagement, I assume?"

What a strange thing to ask. Arranged marriages such as this aren't uncommon in mafia families, but even so, asking so bluntly is quite rude.

"Excuse me?" my eyes narrow as I run through my mental catalogue trying to figure out where I know him from.

He's tall. Not as tall as the Marino brothers, but he must be about 6-foot. He is incredibly lean which makes him look taller. Like a professional cyclist, he is sinewy, lanky, and a bit gaunt. With his slicked-back hair, he looks like a villain from old movies.

It isn't until I realise he reminds me of my emotionless father that I recognise him as my older half-brother. "Oh, Stefan…hi."

He has aged more rapidly than time has passed and now looks much more like our father than when he was younger. At least a decade has passed since I saw him last and he is now middle-aged.

Our relationship, if you can call it that, has historically consisted of both of us happening to attend a handful of events when I was young and I haven't seen him at all since well before I was sent away. He was twenty when I was born; a year older than my mother. We just aren't siblings like the Marinos are.

"Gidday sis," he smiles broadly with his teeth, but it doesn't reach his eyes. "Long time no see. Can't believe you're all grown up. Getting married even!"

"Yeah, it's been a while," I shift my weight from foot to foot, unsure what to say. How does one make small talk with their brother when he is a complete stranger?

"I wish Allegra and the kids were here to see you too, but our youngest, Toby, has a tummy bug. He and Alex would have loved to meet their Auntie Francesca."

Shellshocked by the intensity of Stefan's familial chitchat, I remain silent. Has Stefan simply matured and decided he wants to have a relationship with me now I'm back? Or like everyone else in our corrupt family, does he have an agenda I'm yet to discover?

"I know we haven't had much of a chance to have a relationship, Francesca, but I'm your big brother and I am here for you. I hope you're not being pushed into anything you aren't one hundred percent comfortable with?"

"Um thanks, but I'm okay," I mumble. I'm not foolish enough to trust the man with my true feelings. In the few moments we have been talking I have felt like I'm being circled by a shark.

Wracking my brain for something to say that doesn't involve my wedding, I ask, "So how come you're back in Sydney?"

The false smile is back, but this time I can see his jaw clenching behind it. "Oh you know, we wanted to give the boys a chance to get to know the other side of their family. Repair things with Dad. Now you're back they'll get an auntie too! If you're willing to meet them?"

"Of course," something tells me this isn't a good idea, but his sons are little boys and I like the thought of being an auntie. "I would love to meet them."

"That's great news. Let's swap numbers and we can tee something up. They'll be so excited when I tell them."

Stefan takes my phone and types in his phone number before calling it so he has my number too.

"There we go," he hands back my phone and clinks his beer bottle to my glass. "To family and blood being thicker than water."

"To family," I repeat and take a sip, leaving off the strange second part of his toast. I don't know what to make of this older version of my brother, but it will be nice to widen my social circle beyond my parents and the Marino siblings.

Planting a kiss on each of my cheeks, Stefan bids me goodbye and promises to be in touch to set up a catch-up.

I follow his retreating back as he makes a beeline directly for the exit. It is as if, having spoken with me, he has completed what he set out to do and there is no further need for him to stay at the party.

My gut tells me something is off, but I reassure myself that I will proceed with caution and that my nephews are still too young to be complicit in mafia bullshit.

I do find his overly familiar and affectionate behaviour a bit odd. He has never been more than as polite as he was expected to be towards me. He has never taken an interest in my life or well-being. He has always been a surly younger version of Paul Rossi and I tried to stay out of his way.

As a kid, I was sure he hated me. Like I was somehow to blame for how our father treated his mother by virtue of my very existence.

Across the room, Giovanna and Matteo stand, heads close together as they talk furtively, their eyes trained, like mine were, on Stefan as he hurries out of the door.

Their expressions display suspicion and a hearty dose of hostility and I am trying to figure out why that may be when they both suddenly turn their gazes to me.

Caught staring, I smile weakly and lift my glass to them. They do the same back, but their frowns remain firmly plastered to their faces. I may not be able to read their lips, but I am left with no doubt that Stefan Rossi was not welcome at this party.

I have little time to ponder the dynamics between Stefan and the Marinos before Massi materialises to steal me away to dance.

There is no dance floor and no one else is dancing, but we turn the music up and commandeer part of the lounge. It doesn't take long for others to join us.

This is when I am happiest. When what has happened to me in the past and what will be done to me in the future don't matter. It is just me and my favourite person lost in our fun.

When he first arrived in London just over two years ago, he realised quickly how isolated I was and that I hadn't had anyone to talk to about what happened to me. My boyfriend Gareth was a typically emotionally repressed upper-class Englishman whose parents had silly titles and even sillier expectations of their children. I was expected to look pretty and maintain a stiff upper lip.

Massimo tried to get me to talk and I clammed up. I hadn't expressed myself in so long and managing my anxiety had become a toxic internal war.

So, Massi being the clever guy that he is, resurrected a kind of game Giovanna played with us once when we were little. I was struggling to communicate how I was feeling and she asked me to name a song that reflected my emotions and the situation. She said "Gimme a song" and by the time I had thought of one I was thoroughly distracted from what was upsetting me.

Massi and I do it all the time now and not just when we are sad or stressed. It has become our thing. Finding songs for every emotion and situation. I don't know if Giovanna even remembers she started it.

Observing me as we begin to dance, Massi asks me for a song now, his forehead wrinkled in concern and eyes earnestly trying to see into my state of mind.

"Ummmmm," I think. It is often hard to decide on the perfect song on the spot. It is part of the game, I guess. "Okay, okay. *Supalonely* by Benee.

"The one about a lonely bitch?" Massi laughs with a slight question in his tone.

"Yeah, that's the one." I sing a few of the lyrics about being dramatic and sad in a big world. It's all very melodramatic.

He smiles softly and sadly, and boops me on the nose. "Well sad girl, let's dance. Can't feel lonely when you're bumpin' and grindin'."

Massimo puts on an old-school R&B playlist and we dance like a pair of horny singles in a nightclub hoping not to go home alone.

Soon I'm popping my bum out and circling my hips with Massi behind me running his hands down my sides. We are getting scandalised looks from partygoers who don't realise that Massimo is gay, but we don't care.

Mum frowns at me over Dad's shoulder and in response, I bend over and wiggle my arse into Massimo's crotch. He plays along, slapping it and we burst out laughing.

He's right, it is hard to be sad when you're dirty dancing.

My hair is damp on the base of my head and there is a sheen of sweat on Massimo's forehead. I wrap my arms around his neck and, drunk and emotional, tell him I love him.

"Love you too, Cheska. Always."

"I don't know what I would do without you. I pretty much hate the rest of the world."

"Me too. Always me and you, girl." He grins as we sway together.

"The two secondi mafia brats." *The second course.*

We dance for so long that we avoid having to socialise with anyone else. We are still dancing when we look around and see that the only people left are members of our Marino and Rossi families.

Eventually, my parents leave without me, and Sandy and Peta disappear up to bed. I roll my eyes as I see Elio attempt to discreetly shepherd a peroxide blonde up to his wing of the house.

We all see them tiptoeing upstairs and I'm not jealous, but I am embarrassed. It would have been nice if he could have shown me the respect of not getting his dick wet at our engagement party.

"Hey Ches," Massimo's eyes are twinkling mischievously. "Last one in the pool is a rotten egg." He pauses, challenging me with a raised eyebrow. Being a 'rotten egg' was a terrible fate when we were kids.

I hold one finger up to him and quickly unbuckle the straps on my heels, kicking them under a coffee table. "Ready?"

"Set," Massi grins, crouching like he is about to take part in the Olympic 100-metre race.

"Go!" We both shout and take off toward the pool. Elbows fly as we dodge furniture, the sounds of my squeals filling the room.

Massimo pulls ahead and reaches the glass doors before me and it looks like my chances of victory are dashed.

"Ouch! Shit!" I cry out and grab my foot. Massimo stops immediately looking back to check I'm okay.

"I think I rolled my ankle," I say as I hop toward him. He reaches out and lets me lean on him and as he focuses on my foot I quickly jump out of his reach, dash through the door, sprint the ten metres or so to the edge of the pool, and perform an elegant dive.

The water is cold, but not uncomfortably so. It's refreshing and I relish the thrill of jumping into the pool wearing my mother's expensive dress.

I hear a large splash somewhere nearby as I surface and I wait for Massi to appear.

"Ahahaha! Sucker!" I tease him.

"Come on, that was just bad sportsmanship," he protests. "I can't believe I fell for that basic shit.

"What is wrong with you two?" Matteo calls out as he and Giovanna wander over to us. They're both shaking their heads.

"Jump in," Massimo challenges them.

Giovanna takes a swig of her beer. "Uh, no."

She is stunning with her serious expression and that slightly-quirked dark brow.

"Why not?" I'm doggy paddling to stay afloat but my dress is so tight around my thighs that it's increasingly difficult. I bet I look like a drowning chihuahua.

"Why not?" Gio repeats with a frown. "Well, because I don't want to."

"But why? I'm genuinely curious. When was the last time you did something silly?" I poke my tongue out and chuckle to let her know I'm just teasing, but she stops, clearly thinking about what I've just said. Then, without responding she kicks off her brogues, chucks her blazer on the outdoor sofa, and leaps over my head into the pool.

Massimo roars with laughter. "How did you manage to get her to do that?"

I just wink in response and turn to Matteo. "Your turn, Matty. Don't be a Nigel-no-mates."

"Yeah. Don't be a loser, Matty," Giovanna puts on a sing-song voice from somewhere behind me. It does the trick and with an exaggerated sigh, Matty bombs into the pool creating a mammoth splash. Immediately Massimo is on him, instigating some kind of underwater wrestling.

"Are you drowning?" Giovanna's tone is sharp enough that I'm not sure if I would answer honestly even if I were about to drown. She stands in front of me, tall enough that the surface of the water bobs around mouth level.

"Swimming drunk is reckless," she remarks dryly when I continue to doggy paddle on the spot to keep my head above water. "Swimming in a dress so tight you can't use your legs, well that's just stupid."

"Are you going to help me or just provide running commentary for my untimely death?" I snap.

With an amused snort, Giovanna's hands shoot out and grab my upper arms. Her hands engulf my pathetically small biceps and she tugs me into her body as if I weigh nothing at all.

"Hands on my shoulders," she instructs and I'm relieved to be told what to do. It's like touching her is so off-limits that I'm scared to do it without explicit permission.

"You're welcome. No problem. Any time," she says even though I haven't thanked her. The twinkle in her eye hints at a playfulness I desperately want to unearth.

"How *ever* can I repay you?" fluttering my eyelashes exaggeratedly, I hit her with some sarcasm of my own.

We are face to face as Giovanna walks us both backward to shallower waters. She looks like she is going to say something a few times, but doesn't.

"I can think of a few ways," she eventually mutters and gives me a half-smile that has my heart doing somersaults. The dimple in her cheek deepens and so does the molten pit in my tummy.

Changing the subject she asks, "Are you a bit of a rebel these days, Miss Rossi?"

"Ha! Not really. I mean, the last couple of years Massi and I have had heaps of fun, but I still held down a job and behaved myself mostly." I'm not quite honest about how much of a homebody I am. I don't want her to think I'm boring.

"What were you doing for work?" She is still slowly leading us around the pool, her hands holding onto my elbows to keep me steady. My fingers cling to her shoulders, but I wish I could pull myself closer and wrap an arm around her neck instead.

"Oh, nothing impressive. I did a six-month personal training certificate after I finished school. I just worked at a local gym."

Gio's eyes have softened but she frowns slightly at me. "Why do you say that isn't impressive?"

"Well, look at me, I'm in a pool with three of the Marino siblings. I'm just a girl who worked an okay job that she didn't hate. But it's no career."

Matty and Massimo are leaning against the side of the pool down the shallow end, speaking in low voices paying us no attention. I feel giddy; I have the full attention of Giovanna Marino.

Her wet hair is plastered back and it makes her sharp cheekbones look even more defined. She watches me trace their lines with my eyes.

I bite my bottom lip and now it is my turn to watch her eyes follow my movements. She can't help but lick her lips and smile slowly in response.

"Francesca?" her voice is a low growl and sounds like a warning and a question.

"Giovanna?" I breathe.

She swallows and shakes her head muttering, "Jesus Christ."

Her hands move to my waist and she pulls me into a hug before immediately dragging us both under the water. When we come up she carries me in her arms over to the guys and drops me to my feet in the shallow water.

She can't get away from me fast enough and I'm left with the memory of just those few seconds when I felt her chest against mine and her arms wrapped around me.

"Come on, *cucciolotta*," Matteo's voice snaps me out of my trance. Everyone is exiting the pool.

"*Cucciolotta*?"

He laughs. "That's what we called you when you were a kid because you would follow Gio around like a little puppy dog. It was cute."

My cheeks redden. Does everyone know just how long I have pined after Giovanna Marino?

CHAPTER EIGHT

FRANCESCA

Without opening my eyes I quickly assess the state of my hangover. Not too bad at all considering I drank more than a bottle of prosecco all by myself. I'm a bit woozy, but there is no thumping headache and I don't need to purge the contents of my stomach. *Excellent.*

I roll over and nudge Massimo's bum with my foot.

"Piss off, Ches," he grumbles. He is not a morning person. He also maintains that he is still a 'growing boy' so needs lots of sleep.

"You know, I think that swim last night was a good idea. We've discovered the key to preventing bad hangovers!" I walk both of my feet up his bare back knowing it is winding him up.

"Seriously, Francesca, I'm tired. Go annoy someone else."

The bed creaks as if it too is protesting at my early wake-up and I roll and clamour over Massimo to climb off. "Fine. Catch ya later, grouch."

A lone survivor of the night before, I set out through the quiet house in search of coffee and food. Plodding downstairs to the kitchen, I catch my reflection in the heavy gold-bevelled mirror lining one side of the staircase. Massimo's t-shirt and rugby shorts are huge on me and my hair is in a messy bun atop my head, but at least I had the presence of mind to clean the makeup off my face before going to bed last night.

"Oh. Morning," I mumble to Giovanna as I join her in the kitchen. She looks like she has just come home from the gym in her lycra leggings and fitted

singlet. Her olive skin is shiny with sweat and her hair pulled back in a little ponytail revealing she still has the shaved undercut on the back of her head that I remember.

Drinking from her water bottle greedily, she raises both eyebrows by way of greeting.

"Good workout?" I ask in my best barely-interested, totally casual voice.

"Yeah." She always was a woman of few words, so I don't push the conversation any further. If she wants to talk to me she will. I just need to resist the neediness I feel around her. The desperation to capture her attention somehow.

I busy myself with making a cup of coffee. The giant espresso machine looks far too complicated so I just do a plunger. I'm not precious about coffee like some Italians; I couldn't be after living in England for so long.

"Enough for two?" Giovanna looks over my shoulder.

"Sure. Black?"

"Yes, please."

Well, she's talking to me at least. It is pathetic how happy that makes me. Just having her attention for a second gets my heart racing.

"I'm making eggs on toast. Want some?" She offers gruffly.

"Oh, yes, thank you." I bite my lip to stop a goofy grin from spreading across my face.

Sipping the murky coffee that I should probably have left steeping for a lot longer, I sit at the bench so I can watch her cooking. I'm itching to fill the silence, but I don't. Instead, my eyes catalogue every inch of her body.

She might not be as muscly as she used to be, but Giovanna is still ripped. Her exposed shoulders and arms are defined as if cut out of marble and I want to cling to them like a spider monkey.

An unshakeable desire for this woman has plagued me since puberty and yet if I were to get what I want - her - I would have no idea what to do.

I know how to make a man feel good. Getting them off is easy. As is making myself come. My own body is no mystery to me, but I'm ignorant of the ins and outs of fucking a woman.

Giovanna catches me perving on her and the side of her mouth curls up in amusement. "You alright there, darlin'?"

Warmth rockets up my neck and I blush so hard my face must practically glow, but I don't drop eye contact with her. "Just…looking," I admit.

The tension in the room is palpable and my body reacts with warmth pooling in my lower tummy. The term of endearment she uses for me is enough to send me giddy

"You like what you see?" she murmurs just loud enough for me to hear and my heart takes off racing even faster. It is a cheeky retort tossed over her shoulder as she stands over the stove, but to me, it feels groundbreaking.

"I do." *Play it cool, Francesca. Play it bloody cool.*

Again her lip curls and a dimple appears on the other side of her face. I almost groan at how sexy it looks, but in a split second, she makes her expression neutral again and appears to give herself a shake.

"You're marrying Elio," she states roughly, sliding my breakfast in front of me.

"So I'm told. Wouldn't be my choice."

"You're a good match and it is important for the Family," she continues.

Frowning, I focus on my plate and not the disappointment causing my mood to plummet. "That's all that matters, huh?"

She doesn't respond and a lump forms in my throat. Eight years has done nothing to quell the infatuation I've had with Giovanna since I was a little girl. I'm still the little puppy pathetically following her around.

"You need to take it seriously and make a proper go of it." She is gruff and authoritative. Gone is the flirty woman who was here for a few tantalising moments.

"What if I don't want to? What if I want to go back to the UK? Forget all about this shit?" I'm angry now and I am terrified that I will cry.

"Don't make this harder than it needs to be, Francesca."

I just shake my head at her, gutted that she is just like my parents and her dad. She sees my life as something that can be moved around like a pawn. Sees me as an empty vessel to be married off and filled with babies.

My plate clatters as I slam it into the dishwasher a little too aggressively and I finally lose the battle against my tear ducts. Keeping my head down and hoping she won't see, I move quickly to get out of the kitchen, but she grabs my arm.

I refuse to look at her, turning my face away to hide my tears.

"Francesca," she says softly, but I just shake my head again. I'd rather she didn't pretend to care.

Furiously, I swipe at my cheeks and extract my arm from her grip. She reluctantly lets go and I turn quickly only to run smack bang into Elio's broad, naked chest as he strolls into the kitchen in just a pair of grey track pants.

I'm forced to take a step back and he steadies me before I fall. His face quickly pulls into a frown when he sees the tear tracks on my cheeks and he cups my face in his hands.

"Who's been making my wife cry? That's my job isn't it?"

"I'm not your wife yet," I grumble. He looks over my head at his sister, confused about what has gone on between us.

He sighs and, clearly having received wordless instructions from Giovanna, says, "Come on, come sit outside with me; let's have a chat."

I shadow him out to the outside sofa and the muscles in his back ripple as he raises an arm to run his hand over his short hair. He is a spectacularly good-looking guy. Like ridiculously hot. But, every movement of his body feels calculated to pose and show off. His vanity is second only to his charm.

The sun is already warming up the back garden despite the early hour and I raise my face to bask in the morning light. The salt from my tears dries tight on my cheeks.

Cross-legged, I regard Elio cautiously from the opposite end of the outdoor sofa. He stretches out luxuriously. He is like a lion, lounging under the powder blue sky, awaiting the arrival of lionesses who will kill his dinner and allow him to mount them. I can almost hear David Attenborough's narration.

"I don't want to get married," he admits. *No shit, Elio.* "But that's nothing to do with you. You're beautiful and most men would kill to marry you."

"Hmmm. I don't want to spend my whole life feeling unwanted. I've already had 24 years of it." I shrug.

All the emotions that I have tried to keep at bay for the past 48 hours are threatening to boil over again and I don't think my emotionally stunted husband-to-be is equipped to deal with them.

He is stunning as he tips his head back, the golden hues making his skin look ethereal. A light dusting of stubble coats his chin and his pronounced Adam's apple bobs with each breath.

The picture of masculinity.

On a purely physical level, my body reacts to him even though mentally and emotionally I feel nothing good. His long muscular limbs and strong torso would dwarf me and I can't help but think he probably goes alright in bed, especially given how much bloody practice he's had.

"Come here." He pats his lap. *Cheeky bastard. Do women usually just sit on his lap on demand? Wait, I don't need an answer to that.*

"You hooked up with another woman at our engagement party," I accuse him, ignoring his audacious invitation. "Is she still in your bed?"

"Nah, she's gone." He is indignant but, after a beat, lets out a strangled noise of frustration and rubs his hands over his face. "Look, I did that as a 'fuck you' to my Dad; to show he can't control me."

"Well, I get that obviously, but your Dad doesn't give a shit. It is me who you humiliated."

"I didn't think you'd care. We don't know each other…really."

"It's about respect," my voice catches and a couple more treacherous tears escape. "Neither of us wants this, but you don't have to make it worse."

"I'm sorry. I really am. Come on, come here," he beckons to me, arms open.

Cautiously, I crawl down the sofa towards him. Once I'm in arms reach he yanks me up and sits me on his lap so I'm straddling him.

"What are you doing?!" I squeal. "As you said, we don't even know each other!"

"Relax! I'm not going to try and root you here." He laughs with a glint in his eyes that says he wouldn't say no if I gave him the go-ahead. An opportunist and an arrogant dickhead for sure, I realise that the only thing I can be sure of with Elio is that he will act entirely in his own interest. "And I've known you your whole life technically."

Giovanna is watching us. I see her standing through the glass doors when I glance up. Angry at her earlier dismissal of me, I hope she's maybe a little jealous. She seemed to enjoy my attention before she shut me down. I'm furious

at her for toying with me. As if I need another person yanking my feelings around.

My attention is swiftly drawn back to the man I'm straddling when I feel his cock hardening between my legs. I quickly climb off his lap. His face is plastered with another cheeky smile and I roll my eyes.

"Not today, Satan," I say sternly, pointing a finger at him.

He throws back his head and laughs. He has no problem being the devil.

CHAPTER NINE
FRANCESCA

Without so much as an interview, Deano the frazzled manager of a gym not far from the Marino House shakes my hand and thrusts a generic contract at me. I guess I've got a job.

"Your CV speaks for itself," the swollen gym beast says. I suspect he is just too lazy to conduct any interviews and he'll probably hit on me.

He leads me to a cramped staff room. Gym bags clutter every surface and there is a bin overflowing with wrappers and containers of a variety of health products. Deano digs into a locker full of uniforms and pulls out a couple of branded t-shirts.

"Just wear gym leggings with the t-shirt," he instructs. "Come on, I'll introduce you to some of the team.

Awkwardly I shake hands with several of my new colleagues, smiling and immediately forgetting their names. I cringe at the appreciative gazes of the male personal trainers and hope that this job won't turn into a predator's playground.

"Hey, I'm Sammy!" A bright voice with an accent that hints that she is originally from New Zealand.

"Francesca," I smile warmly back at her genuine grin.

"Don't let the meatheads put you off. They'll try their luck, but if you tell them to piss off they listen." She has been perceptive in picking up my discomfort. "Anyway, I'll catch you around."

I say goodbye and watch the woman I have taken an instant liking to walk away.

As I wait for Deano to bring me a copy of the signed contract, I watch her challenge some of the guys to a pull-up competition which she very nearly wins. Her confidence draws me in and I know immediately that I want to be her friend. From the assertive way she shouts across the gym to the way she banters with everyone, she is the picture of exuberance and completely carefree.

Elio and I are given little time to get used to the idea of our marriage. Outsourcing the practical organising of the wedding to their wives, Dad and Sandy want me signed, sealed, and delivered, like, yesterday, but compromise on an engagement not longer than six months.

There are few things I would less like to spend my time doing than planning a wedding to a man Carly Simon could have written *You're So Vain* about.

I'd rather:

Shove bamboo under my fingernails.

Have a Brazilian wax every day for a year.

Cover myself in syrup and lay down on a nest of fire ants.

Have every man in England explain football's offside rule to me.

Just to name a few.

My lack of enthusiasm is made up for by my mother's abundance of it. If I was still an affection-starved child, desperate for her mother to show interest in her, I would be basking in the sudden attention from Vanessa Rossi. But I'm not. I have long accepted that I won't have a loving mother/daughter relationship until I'm the mother.

That's what upsets me the most about this stupid marriage, I think. I have dreamed for so long about the happy, healthy, loving family I will create with someone who loves me as madly as I love them. Now I appear set to have an awkward and miserable marriage instead.

I have never dreamed of much. Just that. Just to be loved and to love. Family and motherhood.

"You decide," I mumble, propping my head up with my hand, elbow on the Marino's dining table.

It is a conscious decision not to make this easier on anyone involved. I won't fake enthusiasm to make the people forcing me into a loveless marriage more comfortable.

"Francesca," my mother snaps, flapping two essentially identical wedding invitation samples across the table at me. "You are getting married, behave like an adult!"

"Let's cancel the getting married bit and I'll continue to be immature then?" I'm not usually this belligerent, but being amicable and well-behaved has not served me well.

Dragged and dumped from one end of the world to the other and back again.

Naturally, I think I am quite easy-going, a nurturer. A lover, not a hater. But it is difficult to be sweet when your life has never been your own.

The two invitations land on the table with a slap and my mother shoots an exasperated look at Peta who is sitting across from her.

Peta gives her a sympathetic smile, but then turns it to me as well. Not for the first time I wonder how she ended up in this family and in love with a gruff mafia man so much older than her. She is too good, too wholesome for any of this.

"Ness, I think what Francesca is trying to say is that she trusts your judgement on the wedding invitations," her words are gentle and placating. And a very generous interpretation of what I am saying and thinking.

It works to soothe my needy mother's irritation. She sets the embossed, and probably perfumed, pieces of card aside and scribbles something in her leather-bound Wedding Planner Notebook. She bought it from her favourite Swedish stationery shop.

"Right. Elio will obviously have Matteo as his best man and Massimo as a groomsman - "my mother begins, but before I can check myself and maintain my cool air of disinterest I interrupt.

"- No. Massimo will be my maid of honour. Or man-of-honour. Call it what you want."

"Absolutely not, Francesca!" she is as appalled as if I have suggested ceremonial granny tossing at the reception for entertainment.

Poor Peta must be about ready to bang her head on the table. She looks between us as if she is watching a live enactment of *Judge Judy.*

"What are you three plotting?" Just as my mother and I are locked in a death stare-off as Peta's eyes dart between us, Giovanna strides into the kitchen.

I wrench my gaze from Mum and glare at Giovanna. *Enabler.*

"Wedding planning," Mum replies in a treacle sweet tone at the exact time I say, "exploring new forms of torture".

Giovanna snorts and the water she just gulped comes spraying out of her nose. I laugh maniacally and Mum snaps at me again.

"Actually, Giovanna, you could be Francesca's maid of honour..." Mum thinks she's had a fucking brainwave.

"Absolutely fuckin' not," Giovanna says and I follow her up with vehement agreement. Not a snowball's chance in hell.

It would be a final slap in the face to have to stand next to Giovanna while I marry her brother. They will have to carry me down the aisle kicking and screaming.

"Oh, why not?" Mum begins, but Giovanna quickly reminds her of where she stands in the pecking order.

"Vanessa," she warns. "No, and that's final."

Why can't she just say 'no, and that's final' to the whole thing? She is letting me be thrown into a miserable life and doesn't even care.

I look down at my hands in my lap. Relieved that Giovanna won't be my maid of honour, but dejected that there is no one willing to protect me from all the other strategic games of my family.

One day, I always thought, I would have someone who would be willing to stand up for me. Who would put me first. Love me like I'm precious. That love would make up for the lack of it from my parents and the vulnerability I have always felt.

But no. No chance for that now. Elio doesn't love, he lusts. I can't imagine him protecting anything but his own ego. I'm on my own.

CHAPTER TEN
GIOVANNA

16 Years Old

My eyes snap open and in a split second, I transition from deep sleep to wide awake. My room is dark, but through the window, headlights light up our front garden.

My feet hit the floor and I rush to grab a pair of jeans that are hanging over the chair in the corner. Tugging them on, I listen to the sounds of chaos outside and wonder who the gunshots I awoke to were meant for and if they met their target.

Nearly tripping as I yank on a hoodie and rush down the hallway, I hear the backdoor slam downstairs and urgent voices speaking a mixture of Italian and English. I reach the ground floor and, with relief, see Dad barking orders into a cell phone.

A group of Dad's capos, his senior soldiers, are huddled in a circle and I rush forwards to see what they are looking down at.

"Giovanna, what are you doing here?" Fat Tony asks, but I ignore him. I'm not a kid anymore, Dad knows that. He has been bringing me into the family business and I observe everything.

As I draw closer to the group of men, all dressed in suits, one of the men steps aside and I catch a glimpse of the young man lying on the hard wooden floor.

I don't know his real name, but I know the guys call him Patches because he can't grow a full moustache. He has only been working for the *Famiglia* for a year or so and is probably only five or six years older than I am.

Whatever colour Patches' shirt was before, it is now drenched in blood. I count three entry wounds in his chest, but I heard seven shots. Either four bullets went astray or he has more holes in his body than I can see.

His breaths are getting shallower and are being snatched from higher and higher in his chest. Two of the men kneel next to him whispering words of comfort and even though I am no doctor, I know he is not long for this world.

Clutching the gold crucifix that hangs around his neck, the man on Patches' right recites the Hail Mary on a loop and we all watch as the wounded man slips into the clutches of death.

"Giovanna!" Dad barks at me from the kitchen and I hurry over to him after one last look at the body of a man not long out of boyhood.

"How can I help, Dad?" I ask, determined to play my part in the crisis.

The violence has been escalating, but no one was prepared for Alberto to send his men to our front door.

"Take your brothers and get out of here. Out of Sydney. Just drive until you're sure no one has followed you and then head north to the safe house in Noosa," he instructs me. I have a bag packed in the back of my wardrobe for exactly this kind of emergency with cash, a burner phone, and fake IDs for myself and my brothers.

He has barely finished giving me my orders and I am already sprinting back upstairs first to Elio's room and then Matteo's. At 14 and 11, they're both old enough to understand what is going on and spring to action throwing clothes and necessities into bags while I retrieve my emergency pack and head down to our baby brother's room.

By the time I reach Massimo's cot, he is standing, holding on to the bars, and wailing his little head off. Despite my best efforts to calm him with my voice while I pack his bag, he only gets louder and more distressed.

I'm bending over to pick him up when from the corner of the room where a travel cot is set up, another cry sounds. I freeze for a second wondering if I imagined the sob, but a few seconds later a full-on wail joins Massi's chorus.

"Fuck!" I say aloud to myself and hurry over to the other cot. Inside I find Francesca, Dad's right-hand man Paul's daughter. *What is she doing here?*

After a moment's hesitation, I conclude that I can't leave the poor toddler there and after rearranging the bags on my back and Massi on my hip, I wrangle the second crying child into my arms.

"Gio!" Matteo appears at the bedroom door and opens his arms for one of the babies. Massimo happily takes the transition and we hurry downstairs, meeting Elio in the kitchen.

"Dad! Francesca was in Massi's room? Should I take her?" I shout across the room and after looking over at Paul, who nods his head, Dad turns and nods to me.

Peta, Massimo's mum, and Vanessa, Francesca's mum are currently in Bali on a girls' weekend. Things weren't expected to heat up like they have tonight otherwise Peta would never have left her son. Vanessa would have probably still gone. Let's be honest.

Fear makes its first appearance only when I drive the blacked-out Range Rover containing my three siblings and Francesca out of our underground garage. It is too dangerous for us to remain at the house in case of another strike, but leaving also makes us incredibly vulnerable to being attacked or followed.

I hold my breath and, from the front passenger seat, Elio scans our surroundings for any signs of Alberto's men or vehicles acting suspiciously.

"Can't see anything, G," Elio whispers. We have agreed to try to keep the younger kids from being aware of all the danger we are in.

"Okay, just keep watch. I'm going to drive around in circles for a few hours and then we will head into Queensland."

Elio does as he is told, taking his role very seriously. Dad worries that he is too soft and won't be suited to taking over when he retires. He is a bit squeamish, but the kid is super smart.

"Why is Alberto doing this, G?" he asks me after we have been driving for about half an hour in silence.

"Hmmmmm," I wonder how much to tell him. "You know that Dad, Alberto, Paul, and David all went to school together back in Italy right?"

He shakes his head. "Well, I knew Paul and Dad did."

"The four of them have known each other almost their entire lives," I smile across at him before returning my focus to the road.

"How come Alberto wants to fight the others then?" Elio persists.

"Well, the four of them moved to Australia together. They were in their early twenties I think. Our Nonno, Dad's Dad, was already in Australia..."

"Why was he here?"

"Ah, umm. Well, Nonno left Nonna and his kids about fifteen years before that. Not sure why he chose Australia, but he moved here and...well, by the time Dad and his friends arrived, he had a new family."

"Fucking wanker!" Elio's choice of words makes me chuckle. At 14 he uses every opportunity to express himself in 'adult' language.

"Yeah, dog move huh?" I agree. "Anyway, Nonno set up the *Famiglia* in Sydney and was running things by the time the guys moved here. The four of them became Nonno's most loyal soldiers, then his respected capos, and by their late twenties they were his underbosses and closest advisors."

"So Alberto worked with Dad, for Nonno?"

"He did. When Nonno passed on in 1991, Dad took over as the boss of Sydney and most people were happy about it. But, Alberto argued that the four of them had all become Nonno's sons and that Dad was not the natural heir. He wanted a shot at being boss himself."

Elio is hanging on to my every word and has forgotten to keep watch, but I have been checking as well and we aren't being tailed.

"Then what happened?" he prompts me.

"There was a lot of tension. Alberto fell out with Dad and Paul and David. It became obvious that he could no longer work for the *Famiglia*. So he left and moved to Melbourne. I don't know the whole story, but he ended up becoming boss of the Melbourne *Famiglia* and things settled down."

"So why is he fighting Dad now? If he got Melbourne?" Elio frowns.

"Because he still wants Sydney, Elio. He is angry and holds a grudge. He wants Sydney and Melbourne."

"Greedy arsehole," Elio grumbles.

"Yup. He is very greedy. Speaking of which, are you hungry? Let's grab some Maccas!" I have told my younger brother enough for tonight so I shamelessly distract him with the promise of fast food.

CHAPTER ELEVEN
GIOVANNA

"I'll catch you later, G. I'm off on my first date with my future missus." Elio drawls as he pokes his head around the door. Sarcasm drips off him and the way he is dragging his feet you would think he was off to work a shift cleaning toilets, not taking a ten-out-of-ten stunner out for dinner.

"Don't look so excited, little brother," I tease. *I would be like a kid the night before Christmas if I were him.*

He shrugs. "She's fucking hot. It's the marriage bit that I don't like."

I wish he would take this more seriously if only for Francesca's sake. His disdain for the whole thing is going to hurt her. She deserves to feel like her husband is desperately in love with her, but at the very least she shouldn't be made to feel like he is repulsed by the idea of marriage to her.

"Be good to her. None of this is her fault." The guilt for the role I am playing in pushing this arranged marriage is eating at me.

"I never asked for this either. Anyway, better go. Do you think my wife will put out on the first date?" He takes off before I can throw a piece of stationery at him.

He would say he was joking, but he will absolutely try to shag her tonight and if it didn't give me unwelcome and increasingly acute little pangs of jealousy, I would be able to acknowledge that it would probably be a good thing for them. They need to connect and establish some kind of relationship and if they're fucking each other there is less chance he will continue fucking his way around the socialites of Sydney. Maybe.

My cunt throbs to the beat of my racing pulse as I stare down at her naked pussy. She is spread open for me, back arched, moaning my name.

I have to taste her. God, just once before she's taken from me.

Big golden brown eyes stare down at me, darkening as she watches me lower my mouth to her hot, wet core.

"Eyes on me," I mumble into her swollen flesh and she obeys. My tongue dances between her legs and our eyes are locked on each other.

She tastes like heaven.

My need for her is only increasing. I need to see what she looks like when she comes apart in pleasure.

But, I can't see her eyes anymore. Look at me! I need to see you, baby.

Wait, are my eyes shutting? Everything is going dark.

She's disappearing. Where are you going, beautiful?

It's not fair!

"Gio!"

I'm jolted awake by Matteo's voice and a sharp rapping on the open door. Disoriented I look around and realise I fell asleep on the sofa in my office.

Shaking my head as if to blow out all the cobwebs, I croak at Matty to come in. "I wasn't sleeptalking was I?"

That dream was fuckin' filthy and I seriously hope I wasn't narrating it for my brother to hear.

I have never been so attracted to a woman in my life. Another cruel joke played on me by a world that seems to get a lot of laughs at my expense. Not only does Elio get to pretend to be the head of our family while I do the hard graft in the background, but he also gets the girl. Not that he even wants her.

"Nah, but if you're worried about that I'm curious what you were dreaming about!" he winks and saunters in to take a seat in front of my desk.

"Nothing interesting," I reply gruffly. "What's up?"

"There's a lot of grumbling about Elio not being up to the job," he says quietly as if the topic will become less awkward if he only whispers.

"How much is being driven by Stefan being a dirty termite?" I stand and pull two glasses from the drinks cupboard.

Dark amber liquid splashes into one crystal tumbler and then another. I plug the decanter and hand Matty his glass before taking a generous sip from mine.

"Stefan has been busy. He is in the ear of everyone who will listen. But…the concerns aren't exactly invented by him. The older capos are worried Elio is distracted by pussy and partying and…well, he is."

Stefan may as well have stayed in Melbourne. Elio doesn't need any assistance undermining the Family and eroding decades of respected reputation.

A non-committal grunt is all I give him in response to the last part of his sentence. "Have you been able to gauge Alberto's involvement in this? Is Stefan acting under orders from his father-in-law or…?"

Sigh. Never underestimate the ability of 70-year-old men to hold on to grudges. Women are unfairly characterised as the creators of drama, but good grief, Dad and his friends are the perfect examples of how petty, bitchy, and destructive men can be.

It's been, what? Eighteen or so years since Dad put an end to Alberto's attempts to take over Sydney. I was just sixteen when I had to go into hiding with four kids in tow. Alberto's men pelted our home with bullets that night and in the weeks that followed.

All in all, we were nearly two months on the road. The heirs to the Marino *Famiglia.* We had two very close calls with men sent to track us and had to move twice to different safe houses.

By the end of the turf war, I was nearly nineteen and my role was no longer that of full-time babysitter. Sure I still looked after the bambinos sometimes, but I spilled as much blood as any of my father's men in the final days of the conflict.

The idea that Alberto could be mounting another attack sent a cold chill through my bones. My siblings may have been too young to see the realities of the turf wars of the early 2000s, but I remember all too well. We won, yes. But fuck was there a cost.

As is always the way in mafia families, things are more complex now because Paul's estranged son Stefan married into Alberto's family. It was

probably hatred of Paul Rossi that drove Stefan and Alberto's daughter Allegra to pack up and move to Melbourne after they married.

Stefan immediately began to work for Alberto and rose quickly through the ranks. This is why his return to Sydney is so suspicious. He has nothing to gain from being here unless he has a big power play up his sleeve. He has to be here to take power, but whether it is for himself or Alberto remains to be seen.

"Nothing confirmed, but my gut tells me Alberto has at least signed it off. We gotta treat this like he's gearing up to attempt another takeover," Matty echoes my thoughts.

"Yeap. Nothing like a baptism of fire, huh?"

"Well, at least life won't be boring," he shrugs. "By the way, the little birdies have reached the Police Commissioner and he wants to meet with Elio to discuss it all."

"Phil Trotter reached out to you?"

"A young woman in his office who may have had my number reached out asking me to set up a meeting." He winks. Even reserved Matteo is a bit of a man whore; the men in this family, honestly.

"Right. Let's tee it up and see what he knows."

Matteo nods, but he doesn't make any moves to leave. "You aren't going to arrange a marriage for me are you?" he finally says and I can't help but laugh.

A smirk tugs at the sides of my mouth. "Nah, I'll leave you to choose your own wife."

"What about you? You going to find a wife?" This is not the kind of conversation Matty and I usually have. We don't get into each other's love life.

"Ha! Who would have me?" I revert to the self-deprecating humour which is one of my go-to defence mechanisms.

"She likes you. Like really likes you. Be careful." We both know who he is talking about.

"Fuck Matty. So what? Why have this conversation? It doesn't mean shit. She is currently out at dinner with our brother." I'm nearly shouting and I don't usually shout.

"Sorry, G. I shouldn't have said anything." He gets up and walks around the desk to press a kiss on my forehead. He's such a good guy and I shouldn't be mad at him.

"No problem, Matty. I'm meeting some of the capos at *La Fazenda* in half an hour. Doing some recon on how much Stefan has snaked in on relationships already. You coming with?"

"If that's an order then, of course, I'm coming. If not, maybe take Massimo? He needs some experience.

"Good idea. Send him to me. Oh, and Matty, if I give you an order, you'll know."

He smiles and raises an eyebrow. "Yes, boss."

"Love you, Matty," I remind him.

CHAPTER TWELVE
GIOVANNA

Massimo pulls my Range Rover in between the cracked painted lines of our reserved parking spot right outside Sydney's oldest Italian restaurant. Not much to look at from the outside, the interior is warm, intimate, and could be right out of a mob movie. It sits not far from the harbour on a block that was once industrial and dirty, but now teems with trendy restaurant and bar conversions.

But it isn't the Instagrammable location or decor that has the booking sheets full. It isn't even the incredible food which is truly part of Sydney's culinary history. The real reason every Tom, Dick, and Hazza wants a table is that it is hardly a secret that the restaurant is owned by the Marino *Famiglia.*

La Fazenda is run by Auntie Savia and her family. She is my mother's sister, god rest Mama's soul.

Savia's kids do much of the work these days and they keep things above board. We don't run mafia money through it. The only purpose it serves the *Famiglia* is that we hold meetings here either on the family table in the corner or in the private dining room upstairs. It is our home ground.

The interior is warm and cosy. Wood panelled walls are adorned with candlestick sconce lamps casting artful shadows over the tables. We used to have red and white chequered tablecloths, but Savia's eldest daughter Sarah said it looked like we were trying to mimic *The Sopranos.* Now crisp, white tablecloths sit stiffly atop the tables, the excess fabric folding as it drapes.

"G! Massimo! How's it going?" Sarah's dark head pops up from behind the counter near the door. "*Tavola di Famiglia* or upstairs?"

"Hey Sez," the sound of our air kisses punctuates the warm hug she wraps me in. "The Family Table is fine, thanks. A few of the capos will be joining us."

Sarah bustles on ahead, leading us to the large round table we have sat at since before we were old enough to talk. "Are you eating?"

"I'll just have an espresso thanks." I don't want this to be a long discussion. I've been flat out like a lizard drinking all week and I'm about to start fantasising about crawling into bed.

"Same, but I wouldn't say no to some of your cannoli." Massimo gives our older cousin a cheeky grin, his green eyes twinkling.

Patting his arm fondly, Sarah coos "Always for you, baby cousin."

Baz Rossi and Fat Tony arrive right on time which puts me in a more favourable mood. Marginally.

They're getting old and I wonder when they'll make the move into retirement. They're both about a decade younger than Dad though so they could stick around.

Next to arrive is Craig 'The Exorcist' Falconi. He's built like a brick shithouse and his sheer size has heads turning as he reaches our table. He's younger than two capos who arrived before him. Late 40s I would guess.

His nickname is less dangerous than it sounds. He earned it as a young man because of his ability to make spirits disappear instantly when on the piss.

"Craig," I give him a curt nod.

"Giovanna Marino. Always a pleasure, mate." His voice gives no indication of sarcasm, but it is difficult to believe his statement is sincere since I have clocked him in the nose at least twice in the past decade. It's fair to say he has never been a big fan of mine.

"Ah, young Massimo. Enjoying being home, mate?" he says.

"S'all good," Massi mumbles through a mouthful of dessert.

Craig takes a seat at the table and the three men order themselves food and drink. Naturally, The Exorcist orders a double whiskey, shoots it down in one, and exchanges the empty glass for the second double whiskey that Sarah was practised enough to bring along with her.

"Where's our new Don?" Baz Rossi barks, sipping his Chianti pretentiously. He always drinks Italian reds in public, but everyone knows he goes through a box of *Toohey's New* a week at home.

"Elio is a busy man." I wave my arm dismissively. "What do you need? Anything I can help with?"

"Busy like a dog in heat," Baz hisses under his breath and I'm not sure if he intended me to hear him or not.

"All right, Hannibal Lector. With all that hissing you'll be ordering liver and fava beans to go with your Chianti next," I raise my tiny espresso cup to him in a toast, but my *Silence of the Lambs* reference has gone right over his head.

It hasn't bypassed Massi though and he almost coughs up a lung cackling. We've always said Baz Rossi looks like Hannibal.

"You better make sure he marries Paul's girl," Baz warns us and glares at our laughter. "It's only right that we have some Rossi heirs."

"Hey now," Fat Tony interjects in his characteristically amicable way. "Come on Baz, we were all at the engagement party. No need to be issuing threats and whatnot."

Baz expands his glare to include Fat Tony in its range. He is a grumpy bloke at the best of times, but it's like someone pissed in his cornies today.

"Yeah well, Sandy knows the deal," he harrumphs cryptically. But I'm not playing his games so I ignore it.

"Anyway, anything to report?" My voice is serious and flat.

"Your cousin, the one who owns that little bar down at The Rocks. She was visited last week by some gentlemen wearing patches." Leaning back in his chair, The Exorcist regards me dispassionately.

"Fucksake," Massimo mutters and pinches the bridge of his nose. "I'll look into what happened there."

"Seems like the bikies are becoming more active. Bolder," I add.

"It's a splinter group. Some young guys. Ned is getting old and they don't like how tame Satan's Sons have become. From what I hear they're guns for hire now. Mercenaries," The Exorcist stares pointedly at Baz as he concludes his statement.

We know Ned has been having trouble with his nephew, Billy the Kid, so this is not exactly news, but the feeling that some codified and less-than-friendly communication is being passed between Baz and The Exorcist makes me uncomfortable.

I shrug as if I am barely interested. "That's Ned's problem. What use would anyone in the *Famiglia* have for mercenaries?"

The silence that follows is heavy with unspoken information. Baz squirms under The Exorcist's unwavering glare. He looks away only to indicate to Sarah that he would like another double.

"Mercenaries are for people who don't have friends," Massimo breaks the silence.

"Speaking of people without friends, have any of you heard from Stefan Rossi?" Now is as good a time as any to fish for information on the sneaky bastard.

"He is my cousin," Baz spits the words out like venom. "Of course I have."

"Second cousin," corrects The Exorcist. "And you should be careful, it is impossible to wash off the slime that guy leaves wherever he goes."

Lines are being drawn at the table as plain as day. Baz has clearly been entertaining Stefan's ambitions, The Exorcist seems to see this as a betrayal of our trust, and Fat Tony is doing a great impression of Switzerland.

The rest of the conversation is a continuation of sharing tidbits of intel while dancing around the topic of Stefan Rossi. By the time the three capos are standing up to leave, I am well and truly ready for bed.

The meeting has been depressingly unfruitful and has done nothing to quell the growing resentment from people like Baz that Elio is so missing in action.

"Enjoy your cannoli?" I nudge Massimo's empty plate.

"So fucking good. I think I missed Auntie Savia's cannoli more than I missed you."

I chuckle at him wiggling his eyebrows at me. "You cut me deep, kid. Now, tell me what you picked up from that little chat." We are trying to involve him in our day-to-day shit so he can get a handle on how everything works.

"Um. Well, Stefan is getting around the capos and at least some of them are listening to him. I got a weird vibe between Baz and The Exorcist when we

were talking about mercenaries. Mostly we need Elio to man the fuck up and stop leaving the door open for Rossi."

I nod and ruffle his perfectly styled hair. "Good listening, *caro mio*. It's good to have you home."

I could have eaten at *La Fazenda*, but I'm strict about my calorie intake and I know Peta has left some chicken salad in the fridge for me. The woman is an angel, I swear. Mostly for putting up with Dad. She is a lot younger than him and I was suspicious of her when she first arrived on the scene. Despite being only fourteen years older than me, she has been a reliable and supportive stepmother to us three older kids and a wonderful mum to Massimo.

Untucking and unbuttoning my dress shirt, I chuck it over the back of a dining chair and lean against the marble countertop in my tapered dress pants and a sports bra.

I'm shovelling chicken and salad into my mouth, and debating whether to train chest or back when I hear Francesca's laugh carrying up the stairs that go from the underground garage to the hallway next to the kitchen. It sends a thrill up my spine and a flood of heat to my cunt.

He brought her home. My stomach quickly sinks at the thought and I tell myself to snap out of it.

This is fantastic news for the *Famiglia*. They'll fall in love, get married, and have lots of little mafia brats. Stability and peace throughout the land! Happily ever after. *Ugh*.

For some reason it makes me want to forget chest and back and do three hours on the fuckin' punching bag instead.

"Oh hey, G." Elio appears at the top of the stairs. He has an arm around Francesca's shoulders and they both look like they've been laughing.

"Hey, you two. Good date?" I should have run upstairs when I heard her laugh and avoided this painful small talk. Now I'm fuckin' murderous knowing that while I was dealing with shitty senior members of the *Famiglia* he was moving in on quite literally the most beautiful woman I have ever laid my bloody eyes on.

"Yeah it was great," Francesca says softly with a smile. She is trying not to look directly at me and my stomach churns as my brain works overtime trying to figure out if it is because she is embarrassed she ever even looked at me or because she feels the magnetic pull between us too.

Elio lets her go and grabs a couple of wine glasses from a cupboard. "Red? White?" he asks her.

"Red? I don't mind. You choose." She's distracted, her eyes tracing a hot path down my torso and settling on my hard-earned six-pack. Okay, maybe more like a four-pack these days. And, because I'm a pathetic arsehole, I suck in my stomach slightly causing them to ripple and Francesca to gulp slowly. I relish the heat in her gaze.

The marble countertop digs into my lower back, but I will not move from my laidback slouch. It says 'I'm chill, not bothered, totally unaffected'.

Never mind I have to remind myself to chew my food because I am shoving it in my gob with such ferocity. *Self-control, Giovanna.*

"Alright, catch you later, G. We're going to take this upstairs." Elio holds the wine bottle up and chucks his arm back around Francesca's shoulders.

She doesn't say anything to me, but as they reach the base of the stairs she looks back over her shoulder. The intensity of her stare heavy with meaning I refuse to let myself decode.

The churn in my stomach becomes a burn in my chest and I give myself one moment of weakness to feel sorry for myself. One moment to ask why I never seem to get the things I want. Ever. Why I hustle around keeping this family together, but I always end up with the short straw.

CHAPTER THIRTEEN
FRANCESCA

Plush suede leather in dark grey encases the expansive eight-seater sofa in Elio's living room. It is a space that screams opulence. Dark woods and black and grey textures make for a sleek masculine aesthetic that fits him to a tee.

From where I sit on the sofa, Elio's ginormous four-poster bed is visible through the ajar bedroom door.

The dark colour scheme continues there and I can't help but smirk at the absolute certainty I feel that the posts of his bed are set up for restraints and bondage. I'd bet my non-existent life savings on it.

Despite his lounge suite being fit to sit more than his entire family, Elio's right leg presses into my crossed left knee. His closeness is almost overwhelming. The potent scent of his sharp cologne blankets us like a heady bubble. It isn't unpleasant, but it is a lot.

Elio's body language is not leaving any room for doubt that he intends to fuck me. His gaze sweeps up and down my body lingering on my lips, my thighs, my chest, and my neck. He exudes sexual aggression, and dominance, which I'm hugely attracted to, but I'm just not sure I want it from him.

I genuinely didn't expect our night to lead here, but I shouldn't have underestimated Elio's charm. It is legendary after all. How silly of me to think that I could be immune to his silver tongue and panty-melting smiles.

That's not quite honest. I'm having to coach myself to focus on him and only him and to make the best of what is a less-than-ideal situation.

I had a nice time with him tonight. One-on-one, Elio is smart and funny, and engaged. That his phone remained tucked in his pocket for the entirety of our evening has been a welcome surprise. As has his apparent genuine aim to put me at ease.

We dined at a ridiculously expensive and highly exclusive establishment overlooking Darling Harbour. It is tucked on the upper floors of what looks on the outside like an office building, but only those in the know, and willing to pay an arm and a leg for membership, know it even exists.

It has a deliberate old-world approach to service that is very un-Australian. We don't go around calling each other 'sir' and 'ma'am' here. We are famously classless; not so much in the sense that there aren't vast differences in wealth, but in that money doesn't stop us from all being a bit bogan; rough around the edges. My time in England showed me just how relaxed our social interactions are Down Under compared to the motherland.

In their crisp white shirts and tailored black jackets, the staff seemed to be almost role-playing and the pianist in the corner looked like he could have stepped out of an old Hollywood film. It was an experience that's for sure, but one that I would be happy to have infrequently.

Elio didn't seem to be phased by it all, but then he has a membership; this is his world. I'm just a tourist. As he raised his glass of South Australian Shiraz in a toast to us, I wondered how many other women had sat in this prestigious dining room with him; senators and movie stars dining nearby.

Only a fool would think the twinkles in his eyes are just for them. The quirk of his lips has sent tingles through many bodies, his practised sincerity creating the illusion that each one is the only girl in the world.

I hunger for someone whose slow smiles are mine alone.

It isn't that I am jealous. The truth of it is that I don't have any feelings for him whatsoever. What I am fearful of is humiliation and disrespect. When I have so little control over the fundamentals of my life, all that is left to me is my self-respect and dignity.

I will not be the mafia wife who turns her cheek while her husband philanders and makes her the subject of gossip and pity.

My father's first wife was subject to exactly that when he took up with my 18-year-old mother. Although she was far from his first indiscretion. One year

later, Wife #1, Karen, had been discarded and my parents were engaged with me on the way.

I don't blame Karen for the hostility with which she has treated me and my mother in the 24 years since. I would be the same.

The only thing that does make me sad at times is that because my father destroyed his relationship with his older children when he humiliated their mother, I have no relationship with my half-siblings.

Well, I thought I didn't until Stefan's strange familiarity at our engagement party.

He is a year older than my mother, which naturally didn't help the awkward dynamics. My half-sister Claudia is only a few years younger than Mum. I have nieces and nephews, but we have never met. Even before I was shipped off to London I hadn't seen Stefan and Claudia in a few years.

As far as they're concerned I am the mafia brat that resulted from their middle-aged father taking up with a gold digger their age.

Massimo and I jokingly call ourselves the 'Secondi Siblings'. The second course; the main course. Really we aren't as important as the main event at dinner, we are the afterthoughts. The tag-a-longs. The leftovers.

Massimo's relationship with his three half-siblings has always caused me little prickles of jealousy. His situation is a little different from mine though. His mother wasn't discarded as if she were out of date before even reaching menopause. She died. Not that dying is a preferable outcome. It just meant that Peta didn't oust Sandy's first wife, Maria, she just replaced her after she had already gone. Breast cancer killed her and the Marinos still do a lot of donating to related charities.

Peta is a lot younger than Sandy, but still older than all his children. She gets on well with them too. Giovanna and she seem to be friends even. Everyone seems to agree that Peta is too good for her cantankerous husband. She isn't thirsty for status and luxury like my mother, but she has plenty of both.

Witnessing the dynamics of mafia marriages has left me hyper-sensitised to what life is like for mafia wives. Looking over at Elio's handsome face, with its subtle laugh lines and crow's feet, I am reminded that when I am his age I will be 'getting old'. My shelf life is short. His worth will never diminish though.

By the time I'm in my 60s, his mistresses will be my granddaughters' age, if he hasn't disposed of me all together.

Knowing all this and fiercely protective of my dignity, I was surprised to find myself enjoying Elio's company. Sure, I would have traded him for his sister any day of the week, but she has made it clear that she is not an option. Pining for her is only going to hurt me more in the long run.

"If I wanted a wife, I'd want one like you," Elio confessed as we tucked into our delicate starters.

"Is that supposed to be a compliment?"

His face told me he thinks that should be self-evident. "Of course."

"Telling me you don't want to marry me all the time is kind of a buzzkill. I don't want to marry you either. We've established this. We're both here because we think we don't have much choice." I shrugged and popped a spoonful of Moreton Bay bug and veloute in my mouth. It was delicious and I groaned softly. It was reflexive, but I probably could have suppressed it.

"Fuck. Keep making noises like that and we'll consummate our marriage right here," he chuckled.

I looked at him pointedly waiting for him to respond to my earlier statement.

He sighed. "Yeah, I'm here because Dad and Gio won't let up about me getting married. I'm here with *you* because there is no one else I want to marry. I refused to marry you at first, but then I saw you," he flashed me a smile so sexy I bit my lip. "I figure I may as well marry the most beautiful woman I've ever seen if I have to marry."

"Oh come on. Do you tell all the ladies that shit?" My wine glass was halfway to my mouth, but I laugh hysterically.

"Stop laughing, you little shit," he snorted, waving his fork at me. "I'm complimenting you."

Lifting a finger from my glass I wagged it back at him. "No, you're charming me. You're laying it on fucking thick."

He ducked his head and got back to his food. He couldn't stop smiling though and after a spell of silence he suddenly asked, "Is it working?"

"Is *what* working?"

"Am I charming you?"

I paused, thinking. "Against all my better judgement…yes. Just don't fuck with me, Elio."

"Wouldn't dream of it, babe."

My eyebrow raised so fast it nearly disappeared into my hairline.

Sitting in his living room, sipping another glass of wine, I feel a bit like I have willingly walked into a lion's den and am waiting to be eaten. We are doing the dance of predator and prey.

"Did you go to university over there?" he asks me.

"No. I did a six-month course and then worked in a gym. I didn't know what I wanted to be when I grew up and didn't think there was much point dedicating years of my life to something I didn't care about."

"Fair enough."

"What did you study?"

"Law." He takes a gulp from his glass and I think that is the end of his answer, but then he adds: "I love it. It's all I've ever wanted to do."

"Will you have to stop practising now you're, like, the boss?"

He flinches. It is barely perceptible, but I see it. "I haven't practised for years for a firm, but I've been our family lawyer which is a pretty full-on job. Yeah, Giovanna has suggested we hire another lawyer so I can focus on leading the family, but…"

"But you don't like the sound of that?" I ask softly.

"Nope." He snaps out of whatever pensive state he had been in and gently rubs my thigh. "But, I shouldn't be talking about all that stuff."

"I'll be your wife…"

"And you'll thank me for keeping you out of this shit."

He is probably right so I don't argue. I just sit quietly and wait for him to say something. He doesn't, but he does take our empty wine glasses and place them on the coffee table. One of his big hands reaches out and tucks a stray lock of hair behind my ear.

He looks at my face as if he is scanning every feature. Analysing. Self-conscious I bite my bottom lip and avert my gaze.

"Don't do that," he says quietly with a seductive smile. His thumb runs along my bottom lip tugging it from my teeth as his hand supports my chin. "Look at me," he commands.

My tummy is a mess of nerves, but I do as I'm told. His eyes are just like hers. Dark brown with golden flecks. Warm, intense, and terribly sexy. But her lashes are so thick and black and unmistakably feminine that even her brothers' eyes don't compare.

When his lips softly press against mine, I panic for a split second and consider pulling back, but when his tongue slides into my mouth I give myself over. This is the right thing to do. My life has limited options and as far as forced marriages go, things could be far worse.

My reality is that I don't have a single dollar to my name. Sure I have access to the immense wealth of my family and the Marinos, but that only exists if I do as I am told. Running away would plunge me into homelessness and abject poverty. As I said, limited options.

One of his hands slips through my hair to grip the back of my head. The other roams down my side settling in the dip of my waist. He is a good kisser, I'll give him that, but I didn't expect anything less.

Before I know it, I'm lying on my back on the sofa and Elio blankets me with his broad body. I allow my hands to wander, taking in his muscular form. He works out a lot. Just like his sister.

Thinking about Giovanna has me remembering how incredible she looked the other morning when I saw her in the kitchen after her workout. I had wanted to lick the sweat from her collarbone and up her neck and that wasn't an urge I was accustomed to having.

Clutching Elio's shoulders, I will myself to stop imagining they are Giovanna's. It is only going to make things harder for me and it is a pointless exercise. She is not here. She probably doesn't even want to be here. I need to focus on the man whose bed I will sleep in for the rest of my life. Or until he trades me in for a younger model. Fuck.

I focus on the body bearing down on me and kiss him more urgently, wrapping my legs around his hips. He starts to rock between them and I can feel how hard he is through our clothes. I clutch his face with one hand and

with the other I dig my nails into his scalp. He pulls his mouth away from mine and growls in pleasure as I firmly scrape my nails through his buzzcut.

"Jesus Christ," he murmurs.

"Most people call me Francesca." It is a line I have seen in several movies, usually delivered by men, and I have always wanted to use it.

"Pfffft! Cracking jokes huh?" He teases. Then his arms scoop me against him and he is standing. I squeal in surprise and he laughs, walking us into his bedroom.

Another squeal of surprise escapes as he tosses me onto the mattress. I scoot up the bed to rest my head on one of his pillows and watch as he discards his tie and unbuttons his shirt.

"Oooh private striptease," I put my arms behind my head and stick my tongue out.

"Ha ha," he says dryly. "If that dress isn't on my bedroom floor before I get these pants off, you'll be in big trouble, Francesca."

Oh, he likes to play those games, huh?

Tilting my chin and staring down my nose at the stunning male specimen at the end of the bed, I give him my best come-fuck-me eyes and slowly pull my floaty silk dress over my head.

The delicate emerald fabric floats through the air as I fling it at him and he lets it hit him in the face and slide to the ground. He's too busy staring at my braless body, naked except for a white lace g-string.

Enthralled.

At this moment in time, I *know* I have his whole attention. But how exhausting will it be, emotionally and physically, to have to perform like a stripper or a whore for my husband in order to secure his focus for a short while?

Stop thinking, Francesca!

"You just going to stare or are you going to come over here and join me?" My words evoke a confidence I don't feel. Fake it till you make it, right? It seems to work, as his predatory gaze goes up a notch. He looks like he wants to eat me.

Tugging his pants off, Elio crawls up the bed in just his skin-tight jocks. There is no hiding how turned on he is.

He hovers over me holding himself up on his forearms, his hard cock pressed between my legs. "You know this doesn't mean I'm in love with you right?"

I have *never* rolled my eyes so hard in my life. "Trust me, babe. I'm only here because it's been a while and I'm horny."

Curiosity piqued, he asks, "How long has it been?"

"I'm not a virgin so you can get any creepy purity kinks out of your head right now."

"How long?" He presses me.

"You first, Casanova."

"Yesterday. You?"

Unable to control myself I shriek with laughter. He is *such* a manwhore. "Too long." I shrug still laughing. Two years. Not since posh Gareth.

"What's so funny?" He grinds his pelvis into mine to remind me he is still there.

"I'm marrying a manwhore. If I don't laugh I'll cry."

He frowns. "At least I know what I'm doing."

Sighing, I slip a finger into the waistband of his underwear. "There is that. Can you shut up and fuck me now?"

Needing no further encouragement and with a cocky smile plastered to his face, Elio lowers his face to mine capturing my lips with his. This kiss is more aggressive than earlier and quickly he leaves my mouth to trail kisses down my neck to my breasts.

Pushing himself up he takes a breast in each hand and presses them together. He groans. "These are fuckin' beautiful. I can't wait to fuck them."

He shows his appreciation for them by taking my nipples in his mouth one at a time; sucking them until they are hard. Pulses of electricity shoot into my core when he pulls them with his teeth. Just enough to introduce a little pain to the pleasure.

Elio continues to kiss his way down my body until he is positioned with his shoulders between my legs; shoulders so wide that my legs are forced apart and up towards me as he presses against them. He slides a finger underneath the lace barely concealing my sex and into the wetness between my folds. Making a strangled, tortured sound in response to finding me wet, he withdraws his finger and yanks my underwear down my legs.

For a moment we just look into each other's eyes. There is attraction there, but I'm still distracted by the knowledge that despite being set to marry this

guy, he will be off looking for his next conquest the minute he is done with me and I'll be searching for his sister in every room I walk into.

I didn't think this was what being engaged would be like. There should be some security in a lifelong commitment to each other, but with Elio, I will be constantly battling my insecurities. As his wife, I will have no more from him than his whores do.

He lowers his head to softly kiss the hairless skin just above my pussy and I close my eyes. *I'm here now. May as well enjoy it.*

He kisses down my inner thighs teasing me before he hitches both of my legs closer over his muscular shoulders so they're snug against his neck and hungrily dives into my wetness. My back arches and I cry out at the sudden contact with my most sensitive flesh.

Pausing, he smiles against me and murmurs, "You taste so fucking good."

I reached down and claw at his head. My nails drag across his scalp and he loves it just as much as he did earlier. He groans and the vibrations send shivers up my spine.

My hips buck up to meet him as he fucks me with his tongue. "Oh God, yes. Don't stop." I moan.

"No God here, babe. Only me and you," he mumbles, mirroring my earlier joke.

Focusing his mouth on my clit, Elio slides a finger inside me and this time I cry out his name. He fucks me steadily, curling his finger to hit the right spot and sucking on my sensitive little bud.

"I'm gonna come," I gasp and a few seconds later my body is shuddering and pulsing as the orgasm surges through me.

My body relaxes and I feel soft and boneless. "Elio. Fuck." My voice comes out in a rasp. He chuckles.

He kisses my now extra-sensitive clit making me jump and then crawls up my body. Kneeling between my legs he peels off his underwear, rolls a condom onto his raging erection, and puts my legs over his shoulders again. His hands slide under my bum lifting me off the bed and holding me at the angle he wants.

"You look beautiful when you come, Francesca," his eyes are dark, and his voice low.

"Fuck me," I reply with an involuntary eye roll.

Immediately he thrusts into me right to the hilt and I scream in shock and pleasure.

"Oh fuck yes," he groans as he slides in and out, picking up speed. He wraps a forearm around the back of my hips so he can hold me, freeing up his other hand to rub my sensitive clit. It doesn't take long before the warm waves start in my lower belly again and I'm clenching him inside me as I come again.

Without warning, he flips me over and presses my face into the bed with a hand between my shoulder blades. His other arm yanks my arse into the air and he slides into me from behind. Both hands are in the dip of my hips now and he is pounding me hard, our bodies slapping together.

"Yes, I love it like this," I slur into the duvet. There is something about being dominated from behind that drives me fucking wild. "Don't be gentle, please" I beg.

"You like it rough, princess?" he fucks me harder and grabs my hair in one hand pulling my head back towards him.

I can't answer. My mind has separated from my body and I'm capable only of incoherent moans.

Elio stills and then thrusts in and out slowly and deliberately three times, groaning as he comes hard. He collapses on top of me and we lie in a heap, breathing heavy and sweaty.

After a few minutes, he gets up to deal with the condom, smacking my arse lightly on the way. I half expect that he'll kick me out when he returns from the bathroom. He made it clear this was just a fuck whether I'm engaged to him or not.

Instead, he turns off the lights and jumps into bed, tugging me under the navy blue blankets with him. We don't speak and I soon drift off to sleep with him pressed against my back.

He wakes me at some point in the night to have sex again. We're both sleepy, but it is still urgent and hard. When I wake in the morning, however, he is nowhere to be found.

CHAPTER FOURTEEN
FRANCESCA

My intention to avoid Elio for a while is thwarted when I receive a text from him mid-morning.

Elio: Need you to come with me and G to dinner with Police Commissioner today.
Me: Why?
Elio: his wife is coming
Me: I'm not your wife yet
Elio: don't be difficult. Pick you up at 6.30
Me: what if I have plans?
Elio: cancel them

He must have used up all his charm last night when he was trying to get into my pants.

I hate how empty I feel. It's not like I haven't had casual sex before. It is just different when you're supposed to be marrying the guy. And when you're obsessed with his sister.

Well, I hope Elio enjoyed himself because it won't be happening again if he is going to be an arsehole afterward.

What does one wear to dinner with the Police Commissioner? I don't mind being overdressed, but I'll throttle Elio for his lack of information if I'm underdressed.

Raiding my mother's wardrobe once more, I err on the side of formal with a lilac pantsuit and a white, silk camisole top. The lilac pants are tightly tapered and cropped to the ankles and the blazer cinches perfectly at my waist. Patent black pointed stilettos complete the look and I leave my hair out in waves down my back.

If Elio doesn't like how I look, frankly he can just look elsewhere. The masochistic side of me, which seems to be growing lately, kind of hopes he won't approve of my outfit so I can tell him how little his opinion matters to me.

A black SUV pulls up outside my parents' house and Elio gets out of the passenger seat to open the backdoor for me.

Ignoring the now familiar masculine scent of his cologne that wafts over me, I duck under his arm to get in the car wordlessly. A large hand wraps around my upper arm. "Hey?" he says with a frown.

"Um hi?" I look up blankly at his dark eyes, furrowed brows hanging over them.

He grabs my chin and kisses me quickly and we stand staring at each other for a few heartbeats like neither of us can figure the other out. Something just feels off.

Giovanna is driving and my heart does backflips when she twists to look over her shoulder and slowly evaluates my body. Her eyes darken and she swallows hard.

"Francesca," she says.

My cheeks warm from the inside out like I've taken a mouthful of hot tea and I bumble my way through a 'hello'. If my heart doesn't chill out ASAP, its beats will be audible from bloody space.

My backseat daydreaming is interrupted by Giovanna's deep gravelly voice talking Elio through the plan for the meeting.

She could be reading the phonebook and I would still be mesmerised by the strength, confidence, and sexiness of her tones. I've never been with someone who talks dirty, but just the thought of her describing what she wants to do to me in that voice is enough to reduce me to a puddle of lust.

Giovanna seems to know everything about the commissioner. She even coaches Elio on what he needs to say. He just nods along, content to be told

what to do. It is an interesting dynamic between them. I'm surprised his ego allows him to do as he is told. She inspires that kind of confidence, I guess.

"He's under massive amounts of pressure from the minister to explain the escalation in gun crime. I suspect he will be wanting us to solve some of his problems for him. Don't be too accommodating. Let him sweat. But ultimately, we want this sorted too." She rattles off information.

"And what about if he brings Stefan up?" Elio asks.

"Laugh off any suggestion of concerns about your suitability…play up the strength of your relationship with Cheska. 'She's changed my life blah blah…' and act like a man in love. Stefan is nothing but a mild irritant. A fly buzzing around making a nuisance of himself. We will swat him eventually."

"Why is he bringing his wife?" I ask them when I really want to delve into why my half-brother would come up in conversation with the Police Commissioner. I know better than to ask now though.

Chocolatey brown eyes catch mine in the rearview mirror and Giovanna answers, "Because then he can say it was a personal dinner. A social catch-up."

"So I need to do what exactly?"

"Just be friendly and engage with her in small talk."

Seems simple enough. Not sure what we will have in common to discuss, but I guess the weather is always an option.

CHAPTER FIFTEEN
GIOVANNA

The air is thick with the weird vibe between Francesca and Elio. Tension ripples off my brother's shoulders as I attempt to prepare him for our meeting.

I keep snatching glances at Francesca in the rearview mirror and her golden caramel eyes are burdened with a deep sadness. She's achingly beautiful with flawless olive skin in that light purple suit. I almost tell her how beautiful she is when she gets in the car, but I swallow it down.

Elio is concentrating on the folder of notes I handed him when he got in the car. He may be a party boy, but he is intelligent and I am confident he will absorb enough to get us through this dinner.

In the long run, this arrangement is going to drive me nuts. Having to brief him on everything will take ages and we will inevitably get into situations where stuff comes up that I haven't been able to prepare for.

I wish I knew how he really feels about it all. He seemed relieved that he would only be doing the superficial leading and that I am the decision maker. Sometimes I get the impression that he would rather just be my right-hand man, taking care of the legal shit.

This time we are making use of the private room upstairs at *La Fazenda* and I lead Elio and Francesca through the packed restaurant to the stairs next to the noisy kitchen.

Diners stare at us, perhaps because Elio and Francesca are so good-looking, but most likely because they chose to dine at *La Fazenda* knowing its mafia ties, and are thrilled that they have caught a glimpse of us.

The room isn't very big and the large round table takes up most of it with a small bar tucked against the wall. Sarah hasn't managed to get rid of the red and white tablecloth up here and paired with the dim lighting there is definitely a *Sopranos* vibe to it.

Elio pulls his bride-to-be aside. The laughing couple I saw last night disappearing off to Elio's rooms are nowhere to be seen and instead, Francesca looks furious as Elio places a hand on the small of her back.

Out of the corner of my eye, I see him cup her face in his hands, talking softly to her. She shakes her head and shrugs. Finally, he pulls her into a hug and kisses the top of her head.

"Everything okay?" I ask him when he appears at my side.

"Yeah, we fucked last night and I wasn't sufficiently friendly in the morning."

"What did you do?" I wonder if I really want to know.

"What do you mean?"

"In the morning. You said you weren't friendly, so what did you do?"

"Oh, I left before she woke up," he has the decency to look at least a little bit ashamed.

"Yeah that'll do it, mate," I land a soft punch to his shoulder in faux-playfulness.

Inside, bile rises in my throat and jealousy infects me. For a moment I think I'm going to explode. Rolling my shoulders, I crack my neck and focus on bringing my breathing back to normal.

The prickling of the hair on the back of my neck tells me Francesca is watching me and I can't help but look up to check. Her lips are slightly parted and she has a hand pressed over her heart as if to try and stop it from leaping out.

Mine.

She is supposed to be mine.

Where the fuck has this possessiveness come from? She isn't mine and this urge to claim her is fuckin' mental.

The lump in my throat won't budge, but I clear my throat. "Righto. Think you two can keep it together for this?"

They nod just as we hear feet ascending the stairs.

It's game time and Francesca and Elio immediately plaster smiles on their faces. People don't expect me to smile anymore, so I don't bother.

Stepping into my public persona, I fall in behind my brother. He strides forward and thrusts a large hand forward to shake the commissioner's hand. "Mate. Good to see you."

Commissioner Trotter strikes an imposing figure. A cop who made his way up the ranks, he knows how to draw on intimidation when necessary. He's tall, though not as tall as Elio, and has a stocky build with a sturdy beer belly that is putting pressure on the buttons of his dress shirt. Carefully combed grey hair tops a not-unfriendly face and he looks much like any middle-class Aussie bloke with working-class roots.

The men introduce their respective partners and everyone takes their seats at the round table.

As an afterthought, Trotter raises a hand from where he sits opposite me and waves hello. I return a slight nod.

"Let's get some wine in here before we have any shop talk," Elio grins and calls over a waitress who stands quietly in the corner awaiting instruction. "I've been enjoying South Australian reds lately, any objection to cracking a bottle or two of Shiraz?"

God, he's good at schmoozing. All smiles and charm. For the first time, I wonder if Dad maybe got this bizarre shared role spot-on because I hate this shit.

While Elio discusses the wine and orders some bread, I look across him to where Francesca sits. She looks serene and dignified. Not a trace of the firecracker who leaps into a pool in a $5,000 dress for shits and giggles.

As if she can feel my gaze on her, she looks right at me and shoots me a slight smile. I can't help myself and wink in reply and she blushes immediately. A thrill races up my spine. I get a rush from knowing I have the power to make her cheeks flush like that.

Elio is driving the small talk with Trotter and his wife with a discussion of Trotter's favourite rugby league team, the Manly Sea Eagles. *Pull it back now, Elio. Time to let him do the talking.*

Information is gold in our world and if you want to collect it, you need to shut up and listen. I grew up watching Dad listen to his men, saying very little until he was sure he had bled them for every drop of intel they had.

"As much as I would enjoy a social dinner with you both, I know that you didn't reach out to chat about the NRL," Elio keeps his tone light and friendly. "What are you after, Phil?"

Mrs. Trotter looks up from the menu she is perusing with Francesca and eyes her husband nervously. She looks timid, but the kind of timid that you wouldn't want to fuck with in certain circumstances. Like when it comes to administrative processes and organisation. Like a receptionist at a doctor's office; all mild-mannered until someone doesn't use the booking system correctly and then it's all on, passive-aggressively, of course.

"Right. Yes, well I don't need to tell you that gun crime has picked up in Sydney, particularly in the inner city." He pauses, but when Elio remains silent, he continues, "We've seen a sudden influx of some pretty hefty weapons, not your usual handguns and rifles. I'm talking semi-automatics and automatics. Driveby shootings are up 350% on last year and they're more lethal because they're spraying autos instead of firing individual shots."

We all listen and Elio gives a slight nod of his head, encouraging him to continue. I'm proud of my little brother. He is playing this directly from Dad's playbook.

Trotter takes a sip of wine. "As you can expect, the minister is breathing down my neck. Canberra wants to know where the weapons are coming from and who is running them. You have much to do with Satan's Sons?"

Elio's smile is almost condescending. "Not the kind of people we tend to affiliate with, Commissioner. However, my sister has been looking into the weapons influx. I'll let her tell you about her interactions with Satan's Sons." He looks at me as if permitting me to speak.

"We've been concerned about the increased gun violence too and have endeavoured to find out what is going on, but it has been tough tracking the weapons. It wasn't until a relative of ours who owns a small business was hit up

for protection by some Satan's Sons bikies that we started to look into them. It seems Ned -"

"The Outlaw?" Trotter interrupts.

"Yeap, that's the one. He has a control problem. A group has splintered off and gone rogue. I suspect that they are the ones running the weapons."

Francesca's eyes are as wide as saucers enthralled in what I'm saying. Mrs. Trotter, next to her, is equally as intrigued by the discussion. This is probably the most exciting thing that's happened to her in years.

We pause to allow bread and appetisers to be laid on the table. I sip my water, allowing my glass of wine to remain untouched. I'll nurse it until the commissioner has left. Another lesson from Dad: plie your guests with alcohol, but remain sober yourself.

Trotter starts the conversation back up with his mouth still half full of bruschetta. "It's interesting you picked up on the rogue Satan's Sons. Our intelligence has found the same thing. It looks like three or four young bikies, one is The Outlaw's nephew. They've decided to do their own thing. Hooked up with the Arabs and that's where the guns are coming from.

I don't let on that this is useful information; just nod and see if he will say anything else. When he doesn't, I prod a little more. "The young bikies. What do you know about them?"

"Well, they're relatively young. Early, mid-twenties. The nephew is the ringleader. Has a chip on his shoulder by the looks of it. The other two seem to be leeches looking for a quick route to the top."

He has a lot of information about these kids for someone who made out he had just been listening out here and there.

Reading my mind, Elio reinserts himself into the conversation. "Sounds like the boys and girls in blue have done a solid bit of police work. What do you need from us, Phil?"

"The kids are clean. Well, except for a DUI and a wilful damage conviction between them. It's going to take us a while to get anything solid to disrupt them. Unless we're struck with some serious…luck."

Elio smiles slightly. The police are sticklers to the law until their own procedures slow them down.

"People are dying and not just other scumbags. A six-year-old girl copped a stray bullet last week. She was popping into a servo with her dad late at night for ice cream. In her SpongeBob pyjamas. Wrong place, wrong time." Trotter sighs and runs a hand over his brow.

It had been all over the news. Heartbreaking stuff. Trotter isn't above using heartbreak to get what he needs. As much as we are working to our own playbook, so too is the commissioner.

Organised criminals and the police are engaged in a constant dance. There aren't rules, but there are flexible boundaries that we push and pull at. Right now, the commissioner is trying to pull at the heartstrings of the King of Sydney's underworld. Interesting choice of tactic.

"I'm not entirely sure what you're asking of us, Commissioner," Elio nudges him.

If I didn't know better, I would think that the Commissioner was trying to ask us (without asking) to get rid of the bikers. You know...bullet in the head, body in a bag, cinder block around the ankles, and into the harbour.

"I don't know, to be honest, son," the Commissioner sags in his seat and his wife's eyes grow impossibly wide in alarm. "Can I even have confidence that your Family can help when word is you have your own control problem?"

Elio laughs loudly and rocks back in his chair. Credit to him, it looks genuine. "Oh you've been listening to the gossip have you? Don't believe everything you hear on the grapevine. If you're referring to my fiancee's estranged brother Stefan Rossi, well, every family has a pain in its arse and Stefan is our pest."

"Righto, mate," Trotter's eyes slide to the door and he does a poor job of disguising how much he wants to leave. "Lovely meal, thank you. We better be off though."

"You don't want to tell us what you need from us before you leave?" Elio asks gently like he is approaching a frightened kitten.

"Need to think further on it, I think," he says gruffly. "I'll be in touch."

Weirdest meeting I've been to in a while.

The Trotters bustle around grabbing their belongings and Francesca shows them out leaving Elio and me to communicate through raised eyebrows.

"Haven't seen someone leave a dinner that fast since Auntie Savia tried to set you up with her friend's son," Elio laughs to himself.

"Shut the fuck up," the napkin I throw at him falls short, landing on the table between us.

"Giovanna, he's a *doctor*," he continues in his best imitation of our loud and clueless auntie.

My middle finger salutes him while my other hand scrolls through my phone and Elio cackles. The cool and calculated mafia don of a few moments ago has left the building and my idiot brother has reappeared.

"I could hear you laughing from the bottom of the stairs," Francesca snipes, her hands resting on her hips in the doorway.

"Thank goodness. I won't worry about our children inheriting any deafness from you then," he spits back, cold sarcasm replacing his laughter.

He's deadset insane. Sure, Francesca is shitty, but her life has been upended. Cut the poor girl some slack.

If I was him I'd take great fuckin' pleasure in kissing that scowl off her face. He just doesn't seem to realise what he has been handed on a plate. She is perfect. *Fucking perfect*. And instead of thanking his lucky stars, he's pushing her away.

How he handled the Commissioner impressed me so much, but his immediate attitude switch with Francesca pisses me off. He's like an overgrown toddler acting out because he feels insecure or unsettled.

I blame Dad. He has made his talented oldest son a performing monkey not trusted to make actual decisions and stripped away yet more self-respect from a man who despite pretending otherwise, clearly hates himself at times.

As much as I resent doing the thankless work of running the Family businesses only to be dismissed as a mere woman in meetings, Elio has it rough too. He is capable of much more than just being charming. He just needs to figure out what he wants.

~

Back at home, Francesca throws herself down on a sofa in the living area and blows a few flyaway strands of hair off her face. "That was kinda fun," she muses.

Elio looks at her like she just grew another head. "Glad someone enjoyed themselves."

"You hated it? But you were great!"

He pours himself a whiskey and leans against the wall facing her. "Enjoyment isn't guaranteed just because you're good at something,' he takes a sip and pauses. "Only sometimes. Thank fuck I love eating pussy though because I'm a fuckin' champion at it." He winks at her and she rolls her eyes.

"Received lots of feedback, have you?" Francesca mutters and then snaps, "Thanks for offering me a drink by the way."

It looks like this conversation is going to descend into warfare and I'm not keen to stick around to referee. Especially not if Elio manages to charm her into makeup sex.

"You could have asked," he doesn't take the bait. "Anyway, I'm heading out. You can stay here I guess. Or ask G to take you home?"

He's a fuckin' moron. How can such a smart guy be so stupid? He's obviously struggling because I don't like to think he would be so unnecessarily rude to a young woman who is essentially being forced to marry him. Maybe I am giving him too much credit though.

Francesca's face is a picture of shock. Seeing her hurt gives me a pang in my gut. She doesn't deserve this. He's dismissive as if she is some clingy girl he banged and now wants to get rid of.

"Why are you like this?" she whispers. "Would it hurt you to treat me with some respect?"

He rolls his eyes and I can't bite my tongue any longer, "Elio! For fucksake, man."

It's a miracle his crystal whiskey tumbler doesn't shatter as he necks the last of his drink and slams it onto the kitchen countertop. His dress shoes clack across the wooden floor as he strides with purpose towards the stairs to the garage and without so much as a backward glance calls "later" over his shoulder.

"I don't want to marry him," Francesca looks right into my fucking soul with those Bambi eyes. A tear trickles down her cheek and her pain rockets through me as if it is my own.

"I know, *bella.* Let's have a drink; what do you want?" I soothe her.

"Red, please."

Sloshing the maroon liquid into big globular wine glasses, I take a seat next to her. She has her feet tucked underneath her and suddenly looks very young and innocent. Like a little girl wearing her mum's suit.

She is breathtakingly beautiful and I just can't fathom what is going on in my brother's head. He could have come home and taken this absolute stunner to bed. What could he possibly have to do that would top that?

"I wish I didn't let him fuck me. I just thought it would make things easier," she almost appears to be speaking to herself rather than me.

Fuck. What do I say to that? I hate that they fucked, but theoretically, they have a lifetime of it ahead of them. I clear my throat but can't think of how to respond so I just stare into my wine glass, swirling it like I'm at a tasting.

She fills the silence instead. "Are you going to get married?"

"Ha! Not anytime soon," I laugh shakily.

"So your Dad doesn't think you need a wife?"

"Nah, I keep myself in line these days." I shrug.

"And there's no one you want to marry?"

"God, you're still bloody nosy, *cucciolotta*." I lean towards her and nudge her with my shoulder. "Nah, never did end up with the girl of my dreams. Kissed plenty of frogs though."

"If I recall you were never short of options," she casts a cheeky sideways glance my way. I bet I can guess what she is remembering. I am a bit embarrassed that I used to let myself get carried away in front of the kids. It inspired many a painfully awkward Q&A session with little Massimo and Francesca.

"Well, you always did keep a close eye on me," the corner of my mouth tugs up, and I can't help but smirk.

I am just teasing her, but she covers her face in her hands and groans. "Was I really that bad?"

She was. She looked at me like I was the most glorious thing she had ever seen. Like I invented eating Nutella straight out of the jar or something. Everyone put it down to hero worship, including me until just before they sent her away. She would have been 16 and I caught her watching me a few times with a look on her face that told me she didn't want to be me, she *wanted me*.

"No, you were cute. Curious, nosy, and asked waaaay too many questions. You were a kid, darlin'." I splash some more wine into both of our glasses and

lean my head against the back of the sofa. *Darlin'. Little darlin'* was what I called her back then.

Francesca has chucked her purple blazer on the floor and the strappy, silky white camisole against her olive skin is driving me wild. The way her chest rises and falls as she laughs at my shitty jokes is distracting. I can just make out the shape of her nipples and it is physically painful to look away.

I'm fuckin' giddy. One of the most powerful people in this fucking city and I'm tittering and giggling over my brother's 24-year-old fiance.

Jesus Christ, now she's stretching. This is slow torture. The white silk slides up over her taut tanned tummy. Help. SOS. Bring in the fucking chopper and get me outta here.

"Massi told me you've found a job. Congrats," I steer the conversation into safer territory.

"It's just a part-time thing at Strive Fitness. Mostly just helping out around the gym, but I'll get to run a few classes each week for an organisation that brings in patients for rehab. And I made a work friend already!" She's a bit coy and downplays the gig, but seems genuinely thrilled to have made a friend.

"That's great, Cheska. You should be proud of yourself. I know you didn't want to come home, but you're doing good."

Smiling, she gently pushes my leg with a perfectly manicured foot and I catch it. "Thanks, G."

I should let go of her foot, but I don't. I do the exact opposite of what I should do and start massaging it. She bites her bottom lip and stretches her leg out so it is sitting on my lap. My self-control is hampered by the bottle of wine we have all but demolished.

"That feels ridiculously good," she groans and I feel it deep in my cunt.

I'm about to respond with something that I most definitely shouldn't when we are both saved from our poor impulse control by Massimo. He waltzes in from upstairs frowning at his phone, giving Francesca time to slide her dainty, perfectly painted foot off my lap.

"Matty says Stefan has shown up at *Peacocks* and Elio is wasted." He looks up at me. "Check your phone." *Peacocks.* The strip club we've owned for three generations.

Francesca sighs and holds up her empty wine glass. "Massi, can you grab another bottle? I need to forget that I'm marrying an arsehole."

Massimo pretends to be a waiter with a tea towel over his arm as he tops our glasses up, then he pours one for himself and collapses in the plushy dark brown armchair perpendicular to our sofa. "What's he done now, babes?"

"Just couldn't get away from me fast enough when we got back from dinner and now I hear it was because he was gagging to get to the strip club he spends half his life in any way."

Massimo's eyes briefly meet mine and I grimace subtly. We both know our brother and we will have to lie in order to bring her comfort at this point. Regardless of how charming and fun he can be. He is never going to be a faithful husband. He is selfishness personified and poor Francesca is going to be miserable if she doesn't reset her expectations.

She continues, "I'm not being clingy because I want him to be in love with me for fucksake. I wouldn't choose him! But my life is just going to be a shitshow of Elio and his whores. I'll hate myself." One tear falls and then the dam breaks. She sobs, but she is embarrassed so she tries to hide her face behind her delicate hands.

Massimo gets up and drags her onto his lap. He wraps his arms around her and she presses her face into his throat.

He shushes her and whispers comforting words into her ears and somehow I manage to get jealous of my gay brother. I pick up my phone checking the messages in our sibling group chat.

Matty: Rossi is in Peacocks.
Matty: Elio. Opposite you.
Matty: Elio.
Massimo: Is this an actual problem or?
Matty: Where's G?
Massimo: I'll find her

Hmmm. Stefan hasn't been so bold before. He has stayed out of our explicit territory and slithered like the snake he is from capo to capo hissing his

venom behind closed doors. If he is at our club it is for a very deliberate purpose. He is provoking us or making a statement.

"Is Bluey still here?" I ask Massimo as I stand up and stretch my arms over my head. I'm not wasted but there is no way I'm driving. Getting a DUI would be a pathetic 2022 version of getting Al Caponed.

Massimo looks up, confused. "Bluey?"

"Yeah, the larrikin you've had working with you since you got back to Australia. Red hair. About your height. Thinks he's God's gift to women." Italian isn't our mother tongue, sarcasm is.

"I know who he is, G. Just was confused why you were asking."

"Because I'm the boss, Massimo." Irritation is creeping into my voice and he cops one of my infamous scowls. "Is Bluey here or not?"

"He was talking to Fat Tony outside last I saw."

Francesca has been watching our interaction quietly from her perch on Massimo's lap. I catch her looking me up and down as I stand. With my hands in my pockets, my dress shirt unbuttoned halfway down my chest with no bra underneath, I pause to give her time to check me out. Sure enough, she licks her bottom lip slowly not realising I'm watching her.

Fucksake. The last thing I want to do is leave her to go to our fucking strip club. But it is probably a timely escape because my self-control reserves are running critically low. I'm tipsy and wet for her.

Sitting down to tug my leather brogues back on, I order Massimo to go tell Bluey he's taking me to *Peacocks*, and by some miracle the little shit listens, depositing Francesca on his chair gently before heading out the back door.

She watches me do up a couple of buttons on my shirt and throw my blazer on and then beckons me over, curling her index finger. I crouch in front of her chair between her legs and she briskly tidies up my hair for me, running her fingers through it until it sits right.

"Thank you, darlin'" I rasp.

"Not sure why I'm helping you when you're leaving me to go to a strip club," she pouts and it turns me on something chronic. Since when do I get off on being given grief by girls?

"I have your brother to intimidate and my brother to kick up the ass. Not exactly going for a lap dance." I'm still crouching in front of her, our faces are level and the temptation to kiss her is real. Really fucking real.

She leans forward and my brain goes into full meltdown mode. *Fuck, fuck, fuck, what do I do here?* I want to kiss her so badly, but I just can't.

But her face brushes past my cheek and she presses her lips just next to my ear and whispers, "Good." Her voice is husky and it makes me close my eyes, goosebumps scattering over my neck and back.

When I open my eyes she's smiling like a cat that got the cream. She enjoys exerting power over me. Turning grumpy Giovanna into a quivering mess. She's dangerous, this girl. Lethal even.

I grab her chin firmly and bring her face close to mine. "Don't play games with me, darlin'. You won't win." I speak the words so close that she can feel my breath on her lips. She blinks at me but registers no fear. I'm fucked. I'd let her win every day of the week.

CHAPTER SIXTEEN
GIOVANNA

"Do you want me to come in, boss?" Bluey asks as we pull up outside *Peacocks*. It is a discreet building of black glass with entirely indiscreet large purple lettering spelling out the name of our establishment adorning the front side. A huge peacock tail fans open behind the letters.

It has always bugged me that the place is called 'Peacocks' when it is a strip club in which women are the entertainment. Peacocks are male. Nonno should have called it *Peahens*, but that doesn't sound as cool, I guess. And now I think about it, it is really the male patrons who peacock around the place measuring their dicks. Maybe Nonno was being cleverer than I realised.

"Yeah, I'll need you to take me home so don't get on the piss. Hopefully won't be too long."

Bluey gives me a nod and a cheeky grin as he follows me in the front door. How the red-headed class clown ended up working for us I don't know, but he's good value. Funny and, just like my brothers, he is smart when he isn't thinking with his dick.

'Giovanna!" One of the door girls fawns over me. She is wearing leather hotpants with her augmented boobs spilling out of a bejewelled bra. A total gay-for-pay bimbo who would hump my leg for the status it would afford her.

"Ladies," I murmur in response to her and her colleague. In my twenties, I spent a lot more time in *Peacocks* and was a lot friendlier with the staff. I had a posse of lesbian mates who used to love taking advantage of my VIP status at the club. Most of them are married off and have kids now.

The place is busy, but not heaving. We're doing a decent trade this evening, but we always are. Business is never bad when you have a constantly replenishing pool of horny, unfaithful Italian men who want to gather and measure their dicks.

"Bluey, grab me a whiskey, please," I instruct him. "Rocks."

There are two main stages with a mixture of high and low tables scattered around them. Booths line the perimeter of the floor and I spot Elio and Matteo with a group of men in the one that sits right up against the smaller of the two stages.

Bluey places a whiskey in my hand and we weave through the crowds. I'm keeping an eye out for Stefan, but he isn't standing out.

Candice winks at me from the stage. She's nude apart from a diamante g-string. We haven't hooked up for a couple of years, but she's a nice girl and one I don't mind chatting with when I'm here. She definitely didn't have those boobs the last time we caught up though. She grabs them and mouths ' Do you like them?' I roll my eyes but give her a small laugh.

"You distracting the dancers already, G?" Elio's loud voice booms from a few metres away. He is well on his way to oblivion. He sits with his legs spread wide, arms across the back of the booth. Here is the peacock our grandfather named the place after.

"It's a gift and a curse, bro. Don't worry, one day you'll get as much pussy as I do." I say it knowing his mates will react and sure enough they roar with laughter, clinking drinks that they no doubt did not pay for.

"See I tell people you're funny, but they just won't believe me," he shrugs. His ego isn't even slightly bruised by my jab. These are our games. We've always played them. "Move," he tells some drunk bloke with bourbon all down his suit. "Make room for my sister."

Sitting next to him under his mammoth wingspan, I sip my whiskey and scan the crowd. Matteo slides into the booth next to me and even though one of them is hopelessly drunk, I'm happy being flanked by the two of the men I trust the most in the world. A drunk philanderer and a brooding ex-con, what does that say about me?

"What was so urgent that you had to come rushing in here straight after dinner?" I ask Elio. "Did the dancers need help applying their fake tan?"

"Such a comedian, sis. Nah, I just needed to get out of there." His evasiveness is all the more blatant in his drunken state.

"Why?"

"Fuck off, bloody sticky beak." His words are slurred and it takes a few seconds for him to slide his eyes from Candice's tits to me.

"Elio, I was the one left to deal with Francesca. She thinks you hate her. Can't you just try not to be a dick?"

"If I stayed I would've ended up taking her up to bed and fucking her again. It was early and I didn't want to give her the wrong impression."

"The impression that you are attracted to your fiancee and want to spend the night fucking her?"

"Well, yeah. Basically. Look, I don't want to get married. I don't want her to think that because we fuck I suddenly want to get married."

I want to scream. This situation is ridiculous. Both Elio and I want to fuck Francesca, but for different reasons are avoiding doing so. That means, despite being attracted to us both, she is going to bed alone tonight.

"But you *are* getting married. So what does it matter?" I grit my teeth.

Before the pointless circular discussion can continue, Matty whispers in my other ear, "your two o'clock. Next to the stage. Rossi and some stupid fuckin' capos with a death wish."

I follow his directions and spot Stefan at the centre of a group of men. He is attempting to hold court, to look powerful. Unfortunately, it appears a few ill-advised souls have fallen for it.

Azarro. Hmmm. Wouldn't have picked him as a sucker. Mario Azarro, an astute man in his 50s, has always toed the line for my father and I am not happy to see him sitting in Stefan Rossi's little gathering.

La Paglia. Two La Paglias, actually. Fucking morons. And Santoro.

The rest are men I don't recognise. Nobodies. Hangers on. Hired posse perhaps.

"How long have Azarro, Santoro, and the two La Paglias been with him?" I ask Matty.

"Azarro just arrived, I think, and the La Paglias arrived with Rossi."

"Have you had a word?"

"Nah, Elio wasn't...responsive. So I thought I better wait for you."

I turn to speak to my other brother, but a dancer has crawled backwards across the table towards him and he has her pussy in his face. He isn't touching her, yet.

"Sorry to interrupt the heart-to-heart you're having," I nod at the bare cunt. "Are you going to do something about Stefan Rossi starting a pissing contest in your club?"

"Where?" He asks, not looking at me.

"I suspect it is difficult for you to see past the pussy in your face, brother. Next to the stage." I indicate with my glass.

"They're not causing trouble," he shrugs.

"Yet, Elio." I whisper in his ear so that no one else hears, "We can't afford to look weak for a second. Stefan is acting up to prove he can get away with it. He has a capo with him - Azarro - and a few other men from the *Famiglia*."

"So you sort it then, boss," he grins and smacks the dancer's arse so hard that her skin ripples.

"We'll discuss this later," I hiss at him, suppressing all the things I want to scream at him.

Matty and I move across the floor slowly, chatting to patrons and staff we know. We watch the men grow more raucous. They want attention and they'll do something to get it eventually.

"Let's head this off before it kicks off," I mutter to Matty and he shadows me as I swagger over to Rossi's table.

"Stefan. How nice to see you contributing to our takings for the evening," my tone is flat, and my face stoney. "Azarro," I nod at him and run my eyes over the other men in the group.

"Did you draw the short straw, Giovanna," Stefan pulls a face of faux sympathy.

"And have to come and talk to you? No, Stefan, it is always a pleasure."

"No," he laughs and clicks his tongue. "Did you draw the short straw and have to babysit bad boy Elio? The Don that parties harder than he works."

"Watch your mouth, Stefan. You're not in Melbourne anymore," I snap.

"No offence intended," he holds his hands up.

Stefan is putting on a show and a tendril of panic curls up my spine as I worry if I might just be playing straight into his hands. He wants to make us

look like a joke. He wants all of the capos to see him as the strong alternative to a foolish and disinterested Elio.

"No more games," I bark.

I need to step this up a notch. I can't make Elio look better right now, but I can scare the shit out of anyone who is thinking about switching allegiances.

"It is time for you to go home," I step closer to him.

He is just a couple of inches taller than me so I'm able to maintain some physical authority.

"Then you have two choices tomorrow. 1. You fuck off back to Melbourne or 2. You present yourself at 10 am to apologise to our family for the disrespectful, trouble-making snaking around you've been up to and fall the fuck in line. There is a third option, of course, and I promise you if you keep fucking with me I'll happily fire the bullet myself."

"This is all a bit of an overreaction, G -" he sneers.

"That's Giovanna to you, thanks," I interject.

"Giiiiioooooooovvvvaaaaaaannnnnaaaaaa," he elongates the pronunciation of my name. "I'm just here enjoying a few drinks with some friends. Why all the hostility?"

Nope. I will not play his game. He won't get me to justify myself.

"Leave now or I'll have you removed," none of the emotion bubbling away in my gut is detectable in my deadpan voice. Matty and Bluey, flanking me, have been joined by several other members of the Famiglia behind us. The show of strength settles my nerves.

Stefan sits down and rests his arms along the booth behind him, like a cheap, beta version of Elio who for all his faults, looks the part of a mafia boss. "You sure you don't need to check with your brother first, princess?"

My hand goes to the gun shoved in the back of my pants and the biggest of Stefan's goons, an oafish bloke I don't recognise, steps towards me. Instantly Matty and Bluey have their hands on their weapons too.

Stefan laughs and it is unpleasant and cold. His beady eyes narrow at me and I'm struck by how unlike his beautiful sister he is.

His arm shoots out and he hooks an arm around the waist of a passing topless stripper. She squeals in surprise as he hauls her small body onto his lap and paws at one of her boobs.

"All of this is unnecessary," he gestures to our hands resting on our guns, ready to draw at any second.

"What's your name, babe?" I ask the dancer. She is shaking, well aware that she has been yanked into a situation that could end in bloodshed. I need to keep her calm. She is a distraction and I don't want her to become collateral damage.

"Ash," she squeaks. Stefan has her arms pinned to her sides with his forearm across her body, restraining her.

"Let Ash go, Stefan. In Sydney, we don't mess with women and children."

"Then what the fuck are you doing here, little lady? Don't you have some sandwiches to make? Eating pussy doesn't make you a man," his mask slips and falls off completely as venom pours from his mouth.

Sighing and rolling my eyes, I finally draw my gun and walk calmly to stand in front of Stefan. I give Ash a quick reassuring nod and then extend my arm past her to press my gun to the forehead of the pretender. "I would prefer not to shed blood in our club, but you push me much further and yours will paint the floors," I growl.

"Time to go, Rossi," Azarro speaks up, standing to move so that he is angled more on my side of the conflict and I raise my eyebrow at him in question. Fair weather friend. It is a wise move and one that will save his life, but I will never trust him again.

Even the wasted La Paglia brothers are looking uncomfortable now. The wind has changed and they realise they are about to be guilty by association.

"Last chance, all of you," I look at the entire posse. "Get out."

All bar three of Rossi's men scurry off, no doubt hoping that I will forget their faces and their betrayal.

"Santoro," I address the man who remains in his seat next to Rossi. "You are a captain for our Family, I believe."

He nods sharply and looks to Rossi for reassurance or instructions.

"I suggest you run. Do not come back to Sydney. Your lack of loyalty will be remembered and I will never again grant you the reprieve that will allow you to walk out that door right now."

He hesitates and then pushes up from his seat and leaves Stefan, still holding a terrified Ash, with only his hired muscle.

"Matteo, get the snake out of my sight," I command without moving the gun from Stefan's head.

Matty signals to Fat Tony's son, a massive young guy, to assist him. As they approach, Stefan lets go of Ash and she throws herself behind me, clutching at my back. Stefan's narrow, pointy nose and gaunt angular jaw tilt upwards in a display of misplaced haughtiness and he reluctantly allows himself to be escorted out of the club.

"Do not waste my time again, snake," I call after him. "Go back to Melbourne."

Adrenalin continues to surge through my veins as I sit in the dark office above the main floor at *Peacocks*. Spinning my whisky glass on the worse-for-wear wooden desk in front of me, I review how I handled the situation downstairs.

The only reason Stefan Rossi doesn't have a bullet in his head is that his father was my father's *consigliere*, but his parentage won't protect him next time.

I pinch the space between my eyebrows and can't decide if I'm angry or relieved that Elio didn't handle the situation. It makes him look weak that his sister is acting as his proxy, but he doesn't have the same stomach Matty and I have for violence and I'm not sure that he would've been able to show the same strength.

There is a soft knock at the closed door and I call out for the person to enter, assuming it will be Matty or Bluey.

"Hi," a soft, breathy voice says and Ash appears around the door. "I just wanted to thank you for saving me."

I beckon for her to come in and she closes the door behind her. She is wearing marginally more clothing now; she has added a bra and hot pants to her ensemble.

She's hot. Banging body, petite, and pretty. Her blonde hair is pulled back into a voluminous ponytail that reaches mid-way down her back and I imagine wrapping it around my hand.

She approaches me, swaying her hips and telling me with her eyes that she has plans for how she would like to thank me.

"I didn't really save you," I state blandly, leaning back in my chair, knitting my fingers together on my stomach, and resting an ankle on the knee of my other leg.

Her fingertips walk along the edge of the desk as she rounds it to stand next to my chair. "You were so badass though," she giggles and I suppress the urge to roll my eyes.

"And," she lifts a leg and throws it over my lap, sitting to straddle me, "so brave."

I don't move; don't encourage nor dissuade her. Just stare at her heavily made-up face with a slightly lifted brow.

Her palms come to rest on my chest and she inches forward on my lap. I won't lie, I am tempted. We certainly wouldn't be the first ones to fuck on this desk and I'm sexually frustrated from being around Francesca so much.

Francesca.

The blue eyes that stare down at me, hooded in either lust or due to narcotics (maybe both), are the wrong colour. All I want are the caramel-brown Bambi eyes that go with her plush bee-stung lips.

Fuck it. But I can't have her. Will never have her. It is pointless for me to think like this. I need to put her out of my mind. Get laid and move on.

"You wanted to say 'thank you'," I look at Ash's lips as I speak, licking my own suggestively.

She nods eagerly and rolls her hips, grinding her pussy in my lap. "Will you let me show my appreciation?" she purrs leaning towards me.

Enacting what I fantasised about earlier, I quickly reach up, wrap her ponytail around my fist and drag her down for a kiss. It's fine. She kisses fine, but my stomach isn't doing backflips.

I doubt very much that Ash is a lesbian. Her talon-like nails virtually confirm she is not. She might be bisexual, but in all likelihood, this is a power move. All the other girls will know I fucked her two minutes after she leaves the room.

Should I bother? Do I even want this? My brain is being very unhelpful as I try to get lost in the kiss. *Just get off and get out, Giovanna.*

"Do you know how to give head properly?" I squeeze her jaw in one of my hands, pushing her back so I can see her face. Most of the strippers will have slept with women before, but I can't be fucked with an amateur who isn't even into it. "Not suck dick. Eat pussy," I clarify.

She nods again with enthusiasm and I slap my hands on her arse twice and instruct her to get up. Ash sits on the desk and watches as I kick off one of my shoes, undo my pants, and slide them and my underwear down one leg.

"Kneel," I command, pointing to the floor in front of me and she hurriedly obeys. She does look hot looking up at me, legs folded underneath her. Even more so when she takes off her bra and drops it next to her.

Placing my shoeless foot on the chair next to me to open up my legs, I use Ash's ponytail again to pull her up onto her knees so her face aligns with my cunt. "Eat," I tell her and she doesn't need to be told twice.

My head drops back and my eyes flutter closed as I try to focus on enjoying being eaten out, but images of caramel eyes won't leave me alone. I find myself wondering if she has gone to bed now and imagine getting home and slipping in between the sheets to find her sleeping, warm body.

Ash is eating like a champ, but I'm just not getting there. I'm pretty sure the only way I'm going to come is if I pretend she is Francesca.

"Fuck," I grunt in frustration. Keeping my eyes closed, I imagine Francesca on her knees. She would be tentative at first, inexperienced with women. But I'd teach her.

Gripping Ash's head with both hands, I fuck her face and the heat in my core builds.

"Gonna come babe," I groan and she moans into me. It takes all my restraint not to call out Francesca's name when the orgasm hits me. Instead, I just repeat the word "fuck" over and over.

Sitting back on her heels, Ash wipes the back of her hand across her face looking pleased with herself. Fuck, I feel bad for using her. But then she sought me out and she will brag about this to her friends. I don't need to feel guilty about shit.

I waste no time pulling my underwear and pants back up my bare leg and straightening myself up. A big mouthful of whiskey washes away the taste of kisses from a woman who isn't Francesca and I want to be alone.

"You're welcome," I say.

"Pardon?" Ash looks confused as she clips her bra back on.

"You wanted to say thank you. So 'you're welcome,'"

"Oh right," she grins.

"Close the door behind you," I dismiss her, making my disinterest in spending any more time in her company clear.

When she slips out and I'm left in an office that smells like sex and half a bottle of whisky, regret circles my stomach like a drain.

I don't want Francesca any less than I did before Ash entered the office and worst of all, I feel like I have been unfaithful to her.

CHAPTER SEVENTEEN
FRANCESCA

For the first time since we were so rudely snatched from our kitschy flat in Chelsea a couple of months ago, I feel genuinely happy. It is no coincidence that it is the first chance Massimo and I have had to escape the clutches of our deranged families and just hang out like we used to.

My friend Sammy from work is joining us. She and Massi have been getting on just like I knew they would.

We've only worked together at the Strive gym near the Marino house for about six weeks, but she is the only person in my life not trying to push me into something or manipulating me into doing 'what is best for the Family'. Even Massi is a Marino first and foremost.

Sammy's sleek brown hair is always in a ponytail and 90% of her wardrobe is sports bras and exercise leggings. She wears only minimal makeup, but her face is stunning and feminine nonetheless.

Almond-shaped green eyes, a button nose complete with a smattering of freckles, and rosebud cheeks give her an angelic appearance, but having spent many hours at work with her talking shit, I can attest that she is no angel.

Funnily enough, people seem to assume she's gay because she's a complete tomboy, but when I asked she confessed that she was "unfortunately strictly dickly". She's gorgeous and I think I could be attracted to her, but the gravitational pull I feel towards Giovanna makes it difficult to even see other women. There's only room for her and there has only ever been her.

Sammy is everything the people I spend my life with are not. She is unpretentious, quick to smile, and, most significantly, unaffiliated with the mafia. Although I guess her friendship with me probably puts her on some mafia affiliate watchlist somewhere.

She is beautiful. Her Māori heritage gives her light toffee skin which provides a striking contrast to her green eyes. She calls herself a 'Mozzie' - a Māori Aussie. Born in New Zealand, her parents immigrated here when she was a toddler and she speaks with cultural and vernacular influences from both sides of the Tasman Sea.

Her positive attitude doesn't mean she shies away from standing up for herself and others though and to be quite honest, I am a bit nervous about her ever being around Elio. As the only neutral person in my life, I have shared with her a curated version of Elio and my story, and let's just say she is less than impressed with his treatment of me.

Sammy should keep a notebook of all the creative names she has come up with to refer to Elio. Just yesterday she came up with 'Deadshit Douchebagette Ball-bagging Motherfucker'. Whatever that means.

After weeks of enforced dating with Elio - the Deadshit Douchebagette Ballbagging Motherfucker - throughout which I have resolutely refused to reenter his bedroom nor let him in my pants in any other room, we are no closer to wanting to marry each other. We have had some entertaining dinners and fun going out to the clubs, but he has made no attempts to even hide his continuing philandering with any and every woman he fancies. Monogamy is not in our future. Fucking ball-bagging motherfucker.

My future appears to centre around a miserable marriage in which I won't even have my husband's affections to myself during the honeymoon period and the thought of it all has triggered several panic attacks.

The first meltdown was after a nice date with Elio was spoiled in classic fashion when two women were waiting for him when we arrived home. We both knew that I wouldn't be putting out for him as I made the mistake of doing after our first date, but for him to have his booty calls waiting at the house after our date was beyond insensitive. He could have dropped me home. He could have snuck them in later. Rude.

I was more angry at my pathetic stuttering response. I allowed him to introduce them to me for goodness sake. To be fair I was in shock.

He'd sauntered off upstairs with his double act and I had been left standing alone in the echo-y open-plan living space. A silly girl in a slinky Michael Lo Sordo dress, ditched after dinner.

My breath had caught in my throat and I just couldn't dislodge the lump that settled there. When Giovanna happened to pop downstairs to make a cup of peppermint tea she found me hunched over with my hands on my knees, panting like a dog left in a hot car. She talked me into deep breathing and sat with me on the floor for over an hour chatting to calm me down.

The second panic attack hit in the middle of a particularly painful Marino and Rossi family dinner. Massimo sat opposite me and I watched the concern on his face grow as our parents talked about my wedding, when I should get pregnant, and whether I should work. Massi mouthed words of support at me, but listening to them droning on was like acid dripping down my spine.

From the head of the table, Giovanna tried to show me with her hands that I needed to slow my breaths. She could recognise the onset of panic by now.

This time when my breathing seized I knew I had to get out of there. I stood and walked out of the glass backdoors at the Marino house and strode into the pool ruining another of my mother's dresses. Massimo landed in the pool moments later and kept me company as I got my breath under control.

Through the open door, I heard my parents discussing my "attention-seeking behaviour" and I yearned to hear Giovanna's voice cutting them down, but it never came.

Sick of everyone's shit and in need of some escapism, I was excited to throw on a bikini, little linen shorts, and sunnies and slide into Massimo's Range Rover for a day at the beach.

We are heading across town to Bondi Beach, picking up Sammy on the way, and although it is early, on a sunny day like this we will be joined by half of Sydney.

The windows are down, the warm wind whips my hair, and I'm reclining back in the front passenger seat with my tangerine-painted toes up on the dash. Massi is showing his Adonis rig off in just a pair of boardies that reach his mid-

thigh and in true Aussie fashion, he picked up iced coffees for us all on the way, barefoot and shirtless.

We are all smiles as we belt out the cheesy Top 40 hits blasting from his sound system. "Gimme a song, Massi!" I shout.

"K," he thinks for a moment and then tells me to put on *Holy Water* by Noah Davis.

I'm surprised because the song is about coming out and dealing with homophobia, but Massi came out ages ago and his family is fine with him being gay. I contemplate asking him about it, but his furrowed brow tells me that maybe he'd prefer not to discuss it. Now is not the time to deep it.

"Do you guys want to learn to surf with me?" Massi suddenly shouts above the music.

"Today?!" I exclaim.

"No, but this summer."

"Ooh, yes! I do," Sammy calls out from the backseat.

I shrug. "Yeah may as well. Maybe I'll get eaten by a shark and won't have to marry your brother."

"Or find a sexy surfy bit on the side," he winks. "But seriously, I want to learn and Bluey said he'd teach us."

"Of course Bluey surfs!" Even dressed in his mafia man suits, his red hair has a beachy tussle to it.

How exactly Bluey ended up working for the Marinos I am not sure. I remember him from before I was sent away. He had been young then. I'd guess he is about 30 now, maybe Matty's age. He has always been like this little (huge) Aussie stray that was taken in by the Marinos.

"Yeah, he might come say hi later if he can get away from Giovanna."

I eye Massi suspiciously over the top of my sunglasses. "What is this? Are you getting a new best friend, Marino?"

Massimo snorts and denies the charge, but a little slither of emotion flashes in his eyes for a moment and my ever-burgeoning self-confidence crisis has me experiencing a bout of jealousy.

That's all I bloody need.

My self-esteem is already under attack thanks to his older brother and my poor wee heart is already pathetically pining after his older sister. May as well

add some jealousy and paranoia that Massimo will ditch me for Bluey. All I need now is to spend more time with Matty so he can pick an emotion to play with.

"Don't worry, girl," Sammy interjects. "You still have me!"

We manage to find a spot on the beach and lay out our towels. As suspected, it is packed with bodies already. Glistening, tanned bodies. After being in England for so long it is jarring to remember how blase Aussies are about getting our kit off. There are no teeny weenie bikinis in Battersea Park or in Trafalgar Square.

"How has it been working in the family business?" I ask Massi as we lay on our tummies people-watching.

"I've worked for the family since I left high school," he looks confused and a little uneasy about talking about the *Famiglia* in front of Sammy.

"Oh, I mean *back* in the family business," I don't think I realised he was working for the family before he came to London. I mean, he was at university and I just assumed that was it. I was far away, but I still feel like it is something I should know about him. Weird.

"It's better with Dad stepping back," he shrugs.

"Is Elio a good boss? He seems to spend a lot of time at Peacocks." I know I sound snarky, but I do genuinely wonder when he has time to run their massive freighting and logistics empire, all the Family businesses, and the not-so-above-board parts of the Family enterprise.

Massimo lifts his head slowly from where it rested on his forearms and taps his sunglasses down his nose to peer over the top of them. "Francesca," his voice is low and almost like a growl. "Insinuations like that could get you in a lot of trouble. You might be a mafia princess and you can trust me with your life, but babe you can never forget that our families are sharks and they'll rip us limb-for-limb for so much as disrespecting them."

Sammy's eyes widen and I gulp, knowing he is right. I have been given a lot of leeway because my tantrums have just been in front of the Marino siblings, but they now run a feared organised crime family and will no doubt employ violence just as their ancestors have always done in Australia and back in Italy.

"Would he actually hurt her? Like, I know he is an arrogant prick and a total slimy scumfuck, but being violent towards her? That's fucked up," Sammy is horrified. I forget that the amount of violence we are used to is not normal.

"No. But if Cheska goes around questioning his leadership it puts him in a fucking tough situation,' Massi responds.

There is something cagey about the way he talks about this stuff. Like I am only getting a fraction of the picture. It's not just him, it's all of the siblings and their parents, and my parents. It's like everyone is in on some wider plan and I'm being collectively managed. I am expected to be quiet and do as I'm told.

"Speaking of Elio," Sammy grins cheekily, clearly wanting to lighten the mood. "Does he live up to the hype? I don't get how he has women just falling at his feet."

"Are you asking what my brother is like in the sack?" Massi pretends to gag.

Sammy laughs, holding her sides. "Sex gossip is like my favourite thing. Just pretend that we're not talking about your brother."

"I don't know why women go so wild for him. He's a dickhead," Massi shrugs.

"You are like his twin, just younger, with longer hair, and light eyes." I look over the top of my sunglasses at him.

He clears his throat. "And more handsome. Obviously."

"Obvs. Yeah, Elio was pretty great in bed as much as I hate to admit it. We only shagged that one time though. Well, one night. Multiple times."

"You haven't fucked again? I thought you were going to use him for sex right back?" Sammy seems genuinely surprised. I must have forgotten to tell her how I was feeling about it all. I've been unloading this shit on Giovanna, I guess.

"Because he treats me like shit, Sam. I feel my self-respect evaporate after every date."

"I thought you said the dates were all good," Massi frowns.

"The dates are fun. But then he has his booty calls waiting for him when we get home or he goes straight to *Peacocks.* I feel gross. I'd rather not go through the pretence and just have a formal arranged marriage. Separate rooms. Separate lives."

Massi turns on his side, leaning on his elbow, and stares down at me. My own personal solar eclipse. "That sounds miserable though," he says softly.

"Not as miserable as getting to know, and like, maybe even *love*, my husband only for him to traipse mistress after mistress through our lives. Fuck that so much."

"I'm so sorry, Ches. I didn't realise. I thought things were gradually improving," Massi says softly.

"I haven't really talked about it, so you weren't to know."

I flip over onto my back and with my hands behind my head allow some self-indulgent silent tears to trickle out of the corners of my eyes. Masked by my sunglasses, my tears go unnoticed.

Another panic attack lurks in the wings as I think about how much I hate that Massimo's loyalties are now split. We were in our own world in London. We only cared about having fun and each other. Now, my pain is caused by the actions of his family, the family he works for.

I reach out and squeeze his forearm. "I think I'd die without you, Massi. Please - please...I know it's your family, but I need you too."

"You fuckin' goose," he leans over and plants a kiss on my forehead. "I'm not going anywhere. No matter what our mental fuckin' families do."

Sniffing, I nod.

As the sun rises in the sky and we roast alive on the golden sand, our chat chills out and we relax into our usual relaxed banter.

We go for a swim and play around in the waves like Massi and I did when we were younger and roughly the same size. Now Massi manhandles both me and Sammy and throws us over his shoulders like a fireman, tossing us into the salty sea like we weigh nothing.

"Oi! Knock it off, you ratbags!" We all turn to locate the source of the voice.

Bluey stands at the shore with his surfboard under his arm, his other hand shielding his eyes as he cracks a wide smile at us. Naturally, he's wearing a pair of tight blue budgie smugglers which leave little to the imagination. He is covered in so many freckles that there is hardly a millimetre of pale skin between them. His skin looks almost golden.

We wade back towards the shore and he looks me and Sammy up and down appreciatively. His eyes flick to Massimo standing slightly behind me and they hold each other's gaze for long enough that I turn to look at Massi but he looks away.

"Fancy seeing you here," I say in a sing-song voice. "Who knew there were abs hiding under that suit huh?" I give him a wink. He's a good-looking guy. Solid and dependable. He's handsome enough to be attractive but it is his personality that radiates.

"Don't tell anyone my secret!" he jokes. "If they find out I'm not a ranga Homer Simpson, I'll have to beat the women off with a stick. Who's ya friend, Pup?" He has taken to calling me Pup since he found out that the Marinos call me *cucciolotta.*

"A real burden for you," I roll my eyes, laughing before introducing him to Sammy.

His attention switches to Massi. "You got yourself a board yet, little prince?"

My eyebrows shoot up towards my hairline and my eyes dart to Massi, but he has his firmly on the burly redhead. *Little Prince. That's new.*

I can hear the cheeky grin in Massi's voice when he replies. "Not yet, but don't worry I won't let anyone else teach me."

"That's right. I'm poppin' that cherry!" He belly laughs and then jogs into the sea calling back over his shoulder, "I'll come find you guys after."

"Bluey's gonna pop your cherry, Massi," I wriggle my eyebrows at him as we perch once more on our towels.

"Shhhhaaaaaard uuuuup," he drawls, his cheeks growing a little rosier. "Flirtatious straight men are my kryptonite."

"Do you want me to fuck him for you so you can fuck him by proxy?" Sammy asks.

"Are you into him?" He shoots back.

"I mean, yeah he's a good-looking dude. He'd go alright in the sack too, I reckon." she shrugs. "Wouldn't be my first choice, but wouldn't be a chore."

He regards her with curiosity. "Who would be your first choice?"

We weave our way between the sandcastles, towels, and tanning bodies.

"Hmmmm someone with Elio's looks and your personality. And heterosexual obvs," Her eyes twinkle and Massi grins at her. "What about you, Cheska? Who's your first choice?"

I stop laughing and feel bubbles of anxiety gathering in my gut. How I feel about Giovanna is the one thing I have always kept from Massimo. Gathering my wet, salty hair into a messy bun on top of my head, I look out to the sea and try to imagine a world in which nothing is in the way of me walking up to Giovanna and pressing my lips to hers.

"Same person I've wanted forever. But it's ridiculous. I'm marrying Elio and I don't think she would ever want to be with me anyway. Not like I'd want." I don't realise what I've said until Massi clears his throat.

"Ahem. *SHE*? Something you wanna tell us, babe?" Sammy's eyes are even wider than they were before.

I feel the colour drain from my face. I'm not stupid, I know I'm being a homophobic bitch to myself. I've never so much as had a bad thought about Massi being gay and our families are fine with him. I don't know what has made me so cagey about it.

Massi's eyes are wide too and his mouth hangs open. "You did not seriously come out just now!" He gasps.

"Woah woah woah. Hold your horses, okay?" I gather my composure and take a breath before continuing. "It's not that exciting, I'm basically straight. I just have like one tiny bit that isn't quite so straight. Like really small." I ramble on.

He shakes his head baffled. With good reason too. "Babe, we literally partied in gay clubs every week in London and you never said or did anything. What the fuck?"

How can I explain to him that I have never so much as kissed a girl, but that I am incurably obsessed with one woman?

"It just never happened. Doesn't mean I wasn't looking."

"This isn't like FOMO right?"

"What?" Sammy and I ask at the same time.

"You know, rainbow tourism. Identify as bi in your twenties for the clout and then sink into heterosexual suburbia in your thirties." He's teasing me, but there are real questions in there. I know it drives him mad that the gay scene is

full of activists with blue hair who think being gay has more to do with Marxism than having sex with someone of the same sex. His words still sting a bit though. I know my feelings are real, I just never had the chance to act on them because they've always been so focused on one unattainable person.

"This is why I never said anything, you dickhead. It's not an identity thing. I'll happily never talk about it again. I'm much more often attracted to men anyway."

Massi is looking at me like he doesn't know me anymore. I'm regretting saying anything. "Okay then…but when you're paddling the pink canoe -"

"Uh, when I'm doing what now?"

"You know, having a threesome with a couple of no-shows…tickling the undercarriage! Rubbing one out." His cheeky grin grows wider with each euphemism until he's shaking with laughter.

"Riiiight. *Ménage à Moi.*" Sammy has the giggles too. They're both rolling around on their towels like idiots.

"Petting the cat?" I giggle, joining in.

"Buttering your muffin!"

"DJing in the basement - OKAY STOP LAUGHING, both of you! What do you think about? Guys? Gals? Both?" Massi can barely talk between his cackles.

The question quickly brings my laughter to a halt and I am embarrassed, to tell the truth. It is really pathetic. I'm pathetic. And obsessive. "Uh, no comment." I squeak.

"You do wank right?" His eyes are as wide as saucers.

"Pffft! Of course!"

"Then why are you so embarrassed? Omg, do you have a fetish or something?"

"Laaaawwwwwwd help me. No. I just always think about the same person. Always have. Since the first time. Ha! Weird right?"

"Man or woman?" Sammy seeks clarification.

"Woman."

"Who?"

I just shake my head. I can't verbalise it.

"You need to get laid. By a woman. To find out if you're into women or just have a thing for this one. Can you fuck her?" Sammy is so blunt. No wonder her and Massi are gelling so well.

I snort. "I wish. No, not possible."

Before they can delve any deeper into my masturbatory fantasies, Bluey reappears, dripping with water. He stands over Massi and shakes his hair like a dog, spraying him with cold water droplets.

"You dropkick!" Roars Massi, but he's trying his best to suppress a smile. He punches Bluey hard in the gut and then yanks his feet out from under him so he comes crashing down on the sand.

Bluey dives on top of Massi, pelting him with playful punches to the head and shoulders.

Again, Sammy and I exchange meaningful looks.

"This is all feeling vaguely sexual, boys," Sammy comments dryly and Bluey springs back onto his heels and plonks himself on the sand between our towels.

"Nah this shitcunt isn't butch enough for me," Massi jokes, blowing Bluey a kiss.

I look at the huge, muscled redhead with a chiselled jaw sitting next to me and back at Massi.

Bluey just rolls his eyes. "We all know if I was gay I'd top the fuck out of you."

CHAPTER EIGHTEEN
FRANCESCA

16 Years Old

"Why do I have to go? I don't understand." My heart is beating so fast as I look from one parent to the other.

Dad frowns and looks at his watch as if I am wasting his time with all my questions. As if he hasn't just announced that he's sending me away to live on the other side of the world.

I'm 16 and they're shipping me off, but I'm not getting sent away for the usual reasons. I'm not a wayward teen. I have good grades and don't get into too much trouble. No, this isn't about that.

We all know why I'm being sent away. It's because the *Famiglia*, the mafia comes first. And within the *Famiglia*, the men reign supreme. Because it is not only easier to send away a girl than it is to hold the man who wronged her accountable, it is the natural order of things.

My existence is the problem. Not that a man saw fit to take from me what was not his to take. The solution is to remove me from the *Famiglia*, because I am a walking, talking problem.

"Don't make this harder than it needs to be, Francesca," Dad grumbles. He shoots sideways glances at my mother as if to try to catch her eye. He wants to leave her to deal with her tarnished daughter.

I realise at this moment that it isn't just that I don't have a close relationship with my Dad or that we clash. He just feels nothing for me. He

doesn't love me or hate me. I'm just an irritant. Better to place me out of sight so I can be out of mind.

I'm bristling like a cat ready to fight. "Congrats Dad. That's 3 out of 3! 100% of your kids think you're a fucking dickhead!"

"Put a sock in it! Pack your suitcases and stop being a brat! You're not being sent to a bloody internment camp. You're going to your grandparents." I'm satisfied that I am succeeding in pushing his buttons. I'd like nothing more than to make him as miserable as possible.

Wanting to push him further, I stand with my fists clenched and hiss at him, "Tell me why you're sending me away! Tell me the truth! You can't can you? Because you're so fuckin' weak. Can't even stand up to your own brother. I hate you!"

His open hand collides with my cheek snapping my head towards my opposite shoulder so quickly that I think my head might spin off. It's the first time he's ever hit me. I clutch my stinging skin and look at him wide-eyed, but he just storms out of my room without a backward glance.

My mother has been present the entire time. She is the weakest human I think I have ever met. Pathetically chasing around after a man old enough to be her father after she stole him from another woman.

Still holding my face, I ask Mum, "Have you ever stood up for me? Even once?"

"Don't be melodramatic, Francesca. You pushed your father too far."

"So you're just going to let him send your only child to the other side of the world? Or are you looking forward to having no responsibilities again?"

I can see the tears gathering in her eyes, but I don't feel sorry for her. She has allowed him to take every single drop of power from her. She could fight for me. She won't.

I'm not sad in the slightest about leaving my parents. They can fuck right off as far as I'm concerned. Mostly I don't want to leave Massi. We do everything together and I worry about him as well.

Mum keeps trying to tell me how great England is and how I'll love living with her parents. She forgets that I know she ran away from home at 18 and moved to Australia. Can't have been that great.

It should be David being sent away. In another family, he would have been reported to the police and would be locked up for it. The shroud of secrecy would be to protect my feelings and dignity, not to shield him from consequences.

My life might feel like it was worth something in a family like that. Not like a walking vagina punished because a dirty old man tarnished me before they had a chance to sell my purity.

CHAPTER NINETEEN
FRANCESCA

"Here you go. Make sure you wear it today." Elio thrusts a small velvet box into my hand as he walks past me on his way to the kitchen.

He's staring into the fridge as my thumb digs into the lip of the box and snaps it open to reveal a huge princess-cut diamond sitting on a band covered with lots of little diamonds. It is stunning. Absolutely gorgeous. And I motherfucking hate it.

Sick to my stomach, I tilt the box letting the light refract off all the little angles, glistening every plane it hits. Spectacular as it is, it may as well be a ball and chain or a set of handcuffs. And not the fun fluffy kind.

I glare at Elio's back. No glorious sunset. No popping champagne. No lover down on one knee. No surprise. No joy. Just a box thrown at me with as much care as someone might toss a bone to a dog. Probably less.

I always imagined that receiving an engagement ring would be one of my life's memorable moments. Down on one knee, in a romantic setting, they would pledge their undying love and ask me to be theirs for life.

Dreams are free for a reason.

Overcome with emotion, I fight the tears because I have shed way too many of them over this insensitive man and this doomed arranged marriage. Instead, I let rage percolate. The box shuts with a clap and I shove it in the pocket of the lightweight sweatpants I'm wearing.

"Is it really necessary that I attend this thing?" my voice is cold, dead.

"I just gave you a $350,000 ring and I'm copping attitude? And, yes. It is necessary." Elio replies as he saunters around the kitchen island to perch on a stool. He is drinking some kind of pre-workout concoction from a plastic shaker.

"It could be worth $5 billion and I would still hate it," I snap. "Did you have to throw it at me?"

"Oh I'm sorry, did you want me to get down on one knee?" He strides over to where I sit on the sofa to kneel at my feet, sarcasm surrounding his actions like an aura. "Francesca, our parents are forcing us to get married, we've been on a few dates, and from my limited experience you're a pretty good root - will you do me the honour of joining me in resenting family duty and reluctantly getting married?"

Despite my best efforts a small snort escapes. "Pretty good? You seemed to enjoy yourself. But that's beside the point, I don't want to marry you and I don't want to come to your shitty party today either."

"Princess, you don't have a choice. On either front." He digs into my pocket, his hands getting uncomfortably close to intimate areas I wish he had no knowledge of and pulls out the ring box. He slides the symbolic piece of obnoxious jewellery onto my finger easily and I hold up my hand to inspect it.

He watches me curiously and when I don't say anything he shakes his head and asks, "Did you really want me to propose properly?"

"No!" I scowl immediately. "This isn't real, this thing between you and I. But because of it, I'll never experience the real thing. I won't get to feel like the most loved and cherished woman in the world. I get to feel like a piece of property being traded between families. So excuse me for feeling robbed."

"I'm sorry I can't give you that," he says with no emotion nor sincerity in his voice.

"It is what it is." I shrug. Sighing, I get up and brush past Elio's massive form, still kneeling on the floor. "I guess I'll go get ready for this party then."

"It's a pool party. Everyone will just be wearing bathers."

Trying to take the poison out of my tone I fake laugh and respond, "You must have forgotten to mention that. By the way, I'm inviting Sammy from work."

"She hot?"

"Smokin' hot. She's also smart enough to think you're a wanker."

While it is easier living at the Marino house now, that is mostly a reflection of how miserable I was living with my parents.

When Sandy and Dad sat Elio and me down a few weeks ago to inform us that our wedding would be in six months and I would be moving into the Marino house immediately, I couldn't even bring myself to be mad about having my life dragged around again.

I did refuse to move into his wing though.

"No one is under any illusions that you're a virgin, Francesca," Sandy had stated, matter of fact.

Embarrassed at the thought that they might think I was trying to pass myself off as a pure and innocent virgin, I snapped back, "That's not what I'm saying at all. I just don't want to share a room with a man who is still sleeping around. I doubt Elio wants me in his space either. What if he wants to bring a *guest* home."

Elio remained emotionless in the chair beside me. He allowed himself to be railroaded by his father as usual and didn't dispute that he would continue having sex with other women.

"What about after you're married?" Giovanna enquired. She hadn't said a word up until this point. The best and worst part of living with the Marinos was that I saw more of Giovanna. More reminders of what I couldn't have, but also more fleeting moments of contact with her that set my body alight.

I looked at Elio and he looked at me. We both shrugged.

I lost that battle though and I begrudgingly agreed to try living with Elio for a month. After that, I can move into a guest room if I still want to. We are sleeping in the same bed, but I have slapped away every advance he has made in the dark of the night. Thankfully he is often out late and I can pretend to be asleep when he returns.

My olive skin is tanning up quickly now that I'm back in a country with regular sunshine. After my trip to the beach with Massi the other week and daily sunbathing sessions by the pool, I'm a golden brown that is just crying out for white bathers.

I choose a bandeau bikini top with a twist in the middle of my breasts. The bottoms sit high atop my hips and the small piece of fabric on the back disappears into my bum. I know Elio's eyes will bug out of his head when he sees me, but it is in the hope that his sister will join the party at some point that I'm really putting an effort in.

I'll probably go for a swim at some point so I don't want a full face of makeup to melt and leave me looking like the Joker. I just smooth out my complexion with tinted moisturiser, slick on some waterproof mascara, and stain my lips an almost burgundy red.

Chunky wedges with cork heels and thick white linen straps that weave around my ankles, complete the look because I just can't be arsed with standing in stilettos all day.

The ring on my finger is ostentatious and heavy. It is over the top and designed for people to grab your hand and gasp over its obvious value. It is a ring that Elio would choose. One that he wouldn't spend much time looking at.

'Bring me the most expensive, flashy one you have,' he would say.

Giovanna would choose a solitaire. A big diamond, clear and pure, but simple. Just diamond and band. When I start to imagine her grabbing it out of her bedside drawer and sliding it on my finger as we wake together in bliss, I tell myself to stop being a pathetic creep.

"Where have you been?" Elio sounds irritated, but his irritation quickly melts away when he takes in my appearance. He looks hungry like he might drag me into the pantry and devour me.

I register his lust with satisfaction. His wanting me feels like a victory even if only because it gives me a smidge of power over him. "Just upstairs," I reply mildly. I deliberately hid up there until the party was underway.

A cold cocktail in a tall glass with ribbons of cucumber and lemon rind cascading over the rim is thrust into my hands. Of course, he has hired someone to make proper cocktails all day.

Elio's hand on the small of my back guides me around the room and outside. We stop several times so he can introduce me as his fiancee and it is fascinating to watch women one after another ignore me and make eyes at him. He laps it up and I wonder how many of them he has already slept with.

Seizing the chance for a break from schmoozing, I leave Elio and head to the bathroom. Luckily no one is waiting for the loo because I sit on the toilet texting Massimo long after I have finished my wee.

Me: Where the fuck are you?
Massimo: Working
Me: I need you to save me from your brother and his friends
Massimo: I'll be there later hopefully
Me: Can't you ask Giovanna to let you come early? :D:D:D
Massimo: not really how it works. Plus she ain't here
Me: What are you doing?
Massimo: you know I can't tell you that
Me: you're no fun
Massimo: xo

I take my shoes off after about an hour and venture through the forest of beautiful and beautified bodies. Women who could easily grace the covers of Vogue or stomp down a Victoria's Secret runway tower over me and my self-doubts multiply until they're a poison in my blood and a plague on my mind.

It doesn't matter how much I tell myself I am objectively attractive or remind myself of the way Elio looked at my body, I feel inferior and out of place.

Elio used to host parties constantly when Massi and I were little and he hasn't grown up and aged out of it. This kind of social situation will be my reality. I'll be expected to take part and turn the other cheek to his interactions with other women. I see an image of myself pregnant, waddling around all of the models and socialites with a fake smile plastered on my face. I see Elio's look of disgust as he takes in my huge belly and leads a ten-out-of-ten stunner out of the room to find somewhere private.

Here and now, I'm already negotiating with myself as to what is an acceptable amount of time schmoozing before I can excuse myself.

Elio has all but ignored me since the beginning of the party. I watch him sitting on a sofa outside. He's handed a small silver tray and lowers his head to quickly snort two lines of white powder. It is then passed on to the posse surrounding him.

His arm is around a woman I recognise because she is the face of an ad campaign for some zero-sugar vodka RTD. Her face is on the back of buses and constantly on my social media feeds. She's gorgeous, obviously.

If Elio was flirting equally with his posse of women it would be easier to stomach. But he is wrapped up in Ms. Vodka Premix and the feelings of humiliation overwhelm me again. Part of me wants to go over and cause a scene because why-fucking-not at this point? But, that would give the impression that I actually want him.

Looking away, I spot a familiar burly body topped with scruffy red hair. I can't help but smile at the red Budgie Smugglers he's wearing. Most of the men are in above-the-knee boardshorts, but that is so not on brand for Bluey.

Seeing me smile, Bluey wanders over, beer in hand. I don't think I have ever seen a man as comfortable in his body as this bloke. And why not, I guess? He's stacked with muscles.

"I'd ask if you're enjoying the party, but it looks like murder is on your mind," he leans down to drawl in my ear.

"Your boss is an absolute shitcunt, Bluey."

"I couldn't possibly comment, Francesca," he remarks blandly.

"Reckon I can leave yet? Not like he'll notice," I enquire wistfully.

"Why would you do that when you can just have your own fun? Fuck him."

"Listen to the man!" Sammy's arms wrap around my waist and I squeal in delight that she has arrived. "Fuck that toerag's noise. We are going to have fun."

He chuckles. "She's a wise woman. Go find us a spot outside, I'll come find you."

The fabric of the daybed is searingly hot under the heat of the afternoon sun. Enjoying the only just tolerable burn on my skin, I recline and observe Elio and Lady Low-Cal Booze on the other side of the pool.

Leaning back on my elbows with legs stretched out, I must look relaxed, but in reality, Sammy and I are coming up with creative ways I could murder the Adonis arsehole.

"It depends if you care about getting caught though, babe," Sammy jokes. "Anything too bloody will be a nightmare to clean up."

"Hmmm, I don't think I would survive in prison…"

"Are you kidding? You'd be fine! Some butch top dog would claim you and you'd be treated like a queen."

I laugh along with her, but that doesn't sound too bad. I mean, if Giovanna was in prison with me I'd fight every bitch in there to be her girl.

A few men look tempted to stray over to speak to us, but they all know I'm Elio's fiancee, whether he remembers it or not. I look down at the sparkling monstrosity on my hand and hiss.

"Girl, that thing is ridiculous," Sammy shakes her head.

"I know."

Bluey swaggers towards us. He takes so bloody long because every second person wants to talk to him. He is a popular guy. I assess him over the top of my oversized sunglasses. He is good looking and I like him; maybe I should see how Elio feels if I do a bit of flirting of my own.

"Hello, Princess," Bluey presents us with fresh cocktails.

"Not you calling me princess too," I groan.

"You're royalty in our world and you deserve to be treated like it." His eyes dart towards Elio and we both know his comment is dangerously close to life-threatening. He gulps and I think he instantly wants to take it back.

Bluey crawls onto the daybed between Sammy and me and pops a joint between his lips. He produces a lighter from somewhere and given he is just in his budgie smugglers I hope it wasn't tucked in with his dick.

He sucks in, his cheeks hollowing, and holds his breath for a few seconds before exhaling the smoke through his nose.

As the smoke around us clears, I see Elio watching us. His eyes flick from Sammy rubbing sunblock on her thighs to Bluey reclining next to me and over to me.

"Shotgun?" I quirk my eyebrow at Sammy and she grins. I pluck the joint from Bluey's large lips and draw on it hard. Meeting in the middle as we hover over the big redhead, I grab Sammy's chin and seal my lips over hers. Thick smoke pours from my mouth to hers, the smell of damp lawn clippings surrounding us.

Whoops and cheers sound from a group of guys nearby, but Elio doesn't react.

Bluey passes the joint back to me after taking a few more puffs. The way he settles back cradling his head, it looks like he's going to allow the weed to float him off to the land of nod.

"Nap time, you big baby?" I ask and he gives me a cheeky grin, nodding.

Sammy climbs over him and we finish the joint together sitting cross-legged and that's how Giovanna finds us an hour or so later. Seriously stoned and subtly moving to the music.

"Is Bluey still alive?" Giovanna frowns as she approaches.

I want to kiss the lines that are gathering between her brows. She is the most perfect human I've ever seen. No makeup and with her hair pulled into a top knot she is wearing board shorts that come to her mid-thigh and a sporty black bikini top. I'm thankful for my dark sunglasses because I am drinking in her body slowly and thoroughly.

She used to have a full six-pack with a V leading to her pubic area. Now, at 38, she still has her upper abs but her lower stomach has softened a little. I want to kiss that tiny soft pouch of fat that sits between her hips too.

"Francesca, are you alive?" She waves a hand in front of my face.

"Oh sorry, I thought I answered you," I giggle. "Bluey's stoned. Just having a nap."

"You're stoned too, princess," she remarks wryly, winking at Sammy.

"Oh my god, seriously! You're the third person to call me princess today. Do I give off brat vibes or something?"

She chuckles which makes me happy because extracting smiles and laughs from her is my favourite challenge. "Nothing to do with brattiness, darlin'. You're just regal. Take it as a compliment."

Giovanna shoos us over to make room for her on the daybed and Sammy lights up another joint, passing it to me when she's taken a few drags. I blow smoke away from Giovanna's face and picture giving her a shotgun too.

I hold out the half-smoked joint, offering it to her, but she shakes her head and waves her e-cigarette. The way she reclines, running her gaze over the party while she puffs on her vape, has my pulse settling between my legs. The power and confidence she exudes is intoxicating.

My stoned brain conjures a fantasy where I'm kneeling in front of her, her hand roughly in my hair. I shudder. The idea of bending over for her or being dominated by her drives me fucking wild. The rapid dampening of my little white bikini bottoms is evidence of that.

I turn to look at her and find she's watching me already. Panic runs through me for a second until I remind myself she can't read my thoughts. I should stop smoking weed.

The party starts to thin out as some leave to head into town and others go home to crash, wasted from day-drinking. Bluey woke up a while ago, around the time Matty and Massimo arrived home.

We forgo the catering and order a pile of fish and chips that we demolish sitting on the daybed. My face aches from smiling and laughing so much and I can't remember the last time I felt so content or like I belong.

These are good people.

Even if I'm pretty sure they've all killed people before. Even Massimo. I found a gun in his glove box the other day and realised that he is just as much a gangster as his siblings. Not Sammy though. Unless she has a secret past she hides from everyone.

The worst thing about day becoming night is that I have to take off my sunnies and can no longer stare at Giovanna without being noticed. The best part is that when she goes to get herself a sweater, she brings one back for me too and it smells like her.

She catches me smelling it as I pull it over my head so I mumble, "Smells so good." She always smells divine. Not too feminine and not too masculine,

she smells fresh with a slightly heavier patchouli note. There's a tinge of leather there too.

My contentment is only disrupted by the performance Elio and Madame Alcopop are putting on across the pool from us. As their group disperses, they remain glued to each other. The sexual tension between them is electric.

"Look at them. This is insane, G. Why do I have to marry him?" I gesture toward her brother, but I immediately regret saying anything. She looks so uncomfortable. "Sorry, I shouldn't have said anything."

"No, it's fine," she sighs. "I know this is shit. I'm sorry he's treating you like this."

"He's a cunt. I know he's your brother and all, but seriously, what a fucking arsehole," Sammy interjects.

"I never bought into fairytales and all that," I sigh. "But I thought I might end up with someone who at least likes me enough to want to spend time with me. All these experiences I thought I would have, I just won't get now... I've never even been sent flowers, you know?"

"No one ever bought you flowers? Is that important to you?" Giovanna's frowning, trying to understand.

"Never. I mean, the whole idea of giving flowers can be so romantic. Like 'here, I paid way too much money for these beautiful things which will die soon just because I think you're the bees fuckin' knees'. Just because."

"Just because," she echoes. "You deserve all that and so much more."

My frustration can't be contained and I put my head in my hands. "He's the fucking boss now, Gio. Why doesn't he just call it off? He has the power, right?"

When I look up I'm surprised to see what looks like guilt on her face. Elio is the Don now and yet he is the one yanking me along on a line while he dicks models and socialites. He must be a complete psychopath.

"It's Sandy and Paul, *cucciolotta*," she whispers. "They're still exerting a lot of pressure...I can't really say anything more." The guilt is definitely there.

"That's not really good enough though. You guys aren't kids. You're supposed to be in charge now." I shake my head, I'm really angry at Giovanna too. I want her to protect me from this shit, but the reality is that I'm nothing to her beyond a family friend and future sister-in-law.

The high-pitched laugh that has been irritating me for hours drags my attention back to Elio's beverage model. My tongue rolls in between my bottom teeth and my lip as I watch her climb onto his lap. She straddles him in the exact same spot on the sofa that I did when I first got back to Australia. She throws her head back laughing and shaking her ebony curls.

"Fucksake," I grumble. I've been so careful to remain composed, but seeing the pity on the faces of Elio's siblings, Sammy, and Bluey is too much.

Wearing just my bikini and Giovanna's oversized jumper, I stride around the pool toward the man I'm supposed to marry.

I hear an "Oh fuck" from Massimo and "Streuth!" from Bluey. This might not be dignified or composed, but at least it may let me retain a little bit of self-respect.

I'm already yanking the ring off my finger when Elio and I make eye contact. His hands are on the slim hips splayed across him and she keeps bouncing 'excitedly' in his lap. I consider grabbing her hand and ramming the ring on her finger, but this isn't about her. Tomorrow he'll balls deep in another woman.

When I come to a stop in front of the pair, I pause with my hands on my hips, and for a second I'm afraid I'm going to chicken out and scurry off. Instead, I take a deep breath and hold out the ring to him. The Vodka model looks over her shoulder at my outstretched hand and her eyes pop out of her head as she sees the size of the diamonds up close. *Keep dreaming, honey.*

"Can't do it anymore," I tell Elio, managing to take all the emotion out of my voice. "Have to salvage the tiny bit of self-respect I have left. If you have any say in where I get sent away to this time, I'd like to go back to London."

He slowly lifts his hand for me to drop the ring in his palm. "We'll talk about this later," he bites out coldly.

"Not a lot else to say, to be honest," I sniff.

His face is completely unreadable and for once he looks serious. The woman on his lap may as well not be there as he growls at me in a low voice, "You don't want to be making any more of a scene, Francesca." It's a cold warning.

"I have bit my tongue for months while you've performed, not a scene, but a whole fucking parade of whores. I will not marry someone who won't treat me with respect."

The Marino siblings and Bluey are all hovering nearby. They look like a bomb disposal unit moving in on a live UED. Conversations have halted all around us and I have definitely created a scene.

Elio rubs a hand over his super-short hair and sighs. "Go inside, Francesca. We will talk about our marriage later."

White hot rage surges through me at his dismissal and I can't help but hiss through my teeth "Go fuck yourself, Elio," before marching inside.

There's a gasp from the remaining partygoers at the disrespect I have just publicly shown to essentially the most powerful man in Sydney. A pit grows in my stomach as I wonder if he will decide to make an example of me. I keep moving, but half expect to be collared and dragged back in front of him.

I'm only just inside when Elio's voice booms out, laughing and deliberately loud enough for all to hear, "You think she's a firecracker here, you should see her in bed! Side effect of a young wife."

As everyone laughs I don't stick around to hear anymore. Even if I'm still humiliated and powerless, I feel better for standing up for myself. Everyone else might be laughing at the mafia brat throwing a tantrum about infidelity, but at least I can look myself in the eye now.

"Cheska!" Massimo calls, hurrying after me closely followed by Sammy. "Wait!"

I stop and allow them to catch up. "I hate him," I state sadly.

"Right now, so do I," he replies and throws an arm around my shoulders, the other around Sammy. "Wanna watch a movie?"

As the movie ends I stretch my arms above my head, yawning. "Massi? Can I sleep with you tonight? I don't want to deal with Elio."

"Of course, babe."

We walk through the living area to head upstairs. There are still about twelve people chilling outside, but I can't spot Elio. Ugh. I need to go get some PJs and my phone charger from his room. Fingers crossed he's asleep.

I pad down the carpeted hallway towards Elio's wing, steeling myself to give him the cold shoulder if he is awake. I will not talk to him tonight. Not even if he tries to apologise. Charming me will not work this time.

The lights are out throughout his wing and his bedroom door is closed. Tip-toeing through the dark lounge, my gut churns, and something feels off.

Quietly I turn the bedroom door handle in case he's sleeping, but as soon as I get it open a crack it is clear that is not the case. A small bedside light provides just enough light for me to see the RTD model riding Elio like a bucking rodeo bull, her dark curls cascading down her back.

Before I can get out of there, Elio raises his head and smirks at me. Noticing his straying attention, the model turns to look at me too, her expression says 'What are you doing here?'

"Elio," I grind through my teeth. "I literally sleep in that bed."

"I figured you'd sleep somewhere else tonight," he grunts.

"I hate you," I spit at him. "I fucking hate you."

Motherfucker. I want to scream and shout and rant and rave. Instead, again, I walk away. Except once I reach the door between the suite and the hallway, I'm running. It's like ropes are tightening around my chest as the panic sets in. There is no escape from the feeling of walls closing in on me. I know that it won't even take one year of marriage before my spirit is completely broken.

In search of relief, I contemplate throwing myself in the pool again, but I don't want to calm myself down; I want to express some of the rage and frustration that pulses at my temples. Tears are streaming down my face as I charge down the stairs to the living area. Sobs and hiccoughs rack my body.

I wish everyone would just go home. Having drunk strangers gawk at my distress is doubly embarrassing. Seeking refuge from their stares, I find myself running down the stairs that lead to the underground garage. My bare feet hit the cool concrete at the base of the stairs and goosebumps scatter up my legs. Wrapping Giovanna's big jumper closer around me, I wrench open the heavy door and let it thud shut behind me.

Cold, pitch-black darkness blankets me and I shiver as if a ghostly finger has run up my spine. I scramble around clawing the wall for a light switch and am relieved when bright lights burst from the ceiling, walls, and floors, to

illuminate a large collection of cars, motorbikes, scooters, jet skis, and even a segway.

I pace back and forth, weaving between the cars. My tears are drying, but the uncontrollable desire to break free from all the minute ways I am controlled and pushed and pulled only grows stronger.

Maybe I should try screaming. People do that to let out tension, don't they? I'm like 90% sure that the Marinos will have soundproofed this garage. I decide to give it a go, but what I intend to be a powerful roar comes out strangled and half-hearted.

I'm so fucking repressed. I want to be the girl who defies everyone. The challenger. But that has never been me. My survival has been about acquiescence and adapting. For once, I want to be the badass.

I could punch a wall? Except down here, the walls are concrete and that would be entirely self-harming. For the first time in my life, I feel a pull to violence, but I'm impotent to enact it.

I'm still pacing when I pass a tall bin full of sports equipment. Judging by the amount of sand clinging to the equipment it has been used at the beach. A shiny steel baseball bat catches my eye and, before I have time to think, I slide it up and out of the bin and slap it against my other palm. It is heavy; satisfyingly so, and my pulse begins to tap dance as my eyes lock in on Elio's car.

I don't pretend to know a thing about cars. I don't even drive. But I do know that Elio loves his car. It's a sports car, an Italian brand, and it is black-on-black-on-black.

Like a predator approaching prey, I prowl toward the sleek metal beast and my spine straightens at the power I'm about to unleash. A heady mix of adrenalin and empowerment mingle and I have the thought that this could be something I never come back from. What if I love destruction and just keep hitting and lashing out at the world until I'm put in a padded room?

My distorted reflection stares back at me from the driver's side window and I tap the baseball bat lightly on the bonnet. Not heavily enough to damage, but enough to create a percussion beat that serves as a lead-in to what I'm about to do.

My eyes flutter shut and I slowly inflate my lungs like balloons. One breath. Two. And three.

Today, I give myself permission to choose violence.

My first swing hits the sleek black wing mirror sending glass, metal, and plastic splintering and scattering. The second puts a dent in the bonnet the size of Elio's big arrogant head. When I take aim at the windscreen, my inhibitions finally vanish and I let rip with the kind of scream that belongs in a horror film. It is animalistic, raw, and delicious. The tendons in my neck pop out, sweat gathers at the base of my spine, and I scream some more.

Glass flies everywhere. It cuts my feet as I circle my metal prey, slamming the steel bat into its body over and over again. An alarm has been sounding since my first whack connected with the vehicular manifestation of Elio's ego, but I pay it no attention.

My arms ache with the reverberation that rebounds with each swing and hit. With all the adrenalin surging through my veins, I barely register the pain from the rebounding force, but tomorrow I will pay for it.

A movement to my right has me snapping my head around, bat held up ready to strike. Giovanna stands a few metres from the car with her hands up as if to indicate she isn't armed. Her mouth is moving and I think she is saying my name. I force myself to concentrate, to hear what she is saying.

"Francesca," her voice is low, calm, and reassuring. "Darlin', pass me the bat."

I stand, unmoving. Massimo appears in the internal doorway, followed by Matteo and Sammy.

"Elio has finally literally driven a woman crazy," Matty mutters and earns himself a scowl from his sister.

She is reaching out for me and the concern in her eyes throws cold water on my rage. My shoulders sag and I let the bat clatter to the ground. Her eyes don't leave mine, but she flinches when the tears begin to trickle down my face.

"Stay there, *bella*," she points to my bleeding feet and I suddenly begin registering the pain from walking around on broken glass. "I'll come get you."

The glass crunches under her Nike sneakers and she approaches me like I am a scared, abused animal she doesn't want to startle. She cautiously touches my shoulders and then sweeps an arm under my legs to pull me into a bridal carry. I let my head drop down onto her shoulder and begin to dread the moment she will put me back down.

Her scent surrounds me and I'm simultaneously comforted and aroused. I go to tuck my face into her neck but hesitate.

Massimo offers to carry me up the stairs but Giovanna just shakes her head and walks past him. She strides up the stairs like I weigh nothing and I want her to stride right past the kitchen and living area and carry me up to her room.

'Hey hey hey," Giovanna's voice is gentle and concerned as she peers down at my tear-streaked face. "What's happened?"

I cling to her, arms around her neck. Her hand cups the back of my head and now I throw caution to the wind and bury my face in the warm nook of her shoulder. The panic subsides a little as I inhale her scent.

"He's humiliated me again," I manage to get out, but the embarrassment makes it difficult to admit what happened. "He is fucking that model in our bed. His bed, I guess. But I'm supposed to sleep there."

"What?!" She wasn't expecting that, though really what else was it going to be about? "He's pushed this too fuckin' far," she says to Matty and Massimo.

She gently deposits me on a sofa in the lounge and instructs them to sort out my feet. Then she marches down the hall towards Elio's suite and I'm worried she might choose violence today as well.

CHAPTER TWENTY
GIOVANNA

"OUT! Now!" The words roar out of me with more explosiveness than I intend as I slam into Elio's room. His pale arse is bobbing in the air, one impossibly thin leg draped over his shoulder, as he pistons in and out of the simpering idiot he's had hanging off him all day.

"What the fuck?" he roars right back at me, looking over his shoulder to where I stand in the doorway with my hands on my hips. He's a fucking moron. A complete idiot. "You get out," he adds.

"Girl," I address the woman; she's a stranger to me. "Clothes on and out of my house now, thanks." She unfurls herself from Elio and sheepishly climbs off the bed.

"You can pull rank over a lot of things, Gio, but not over where I stick my dick," Elio spits at me as he tugs on a pair of sweatpants.

I grit my teeth. "Your inability to exercise control over your dick is what is causing problems!"

Dressed haphazardly, the young woman tentatively clears her throat. "Yeah, so I'm going to go now?" Her voice goes high at the end of the sentence and it sounds like a question.

"Elio," I bark. "Are you going to see your friend out?"

He looks like he's on the brink of throwing something at me. His anger swells and surrounds him like a mist, but he does as he is told, leading the woman out of his suite and into the hallway.

Incredulous that I'm having to do this to my 36-year-old brother, I follow the pair of them to ensure she leaves the property.

"Aren't you lucky you can go running to mummy? Pathetic!" Elio taunts Francesca as he stomps past her towards the back door.

Mummy? Haven't been called that before. A girl I was seeing a few years back used to call me 'daddy' in bed. Weirdly, I didn't mind that so much. It was kind of hot. I'm not sure 'mummy' has the same effect.

"Time to go!" Elio bellows at the stragglers from the party as he crosses the great open living space. "Now, thanks!" They scurry around collecting their belongings, hearing the fury in his voice. In a matter of minutes only Francesca, my brothers, Sammy, and I remain.

"What the fuck is wrong with you, you piece of shit?" Sammy rushes at him. Her fury would be more intimidating if she didn't have to tip her head right back to look up at him. "I hope you catch 17 STDs from your hoebags and your dick falls off!"

Massimo scoops Sammy up and drops her in an armchair from where she continues to call Elio an eclectic and impressive list of names.

"Francesca!" Elio shouts, glaring at her from a few metres away. "You want to fight your own battles, princess? Or are you leaving it to mummy and the fuckin' Kiwi chihuahua?"

I have never seen him like this. Sure he has always been an egotistical twat, but usually he is oblivious to or reckless with other people's feelings, not downright cruel. Either the marriage or the new role he has in the family seems to have tipped him over the edge. Probably both.

Francesca stares wildly from the sofa looking like a disheveled fucking angel. She's still wearing just the jumper I gave her over the top of her bathers. Her golden brown legs and feet are in the air as Matty plucks pieces of glass out of the soles of her feet with a pair of tweezers. Looking at her legs in the air gets me ridiculously wet and I quickly raise my gaze back to her face.

Her face is haunting. Those big doe eyes look so afraid and tired.

"I told you not to fall in love with me," Elio shoots at her, exasperated. *Arrogant son of a bitch.*

Fury has her innocent eyes narrowing at him. Her chin tilts a little in the air and her shoulders go back. Where she had been a nervous little girl a few seconds ago, now she looks fierce.

She slaps one of her thighs, laughing. Almost deranged, she is cackling like it is the funniest thing she's ever heard. "Love? You've got to be shitting me, right?" She sneers, "I don't love you! I'm embarrassed by you! I don't want to marry a man so pathetic he is ruled by his cock and incapable of treating me with respect."

He blanches and she continues. "I was willing to give things a go at the start because I've been so fucking conditioned to do as I'm told by this psychotic family." She sounds bitter and regretful. "But now? I wouldn't piss on you if you were on fire."

The corners of my mouth twitch and I want to smile. He's getting his arse handed to him and he couldn't deserve it more. Massimo and Matty are also smothering smiles and observing the scene with a mixture of shock and entertainment.

"When did I ever promise you monogamy? Huh? You are a mafia princess, for fucksake! You know how this works!"

"You could have exercised a little discretion, dickhead! And we never talked about it. You just assumed you could treat me like shit. But I grew up watching our dads too and I don't want it! I don't want that life!"

Elio turns away from her, his hands on his head, and paces. After an awkward silence, he stops and looks at her. "Well, you won't be carrying my dick around in your purse, princess. You will do as you're fucking told and not undermine me!" Then he stops suddenly looking at what Matty is doing. "How the fuck did you get glass in your feet?"

I expect her to look sheepish, but her stare is defiant and satisfied. "I needed to get the anger out of my system," she shrugs.

We watch the blood drain from his face. He looks around the room maniacally searching for the damage she has inflicted. "What did you do?" he growls.

"I smashed up your car with a baseball bat," she states calmly.

Elio chokes in shock and I get ready to restrain him. He is the least violent of the four of us, but fucking with his car is just about the worst thing you could do to him. "WHAT. THE. FUCK. YOU CRAZY FUCKING BITCH!"

Francesca's mouth opens to scream back at him, but I think this has gone far enough. I interject calmly, "Enough." When I see I have everyone's attention, I continue, "Elio you will be in my office at 10 am tomorrow. Massimo and Matteo, I need you to be there too."

The three of them nod obediently. "Massimo, please get Francesca what she needs out of Elio's room. Elio you wait here and calm down. I don't want to hear any more bullshit tonight."

Elio is already running down the stairs to the garage and his roars of fury can be heard through the open door as he takes in the state of his car.

Francesca eyes me curiously before smiling sweetly unleashing butterflies in my stomach. 'Thank you' she mouths to me and I give her a quick nod in response, but remain stoic, hiding the anarchy she creates in my nervous system.

CHAPTER TWENTY ONE

FRANCESCA

The house is modern, square with lots of glass. The lawn is precisely manicured and the hedges are so evenly pruned that it looks like a leveller has been used to make the tops perfectly flat.

The houses on either side are just as large and despite varying slightly in colour palette - greys, instead of beiges - are cut from the same design cloth as the Tetris block building in front of me.

I start up the path and note that there are no bikes or toys on the front lawn. It doesn't look like a home for a young family. There is no indication that two boisterous boys create carnage as they play and grow here.

It is, however, exactly the type of house I would picture my big brother living in. It is austere, clinical, a show home.

Doubt forces its way into my thoughts and I question what I am doing for the thousandth time since I left the house.

I didn't tell anyone where I was going. I told Massi that I was going to the gym and I'm not accustomed to lying to him. It doesn't feel good. No one even knows that Stefan and I have been in contact.

I suspect they would not be pleased if they were aware given the unspoken hostility I have seen creating thick tension whenever Stefan is in the same room as the Marino siblings.

That's their problem though. I'm entitled to have a relationship with my own brother and I want to get to know my nephews.

It would be nice to have family that isn't using me for whatever agenda they're pursuing. Something normal.

Sure, Stefan comes off as uptight, but since exchanging numbers at the engagement party, he has been the only person checking in and asking me how I am. He seems to care about me. He's certainly the only one who questions whether this arranged marriage is the best thing for me.

Before I have even reached out to press the doorbell, the large, heavy door is flung open and two little boys launch themselves at me.

"Auntie Francesca!" the older one exclaims, wrapping his arms tight around my middle. "We're so excited to meet you!"

Behind them, Stefan appears with a small smile on his face. He looks strange out of a suit. Barefoot and in jeans and a white t-shirt, he doesn't look quite right. He is a man that doesn't suit casual and never looks relaxed.

"Sorry about these two rascals. They've been beside themselves with excitement all morning," he chuckles.

I brush the hair out of the little one's eyes and smile down at them both. "Best greeting ever!" I exclaim. The joy in their little faces warms me and I blink back tears.

"I'm Alex and I'm nearly seven," the oldest boy announces proudly, his grin revealing a missing front tooth.

"Hello, Alex! I guess you know I'm your Auntie Francesca. And, you must be Toby then! How old are you?"

Shyly, the youngest Rossi looks up at me and whispers, "Four." He holds up three fingers and Alex rolls his eyes before gently pulling one more of his brother's fingers up.

I follow my brother and his two children into the house and I'm struck again by how unsuited it seems to be for a family with children. *Where is the chaos? The toys?*

In the kitchen, Stefan introduces me to his wife Allegra. She is just as severe as he is. Uptight and cold, though she attempts warmth. Looking at the pair of them, I am not sure how they produced two such excitable young boys.

We kiss each other on each cheek and Allegra says, "It is so nice to have you here, Francesca. So nice for Stefan to have a family member who isn't just

out to use him. It is so sad that your father has so little care for his children." Her voice is fluttery, and soft, and sounds far too young for her.

"Allegra," Stefan softly reprimands her. His face says, 'Be quiet' and there is something awkward about their interaction.

"No, no, Stefan, it's fine. I get it. I feel the same," I smile reassuringly and they all smile back at me.

We have coffee and nibble on a selection of baked sweets Allegra has made. The boys are remarkably well-behaved for kids so young. They sit sipping frothed milk and listen to their parents asking me questions about my time in Britain. They're bored, I can tell. But they know better than to express it.

We walked through a sparse hallway and into even sparser rooms to reach the living room and I hadn't seen a single thing that would hold the interest of a four-year-old or a six-year-old.

Everything in the house is hard with sharp ninety-degree angles. Blocks of cold murky colours are cast against concrete and dark slate. It is impressive and expensive but belongs on the pages of some painfully obnoxious design magazine rather than housing a young family.

"So you've been back in Sydney for two years?" I ask when I finally spot a break in the conversation.

Stefan clears his throat and places his hand over Allegra's where it rests on the polished concrete dining table. "Yeah, god time flies doesn't it, *cara*? Can't believe it has been two years."

Allegra nods dutifully.

"So you're here for good?" I don't know why they would want to be. The Marinos don't like him and they run the scene here. And, if he wanted to patch things up with Dad...he hasn't made much progress in the past two years.

"We're playing things by ear," Stefan answers cryptically.

"What about your Dad, Allegra? You're not needed in Melbourne?"

Stefan subtly squeezes Allegra's hand and her childlike voice speaks. "Oh no, Dad has my brother. We wanted to...you know...give the boys a chance to see the other side of their family..."

"The truth is," Stefan interrupts. "That is only part of the reason we moved. You are the other part."

"Me?" This makes no sense whatsoever. "I was in England two years ago though?"

"Yes, but I got wind that Dad was going to marry you off and well, I couldn't stand by. I failed you though, Francesca. Here we are two years later and you are engaged to that prick Elio." He throws his hands in the air in exasperation.

Two years ago. Dad was planning to arrange a marriage for me two years ago. I was engaged to Gareth the posh Englishman two years ago! What was he going to do about that? Just get rid of him?

But, I did get rid of him. After Massimo showed up and talked some sense into me.

After Massimo turned up and talked some sense into me.

No. Massimo would have told me if he had been sent by his father or mine. We tell each other everything. Don't we?

"Francesca?" Stefan is leaning forwards, concern etched on his pinched face. "I'm so sorry for failing you, *tesorina*. But I won't give up."

His dark, almost black eyes meet mine, but I don't find reassurance in them. If anything, I feel trapped, and claustrophobic. Smothered.

"Thank you so much for coffee," I say and in my rush to stand bang my hip on the stupid Flinstone's table that probably cost $50,000. "Excuse me, but I just remembered - I have to go. It was so lovely to meet you Allegra and you boys. Please let's catch up again soon?"

Without waiting for an answer I rush out of the house, Stefan calling after me.

CHAPTER TWENTY TWO
GIOVANNA

"Knock knock", Matty says as he hovers in the doorway to my office.

"Come in," I say wearily. I've been working for about two hours already and it's 9.45 am on a Sunday. Shortly I will have to deal with the unnecessary bullshit Elio has caused while everyone goes around treating him like he's the Marino Don. Life feels a little unfair right now.

I motion for Matty to close the door and take a seat. "Matty," I whinge his name like a plea. A plea for what, I'm not sure. Guidance? Support? Solidarity? I wouldn't speak to anyone else like this, but as we've gotten older my second brother has become my best mate. "What do I do?"

Matty and I are so alike and so very different from our brothers. We get each other and don't need to create noise to be heard. Like me, Matty is dedicated to the family and our businesses. When Elio is at Peacocks or doing lines off a stripper's arse on a yacht in Sydney Harbour, the pair of us don't stop hustling. We also have the stomach for violence that Elio seems to lack.

Matty grimaces showing he appreciates how difficult the situation is. "Fear and humiliation? Either that or chop off his cock and don't let him leave the house." He jokes, but there is some truth to it. Usually, violence or degradation are the two key tools for punishment in our world. Punishment and control.

"Francesca's method of revenge was pretty effective last night," I remark grimly. Effective and fucking hot. Seeing her undone like that was kind of earth-shattering. If she hadn't been so upset, her wild eyes and uncontrolled screams might have had me bending her over the crushed bonnet of Elio's car.

Matty cracks a rare unabashed smile as he remembers the scene we rushed to last night after the alarms started going off in the garage. "It was beautiful. Just need a soundtrack and some slo-mo."

My stomach clenches at his use of the word beautiful even though I know very well that he was referring to the destruction she wrought rather than the woman herself. *Why the fuck am I jealous anyway?* Our other brother is going to marry her for fucksake.

"The way she just matter of fact told him she smashed up his car with her legs in the air…" I shake my head with a small smile.

"You just like that she had her legs in the air," he winks and I run a hand over my face.

"Don't beat yourself up, G," he continues. "She looks at you like you're the only thing in the world that matters. Like she would die for you or be on her knees for you in a second. I'm impressed by how restrained you're being, to be honest."

That might be the most I have heard him say in one go since he got out of prison a couple of years ago. I was there to pick him up, the solid, harder-looking man who replaced my formerly lean and laid-back brother.

The real difference was in his eyes though. As I took his cheeks in my palms and searched his face for the pain I knew would be there, I suddenly saw what people mean when they describe someone's eyes as "haunted".

Matty had quickly risen through the prisoner ranks, his reputation as the son of the Don of Sydney bolstering his credentials. It wasn't long before he had the run of the place, but ruling free criminals is one thing, ruling criminals in captivity is another.

Violence is the only true currency and the only true tool to maintain or challenge social order behind bars. Matty lived with the very real constant threat of murder by shanking or the fists of a rival for four years. He slept little and lightly, afraid to be vulnerable to attack. Not that he ever could afford to show so much as a sliver of fear.

It wasn't until we sat together in the backseat of one of our SUVs, shielded by blacked-out windows, that his face crumpled. The ruthless mafia prince who scowled at everyone as he strode out of the prison in a sharp suit we had

delivered in advance disappeared to reveal a broken man and the true pain and exhaustion he felt.

Elio drove us silently home while I held Matty's head to my shoulder and rocked him while he cried. We didn't talk. Matty cried, I held him, and Elio drove around Sydney in circles until we were all ready to put our mafia masks back on and face our father.

Free for the past two years, Matty is no longer broken, but he isn't the same man he was. The most violent of my brothers, he is also the one I'm most protective of.

He regards me with gentle affection as he drops his truth bombs on me, but I shake my head with sad resignation.

"Yeah well, there's no sense in me creating some Romeo and Juliet bullshit situation. What's the point in torturing us both," my glumness isn't new, but expressing it is.

Massi arrives right at 10 o'clock with a grin on his face. "I can't stop smiling every time I think about the moment Elio realised Ches had gone feral."

"How is slugger this morning? She okay?" I ask.

He shrugs. "Fed up, but okay. Surprisingly she has no regrets. She's gone to the gym."

Even though I want to ask more, I don't. I don't want to seem too interested in Francesca. Talking candidly with Matty is one thing, but Massimo doesn't have the same levels of discretion, especially when it comes to Francesca.

"Call him," I instruct Matty when Elio still hasn't arrived at 10.15. *Fucksake.*

"Bro, where the fuck are you?" Matty growls into the phone.

"Yeah, well hurry up."

I raise my eyebrows in question.

"Still in bed," Matty mutters.

"Jesus Christ! He has three minutes or you two are going to physically bring him to me."

By the time he strolls in a few minutes later in sweatpants and a t-shirt, my blood pressure is through the roof and I'm ready to go off.

He shuts the door and goes to sit down. "No. Stand," I command him and he balks but obeys.

"You're going to shut the fuck up and listen," I tell him in a low, calm voice. "You might get to play pretend King out there, but at the end of the day, you answer to me. You are playing a role, nothing more. When I tell you to do something, you fuckin' do it. When I tell you to cut the shit and act your age, what do you do?"

He pauses, resisting for a few seconds, and then grinds out, "Cut the shit and act my age."

"Yes. You do. This tantrum you've been having about marrying Francesca ends now. Would I have cut this deal with Rossi? No. Arranged marriages aren't my thing. But Dad set this up before he retired and he will be a fuckin' nightmare for all of us if we don't follow through. If you have another suitable woman you want to marry, hurry up and speak up, now. If not, count your lucky stars that you haven't been set up with a howler."

He is looking at the ground and I'm relieved to see a sheepishness creeping into his posture. I'm getting through to him, I think.

"Look at me!" I bark. His eyes meet mine and interestingly the animosity in them seems to be waning too. Strangely, I think I see relief settling in the dark brown eyes that look so much like my own. "Treat her with respect. The pair of you need to figure out what kind of relationship you'll have, but the public displays of disregard for her feelings stop. Your dickhead behaviour has created the issues. I seriously do not want to have to talk to you about this again. We have much more serious shit going down that we need to be focused on. Understand?"

"Yes, boss," he answers immediately, looking far more settled than he did when he first entered the room full of faux-bravado and very real resentment.

"When you leave this house, or when you have guests here, you are on display as the Don. We cannot afford for word to get out that we are weak because our Don is too busy indulging in piss and pussy to do his fuckin' job. You need to act the part. The men need to have confidence in you and respect you. Otherwise, we are fucked, Elio. Do you care if we are fucked?"

He nods. "Of course, I care."

"Then brother, for the love of God, fuckin' start acting like it."

Elio takes a deep breath and speaks to all of us. "I'm sorry. This isn't the life I wanted, but I know I'm not the only one who feels like that. I'll straighten

up my act. I just don't know how I'm going to get Francesca to stop hating me though..."

I snort. "Well, I've got her scheming traitorous brother to worry about. You're going to have to figure out the mafia princess all on your own."

CHAPTER TWENTY THREE
GIOVANNA

32 Years Old

The bitter taste of vomit lingers in my mouth and thumping rage has my heart leaping out of my chest as I take the stairs two at a time.

There's a loud crack as the door flies open with so much force it collides with the wall. I linger in the doorway for a moment sucking in a few deep breaths to bring my fury down to a level where it can be harnessed rather than unleashed.

Dad looks up from his desk impassively, but Paul and David Rossi just about jump out of their seats.

In two strides I'm in front of the monster with my fist closing around his collar as I yank him up out of his chair. His head connects with the wall with a dull thud and I shove my forearm into his throat.

"What are you doing?!" exclaims Paul. He hasn't left his seat to assist his brother, he just sits waving his arms as if that will help. "Sandy, what is she doing?"

Dad sighs. "Giovanna?"

"TWO YEARS AGO!" I explode. "This sick fuck fucking t-touched - fucking *assaulted* - Francesca and is somehow still breathing two years later!"

"Ah, yes," Dad takes his reading glasses off and drops them on his desk.

Paul splutters and finally stands, reluctantly moving towards me before lunging for the arm I have on his brother's throat.

Without removing the arm, I swing my other fist around and clock Paul across the face. There is a sickening crunch as his nose breaks and blood pours

from his nostrils. Deep claret descends like a splitting river down his chin to drip all over his crisp white shirt. He staggers back into his chair.

"Fuckin' bitch!" He splutters, trying to catch his own blood in his hands. "Mate? You really not gonna stop this?" He looks at my father aghast.

Landing a couple of solid hits to David's head and ribs, I glance over to Dad. He's sitting back in his chair watching and raises a hand to silence Paul. His face is expressionless, but a slight, barely perceptible nod tells me that I have his permission to kick the shit out of this utter scum.

David's face reddens, his body screaming for oxygen as I force my forearm hard against his windpipe. "You deserve to die, you piece of shit. Your mates are too piss-weak to put a bullet between your eyes, but I'm not," I growl, my face just centimetres from his.

"Sandy, mate! She's mad as a cut snake!" Paul appeals again.

"You make me sick!" I shoot over my shoulder at him. "She's your daughter, Rossi! You're seriously defending this piece of shit after what he did?"

He goes silent, dabbing at his nose with his sleeve.

My fist connects with David's abdomen once, twice, three times. He tries to double over, but I still have him pinned to the wall. He gurgles, trying to speak and his hands claw at my arm, leaving bright red gouges up my forearm.

"Shut the fuck up, David. Take the fucking beating," Dad's voice is cold. "The girl was sent away. You've had it easy. Just take your medicine."

My head explodes. His medicine? This is hardly enough of a punishment. We don't involve the police in our business, obviously, so Francesca will get no justice from the system. But if I was in Dad's seat, our justice would have David wishing he had the police to deal with instead. He deserves to suffer a painful death after his genitals have been separated from his body. Cinder Block round the ankles and into the harbour.

Our world is run by men and I've transcended a lot of the bullshit despite my sex, but the old boys will protect each other to the bitter end. No consequences when you're at the top of the mafia tree. That's why I'm here to dole out my own justice.

Raining punch after punch down on David's paunchy body, I don't ease up until he is struggling to stand. Withdrawing the pressure on his neck, I stand

back and allow him to slide down the wall to collapse on the carpet. His breathing is laboured, but he has suffered no major damage. Unfortunately.

Pulling a small hammer out of my jacket pocket, I kneel next to him. "Spread them!" I shout in his face, tapping his hand with the head of the hammer. David whimpers and slowly splays his fingers on the small wooden side table next to him.

"You. Will. Not. Be. Able. To. Wipe your arse. Or pick your nose. Or touch things you aren't fucking supposed to. As each of these fingers slowly heals, I want you to remember that if you touch another girl, I will chop your hands off."

One by one I slam the hammer into every single one of his knuckles, shattering the bones. He wails, snot and tears running down his face and I have never hated someone so much in my life. Revolting.

I tuck the hammer away and produce an ultra-sharp hunting knife from another pocket. David begins to whimper and tries to drag himself away. A pool of urine accumulates on the carpet between his legs and I sneer at him, "You'll clean your piss off Dad's carpet, mangled fingers or not."

I bring the knife down swiftly and slice through the buttons on the monster's dress shirt like butter, exposing his bare chest. I crouch next to him attempting to avoid the yellow puddle.

"Ppppplease," he stutters through swollen lips.

"Get fucked. You don't deserve my mercy." The tip of the knife pierces through the skin in the centre of his chest. Dragging the knife slowly down the centre of his torso to the top of his belly button I split him open just enough to scar. Back at the top of the cut I slice a curve out towards his nipple and leave him with a giant bleeding 'P' that will scar and be with him forever. Let him explain what it stands for. Paedophile or predator works for me.

Standing, I send my boot into his side a handful more times before spitting on the cowering bleeding mess.

"I will kill you. I promise you that David. One day Dad won't be here to protect you and I will finish this. Time won't make me forgive you and I won't fuckin' forget either. You are on borrowed time." With one last kick, I storm out of the office glaring at the pathetic men who have enabled and protected a predator.

CHAPTER TWENTY FOUR

FRANCESCA

Despite knowing I am jumping to conclusions and that I should give Massimo the benefit of the doubt, my Uber ride back to the Marino house could have been powered by my rage alone.

The kind of fury that only last night saw me destroy a luxury vehicle worth hundreds of thousands of dollars.

The percolating bile that poisons me from the inside is foreign to me. I've done sad. Boy, have I done sad. The kind of depression that settles on you like a damp blanket of misery weighing down your limbs and dousing you in lethargy. But anger has always been a secondary emotion of little potency for me. Probably smothered by depressed apathy so that it manifests only bouts of frustration that giveaway to self-pity and sorrow.

Somewhere over the ocean on my Air New Zealand flight to Sydney, something shifted in me. Or maybe it was the moment I found out my future had already been packaged up and traded to a man incapable of chivalry and common decency.

I don't know.

I just know that I am not the Francesca who dragged her feet into Heathrow, unwilling to return to Australia but putting up little fight.

And now, if I am to find out that the one person I trust in this world has been involved in the whole sorry affair, that might just be the final crack in the veneer. My heart will break and my faith that this world holds anything decent for me will seep out.

The sounds of laughter and music can be heard the minute I step onto the staircase from the underground garage at the Marino House.

Another party? Christ. If I have to see another influencer humping Elio's leg I'll get the itch to take the baseball bat out for another swing.

I'm not exactly dressed for a party either. I wore gym gear to Stefan's house to support the alibi I gave Massimo. Leggings, sports bra, and trainers. All in black.

"Tiny, you shit cunt!" I hear Bluey's booming voice as I enter the kitchen and grab sparkling water from the fridge.

Relief takes the tension out of my shoulders when I look out into the back garden to see that despite the raucous noise there are only a handful of Marino soldiers lounging in the sun, drinking beers.

Massimo is in the centre of the outdoor sofa looking up at Bluey who is poised to leap off a bar leaner into the pool.

He is pointing at Tiny, Fat Tony's son, and shouting, "How can you even have a stag-do without strippers?"

Tiny is getting married soon. His bride-to-be is a cousin of the Marinos, Sarah. Cute couple and it sounds like Tiny knows what side his bread is buttered on if he is declining strippers. Good. These men could do with spending time with men who respect the women in their lives.

"Well, I'm not bothered if we don't do strippers," Massimo shrugs with a smirk.

"Not helping, Massi. Be an ally to straight blokes!" Bluey flips off the high table dodging the empty plastic water bottle Massi throws at his head.

I haven't seen this 'lad' version of Massimo. It was just us and whoever we partied with when we were in London.

Seeing him hanging out with the guys and engaging in all the masculine banter gives me a knot in my stomach. Insecurities make their way to the surface and panic claws at my airways.

If this is his scene, hanging out with me must be a total drag.

The thought occurs to me that I might be feeling like this because I am already feeling paranoid about what he has known about my arranged marriage. I don't have much room for reason and logic right now though.

"Hey Cheska," Bluey calls out from the pool and the other guys call out hellos as well.

"Massimo, can I speak with you please?" I ask him after a half-hearted wave to the others.

"Sure, what's up?" he smiles.

"Like, privately...please?"

His smile disappears and his brow creases. Standing and draining the last of the beer in his bottle, he nods and follows me into the house.

I lead him over to the window seat in the far corner, diagonally as far from the back garden as possible. He sits and looks confused when I put enough space between us to prevent any touching.

We don't do personal space. Not with each other.

"Ches, what's going on?" he can't hide the real concern in his voice.

Taking a big breath, I just blurt it out. "When did you know we were going to leave London? A-and that I was going to be...married off?"

Resignation dawns on his face and I know in a split second that Stefan was right. Maybe he is just looking out for me. Being a big brother. Better late than never, I guess.

"Look, Ches -"

"I don't want to hear any bullshit, Massimo. I'm already ODing from your brother."

"I knew we were going to get brought home," he drops his head. "But there was no point trying to fight it so I didn't want to ruin our time by worrying you..."

"That wasn't your call to make. We could have made a plan or something. We could have hidden!" We could be living in a quiet Spanish village right now. Or somewhere in the Swiss Alps. We had the time and means to avoid this clusterfuck, but we didn't because we aren't on the same side like I thought we were.

Massi furiously runs a hand through his golden brown locks in a gesture that is infuriatingly like the one his eldest brother makes regularly. "You don't think our families don't have the ability to track us down? Come on, Francesca!"

"We - We had money and we've made friends all over Europe..."

He looks at me with a mixture of pity and disdain at my naivety. "That money would be turned off like a tap and they know every single place we've visited every single contact…"

"You were reporting back this whole time?" It is meant to be a statement, but it comes out more as a question. Or was it vice versa. I don't know. The bottom is falling out of my world and I am in agony.

Massimo nods sadly, eyes cast down and my hand itches to reach out and slap him across the face.

"Why were you in London?" my voice is dead, and my heart is already breaking.

"To be with you," he answers.

"Because your Dad sent you?"

Silence.

"To get me to break up with Gareth?" I guess.

"That was part of it," he mumbles before looking up and exclaiming, "but he wasn't right for you, Ches! I would've told you not to marry him anyway!"

"You mean like Elio is so right for me now?" I hiss at him and the poison that is coursing through my veins toxifying every good memory I have of my best friend pours into my words.

He is silent, once again. Guilt is woven through every feature of his face and I can tell his heart is breaking too. But he did this to us. He broke us. He betrayed me and ripped my soul out through my throat.

"Fuck you, Massimo," I whisper.

Numb and barely registering the tears pouring down my face, the sobs heaving in my chest, I get up and walk away.

CHAPTER TWENTY FIVE
SANDY

Two and a Half Years Ago

"Can someone tell me why I have been *summoned* to this meeting?" Irritation masks an uncharacteristic thread of anxiety that I am carefully avoiding pulling. "Last time I looked I give the orders and you lot obey them."

Eight Italian faces, the youngest in his forties, stare back at me from around the table. All dressed in expensive suits and with roughly the same haircut, the only real differences between one man and the next are age and the degree to which indulgence has taken a toll on their body.

My thread of anxiety would be more like a thick corded rope if not for the fact that the meeting is being held upstairs at the restaurant I own, *La Fazenda*, and I am sitting in my usual chair. The boss' chair.

The private room above the restaurant is small and with so many of us crammed in the air is stifling. Trickles of sweat are running down the temples, necks, and backs of every man present.

Physical discomfort doesn't appear to be the only kind of stress being experienced by those around the table either. Tension as thick as humidity right before the rain breaks blankets the room.

I seriously hope these fuckers aren't about to do something stupid.

Some of them have gone soft in the years of relative peace we have had since I smacked back Alberto Romano twenty or so years ago. They have

forgotten that power and peace must be actively defended. To take either for granted is often a fatal error.

"I haven't got all fuckin' day," I bark when no one responds to me. "One of you spit it out."

To my surprise, it is my oldest friend, Paul Rossi, who speaks up after clearing his throat and glancing around at the others. "Boss, the capos asked to meet with you today because they want to discuss your succession plan," he begins.

"You've made it clear that Elio will take over when you retire...but the capos have come to me with some concerns about Elio's...apparent disinterest in the family business and a keen interest in partying."

Rage is my knee-jerk reaction. My succession plan is entirely up to me. I could hand over to Crocodile fuckin' Dundee if I wanted to.

It is also unsettling to know that my men, supposedly loyal men who would die for me, are thinking so deeply about the world without me in it.

The problem is Paul isn't wrong. Elio is probably the least suited of any of my children to lead the *Famiglia*. Giovanna is the most capable but is female. Matteo is soon to be released from prison after a four-year stint and Massimo is only 21 years old.

That leaves my oldest, least bloodthirsty son. He thinks I don't know he avoids the more violent aspects of our work, but I know Giovanna and Matteo have covered for him ever since they were knee-high to grasshoppers.

But there is no fucking chance whatsoever that I will be succeeded by anyone other than one of my children. Ya fuckin' dreamin'.

"Been discussing my demise, have you? Will I be retiring soon? Do share your insights..." I growl at the room.

"Come on mate. You and me, we're turning 68 this year. The guys just want to be sure there is an ironclad plan for what happens when we no longer have you to lead the *Famiglia*," Paul sweet-talks me, soothing me and my gripes as he has done for more than half a century.

"Elio will take over from me. It is my job - and yours - to ensure that he is ready and capable when the time comes," I'm not telling them anything new and I get the feeling they have a lot more to say on the matter.

"Boss, if I may," Baz Rossi speaks up. "Elio will have all the support he needs. But we need to make sure we have some… measures in place that ensure that we are able to provide…guidance when he needs it. And, I'm sure you appreciate that we need to protect our interests too."

Baz is Paul and David's first cousin. As is the man to his right, Joseph Rossi. And, across the table from them, Champ Brown is also their cousin through his mother's side of the family. There was a real influx of Rossis when I took over the *Famiglia.* Paul became my consigliere and then it seemed every relative he had back in Italy wanted to move to Sydney.

The Rossi guys have always been loyal soldiers and capos, but with so many men from one family sitting around the table, I have always been aware of the power bloc they could form. A niggly feeling in my gut tells me now could be the time that they use their numbers advantage.

"I'll just lay it all out, shall I?" Paul speaks confidently to the room and why shouldn't he be confident? He has been my closest advisor my entire life and he is a Rossi. "We are all loyal soldiers to the Marino *Famiglia,* however, we have a suggestion as to how we could ensure that we are even more tightly bound to the future of the *Famiglia…*" He pauses for effect and to take a deep breath. "Five of us here are from the Rossi family and if Elio were to marry a Rossi it would bind our families together and his heirs would be Rossis too."

My eyebrows shoot towards my hairline. An interesting suggestion and one that I think I can quickly get on board with. I couldn't give a monkey's who Elio marries so long as she behaves as a boss' wife should.

It makes a lot of sense to provide an extra reason for the Capos to be loyal to Elio when they don't have the highest opinion of him.

"Of course, the other alternative…" Baz pauses and licks his lips nervously. "…would be to bring in a Rossi instead of Elio. Stefan Rossi could unite Sydney and Melbourne…"

Heat rises from my chest and up my face. "Are you threatening me with a takeover, Rossi?" I ask him as I press my palms into the table and stand, looming over the table.

"No, no!" Paul jumps in. "Why anyone would want my son in charge of anything I don't know. He couldn't punch his way out of a wet paper bag. No, our best option is to marry Elio to a Rossi."

Still bristling, I give Baz a stare imbued with so much scorching aggression it is a wonder his Brylcreemed hair doesn't catch fire. "Don't," I point a finger at him. "...you *ever* threaten me again."

The room is quiet for a moment and Baz stumbles over an apology.

"Which Rossi do you suggest my boy should marry?" I direct my question at Paul.

He grins and I know what his answer will be before he has even said it. "Francesca."

CHAPTER TWENTY SIX
FRANCESCA

"Someone sent you flowers!" Sammy punches me in the upper arm and circles me bouncing in a fighter's stance.

My fist shoots out and I'm sure it will connect with her shoulder, but she easily deflects it.

Dropping the goofy grin, she resets my arms in the correct stance and kicks my feet further apart. "When are you going to let me turn you into a fighter?" she asks again. "Look you've even got the *Million Dollar Baby* double-braid going on today!"

Sammy is waiting for a client, she trains athletes, mostly fighters, but also works with a women's rugby league programme. She is the fittest person I know, loves running, and plays all sorts of different sports just for fun. Lean, but solid, she has an arse on her that leaves men and women drooling in her wake.

"Sammy, whatever gave you the impression that I want to be a fighter?" I try to tickle her instead, but her quick reflexes deflect my hands again.

"All women should know how to fight," she says simply.

"Yeah self defence, I guess. But I prefer to wage my wars with words," I wink at her.

"Oh yeah sure, definitely looked like it when you were taking a steel baseball bat to your fiance's Ferrari," her sarcasm extends from her voice to her facial expressions.

As we approach the front desk I spot the hugest bouquet of flowers I've ever seen. They're a gorgeous bunch; full of peonies, roses, and lavender. All

pink, white, purple, and green. My first thought is that they are from Massimo, an apology gesture. My second thought is that someone has ordered flowers on behalf of Elio and constructed an apology gesture for him. He definitely won't have come up with the idea all on his own.

I'm wrong on both counts.

"They must have cost $500 at least," Sam speculates next to me.

"Is there a card?" I ask and Sammy digs one out of the side of the bouquet.

The cream card with a gold embossed daisy on the front contains a message of two words and a signature of a single letter.

Just because,
G

Despite the emotional turmoil of the past couple of weeks, I find myself biting my lip and allowing the little warmth in my chest to spread into a wide smile.

I am still furious with her and the rest of her siblings. Especially Massimo. But she listened when I said no one had ever bought me flowers before and maybe I'm just so attention and affection-starved that this is all it takes to chip away at my fury.

Just because. Giovanna Marino thinks about me! I pull out my phone and snap a photo of the flowers and send it to Giovanna:

Me: Thank you. Very sweet x

I remind myself that this is just a brief intermission and that normal programming of righteous anger will resume shortly. There should be no one left in the Marino and Rossi families that I trust. But, it's hard to be angry at her. Her life has been dictated to and controlled by her father too in many ways.

Plus, all my energy is going into being mad at Massimo. It has been two weeks since I spoke to him. By far the longest we have ever gone without talking.

He has left messages, texts, and emails. He has knocked on the spare bedroom that is currently mine and begged to talk. Giovanna, Matty, and even

Elio have tried to intercede on his behalf, but the pressure on my chest, and the lump in my throat, remind me that the hurt he has caused me is still raw.

I tuck my phone away so I'm not tempted to keep sending Giovanna messages, confess feelings I shouldn't, or beg her to intervene and cancel my wedding.

But I'm still smiling to myself as I do my rounds, tiding away weights and wiping down equipment. I bite my lip thinking about her going online to order me flowers or maybe she called up and ordered over the phone. Either way, she was thinking about me and wanted to make me feel happy.

Distracted by my burgeoning fantasies of a future with my soon-to-be sister-in-law, I don't notice the three men dressed in jeans and patched leather jackets as they approach me. They're not talking to each other and their movements are preplanned. Organised.

It's quiet, mid-afternoon. Too late for the yummy mummies and too early for the after-school and uni crowd. Sammy has disappeared into one of the studios to train a client and looking bored and unamused, our receptionist is on the phone.

I squat down to lift a twenty-eight-kilogram dumbbell that some arsehole has left in the middle of the gym floor. They clearly missed the sign that says *'If you're big enough to pick it up, you're big enough to put it away'.*

Heaving the weight into the nook of my forearms, I carry it over to the rack and awkwardly manoeuvre the weight trying to line it up so I can slot it into its rightful place. Suddenly, a large hand covered in tattoos reaches from behind me, grabs the weight, picking it up with ease.

Unaware that anyone was behind me, the intrusion gives me a fright and I jump away from the man as he puts the weight back on the rack for me.

"Um thanks," I mumble and turn to walk away quickly so he won't have the opportunity to strike up a conversation with me.

"No problem, princess." Princess, again? What is it with everyone calling me that lately? Is this just his way of coming on to me? Because even if I was interested, calling me that would have turned me off.

The way he said it felt like he was using it as a title though, rather than a term of endearment.

Reluctantly, I lift my gaze to his face, and the smile I find there frightens me. It is lecherous and threatening despite his young, handsome features. I'm all of a sudden very aware of my size disadvantage and regretting my complacency about self-defence not fifteen minutes ago.

I'm only just taking in his large presence and the fact that he is not dressed for the gym when two men in similar patched leather jackets appear on either side of us. My heart rate picks up and I know instinctively that these men know exactly who I am. They aren't surrounding me by accident.

They know who I am to the *Famiglia.*

Pushing my shoulders back and I look down my nose at the intimidating trio. "Can I help you, gentlemen? Considering a membership?"

My efforts to play it cool are unlikely to be successful if my pulse doesn't slow the fuck down ASAP, but I will fake confidence and calm even if I don't feel it.

"We were just in the neighbourhood and thought we'd come to say hi," the guy who helped me with the weight says.

He seems to be the leader. He's bigger and appears slightly older, maybe mid-twenties, and his buddies look to him for direction.

He isn't Italian, or if he is, whatever other heritage he has is dominating his genes. Dark blonde hair is pulled up roughly into a bun at the back of his head. It looks wind-swept and scruffy, not at all like the hipster man-buns you see behind the bars of every trendy bar.

If I wasn't so instinctively terrified by the man, his deep blue eyes would be enchanting. The depth of colour in them is almost unreal. His strong, straight nose and square jaw provide a masculine contrast to the beauty of those deep ocean-blue irises.

"Say hi to who?" I furrow my brow and look around.

"You, of course, princess," the shorter of the three men answers. His hair is long, lank, and greasy and I bite back the urge to snidely recommend him my favourite brand of dry shampoo.

Stepping back, I inject all the steel into my voice I can muster and say, "You must have me confused with someone else. I don't know you." I turn sharply to get out of there, but I'm sandwiched between the squat racks and the three patched bikers.

"No, we know exactly who you are, *Francesca*," the leader is taking pleasure in frightening me. He drags my name out like he's tasting each syllable and looks me up and down as if I'm next on the menu.

"Check out the rig on her, Billy," the short guy whistles and leers at my body. "You sure we can't take her with us?"

Billy. His question was directed at his blonde leader.

"What do you want?" I snap.

The three of them are crowding me. Getting closer and closer. The way they prowl around me is like a group of hyenas circling a carcass. There's nowhere for me to retreat to and the few people around aren't paying us attention.

"Tsk, I told you. We are here to say hi," His mouth curls into an even wider grin revealing perfectly straight white teeth. *Who knew bikers went to orthodontists...*

"Well, you've said hi. I'd like to get back to my work now, thanks," I try to push past them, but a set of large tattooed hands shoot out and grab me by my pitifully under-developed upper arms.

"Ouch," I cry out as the grip pinches me. I'll have fingertip-shaped bruises there tomorrow. Fingertips the size of bloody apricots.

"Actually, we were wanting to talk to you about Elio Marino." The biker doesn't let go of me, but he does loosen his grip a bit.

"I'm not his secretary," I retort. The men chuckle, sharing dark, amused looks over my head.

A hand belonging to the guy with the greasy hair quickly wraps around my neck so my chin rests between his hairy thumb and forefinger. The fingers squeeze slowly, increasing pressure and I attempt to push down the growing panic. But the terrible emptiness in my chest swells and the blood rushes to my head. I begin to feel lightheaded and my vision blurs as I scratch desperately at the hand squeezing the life out of me, drawing blood.

At least I will have his DNA under my fingernails if they kill me. The dark thoughts provide cold comfort.

If they ever find my body.

How is no one seeing this? I want to scream for help, but I'm just gasping and gulping like a fish out of water. *This would be such a shit way to die.*

"We're talking to you, not him and we are telling you it would be a really bad idea for you to marry him, princess."

"Why - do - you - care?" The meaty hand relaxes for a moment so I can rasp out a response.

"We don't. We're just paid to relay the message," the alpha of the pack grins and his sidekick squeezes my neck tighter. "All you need to know is that if you don't stop the wedding, you won't make it to the honeymoon."

My eyelids flutter as I try to nod to show I understand. I'm sure that I'm about to slip out of consciousness when he finally lets go of my throat and pushes me away.

Gasping, the sounds I make are barely human. The desperate rasp as I suck oxygen into my empty lungs is like nothing I have heard before. It is the rattling, ugly sound of life snatched from the jaws of death.

"Is everything okay over here?" a woman who looks to be in her 50s stands hands on her hips trying her best to look confident and formidable. I'm filled with affection for this one stranger brave enough to check on me.

The leader of the trio turns to her and plastering a huge smile on his face switches on the charm. His performance would put even Elio to shame. "We were just checking the same thing. We heard her choking, but it turns out her water just went down the wrong hole."

"You okay?" she asks me directly as the bikers stride out of the gym and I nod with a weak smile. Bless her, but I do not need the police being called.

CHAPTER TWENTY SEVEN
FRANCESCA

"Oh you're home," Massimo's tentative and guilt-laced voice cuts through the simmering remains of my panic attack. I'm soaking wet, sitting on the daybed by the pool with my arms wrapped around my legs. Even though it's a scorching day, I can't stop shivering.

"You been swimming in your clothes again?" He wanders towards me.

He seems to want to clear the air and takes the fact that I haven't run off as encouragement.

I don't raise my chin from where it rests on my knees because I know the minute I do the bruising on my neck from the biker's massive fist will be visible.

Making up a tummy ache, I scrambled out of the gym shortly after I heard the motorcycles tear out of the car park. I took the half-hour walk home to try and calm my nerves. Unsuccessfully.

Growing up around the mafia has meant I have seen plenty of glimpses of violence and law-breaking and I have always known there is a strong possibility I could be targeted by enemies of my family or the Marinos. Today was the first time that I experienced it.

The bikers were rough, a different kind of criminal from the ones I live my life with. My criminals come in Armani suits and are wined and dined by the establishment. Bikers are outlaws; they don't pretend respectability. They smell like petrol and leather, and the danger they present feels dirtier.

Even though the blue-eyed biker with the man-bun is objectively very good-looking, I was repulsed by his griminess. Without their leader's

attractiveness, the other two bikers looked even rougher. The way they salivated over me, pointedly staring at my breasts and bum, sent a shot of terror to my brain. It was that implicit threat that they could take me and use my body however they wanted that has left me shaking like a leaf.

Years of therapy have done wonders for my ability to ride the waves of inevitable triggers. Where my parents shipped off a traumatised and broken girl without a thought of how to remedy her pain, my grandmother at least had the presence of mind to send me to a psychologist once a week.

Undoubtedly I'm still a hot mess. Therapy doesn't fix anyone. It doesn't take away what happened. If it's successful it simply teaches us how to live with our traumas and push on with what we have left.

I'm sure the Marinos and my family have their opinions about why I jump in the pool in my clothes so often. My parents probably put it down to attention-seeking behaviour. Massi doesn't question it. Maybe Giovanna and Matty think I'm crazy. Elio would need to care about me to form a proper opinion.

The truth is that one of the coping mechanisms I learned for managing distress is to use acute changes in my five senses to jolt myself out of a spiral. By focusing on the physical, the emotional and the mental can get a break. The shock of jumping into a cold pool seems to have become my go-to tactic since returning to Australia.

"You're shaking. Are you okay?" There is concern in Massi's voice and he hurries over to where I sit. He wraps his arms around my hunched-over form and drags me closer to him. "Francesca, has something happened? Oh my god…was it David?"

I quickly shake my head at that and an involuntary shudder follows. Lifting my head, I expose my neck so he can see the red fingerprints and the bruises that are already forming.

"What the fuck! Who did this?"

Clearing my throat sends searing pain down my oesophagus and it is becoming increasingly hard to swallow. "Bikers…came to the…g-gym," I rasp. I can barely speak.

Immediately, Massimo pulls his phone out.

"G. Where are you?" He barks into the phone after a few moments.

"Come down to the pool. Bikers went to Francesca's work."

"She's shaken and they've...they've strangled her or something."

She must have hung up on him because he puts the phone back into his pocket. He holds me tight, rocking back and forwards and barely a minute has passed before we hear Giovanna hurtling down the stairs, across the living area, and out the backdoor.

I look up from where I have tucked my head into my knees again and see Giovanna striding around the pool toward us. She's in her usual tight, tailored suit pants with a crisp white dress shirt tucked in. Her face is a picture of terror and fury and, even in my quivering state, my heart skips a beat.

She drops down to her knees in front of where I'm perched on the daybed and gently tucks a damp lock of hair behind my ear before gently guiding me with her fingers under my chin to lift my head so she can see the damage.

She hisses when she sees my neck and her eyes lock on mine. "Who did this to you, darling?"

I swallow and try to clear my throat again and Massimo quietly informs her, "She's struggling to speak."

"Three. B-b-bikies," I manage to get out and I see Giovanna make eye contact with Massi. "One was c-c-called B-b-billy."

"Jesus Christ," Giovanna murmurs. She's still crouching in front of me. She's so close I can see the emotion in her dark eyes, even as she maintains a staunch expression. "Francesca?" she asks me softly, her hands cupping my face. "Apart from...what they did to your neck...did they hurt you anywhere else? Do anything else?"

I shake my head and relief washes over her. "And did they tell you what they want?"

"T-t-told me not to marry...Elio."

She turns to Massimo. "Have you called Elio?"

He looks sheepish as if he has realised that he should have. "Not yet." He gets his phone back out and hands it to Giovanna.

"It's me, Elio."

"Get home now. Bikies visited Francesca at work."

"She's... mostly fine, but you need to get here."

"See you soon."

She hands the phone back to Massi and tells him to get hold of Matty as well.

"I-I don't w-w-want to see Elio," every word feels like it is scraping sandpaper up the inside of my throat.

Giovanna looks down for a second and then moves so she is further away from me. "He wants to be here for you. Give him a chance to make it right." Her words don't match the reluctance I hear in her voice.

"I. Don't. Want. Him." My hand shoots out and grabs one of her's and she lets me intertwine our fingers briefly. Massimo is pacing near the back door, on the phone.

Giovanna drops my hand, stands, and comes to sit next to me on the daybed. My disappointment at the loss of contact is quickly soothed when she picks my hand back up again and presses a brief kiss on my knuckles.

"Look at me," she whispers and for a moment I feel weightless as the strength of her gaze envelops me. "I know this is hard, darlin'. But, this is duty. I need you to give Elio another chance…even if it isn't what I want."

This is the closest we've ever come to acknowledging the attraction between us. The terror and pain I'm feeling is relieved by a hit of elation. *She wants me.*

She squeezes my hand gently and I just keep shaking my head. "O-only t-t-thing I've…ever wanted," I whisper so quietly, I'm not sure she hears and I let the sentence drop, incomplete.

A couple of tears run down my cheeks and she lets go of my hand to swipe them away with her thumbs.

She gives me another intense stare. "I will always have your back. No matter what. I'm here."

My heartbreaks. She's going to force me to marry him even if she doesn't want it to happen and I'd rather be choked again.

CHAPTER TWENTY EIGHT
GIOVANNA

"Peta, this looks bloody delicious," I collapse into my chair at the head of the table. My stepmother has made her classic Australian 'Chicken Parma'. It's Chicken Parmigiana, but Aussies had to 'boganise' it.

Massimo kisses his mother on the top of her head and sits down to my left. Peta beams over at him, her pride and joy. Matty is already tucking into his dinner on my right and Dad sits opposite his wife.

"Where's Elio?" I ask the table. I've been trying to track him down all day, but have had no success.

It's frustrating because in the week after the bikies threatened Francesca he was really good. He comforted her and looked after her. I could see her starting to relax around him again. Of course, I knew he spent several evenings at Peacock after she had taken herself off to bed in the guest room.

Both of my brothers shrug and I let out a sigh. Dad raises his eyebrows and I can tell he wants to ask questions, but he holds his tongue. Eventually, after a few minutes of quietly tucking into our dinner, he speaks, "Peta, did you get the venue booked for the wedding?"

"Yeap, *Long Reef Golf Club.* Invitations have gone out," she reaches out and pats his hand as if to reassure him it is all in hand.

"Good," is his punctuated response.

I received my invitation. It was left on my desk a couple of days ago. If the fireplace had been lit I would have thrown it in.

I don't want to think about the fucking wedding. Don't want to talk about it. I pretend to be bored by the whole thing, but the truth is it makes me nauseous that in just under four months Francesca will be a Marino, but not mine.

Dad's voice booms across the table. "How is Francesca doing?" He directs the question at Massimo as the person most likely to know.

Massi finishes his mouthful of breaded chicken and glares at Dad. "She's pretty messed up actually. Don't know that she'll ever trust me again…" he pauses, swallowing down emotions.

"You did what was needed for the family," Dad tells him gruffly.

"What about what is best for her though? I am supposed to be the one who has her back when no one else does. She doesn't deserve all this," Massimo slams his glass of water down on the table and everyone jumps.

"Where is she?" I ask.

"At work."

"What? She's gone back there? Who allowed that?" I explode with a ferocity that surprises me.

He raises a shoulder. "She wanted to get back to normal. Bluey is going everywhere with her now."

"Strewth. Make sure he doesn't have a crack at her. All we need is her knocked up with a redhead," Dad sure has a way with words. Matty snorts, but Massimo looks furious.

"Dad! What the fuck," he slams his cutlery on the table.

Dad looks baffled as if he can't imagine anything wrong with his comments. "What? The ratbag is worse than Elio was at his age."

Massi scowls and shoves a pile of salad in his mouth aggressively.

"I'm sure Bluey has enough sense to be professional," I murmur. "I wouldn't have chosen anyone else to protect her."

After dinner, I sit down opposite Dad in my office. It is strange to be behind the desk with him on the other side. He's looking very tan, but then he and Peta did just get back from a week in the Whitsundays.

I place a glass of whiskey on the rocks in his hand and cradle my own. We sit in companionable silence, the joyous sounds of Massimo regaling his mother with an elaborate tale in the kitchen waft in the open door.

"Should I be worried about your brother?" Dad breaks the silence. He's asking about Elio and it isn't about his health and well-being. Dad still has a foot in the family business and while I value his mentorship, his meddling is doing my head in.

"Mmmm. For me to worry about, Dad," I answer flatly.

"I know that, Giovanna," he responds a little testily. "I'm not blind or deaf though and I can see he doesn't have the respect of the men. It's a problem."

No shit it's a problem. The men who dedicate their lives to working for our family see a playboy prince who is more interested in getting his dick wet than being a good leader.

"I'm doing my best. You wanted this split leadership thing..."

He doesn't say anything for a moment, just sips his drink. "He needs to pull finger."

"Yup," I sigh, popping 'P' at the end of the word. As if I haven't been battling him on this every time he is in front of me.

Bitterness poisons me and I focus on pushing it back into the box I keep it in. It wants to distract me with thoughts of how bullshit it is that I couldn't inherit Dad's role outright. It wants me to rage about having to sit and watch my hedonistic little brother sit in my seat and fail to live up to expectations.

"Has he managed to fuck things up anymore with Francesca?" Sandy asks.

"He's been better the past week. I don't know that she'll ever forgive him though." I pause and then continue, "She doesn't want her parents' marriage, Dad."

Sandy grunts. "Her parents don't want that marriage."

"Dad, he doesn't want this either."

"Chris, Giovanna. He's made it very fucking clear he doesn't want to get married. You don't need to remind me," barks Sandy.

"I mean he doesn't want any of this. He's running away. Avoiding. I duno if he's admitted it to himself, but he doesn't want to be Don."

"Tough!" Sandy growls. "These are the cards he has been dealt."

"Maybe it would be best for the family if he wasn't the Don," Matty appears in the doorway and he is speaking very carefully. It is practically blasphemous what he is saying. "Gio has the men's respect. It doesn't matter that she is a woman or gay."

The way we all hold our breath it is as if all the oxygen has been sucked out of the room. Our collective stress level heightens and we all assess each other, waiting for someone else to speak first.

CHAPTER TWENTY NINE
FRANCESCA

"Literally every man here, except the one in the Hawaiian shirt over there, is drooling over you. And Hawaiian shirt guy only isn't because he is too busy chewing the inside of his face off," I elbow Massi in the ribs and he grimaces at my comment and the jab.

Massimo's ability to bring a gay club to a standstill is nothing new, but it is always a sight to behold. I swear some of these men would divorce their husbands for one night with him.

"You're attracting plenty of looks from the ladies yourself, Ches."

"Lol, whatever. They all assume I'm a fag hag just tagging along with you."

"Maybe. But now I know you're a little bit bi you might just have to make some moves," he orders us a pair of whiskey sours and we find a high table and stools to perch on.

"No way! I told you. My attraction to women is *very* exclusive."

He keeps pushing me. "So if your lady obsession walked in tonight you'd make a move?"

I think for a moment. The idea of making a move on Giovanna terrifies me. "Honestly? Probably not."

Desperate to change the subject I delve into a topic I've been wanting to bring up with him. "Hey Massi, I overheard something the other night - "

"You need to be careful about repeating things you heard, Cheska. Seriously."

"I know. I'd only ask you. It's just that I heard Gio, Matty, and your Dad talking about Elio..."

He tenses and I can tell he doesn't want to continue this conversation. "What about?"

"Matty said Giovanna would do a better job..."

"You shouldn't have heard that and you should forget it," he snaps.

Awkward. Things haven't been the same between us since I learned he was babysitting me with a hefty dose of manipulation while we were in London. I know we've had lots of shit to deal with but I miss my carefree friend. Massimo is way too serious and stressed in Australia.

We fall into a people-watching silence and sip on our drinks. It's still pretty early in the night so the dance floor isn't packed yet, but there is plenty of entertainment on offer.

"Are you glad we came back?" I venture a new conversation.

"Mostly, yeah," he agrees. "Weather is better for a start. Missed my family too. We had fun over there though, didn't we?"

"We sure did." *Even though it was all a lie.*

"How are you doing?" He asks gently.

"It's been kind of a mindfuck to be dragged back here. On top of everything else, you know, seeing...well, just being in the same room...as *him...*"

"I'm so sorry, babe. I'll never let him hurt you again. I promise."

I give him a small smile. I believe him. I trust that he would take David out if it came to it. It's all the other hurt that he can't help with. All the collateral damage that has torn me up for eight years.

"No one did anything, Massimo," my voice cracks. "They just sent me away. He had...no consequences."

"That's not one hundred percent true," Massi says cryptically. "Giovanna did."

I frown. I've never heard this before. "What?"

"Yeah...she asked me what happened because our parents were keeping it under wraps. So I, uh, told her and she lost it. This was like two years after you left."

"She did?"

"Yeah. You know what she's like. Did you really think she would do nothing?"

Giovanna has always had a strong sense of justice and has always been more than ready to dole it out when the police and establishment fail to do so. Perhaps that's why I feel so hurt by her apparent inaction in both the David situation and my forced marriage. I expect more from her. More than anything I crave her protection. "I didn't even know if she knew. For all I knew, they buried it after they put me on a plane."

Massimo rests his forearms on the table and leans toward me. Lowering his voice he tells me, "Babe, Giovanna broke every single one of his fingers and gave him the beating of his life."

Stunned doesn't even begin to describe how I'm feeling. I'm speechless and overcome with a cocktail of competing emotions. There's pure relief that someone actually did something, anything. Discomfort loiters around the edges as I realise that the knowledge that Giovanna avenged me fills me with warmth. I must be a mafia brat through and through to get warm and fuzzies from such violence.

"Does Sandy know?" I finally ask.

"He was there. Your Dad tried to intervene, but Sandy stopped him and let Giovanna thrash him."

Bitterness floods my emotional cocktail and I sneer sarcastically, "Cheers Dad."

We sit in silence, processing our heavy conversation in the middle of a busy gay bar. It's amazing how much lighter I feel knowing that he suffered just a little bit because of what he did. He wouldn't have been able to wipe his arse for months. Just imagining Giovanna unleashing on him gives me a boost of strength that I haven't felt in a long time.

"She'll kill him if he touches you again," he mutters just loud enough for me to hear. "She promised him."

The campy DJ looks like is trying to hit every stereotype in flamboyant-gay-man bingo. He is topless, in very tight denim cutoffs, and neon pink sunglasses. Before we started drinking we rolled our eyes and contemplated leaving to go to a straight club.

"Does everything always have to be so fucking extra?" grumbled Massimo. He tends to reject anything camp and resents being stereotyped. He's very masculine and it often takes people a while to clock him as gay.

Several cocktails and a couple of tequila shots later we are belting *Just Like A Prayer* at the top of our voices and making friends on the dancefloor. Alcohol has dissolved our snobbery and the heaviness of our earlier conversations forgotten.

Massimo hoists me up by my hips and I throw my arms out wide, my head back and sing. He spins us around and I feel like I'm flying.

"You two are fuckin' wackos," the unmistakable drawl of Bluey snaps me out of my moment and Massimo lets me slide to touchdown on my feet.

He scowls at Bluey. "What are you doing here?"

"What? Am I not allowed? They must have forgotten to check my 'Heterosexual Card' on the way in," he teases, but there is a little bit of an edge to his voice.

"But, why *are* you here?" I ask. "Feeling a bit curious? Wanna try some dick?" I cringe at how crass I am when I've had a bit to drink.

He laughs, but Massi doesn't. "Nah, I'm here with Gio. She's meeting some mates. I should go back and lurk near her."

I whip my head around and look in the direction he points. Sure enough, there's Giovanna. God, she's perfection. How does just seeing her liquify my insides every time?

She wears black ripped jeans, a white t-shirt, a leather jacket, and a slouchy beanie. One of her friends is talking to her and she frowns, sipping beer from a bottle. I nearly go cross-eyed imagining what it would be like to walk over, slide my hands up her chest, and press my lips to hers.

"You're staring," Massimo whispers in my ear from behind and I jump. I'm lucky I'm not drooling as well.

Shaking my head briskly, I snap at him, "No I'm not!"

"Reow! Easy tiger. No need to take my head off," he teases, making camp claw movements with his hands.

I laugh weakly. I'm half distracted by Giovanna's presence and half terrified that Massi noticed me gawking.

"What's wrong with you?" He takes a sip from his cocktail and fixes me with a suspicious stare. "You're blushing."

My eyes slide over to where his sister is standing as if I have no control over them at all. He follows my gaze, eyes narrowing.

"You *are* staring, Francesca Rossi!" he accuses.

My eyes snap back to his face and I open my mouth to say something, anything, but nothing comes out. I could blame the alcohol, but really I'm in a state of shock over the electric attraction I have to Giovanna.

"No," I finally half-heartedly object. "I was just looking…to see what Gio was doing."

One of his eyebrows arches into a quizzical expression and he shakes his head.

"You're a weirdo. Got a few roos loose in the top paddock …" he starts, but before he can finish the train of thought, he suddenly asks, "Oh my god. It's her isn't it?"

Gulping, I play dumb. "What do you mean?"

"My sister is the one, isn't she? The only one you wank to."

After slapping him playfully on the arm, I pause. I'm too drunk to lie convincingly. My shoulders droop and, reluctantly, I nod.

"Holy shit. Since when? Makes sense though. You followed her everywhere!"

We stand at the side of the dancefloor, watching his big sister chat with her friends not far from us.

"Since forever. She is everything, Massi. I can't believe I'm telling you this now." In my drunken state, being in unrequited love with my best friend's big sister feels like the most painful and awful thing to endure.

"Oh babe," he pulls me into a hug. We sway as if slow dancing to the high-tempo club beat. "You know what's fucked up? You're going to be fucking my brother while thinking about my sister…."

We laugh, clinging to each other and to our own stomachs. "Gotta laugh or I'll cry," I wheeze.

After much protesting, I allow Massi to drag me over to where Giovanna and her friends are hanging out. I scan the women trying to assess if any might be Gio's type, but the truth is, I don't know what her type is. The women I saw

her with when I was younger were pretty femme if I recall, but that was a long time ago.

I'm unimpressed to see that the most feminine woman in the group is standing next to Giovanna with her hand on her shoulder. She's just wearing jeans, but has a face of makeup and long straightened hair.

I hate her immediately.

The feeling takes me back to when I was young watching Giovanna make out with her friends beside the pool. I turned into quite the green-eyed monster and it looks like I still have the potential to do that as an adult.

I'm suddenly self-conscious of my high-waisted tight leather miniskirt and tucked-in sequined camisole. I'm one of the few women in high heels and I look like a tourist. Or a fag hag. A straight woman dropping into a gay bar to gawk.

The establishment is full of glaring symbols of gayness. Cues worn to signal belonging to the group. Blue hair, facial piercings, undercuts, and pieces of rainbow clothing. None of them are my style, but maybe I should have made an effort to not look quite so fucking straight.

We are only a few metres away when Giovanna spots us. She raises her eyebrows and beckons us over. "Fancy seeing you two here," she teases dryly.

I look up through my eyelashes at her and give her my best seductive smile. She holds my gaze for a second longer than she should and the muscles on the sides of my tummy contract.

"This isn't your usual scene, is it Francesca?" she remarks. *What a loaded question.*

"I'm sure you know what they say about assumptions, Giovanna," I take my bottom lip between my teeth and half smile. She swallows hard and the muscles in her neck and jaw flicker in a way that has me dreaming about kissing those spots.

Massimo leaves us leering at each other and sidles off to speak with Bluey. He is subtle, but I wonder if he would've done so if he hadn't just learned that I'm in lust, and love, with his sister.

Giovanna introduces me to a few of her friends and it brings me great satisfaction to see her shrug off the hand that had remained determinedly on her shoulder. The woman the hand belongs to, Bex, looks put out. She flicks

her sheet of shiny straight hair over her shoulder and glares at me as if she senses immediately that I'm competition.

I inch a little closer to Giovanna, taking advantage of the crowded room and the bustle of bodies until our arms can't help but brush each other every time we move.

"You having fun, Ches?" she ducks down and places her mouth next to my ear. An involuntary shiver runs up my spine and she must feel it because she chuckles softly and places a hand on the small of my back.

I feel like I'm dying and I'm not sure if I'm heading to heaven or hell. The lightest of her touches has my heart racing. A second of eye contact catches the breath in my chest.

"I'll have fun if you dance with me," I reply in a wild stab at being bold, hoping and wishing she will ignore all the reasons she should say no.

For a moment we stand chest to chest, our bodies touching ever so slightly when our exhales synchronise. She looks down her nose at me, thinking and serious and I swallow the urge to reach up and run a finger over the scar in her eyebrow. I can't imagine her face without it. The imperfection makes her infinitely sexier.

After a beat, she sighs as if defeated. She finishes her beer in one smooth gulp, drops the empty bottle on a nearby bar leaner, and takes my hand, leading me to the dancefloor.

Fuck. I didn't think about what to do if she actually agreed to dance with me. My hands begin to tremble and Giovanna squeezes the one she holds in her own gently. She casts a sexy grin over her shoulder and I swear my brain shortcircuits.

At first, we kinda just dance next to each other, bumping occasionally. I know I can dance well enough that I don't look awkward. I'm somewhat of an expert in dirty dancing, thanks to Giovanna's little brother.

Massimo, not Elio. And not that he ever let me dance with anyone else.

I push down a small wave of anger at the realisation that Massimo was preventing me from dancing with any other men under orders.

An expert at dirty dancing with my gay best friend who was paid to babysit me. Pathetic.

After a few songs I begin to relax and no longer feel like my heart is threatening to go into cardiac arrest. She is loosening up too. She is more of a contained dancer than I am. The classic butch two-step with minimal upper body movement. But, we are moving in sync with each other now. My fluid sensuality meeting her strong sexual energy.

Madonna. Whitney. Mariah. Beyonce. This DJ loves his pop queens.

As we jump around to Lady Gaga's *Alejandro,* singing along with everyone else, Giovanna smiles so widely at me that it feels like my heart swells and is too big for my chest. Her whole face changes when she smiles and because she so infrequently bestows them on anyone, it feels like a gift.

The music changes and *GAY 4 ME* by G Flip and Lauren Sanderson comes on and all the women in the room squeal and holler. The dance floor is suddenly full of more women than men.

I bite the side of my bottom lip, thinking about how relatable the lyrics are and Giovanna laughs, cupping my face with both hands. "You're fuckin' adorable," she shouts above the music, and my heart stutters and then soars.

I turn to face away from her but move closer, my bum pressing back into the front of her jeans. Closing my eyes I swivel my hips and gyrate. I'm not giving her a lap dance, but I am telling her that I would if she asked.

Unable to see her reaction, I cross my fingers that I'm not pushing things too far. What if she just walks away? Leaves me on the dancefloor alone?

It feels like an eternity has passed when one of her hands snakes around my waist to press on my lower stomach, dragging me in closer to her body, and it makes me want to punch the air in excitement.

Her breath is warm by my ear and I lean my head back on her shoulder briefly.

"Are you a little bit gay, little darlin'?" Her voice is a sexy growl. I love when she calls me 'little darlin'. Her deep, rough voice shaping the gentle words just for me gives me butterflies.

"Only for you," I respond, turning my head slightly so our breath mingles between our dangerously close mouths. I can't see her reaction, but I hear her sharp inhalation and she keeps moving with me, touching me.

Her splayed hand hasn't moved from my lower stomach and I curse the leather of my skirt that is preventing me from feeling her skin on mine. As it is, her hand may as well be on fire, the heat from it is setting me alight.

She finally spins me around when *she calls me daddy* by KING MALA begins to play. I giggle to myself remembering how Elio accused me of 'running to mummy' when Giovanna stood up for me.

"What are you laughing about?" She tightens her grip on my waist and I wind my arms around her neck. Our chests press together and even though two bras and our tops separate us, the feeling of our breasts pushed together is possibly the single most erotic thing I have ever experienced.

"The song just reminds me of Elio saying I ran to 'mummy', but you're probably more of a 'daddy' to be honest." I blurt it out and then duck my head into her shoulder in horror. Her shoulders begin to shake as she laughs.

"That sounded weird," I squeal, pulling my head back to look at her with an embarrassed grimace on my face. "Oh god, just forget I said it!"

The words keep tumbling out of my mouth and I immediately want to scoop them back up, but Giovanna's eyes darken and she doesn't seem weirded out.

It's her turn to drop her head and she rests her mouth against my neck for just a second, groaning, "You are trouble. So so much trouble."

We dance for another song or two, but our movements become less and less sexual. It is like reminding herself of how much trouble I am has broken the spell and she pulls away.

"I need to stop now, Francesca," she forces out eventually.

"What's wrong?" I ask, taking in her furrowed brow and tortured expression. Our faces are so close I could just lean up and kiss her. Instead, I give in to my earlier temptation and trace a finger over the scar in her eyebrow, waiting for her to respond.

"We just can't..." She is struggling to find the words to express herself. I don't want to push, but I desperately want to know how she feels.

"Give me a song," I say as softly as I can with all the noise surrounding us. "Remember how you'd say that to us? Give me a song, Giovanna."

She presses her forehead against mine and makes a humming noise as she thinks. We stand like that, barely moving, for what feels like ages. I'm just about

to give her an out when she leans back and with eyes smouldering with an emotion I can't pinpoint, says: "Iris."

"Iris?" I repeat. *Who is Iris?*

"Yeah, the - Dolls," she elaborates. The music gets louder and I can't quite make out the name of the band.

"Huh?" *Did she seriously say The Pussycat Dolls? Was one of them called Iris?*

A sad smile dances across her face and she shakes her head. "Nevermind, darlin'. Thanks for the dance." She takes my hand and leads me off the dancefloor back towards her mates.

"What the fuck, G!" A particularly outgoing woman dressed similarly to Giovanna exclaims. "Where have you been hiding this babe?"

She gives me a big suggestive wink.

"Don't be a fuckin' pest, Azra," Giovanna punches her in the upper arm hard enough to hurt, but her tone is joking.

Azra is undeterred and directs her comments to me, "Hey beautiful, what are you doing wasting your time with this grumpy old woman?"

Giovanna scowls and rolls her eyes. She's let my hand go and I hate how empty it leaves me feeling. I want to snatch it back and have her symbolically brand me as hers.

"She's engaged to my brother, dickhead." Giovanna retorts flatly.

And there it is. Reality, that bastard.

Azra's eyes bug out of her head and she looks from me and back to Giovanna as if trying to see if we are taking the piss. "Which one? Does he let anyone dance with her like that or are youse just keeping it in the family?"

"Elio," she answers. "And I have no idea what you're talking about." Azra goes to protest, but Giovanna repeats herself in a firmer tone, "No idea, Az."

Making it clear the discussion is over, she turns around and beckons Bluey over. He's engaged in an intense discussion with Massimo and they're both frowning as they join our group.

"Take Francesca home, Massimo," she orders.

"What?! I don't want to go home!" I'm indignant. I'll decide when I want to go home. What the fuck is wrong with her?

"Because I said so," she barks, grabbing my chin between her thumb and forefinger. "Do as you're told."

"Fine, I wanted to get out of here anyway," mutters Massimo, shooting a furious glance Bluey's way.

My lips purse into an involuntary pout and my eyes narrow to glare at Giovanna. She scoffs as if my anger is a source of amusement for her and pulls me unexpectedly into her arms. I melt in an instant as if I hadn't been ready to square off with her moments before.

She tilts my chin up to look at her and I feel giddy. People are watching, including Massi and Bluey, and I know that is not a good thing, but all I can feel is the thrill of the surge of need that shoots to my lower stomach and settles between my legs.

"I need you to go, darlin'. I'm gonna kill the next person who hits on you or drag you out of here like a cavewoman and I… we just can't," she whispers just loud enough for me to hear. "You understand?"

I'm nodding as if I am in a trance. She hypnotises me with eye contact. With touch.

"Come on, Cheska," Massimo orders. He plants a kiss on his sister's cheek and gently tugs me by the arm.

"Bye," I say weakly to Giovanna. My brain has completely checked out and her friends are watching us like we are in a soap opera.

"Bye, *bella*," she replies before turning away and accepting a full bottle of beer from Azra.

CHAPTER THIRTY
GIOVANNA

Jesus fuckin' Christ. I'm 38 years old. Nearly middle-aged. Fuck, wait. Am I already middle-aged? If I do another 38 years I'll be 76. Decent innings in a mafia family. Fuck. I'm middle-aged.

What am I doing, at 38 fucking years old, going out and getting munted on a school night? Mind you, every night is a school night these days. I don't exactly get to clock off for the weekend. Especially not when my shit of a brother goes completely MIA when he is supposed to be at least pretending to run the show.

Despite taking more than the recommended dose of painkillers before leaving home, my head is pounding. My throat is drier than a box of Weetbix even though I distinctly remember force-feeding myself a litre of water before I hit the hay last night. Worst of all, no matter how thoroughly I showered this morning and how much perfume I have doused myself in, any perspiring I do today will smell like beer and whatever spirits Az was handing me once we got to *Peacocks.*

I grabbed a coffee on the way into our office building in town, but the caffeine hasn't helped as much as I had hoped. Or at all. I haven't touched drugs for about five years now, but Christ, a bump or two of coke wouldn't go amiss today.

Usually, I'd enjoy looking out at the view from our obnoxious glass elevator, but today I face inwards towards the doors because I'm scared I'll

projectile vomit the remains of my greasy drive-thru breaky at the sight of the world disappearing below.

What a hot mess.

I'm too old for this shit. Odds are this could turn into a two-day hangover as well. Who am I kidding, could be a triple-day torture.

This is my punishment, or maybe my penance, for giving into temptation and allowing myself to get into trouble with Francesca last night. I clearly cannot be trusted to have any alcohol around her.

Last night I played with fire. But those eyes. Those bee-stung lips. Her legs in that leather skirt. *Fuck me sideways.*

It's been a while since I felt out of control like I did last night. Giving in to my emotional or physiological yearnings isn't something I have the luxury of doing anymore. Not when they centre around Francesca Rossi anyway.

It is in my nature to maintain dominance, and control, and to be in charge. I need control to operate, to survive. I'm sure a therapist would have a field day delving into the reasons why that is.

Even before Dad dumped everything on me and Elio, my responsibilities to the *Famiglia* required total discipline. I've learnt the importance of knowing everything about everyone, in any room, at any given time so that when I make a move it is informed.

My world is often chaotic and I find calm in directing traffic, in command of the strings I'm pulling. Mitigating risk factors and crossing out potential vulnerabilities is calming in itself.

The gym is almost a spiritual place for me. It represents structure, routine, and discipline. I've always used exercise as an outlet for stress and it shows in my body. Every muscle has been carefully developed by focused regimes and strict adherence to a nutritional diet.

I'm well aware that my friends call me uptight and the control I exert over myself is often not appreciated when I wield it over others. But now the survival of the *Famiglia* depends on me and my discipline.

Usually, I can shake off a girl who is being too keen. Communicate my disinterest in blunt terms. Get on with things. But as much as Francesca is way too keen on me, I'm just as much too keen on her.

It is more than just physical attraction and that's saying something because every inch of her is stunning. It is her sweetness and sass, her resilience, and her exuberance. It's the insane chemistry that crackles between us even if we are on opposite sides of a room. Even the ultra-feminine scent of her perfume is enough to drive me to distraction.

Last night when I had her in my arms on the dance floor, my brain was flooded by temptation screaming at me to take her for myself. It reminded me that Elio has treated her like shit and she deserves so much better. God, I want to be the one to give her everything she deserves.

She is probably still fuming that I sent her home with Massimo, but I had to get her out of there. The last of my defences didn't look like they were going to hold and I couldn't risk it.

My duty is to the *Famiglia* first and foremost.

The thought of those huge brown eyes, framed with thick black lashes, looking up at anyone but me makes me fuckin' homicidal though.

She has always looked at me like I am her hero, but now it's that and so much more. It's like she thinks I could prevent nuclear war, cure cancer, and make chocolate calorie-free all at once. Her beautiful open face hides nothing and it says plain as day that she would hand me her heart if only I would take it. *I want to take it.*

I remind myself over and over that she is marrying my brother. She is also fourteen years younger than me and I used to babysit her! A not-insignificant detail that I keep overlooking.

Demonstrating exactly how much younger than me she is, she had never even heard of *Iris* by the *Goo Goo Dolls*. It is probably a good thing. Choosing that song was a moment of weakness.

It's a cruel world. A cruel, cruel world. I've had girlfriends over the years, but I tend to end things before they get too serious. Our world is very different from the one most Aussie women live in and I've never met one who I thought would fit. Who would cope with the violence, and criminality, and be able to navigate the often archaic social dynamics.

It's not that I'm afraid of settling down. I just want to do it right and I've always thought it would only work with a woman who already knows my world.

Sadly, there isn't an abundance of lesbians kicking around Italian mafia families. Not ones that are out of the closet anyway.

It seems beyond cruel that here is the most beautiful woman I have ever seen in my life, who has grown up in the mafia and shows me she wants me, and my Dad is marrying her off to my little brother. Murphy's Law. Cue *Alanis Morissette.*

The safest thing for me to do is stay the fuck away from her. Especially when my blood alcohol level is sky-high.

The doors open on the 26th floor and I banish Francesca from my thoughts as I approach our reception desk. "Morning, Chelsea," I croak, failing to disguise how rough I sound. "Is Elio in?"

Cheery and professional as usual, Chelsea replies that she hasn't seen Elio since last week. She's probably in her mid-thirties and is one of the most thoroughly pleasant people I have ever met. Marino Corp is the legal and legitimate part of our business and despite knowing what our family is famous for, Chelsea has diligently played Captain Oblivious for about four years now.

"Would you like a coffee, Giovanna?" she asks.

Looking into my empty takeaway cup I thank her, "God, yes, please. One hasn't done the trick."

As expected, the door to Elio's executive suite is shut. I roll my eyes to myself as I read his name on the door above the words 'Chief Executive'. The man hasn't a clue about what is going on in this building. He's here so infrequently that staff are already whispering and wondering if the company will tank now Dad has left. Never mind, I've been running the corporate side of the *Famiglia* with Dad for years now.

Even pushing the door into my own, more humble office takes far too much energy and I sink into the seat behind my desk with pathetic relief. I'd prefer to be working out of home, but it's important that I'm here if Elio isn't.

"Here you go," Chelsea says brightly, placing a perfectly made coffee in front of me.

"You're a legend. Thanks, Chelsea. When Matteo gets in can you tell him to come see me please?"

"Sure. Hope that one hits the spot, but if you need more caffeine let me know!"

Half an hour or so later, Matty pokes his head around the door. "Morning, boss," he mumbles.

"Hey mate," I yawn.

"You look a bit worse for wear. Out on the turps last night?"

I drop my head to my desk and pretend to sleep. "Yeah, went for a few and it turned into a big night. Now, I suffer."

He chuckles, smug that his head isn't pounding. "Seems like I'm the only one who didn't get hammered last night. I saw Massi and Francesca looking very dusty this morning."

Time to change the subject. "Don't suppose you've seen our other brother recently?"

He shakes his head. "What's today…Thursday? Hmmm, don't think I've seen him since the weekend."

"Jesus Christ! This is a joke, Matty. What's going on in his head?" I pull my hair in frustration.

Elio attends one meeting in every five and signs off everything rather than reading what it is and applying judgement. It's lucky our executive leadership team has been with us for so long that we can trust them not to take advantage of the disinterest he shows. Not that I'm not keeping a close eye on things.

Events he is good at. He never misses a liquid lunch or tickets to the footy. He schmoozes better than anyone I know, but that just isn't enough.

"He doesn't want this. He doesn't want to be the boss. He doesn't want to marry Francesca. He's running away from his problems and responsibilities."

The very things I want, that I have waited for, he has on a silver platter, but he doesn't want them. He would rather hide behind a bottle, between the legs of strangers.

"Nightmare. Anyway, we need to sort out the fuckers who threatened Francesca. You said you've tracked them down?"

Energised at the prospect of enacting violence, Matty sits up straighter. "The guys picked up two of them this morning. Not the ringleader though, the Billy guy. He's ghosted."

"Where are they? The other two."

"Should be arriving at the warehouse shortly," he grins. "You coming with?"

The men terrified Francesca. They left her with bruises. I wouldn't miss this for the world.

"Yeah, why not," I respond.

~

There is something disturbingly comforting about walking into the warehouse. It's been several months since I had to get my hands dirty and, as much as we aren't supposed to admit these kinds of things, there is nothing like the buzz of fucking up someone who has fucked you over.

It's an unbranded, unremarkable warehouse in the middle of a quiet industrial district. It has been in the family since before Dad moved to Australia. Nonno got creative with property records at the time and now two generations later it is virtually impossible to trace the place back to us.

Mostly we use it for shifting our less-than-legal product, but in the basement, we have a dedicated room for extractions and cleanups. It is kitted out with every tool imaginable for extracting the truth from someone or cleaning up a loose end.

"Those things are going to kill you," I nudge Fat Tony, looking pointedly at the cigarette dangling from his lips, and take a drag from my vape. He's standing in the utilitarian atrium of our warehouse. It's all brown and concrete and in serious need of renovation.

His face lights up and he wraps me in a boney hug. There is not a gram of fat on Fat Tony. Rumour has it that he was skin and bones from birth.

"Just wait, we'll find out in ten years that those wanker puffers are even worse for you. Don't ask me to donate you a lung," his eyes twinkle in his weathered, wrinkly face as he jabs his burning cigarette at my vape. He must be in his late 50s, but the scrawny bastard looks about 100.

"You know as well as I do that we are more likely to cop a bullet than a cancer diagnosis," I grin. I miss working with the guys. The banter is morbid and we all know we're on borrowed time. It makes for a unique brotherhood. A brotherhood that at some point decided to open its arms to this tomboy dyke.

Fat Tony nods towards the elevator. "What's so special about the brats downstairs that the big guns have come to sort them out?"

"I'm not the big guns, Fat," I roll my eyes.

"Aw come on, G. I know I'm not the sharpest tool in the shed, but even I can see who's running the show."

I purse my lips, annoyed that I have to keep repeating the lines of loyalty to my brother like I'm a politician on the campaign trail. "Elio is the boss. I'm off downstairs. Say hello to Cath from me."

Matty is already in the basement laying out a selection of tools. He's taken off his blazer and business shirt and is wearing a singlet tucked into his dark trousers. I stroll into the sparse space rolling the sleeves up on my dress shirt and raise my eyebrows in greeting to two of our guys who have been tasked with standing guard over the prisoners.

The residual odour of bleach from previous clean-ups gives the place the smell of a hospital and an indoor swimming pool. The scent is nostalgic for me. This is where Dad taught me that leaders sometimes have to use fear and violence. It is where he showed me that the boss must be willing to do what he asks of his men.

I was about 12 the first time I was allowed down here. Maybe 14 when I witnessed my first cleanup. Seventeen when I was allowed to pick up the tools myself.

I was born to be mafia, I have no doubt. But it was Dad who crafted me into a ruthless killer. I don't thrive on the bloodlust as much as Matty, but I feel the thrill and the power. It is intoxicating.

Elio avoids coming down here as much as possible. I honestly don't know that he has even killed a man before. Something that would make him a total anomaly among dons. He's the gentlest of us; the lover of all things light and pleasurable. The worst possible one of us to be Don.

My phone rings in my pocket and I'm about to silence it when I see it's Elio calling.

"Good to see you're alive," I answer with a growl.

"What are you doing at the warehouse?" He barks.

"You would know if you had been around the past week." My voice is a lot calmer than I feel. I want to rage at him. Demand he acts like a 36-year-old man and not a petulant 20-year-old who can't think beyond the next party.

"Baz just called and said you're running a clean-up without him." He has the temerity, the fucking audacity, to sound irritated and he is so lucky we are conducting this conversation over the phone because if he were in front of me I might just headbutt him.

"Why would that be any of his business?" *Or any of yours given you don't take any interest in Famiglia business.*

"Because he is one of Dad's capos and he is still advising me."

"Advising you on what?! How to achieve an even fucking tan?" I explode, managing to make Matty's head jolt up in surprise. He scowls and returns his focus to his tools of torture.

Pinching my nose and breathing deeply, I lower my voice so the two soldiers nearby can't hear. "Have you forgotten your role in this is to sit still and do whatever I motherfucking tell you? Can you just show the fuck up and play pretend like you're supposed to!"

There's a silent pause and I can almost hear the cogs in his brain going.

"Right. Baz wound me up and was saying that Dad expected him to advise me. I'm hungover as fuck and not thinking straight," he sighs and that is as close as I'm going to get to an apology from him.

For a smart guy, Elio is easily manipulated and Baz knows that. Fuckin' snake.

"Next time he calls you, remind the cunt who is in charge. And stop listening to him, for fucksake. The circle of trust is us siblings now. Dad gives advice, but it's me, you, Matty, and Massi in charge now. Don't trust anyone else."

He grunts in agreement. "Righto. I need to sleep this hangover off, but I'll give you a buzz later and catch up on things."

"Wish I could sleep my hangover off," I mutter to myself after he has hung up.

Now even more frustrated and irritated, I stomp over to the two men tied to chairs in the middle of the room surrounded by plastic drop sheets. They have paper bags over their heads and their arms are tied behind them with zip ties.

"Didn't you feel like stringing them up from the ceiling?" I call over my shoulder to Matty.

"Nah, I didn't wanna waste time. I suspect this won't take long," he replies, pushing a trolley containing his selected tools toward me.

As it rolls over the slightly uneven concrete the steel implements clang and clatter. The sound has the trussed-up men whimpering and squirming, terrified by the approaching pain instruments they cannot see.

Matty brings the trolley to a halt and saunters over to yank the bags off their heads, crumpling each paper bag and tossing them over his shoulder. Finally able to see, they whip their heads around wildly, trying to take in their surroundings as quickly as possible.

Not only are they younger than I expected, but I quickly realise I've seen them before.

"You've been in my club, " I don't ask, I tell them and while one of them slowly shakes his head, the other nods keenly.

"Ooosh. Not a great start boys," I laugh as they look furiously at each other, desperate to communicate and get their stories straight.

"Where's your fearless leader, Billy? Why's he left you to face the music?" I continue.

They are trading looks again, but don't reply.

I tut. A slow click of my tongue and a shake of my head.

"What do you think I'm going to do if you don't start replying? Huh?" My gaze lazily slides over to the tools on the trolley.

"W-w-e don't know where Billy is," one of them trembles as he speaks up.

"But it *was* you two and Billy who threatened Francesca Rossi while she was at work?"

No answer.

I put out my hand and Matty slaps a small hammer onto my palm. He knows I like breaking fingers.

"Y-y-es, it was us," the same guy shouts while his buddy glares at him. We have identified the loose lips of the pair.

"Did you think it was wise to threaten a Marino? You know she is marrying into our family, yes?"

When my question is met with silence, I turn and call out to our guards. "Bring over a table and untie their hands."

The two bikies are red-faced and sweating, engaged in a silent argument about what they should and should not say.

Once the *Famiglia* soldiers have the quivering bikers' hands flat, fingers splayed on the tabletop, I tap the hammer lightly on the wooden surface. "If you don't answer this next question, I'm going to break one of your thumbs. One *each*. Why did you threaten Francesca?"

The silent bikie shakes his head as if to say 'I'm not saying anything'. I shrug and bring the hammer down hard on his thumb, shattering the bones and causing him to cry out in pain. He thrashes around trying to pull his injured hand into his chest, but our soldier is much stronger and holds his hand in place.

Immediately his chattier friend pipes up. "We were told to scare her out of marrying Elio Marino! That's all!"

"That's all," my voice is almost a whisper, but I swear it could freeze Sydney Harbour on a summer day. "That's all? Francesca's delicate neck was black and blue for a week. Was it your hand that left those marks on her?"

The talker shakes his head profusely while his buddy whimpers quietly.

"Who left the marks on her?" I ask them both.

"Not me," sobs the talker, instantly dobbing in the man next to him.

But suddenly the other man has something to say too. "It was Billy!" he gasps, glaring at the man next to him as if to dare him to contradict this accusation.

"Convenient given he isn't here," I sniff and turn to my brother. "Jesus, Matty. These two are just kids. They probably think when they get shot they'll go back to the beginning of the level to respawn."

At the word 'shot' the talkative biker starts sobbing and begging for his life. The other guy is hunched over his mangled thumb, breathing heavily.

"I don't think they have much useful information, G," he says and I agree we aren't going to get anything substantial from them.

"Shall we just get to the punishment then? I've got a busy afternoon," I push my sleeves further up my arms, nearly to my elbow.

"W-w-what's our p-p-punishment?" the talker asks. Pathetic little whiner. We were taught to shut the fuck up if we were captured by enemies.

"Well, I could kill you. Easily. But I want you to go tell your mate Billy what will happen to him if he even thinks about doing something like this again. Can you pass on the message?" They both nod at me, relieved.

Their relief is short-lived when I ask Matty to pass me a meat cleaver. "You do one and I'll do one," I tell Matty and he nods. The biker's eyes widen and panic sets in once more. Chatty lad's begging goes up a notch and the smell of urine overpowers the scent of bleach in the room as he pisses himself. Gross.

"You're each going to lose a hand. But because I'm nice, I'll let you choose which hand."

My face and white shirt are splattered with blood as we head back upstairs and I feel much better. The swing and clunk of the meat cleaver slicing through flesh and bone echoes in my mind. Retribution always feels good.

No one fucking touches Francesca Rossi. I want those little bikie birdies to sing. I want them to tell everyone who will listen that if you fuck with Francesca, you will get fucked up by the Marinos.

CHAPTER THIRTY ONE
GIOVANNA

32 Years Old

"Mum, honest to God, I will spit in the cunt's food if he is invited to one more family dinner," the venom in Massimo's voice makes me do a double take.

Peta has a saucepan on every ring of the stove and she is in full Sunday dinner mode. One hand is on her hip and the other holds a wooden spoon, red sauce dripping from it onto the floor as she gapes at her gigantic man-child.

"You're going to spit in who's food?" I ask, smacking Massi lightly on the back of the head as I slouch into the kitchen in search of a Gatorade and some painkillers. Hangovers are worse in your 30s. It's all downhill from here.

"Oh, no one! Your brother is just being a hormonal teenager!" Peta is shrill and Peta is never shrill.

I narrow my eyes. "Well, *that* was convincing, Pete..." Especially since he is hardly a spotty prepubescent kid. He's 18 and well over 6ft tall.

Massimo is glaring at his mother with a ferocity I have never seen before. It is unsettling. These two are usually as thick as thieves. He is a mummy's boy and Peta thinks the sun rises and sets on his big half-Italian head.

"He's just grumbling about having to spend time with all of us old folks, right Massi?" Peta persists, this time with a false smile so tight it is practically a grimace.

"Whatever," Massimo responds, rolling his eyes and pushing off his stool. He thuds past me and out of the kitchen without a backward glance.

"Just…don't, Giovanna. Please?" Peta pleads, shoving a tray of butterflied lamb into the oven.

I grunt and take a big gulp of my Diet Coke. I'm smart enough to drop the matter now, but there is no way I won't be extracting the truth from Massimo as soon as possible.

The opportunity presents itself just after dinner when all of our guests have left. Massimo finishes loading the dishwasher with Dad and dashes upstairs to his room.

He already has his gaming headset on and is sitting in front of his computer when I let myself into his room a few minutes later.

"Have you ever heard of knocking?" he snaps. He doesn't want to talk to me, I can tell that much. He's clever enough to know that I have questions following the cryptic and highly suspect incident in the kitchen today.

"Learn to lock your door," I respond blandly and step into his room. "What the fuck died in here, you fuckin' animal?"

Holding my nose, I pretend to gag and look around for the source of the putrid aroma.

He glares at me, offended at the suggestion that there might be an unpleasant smell in his room. "Get. Out."

"Nah, we need to talk," I take a seat cautiously on his unmade bed. Who knows what could be lurking in the pile of sheets. Crusty socks, half-eaten snacks, a bloody possum, who knows.

"Don't feel like chatting. Maybe another time."

"Turn that thing off, Massimo. I'm not fuckin' around," I lower my voice menacingly and the kid knows it is time to cut the attitude.

With a flourish that is distinctly teenaged and just a little bit camp, he tosses his controller aside and rips his headset off. "What?"

"You know what. Whose food do you want to spit on?"

His eyes are suddenly very preoccupied with the carpet. Emotions are bubbling very close to the surface. He is sad, but he is also full of rage that I don't usually see in him.

After exhaling slowly he finally looks up, but his shoulders remain hunched over as if to protect himself. "Do you seriously not know?"

A flash of irritation threatens to derail my patient attempts to cajole my youngest sibling into telling me what I want to know. Of course, I don't bloody know. That's why I'm asking, bloody hell.

"I wouldn't be asking if I did, Massi. Now, come on. Spit it out."

"David. Uncle David. I want to spit in his food," he rushes out and then returns his gaze to his floor. "Want to do more than that."

Huh. "Can't say he is my favourite person and he is a creep…"

Before I can complete my sentence, Massi interrupts. "He's the reason Francesca is gone."

"That was two years ago…" I don't understand why this is all being dredged up now. "I'm going to need you to break this down for me."

And with that, he starts speaking and like opening the floodgates it all comes out. "Remember that party just before she was sent to England? It was here, but you were away in Melbourne."

I nod. I do remember. Mostly because the vibe was so off-kilter when I got back. Everyone was on edge and Francesca was gone. I had a lot of shit going on in my life at the time so I kinda just left it be and it went away.

"Heaps of people were here. Was one of the rowdier parties we've had at the house. And me and Ches had been watching Parks and Rec in the TV room. We weren't drinking or anything. Just had pizza. It got late and we were sleepy, but we decided we would watch one more episode. Cheska left to go to the bathroom first…I-I must have drifted off to sleep on the sofa. When I woke up she wasn't there. Checked my phone and I'd been knocked out for more than half an hour. I thought maybe she left me there 'cause I was sleeping -" he continues, swallowing hard.

"I went looking for her but she was nowhere in the party so I went upstairs. I thought she might have crashed in my room or something. She wasn't there, but when I was walking back to the stairs I saw a light was on in the spare bedroom. The one down Elio's end. Light was like coming under the door. No one goes in there and I thought 'That's weird'. I went to have a look." He stops, clearly not wanting to revisit the memory, but after a few seconds and a deep breath, he continues.

"I found her…and him," he looks up, fury blanketing his expression. He doesn't need to say more. I know. *I know.* Better than anyone else. "She was fighting him off, but he…he already had her pants off…"

Rage explodes behind my eyes and it takes everything in me to remain composed for Massimo's sake.

Instead of seeing red, I see black. Blackness clouds in and I'm swamped by the overwhelming urge to tear the limbs off David Rossi. There is a special place in hell for men like him and I'm happy to help him get there on an express ticket.

CHAPTER THIRTY TWO
FRANCESCA

Fat Tony's son is getting married to Auntie Savia's daughter and it's a massive deal because it is the first time in years that mafia brats are choosing to marry each other instead of shacking up with Aussies and drifting away from the *Famiglia.*

I have been informed that not only will I be attending the big event, but Elio and I will be resuming our own pretend relationship and going together. We have barely spoken since our screaming match after his pool party, but it seems he has been given the same hard word I received and we are again being thrust together.

The only thing that sparks the excitement that had me dress shopping and getting my hair and makeup done is the thought of Giovanna's reaction to seeing me all dolled up. After our night at GAYBAR over a week ago I have only seen her in passing.

She's avoiding me, I think.

That brief time on the dancefloor and the way she touched me and looked at me, tell me that the avoidance isn't about not wanting to be around me. I know she wants me now. It is about avoiding temptation.

I can still hear her deep voice next to my ear, giving me shivers, and feel her hand skimming my back. Seeing her crave me as I crave her has sustained me in the days since. Her approval was all I wanted once, but now it is her desire. I need her to yearn for me. I want to watch her suffer as I do.

Tonight, I am determined, desperate even, to get another hit of Giovanna's attention. Even if she won't touch me and even though we will be surrounded by family, I will burn for her in the hope I can set her alight.

My dress reaches right down to the floor. It is a deep emerald green corset that flows into looser satin folds with a side split that reaches my upper thigh. All silky satin, it is the most beautiful thing I've ever worn.

Elio is wearing a classic black suit without a tie and with his white dress shirt unbuttoned far enough to show off more than a sliver of his chest. It is simple, but as always he oozes sex appeal, style, and wealth.

With one last coat of shimmering body powder swept over the leg that is exposed by the deep slit in my dress and a slick of gloss applied over deep burgundy lipstick, I steel my spine and make my way downstairs.

My parents and the Marino family must be all gathered in the big living room. I'm fashionably late to the pre-drinks Peta organised and Massimo has already been sent up to see where I am three times.

My heels click against the polished stairs and I steady myself with a hand on the wall. My heart races in anticipation of Giovanna's serious face frowning as she takes me in and tries to resist how I make her feel. I won't let her avoid me tonight.

Elio appears at the bottom of the stairs and offers me his hand. He's smiling, but I can see the tension behind his eyes. I give him a polite smile in return and allow him to lead me into the room.

"You look incredible," He says in uncharacteristic seriousness and I, again, grant him a small smile. The way his gaze caresses me, showing clear appreciation for how I look, is no longer pleasantly validating. Now, it's an irritant.

Any attraction I had for the guy is dead and buried. His behaviour has tarnished his good looks and rendered his charm impotent. No matter if he is on his best behaviour tonight, I will not be entertaining any attempts to get me into bed.

There's a gasp from Peta and approving noises from my mother, and then my searching eyes find Giovanna. Just as I hoped, she drinks in my appearance thirstily and looks like she's been sucker-punched. But, I only get a split second

of satisfaction at the lust in her expression before my stomach bottoms out and reality whacks me in the face.

Giovanna and I are staring at each other, a live current surging between us, when a hand slides around her bicep, and Bex from the club last week appears at her side. A smug smile hangs on her face and the way she clutches at Giovanna makes it clear she is here as her date.

It's my turn to be sucker-punched. All the air leaves the room and I can't help but clutch at my lower stomach as if I truly have taken a blow. Giovanna sees it too. Her eyes zero in on where my hand presses, guilt flashing across her face.

I take a step backward, all of the confidence I basked in all day has been sucked away. At the same moment, Dad catches sight of me and his lip curls up in distaste. "Go and change, Francesca. You're not wearing that," he snarls.

My face falls. This could not be going any worse. I half expect someone to stumble into me and pour a drink over my beautiful dress or for one of the decorative candles in the dining room to set my hair on fire.

"You disrespect me and your fiance," Dad nods towards Elio, "dressed like that. Everything hanging out."

Elio opens his mouth to say something, but Mum jumps in for once, pleading, "Oh leave her alone, Paul. It's just a bit of leg."

The look I give my father is pure hatred. "I'll wear whatever I want."

"Well if you're happy looking like a slapper," he sneers and I'm struck again by how thoroughly Paul Rossi shows his displeasure at the existence of his children.

We barely have time to recover from the awkwardness of my father's comments when fate delivers something worse than a ruined dress or burnt hair. The back door opens and we all turn to see Uncle David walk in as if he has every right to be here.

My eyes raise to the ceiling and I shut them briefly, wondering if I'm in my own version of *The Truman Show* and everyone around me are simply actors torturing me.

Tears well and rumbles of fury roll through my chest. I have a choice. I can cry and run back upstairs; refuse to go to the wedding. Or, I can unleash my anger and cause a scene.

"It's funny you think I look like a whore in this, Dad. I was wearing sweatpants and a t-shirt when your brother r-raped me." The room goes silent and the silence gives me some strength back. God, I wish I hadn't stuttered though.

David stops in his tracks on his way across the great room. Perhaps this is the first time he has ever heard the words that describe his vile actions spoken aloud. Maybe if someone had stopped and said the words it would have been more difficult to usher me out of the country and allow him to carry on as if nothing happened.

If looks could kill, Giovanna would slay him right here and now. Forget looks, given the opportunity she would kill him with her bare hands.

"What are you afraid of, Dad? The worst has already happened!" I continue in righteous fury. "And what I was wearing didn't save me."

Embarrassment slips past my shield of fury and leaves my cheeks scorching and my stomach swirling. Airing my dirty laundry isn't cathartic. It hurts me just as much as it inflicts blows on my intended targets.

"What is David doing here? Have I not made myself clear?" Giovanna growls looking around the room before settling her searing gaze on Dad and Sandy.

Dad sniffs. "He is my brother," he states as if that is explanation enough.

"And I am your daughter," I whisper, annoyed that he can still hurt me with his lack of paternal affection. Am I so insignificant? So disposable?

"Isn't it about time we left the past in the past?" David lurks on the periphery of the large entertaining space. His eyes gleam hungrily at our gathering. Pathetic attempts to reinsert himself into the *Famiglia* make him look creepier, needier.

"Out," Giovanna commands, breaking the silence. She steps forward and addresses the room. "*He* is not welcome in this house. Ever. Now fuck off, David."

He turns on his heel after ascertaining that his brother isn't going to step in. He scampers off and I wish he'd take my Dad with him.

"Well, this has been fun!" Elio breaks the tension. "Francesca, you look beautiful. What would you like to drink?" This time the small smile I give him

is genuine. He's an arsehole, but unlike my father, he has some redeeming features.

The room quickly splits in half by generation. My mother coddles her husband, soothing his bruised ego while Peta gives Sandy grief, about what I'm not sure. In the meantime, Elio has thrust a glass of rose into my hand and his siblings gather around to comfort me.

Despite my intentions to hold Giovanna's attention tonight, I am the one avoiding her eye contact. She stood up for me and while I'm grateful, the whole incident was rather humiliating. The mere knowledge that she knows I'm broken makes me nauseous.

Therapy has taught me to challenge my self-destructive thinking, but no matter what I do to resist it, I can't help but feel dirty, used, broken, and defective when I think about what happened to me. I don't want Giovanna to see those cracks. I don't want her to be exposed to the ugliest parts of me.

On top of my self-loathing and even though I have no right to be angry that she has brought a date - I'm here with her brother after all - a green-eyed monster beats on my chest. Rationality tends not to be found around feelings as strong as those that I have for Giovanna.

Bex has a vice-like grip on Giovanna's arm. Even though she's wise enough not to be openly hostile to me, I can feel her dislike radiating in my direction. That she heard my darkest secret makes me want to scream.

Her own green-eyed monster is plainly causing her trouble too. She saw us last week. She saw our chemistry and how Giovanna shrugged her off to talk to me. She watched us dance and saw the touches, the smiles, our closeness.

I return her dislike with pure, cold indifference.

Her pitch-black hair is pulled into a tight ballet bun on the top of her head. She's sorted out her regrowth since last week, I notice snarkily. Bex is naturally pretty and her makeup draws attention to her striking blue eyes. Curvier than me, she fills out her black halter-neck bodycon dress well. She's attractive, no doubt about it, and I totally hold it against her.

"Who do you want to punch more right now - your Dad or Bex?" Massimo murmurs into my ear, pulling away to grin and wink.

'Both', I mouth to him and he sniggers. 'Fuck my life', I mouth again. He gives me a sympathetic grimace.

"You're way hotter than her, babe" he whispers just as Matty appears behind us.

"Hotter than who?" He asks and I cringe.

Neither Massimo nor I say anything, but Massi's eyes slide over to land on Bex. Matty frowns and his sister looks up just as he is assessing the situation and her gaze automatically snaps to me, a morose look on her face. He turns to me, head tilted.

"I told her to have some fuckin' self-control," Matty mutters to himself.

"Nothing has happened, Matty. I'm just doing the puppy dog thing," I sigh.

He shakes his head and places his face in his hands. "This is some Home and Away shit. Am I the only one without drama in this family?"

"Hey!" protests Massi. "I know you've been a bloody boy scout since you got out of lock up, but I'm not a drama llama either!"

But when Matty raises his eyebrows and gives him a look loaded with meaning, he concedes, "Fine." Hmmm. I'll file that away as something to ask Massi about later.

I'm successful in avoiding Giovanna and Bex for the entire pre-drinks and drag Elio into a car with Massi and Matty leaving them to travel alone to the wedding. They sit directly in front of us in the church and I'm treated to a closeup experience of Bex's flirtation while we wait for the bride to arrive. It is uniquely infuriating and I spend the time daydreaming about dragging her out of the church by her hair.

Sarah is a beautiful bride in her white sleeveless gown. I don't know her very well, but she is cousins with the Marinos so I've seen her around. She manages *La Fazenda* for her mum these days. Even without the personal connection, when she catches the eye of her awaiting husband, the look of pure adoration on her face has me tearing up. I turn to look at Tiny, standing at the altar, and see the same expression on his face. I wipe a stray tear from my cheek and notice that Giovanna, in the row in front, isn't watching the bride, she's fixated on me.

Quickly averting my eyes, I focus on the huge guy dwarfing the priest at the altar. Just like his dad is ironically Fat Tony, Tiny is the opposite of what

his name conveys. He is about 6'6 and built like a brick shithouse. Come to think of it, I can't think of what Tiny's real name is off the top of my head.

"That'll be you two next," Bex says in a cloying, sickly sweet voice as she looks over her shoulder at Elio and me. "You must be so excited." Giovanna blanches.

It is agony to know that I will not experience the emotions that Tiny and Sarah are feeling as they meet at the altar. My husband-to-be won't get choked up and think he is the luckiest man on Earth. He will drag himself to stand and wait for me because his family has him over a barrel.

"As you can see we are both super enthused by the thought," I remark dryly, sharing a conspiratorial look with my fiance and not caring about pretence for a split second. At least we are united in our disdain for our arranged marriage.

She quickly turns back to face the front and again attaches herself to Giovanna's side.

I wish I knew what Gio was thinking. Is she really into Bex? Or did she bring her because I would be with Elio? She must know by now that I would give anything to be standing next to her.

As we sit down to endure a long Catholic wedding service, I sigh and mutter, "I need to get drunk". On either side of me, Massimo and Elio reply, "Me too" in unison.

CHAPTER THIRTY THREE
GIOVANNA

The regret is instant. Bringing a date to Tiny and Sarah's wedding feels like the worst idea I've ever had the minute I see Francesca's face fall. Then her prick of a father has to stick the boot in and then David dares to show his ugly fuckin' mug. What a complete shit show.

Logically, there is no reason I shouldn't bring a date. I'm single and owe Francesca nothing. She's marrying my brother. The whole reason I asked Bex to come was to provide a buffer and reduce temptation after what happened at GAYBAR last week. I knew Bex would be all over me like a rash and that would make it difficult for me to be alone with Francesca.

Naturally, now I desperately need to speak to her privately to check she's okay, but all I can do is pathetically watch from afar and try not to get shitty with Bex.

I could throttle her when she makes a comment about Elio and Francesca being "next" down the aisle. She has always come across as pretty chill, but I told her their marriage is arranged and her comment was deliberately inflammatory. She wanted to take a jab at Francesca.

Bex is a good-looking girl and looks great tonight. Ordinarily, I would be planning to take her home with me at the end of the night, but not tonight. An angel, spectacularly beautiful but tragically neglected, has disrupted every nook and cranny of my life. Nothing feels right anymore. The only thing that brings me peace is the stolen moments with Francesca.

It's like I'm pulled into her orbit whenever she enters a room. To drag my attention from her is as much of an impossibility as defying physics itself. I'm alert to every twitch of her lips and furrow of her brow and I foresee a life of torture where I am left to observe her every move as she marries Elio and has his babies. The only thing I can imagine would be worse is the alternative, a life without her in it at all.

How could she not mess with my head when she looks like that?

She's the picture of elegance as she stands next to Elio in her deep green dress. Even the way she delicately holds the stem of her wine glass between her forefinger and thumb, bringing it slowly to her lips, is graceful. The gentle way she tosses her hair off her shoulder drives me as wild as the way she rolls her soft lips together to ensure her lipstick remains evenly spread.

All week I have been torturing myself with the memory of how good she smelled when we danced and how perfect it was when I had her in my arms. All week I've avoided her because I can't have her, but I can't resist her.

I'm punished by her haunted expression every time we make eye contact. She looks sad. Like I have betrayed her or broken her heart. She has no idea that I'm breaking my own as well.

I find myself sitting alone, nursing a glass of red wine and thanking the universe for giving me a reprieve from Bex. She went to the bathroom a while ago; I'm hoping she has made a friend and is entertaining herself.

From my seat, I can see most of the room. It staggers me that after a lifetime of being a part of this wider *Famiglia*, most of these people now technically work for me. There are a few non-*Famiglia* guests; you can spot them because they look like they've been taken on a safari. They probably think nothing of me, the dykey, grumpy woman in a suit, but the striking mafia men in their suits, towering above six feet leave them in awe.

With a loud sigh, Dad lowers himself into the chair next to me. I can practically hear his bones creaking. As is the case every time I look at him carefully these days, I see a rapidly ageing man. He needed to retire, there's no question about that. I wish he would've brought me in on everything sooner though. This has been a baptism of fire.

"Papa," I acknowledge him and take a sip of scotch.

His lined face registers surprise. "You haven't called me that since you were a kid," he states.

"Yeah, well, I guess I'm feeling nostalgic," or maybe it's just that he looks more like a Papa now that he isn't the guy in charge.

We watch the room for several minutes and many guests cast glances our way. They know I have always been Dad's protege, even if I was too 'flawed' biologically to inherit his 'kingdom'.

I've lost count of the number of times I've heard "If only she was a boy". My answer is usually "If only we didn't operate under archaic rules that would rather see an unsuitable male than a perfectly suited female lead the family". Dad would then inevitably start a lecture about the importance of tradition and ritual in maintaining power.

"He's a good boy," Dad nods towards Tiny, his arms wrapped around his new wife on the dancefloor. "His Dad has always been good to me. Tiny will be loyal to you."

"You mean to Elio," I murmur, dispassionately.

He makes a frustrated sound and throws his hands in the air. "You know what I mean." Then briskly changing the subject he asks, "Has your brother pulled finger and started treating Francesca right?"

Maybe it's because of the drama before the wedding or because I've been forced to think more about David since Francesca returned home, but I find my usual controlled demeanour shaken by this comment. "Treat her right? When has anyone in this *Famiglia* ever treated that poor girl right?"

He surprises me by grunting in a kind of acknowledgement. "I regret that you know?" I just about choke on my own spit. Alessandro Marino doesn't admit regrets.

"I should have exiled him, but it was an unstable time and Paul and David were keeping the ship steady… Did you know Fat Tony didn't speak to me unless he fuckin' had to for about a year because I let the scumbag hang around?"

I shouldn't be surprised, but I had always felt like I was the only one who was willing to deal with David. "You know I've always looked up to you, Dad. I've always known I'd be working for the *Famiglia* for life. But, Christ, that changed how I saw you."

He swallows hard and his flash of vulnerability rocks me. "You won't understand all of the decisions I made and I won't understand all that you'll decide," he grinds out eventually.

I lower my voice and look Dad dead in the eye. "I will kill him," I whisper.

"I know and when that time comes he will deserve it," Dad claps me on the shoulder.

He levers himself back out of the chair with some effort and makes his way over to where my stepmother is talking to Fat Tony and his wife Kiri. Even with his slightly stooped posture and aged appearance, he manages to ooze power and command respect.

I allow myself a brief moment of exasperation for the man and the way he somehow, despite it all continues to command my respect too. His failure to push past archaic sexist traditions when Elio is so clearly not cut out for leading the *Famiglia* is a small, but persistent wound that still weeps. It is mostly under control, but it wouldn't take much for it to become a festering infected mess.

Peta spots Dad making his way over and a genuine bright smile takes over her pretty face. My stepmother is only fourteen years older than I am, but I have never doubted the unfathomable devotion she has for my often cantankerous father.

An unexpected stab of jealousy irritates me as I watch Dad embrace her as if he has been away from her for months, not twenty minutes. It's the same stab that I felt watching Sarah's face light up at the sight of Tiny waiting at the altar. Their love and obsession for each other is as plain as day.

It must feel incredible to ache for someone and know that they are yours. To hunger to touch them and be able to do so. To wake in the morning and watch the face of the one you love sleep peacefully yet to open up to the world.

"You're deep in thought," Bex's voice makes me jump. She slides in to occupy the seat Dad has vacated." What are you thinking about?"

'Oh you know, love and shit. The stuff people think about at weddings," I wasn't entirely lying.

She seems surprised. "You want to have your turn down the aisle?"

"Sure, one day," I drain the rest of my scotch. "I'm not opposed to settling down," I clarify, "it just hasn't happened yet."

Her eyes light up and I immediately regret my honesty.

"That's *very* good to know," her smile matches her voice for seductiveness and it is laced with meaning. I curse myself; I do not want to give her any false optimism that anything is going to happen between us.

"Can't see it happening any time soon though!" I quickly add and her hopeful expression falters.

Luckily, I'm saved from further discussion of the topic by my phone vibrating in my pocket. Seeing it is one of our guys who is on duty and not attending the wedding, I answer it.

"Yes?"

"Just a heads up, boss. Billy the Kid has popped up back in Sydney. Seems he's heard about his two mates being um…handicapped…" a drawling Italian Australian accent informs me.

About time. We've been trying to track down the leader of the attack on Francesca at the gym, but he had gone to ground. His Uncle Ned, leader of Satan's Sons swears his nephew has gone rogue with his current activities and based on our surveillance I am starting to believe him. Someone else is bankrolling Billy.

"Do we have eyes on him now?" I ask quietly, but I know Bex is listening with interest. She's the epitome of a tourist. This is all very exciting and novel for her.

"We had a tail on him but lost him about half an hour ago. We're a bit short on men, what with the wedding…"

Shit. I should've been meaner and made more of the guys miss the celebrations. I left a real skeleton team to handle business for tonight and it could cost us. "Keep looking for him. We're heading to *Peacocks* after this. Update me after your shift."

Bex's small hand slides up my leg from the knee to rest suggestively on my upper thigh. "It's hot when you're in boss mode," she purrs at me as soon as I hang up.

"I'm not the boss," I reply sharply. "Elio is."

She leans in closer, "It seems like you are. I like it."

"This isn't a roleplay from some Netflix mafia romance, Bex. I'm not the boss. Stop trying to make it kinky," I am unnecessarily harsh. She's embarrassed and I feel bad immediately. "Look, I'm sorry. It's just not a game, okay?"

She looks at me with big, wide eyes and it does nothing for me. How could it when I've been ruined by Francesca's doe eyes? Speaking of which, I look up to find her and see she's observing us from about ten metres away. Her gaze is fixated on Bex's arm and our intimate stance.

Pain shrouds her expression and she physically winces. Reflexively, I push Bex's hand off my lap, and even though I don't want to cause her any pain, a frisson of excitement zig zags through my chest at the knowledge that Francesca is jealous.

God, she's achingly beautiful. She's everything I love about women. Soft skin, silky hair, pillowy lips, and a decadent, feminine scent. I blatantly watch her chest rise and fall, she's affected by my attention.

Her breasts push gently up against the sweetheart neckline of her dress. Golden skin curving against emerald satin. I almost close my eyes imagining for a second what it would be like to dust her chest with kisses and then run my wet tongue along the swell of her breasts. A tug of the front of her dress would have them spilling out so I can suck one of her nipples into my mouth. This is exquisite torture. I'm wet just thinking about it.

The alcohol has my mind taking the fantasies further and soon I'm wondering if it would be all that bad for me to take her in the bathrooms here and now. *Elio doesn't even want her*, drunk Giovanna reasons. The thought of sitting her up on the counter and sliding my fingers inside her while my tongue fucks her mouth has my cunt throbbing.

But I won't fuck her in a toilet. Not the first time, anyway. If I ever let myself have her it will be in a bed where I can take my time and worship every inch of her body.

Bex follows my stare and stiffens when she sees Francesca quickly turn away. "Why did you even invite me, Giovanna?" she asks bitterly. "You're obviously obsessed with your brother's little moll."

"Don't talk about her like that," I bite out sharply. "I told you that I wanted company, but it wasn't a romantic thing. You said you were fine coming as mates."

Bex rolls her eyes and stands up, "I'm leaving," she spits, thankfully it's quietly. "Call me when you've got over your crush."

Well, don't hold your breath because I won't be getting over that mafia princess before there is a cold day in hell.

A wave of relief cascades over me as Bex gathers up her clutch and phone and charges out of the room. "Bye," I call after her mildly. Thank fuck for that. I'm never bringing a date to something again…unless it's the real deal.

CHAPTER THIRTY FOUR
GIOVANNA

Those of us kicking onto Peacocks pile into town cars and like a cavalcade we travel through Sydney's backstreets.

The headrest props my head up so my gaze is directed towards the ceiling and I don't have to actively observe Elio and Francesca sitting opposite me. That I got stuck in their car is yet further evidence that the universe is determined to fuck with me.

An inexplicable unease settles over me that has nothing to do with the couple and everything to do with the update I received from the guys on shift just before the reception concluded.

"We managed to get back on his tail," the young and enthusiastic voice told me as I sucked on my vape just outside the hotel lobby. "He has arrived at a sort of warehouse in Chinatown -"

"In Haymarket?" I interrupted him, my pulse picking up.

"Yes. There are four blacked-out SUVs without number plates sitting outside. BMWs. Look like X7s but haven't been able to get that confirmed yet."

"And is there any movement? What are they doing?"

"Nothing yet. He is inside. Bit weird that a pack of bikers have cars waiting outside for them…"

"Mmmm weird for sure," I agreed before asking him to keep me abreast of any changes and hung up.

It can't be a coincidence that we have been celebrating at the Rydges just a matter of streets away from Chinatown. I don't believe in those kinds of coincidences. Though if they were looking to strike against us they have left it too late. We were all gathered in one place up until five minutes ago.

My phone vibrates in my palm, alerting me to a text message. It reads: **All four BMWs on the move. Armed.**

Fuck. Something is going down. I have a bad, bad feeling that has my hair standing on end.

I group call Massi and Matty who are in separate cars in front of us.

"Miss us already? We literally just left, G," Massimo's voice slurs reminding me that none of us are in peak physical condition to be dealing with an active threat right now.

Switching to speakerphone so Elio can hear as well, I cut to the chase. "Bikers are up to something. Our guys tailed Billy the Kid to a warehouse in Chinatown and they all just piled into SUVs…armed."

"Shit," mutters Matty. "That's fucking close…"

"Yeap. This could have nothing to do with us, but given I just removed the hands of two of Billy's best pals I'd say we are high on his shit list." I respond.

"Connor," I get the attention of our driver, a half-Irish, half-Italian beefcake. What a combo. Christmas in his household must be nuts. "Be alert for four BMW SUVs, no plates. Possibly X7s."

Massi and Matty relay the message to their drivers and they all shift from glorified Uber drivers into protection mode, their real area of expertise.

Francesca has been silent throughout the exchange, but the terror in her expression is evident when I assess how she is doing. She sits with her knees pressed together, hands clasped together in her lap, and despite sitting next to Elio they aren't touching. It is like there is an invisible wall between them.

"You okay there, Cheska," I ask her, mentally willing my brother to put his arm around her or something to make her feel safe.

She nods vigorously, but her face doesn't display any less terror. "I'm fine," her voice is small and I have the sudden urge to vomit at the thought of her being caught up in such a potentially dangerous situation.

"Just stick to Elio no matter what happens, okay? We won't let anything happen to you." When Elio makes no moves to draw her in, I reach out and

squeeze her clasped hands in one of mine. She gulps and I mirror the action. It takes every ounce of my discipline to return my focus to my brothers when all I want to do is pull her into my lap and keep her safe.

CHAPTER THIRTY FIVE
GIOVANNA

The guys reckon my body isn't capable of fear. Some of them have said I must be a kind of psychopath or something and to be honest, sometimes I have wondered. I'm not a serial killer who murders people for shits and giggles, but I have killed more than once. I don't get off on it or anything, but I was dead calm on each occasion and I haven't lost any sleep about it. Mostly I lose sleep over the fuckers I haven't killed yet.

But, tonight I finally get conclusive proof that I am not a psychopath.

I experience fear so acute it is like a hot knife slicing up my spine. The bottom falls out of my stomach and I finally understand what people mean when they say 'time stood still'.

We have been so fucking complacent that it kills me to even think about it. Sitting ducks. Cocky, over-confident, morons. I approached security for this wedding with the naivety of a kid who has only lived through peacetime. Lax.

When we are safely home and Francesca is tucked up in bed, I will dedicate some serious time to beating myself up about this, but right now I need to focus.

"Traffic lights ahead. To our left. BMWs, no plates," Matty's voice comes through the speaker calm and direct.

"Okay, we are definitely the target. They will try to get us off the road somewhere less populated. Adjust routes accordingly," I command. "Seatbelts on, everyone."

Francesca's hands shake as she tries to pull her seatbelt across her body and I quickly take it and secure it for her. "Deep breaths, darlin'. We'll all be fine," I whisper to her gently and she just nods mutely.

As the last car in our cavalcade, we are in danger of being targeted first and all we can do is watch as the four blacked-out vehicles turn in behind us.

Just as we can't see into their cars, they can't see into ours, but I don't doubt they know which of us is in each of our three vehicles. They had eyes on us, watching so they knew when we were leaving and we made it fucking easy for them.

Our drivers stick to busy roads, but it is two in the morning and as soon as we are out of the central city the streets become quieter and quieter. Other than looping back around and heading back into the city, we are short of options. We can drive around in circles all night, but eventually, we will run out of gas.

"Get your weapons," I bark, kicking my heel back against the false compartment under my seat. The leatherbound panel pops out and I pull a semi-automatic from the cavity and check the handgun in my shoulder holster is loaded. Elio does the same.

"I don't know how to shoot," squeaks Francesca.

"We've got you," Elio says, finally turning his eyes to her. He better fucking have her. If he doesn't keep her safe, I'll…I don't know what I'll do.

"On the move, boss," Connor catches my eye in the rearview mirror and I whip my head around to see the BMWs speed up and move into the empty lane for oncoming traffic.

Here we fucking go. I quickly kiss the crucifix that hangs at my neck out of habit. It was my mother's and despite my complicated relationship with Catholicism, it brings me some measure of comfort.

Craning my neck I see the first BMW swerve in front of the car leading our cavalcade which carries Matty and the two other guys who served as Tiny's groomsmen with him.

Immediately, the rest of the BMWs move to box us in and the front car slows forcing us all to slow with it. Up ahead the night seems to swallow up the road as street lights become dispersed at less frequent intervals and there isn't a house in sight.

The dark, manicured expanse of a large golf course sprawls to our right, and some kind of nature reserve to our left. The perfect spot for an ambush.

The SUV tailing us surges forward so close it may as well clip itself onto our tow bar and the windshield, unable to be tinted so completely black, reveals two men dressed all in black as if they are members of some kind of special ops team. The one not driving holds a massive semi-automatic across his chest.

"If we can just get to the residential area on the other side of the golf course we should be good," remarks Connor through gritted teeth, his hands gripping the steering wheel hard.

"They won't let us," I respond matter of fact and emotionless. "They will run us off the road shortly. Everyone brace and then get the fuck out of the cars. Use them as shields and shoot to kill."

The words have barely passed through my lips when, as one, the BMWs pull back slightly before accelerating forwards. We are all hit from the side and the rear with a sickening symphony of crunches and shrieking metal.

Francesca's eyes meet me in the fraction of a second before we are hit and the fear in them cracks my heart. She should be safe and protected. She may have been born into this world, but she was born to be revered in it, not to be on the front line facing guns and thugs. I swear a silent oath to myself that I will get her out of this safely and it is as if she hears my thoughts because the fear in her expression is mellowed slightly by a look that conveys trust. Faith that she will be safe so long as I am there.

Instead of scrunching my eyes shut on impact, I'm unable to rip my gaze from her body as it is rag-dolled from one side to the other, kept from hurtling into the door by the seatbelt across her body.

Searing pain shoots through my left shoulder as my body slams against the car door, but adrenalin has me ignoring it and moving swiftly to unfasten my seatbelt and then Francesca's as soon as our spinning car crashes to a halt on its side.

Climbing between the front seats, I help Connor kick out the cracked windshield and then reach behind me to drag Francesca through the seats and out through the hole where the glass was. Elio follows one hand on her back, pushing her along after me.

Gunfire begins almost immediately in rapid bursts that rip through the night.

I chance a look across at our other two cars and see that Matty's car now sits on its roof, wheels still spinning in the air, but the car Massimo was in remains the right way up.

Everyone appears to be present and accounted for, crouching behind our vehicles and returning fire where possible.

"Fuck!" Bluey's voice roars through the darkness and I know he has been hit.

"No, no, no, no!" Massimo's voice follows and sensing weakness, our enemy focuses on our middle car.

"Hold here," I whisper to Elio urgently. "I'm going to cover Massi and Bluey. Get Francesca to those trees if they move in." I point to a cluster of large trees that will provide sparse coverage, but in the absence of other options appears the safest place for her.

He nods once and focuses over the upturned car at the bullets flying towards us.

Half expecting white hot nuggets of metal to punch holes in my body, I sprint from our car to crouch behind Massimo's. It only takes a few seconds, but my senses are alight and my hair stands on end as I dash past death.

A bloody wound saturates Bluey's shirt in red, but a quick inspection shows that the shot went straight through the flesh in his shoulder. He'll survive this injury, but there is a very real chance he will cop another bullet or 20 if we don't hold them off.

"Put pressure on it," I yell to Massimo over the gunfire and he tears his suit jacket off, using it to stem the flow from his friend's shoulder.

Angling my body to make myself the narrowest target possible, I peep across the bonnet of the car we are using as a shield and count nine gunmen, plus a man loitering near each car ready to jump into the driver's seat.

We are fucked. I can't see how we can hold them off. We are caught with our underwear down. Outnumbered. Outarmed. Out of fucking luck.

I'm desperately wracking my brains for some kind of plan that will get us out of here alive when Matty and the groomsmen leave their car as it goes up in flames, dashing to shelter with us.

Breathless, Matty joins me in assessing the situation. "Don't like our chances, sis," he says remarkably calmly.

"We hold them off as long as we can and never stop fighting," I tell him. "No surrender."

My words turn to ash in my mouth as I look toward the car I left Elio and Francesca behind just in time to see him shove her toward the trees I pointed out earlier. She stumbles in her high heels but is able to run surprisingly fast.

For the first time in my life, I consider if surrendering might be the best option if it only means that the beautiful Bambi-eyed woman will live. But, I hardly have time to absorb the thought when a man in black appeared out of nowhere from behind Matty's burning car. He sprints past us, firing a few unsuccessful shots in our direction.

Another of the men provides cover for him, sending bullets across the bonnet and rear of the car, preventing us from taking the sprinting man out.

My heart rate must be going berserk, but as I helplessly watch the man reach Francesca just before she can reach the shelter of the trees, it feels like it is pulled back to a slow, deep beat that booms in my ears.

We all stand dumbfounded like cuckolds as Francesca's assailant twists her into a headlock and promptly holds a huge knife to her throat. He begins to walk her towards us, confident that we will not risk shooting at him while he has her as a shield.

"Jesus. Fuck!" Massimo shouts, looking up from Bluey and realising his best friend has a knife to her throat. His voice carries the fear - that hot sharp steel slicing through veins - that I feel in my bones.

"Over here, all of you," the knife-wielding piece of shit barks at us, removing his weapon from Francesca's throat for a second to indicate he wants us all in front of the middle car that Massimo and Bluey were in.

We comply, tossing our semi-automatics to the ground as instructed and he drags Francesca keeping her body between us and him. The one remaining BMW is just a short sprint away from his back and his three men wielding guns move to flank him.

My first instinct is to intervene, but Elio needs to take control. These men, whoever they are, think he is our don and he needs to act accordingly. We are all looking to him for an indication of how the fuck this diabolic situation is

going to be handled. He remains still and I watch him with desperate intensity, willing and wishing him to do something. Anything. His eyes shift to meet mine for a fraction of a second and I imbue my gaze with as much meaning as possible, telling him to step the fuck up.

"What are you doing?" Elio asks the man simply. *Come on, brother. Put some menace in your voice, for fucksake.*

"Showing Miss Rossi the life she has to look forward to if she marries you," the man spits back. "Never safe; not even around family and friends. Always looking over her shoulder."

What the ever-loving fuck. She is the target, not just a woman unfortunately caught in the chaos. That's why they all left. They had their girl. They were never meant to kill us all. They just wanted her. Our Francesca. *My* Francesca.

Shifting my attention from my brother, I meet her eyes. As round as saucers, light-toffee coloured, I could stare at them forever, but at this moment they are killing me. She looks beyond beautiful and as dignified as ever, but the terror is radiating off her.

'It's okay', I mouth to her. 'It'll be okay'. Her lip quivers in response, but her posture remains rigid and aloof. Her nose is slightly tilted in the air in haughtiness as if to flip the bird at her assailant and show she is unbreakable. My little darling is shaking like a leaf though.

The man fists her hair, yanking it back to expose her neck further. I swear I can see her pulse beating under her skin from where I stand. He presses the knife hard enough into her flawless skin that it breaks skin and blood trickles down towards her sternum.

She whimpers and rage courses through me, eating up much of the paralysing fear that had arrived first. This fucker is a dead man. He was a dead man the minute he even thought about touching Francesca. I bare my teeth but force myself to remain still.

Elio is dithering. Asking too many questions and not applying any pressure. The guy with the knife feels like he has the upper hand and right now, he does. *What are you doing, Elio?*

I know he must be carrying another weapon somewhere. My handgun is suddenly heavy in the shoulder holster under my blazer.

Matty catches my eye. He is worried Elio doesn't have this in hand too. Massimo is still crouched next to Bluey and I can hear his heavy breathing. We are all at a standstill.

"Are you just going to sit there and watch me cut her tiny throat?" the man in black taunts Elio and I want to scream at my brother to fucking do something.

"I'm trying to work out your angle," Elio replies simply. "What is your endgame? You think you're going to walk away from here?"

The longer this drags on, the more Elio's authority will diminish. The fuckin' dog cunt facing us should be lying in a pool of his own blood already, a bullet between the eyes. I'm getting itchy to jump in and take control.

"This ends one of two ways. Either she comes with me now or her life ends here in the middle of a deserted road. The choice is yours and hers."

"If I let you take her, what happens next?" Elio asks and I want to fucking shoot him. I can't believe he is even entertaining this.

"She is kept…*safe* so long as your marriage is called off. If not, she pays the price for your failures," he states plainly.

"Why do you care if we marry?"

I can't take it any longer. As Elio mulls over what he is hearing, Francesca lets out a sob and it breaks my heart in two. She's trying so hard to be brave, but she has a fucking huge knife to her throat. She's bleeding just enough for it to be alarming without doing any real damage. I see her taking in the bright red streams charting a course down her neck and chest.

"It's okay, darlin'," I try to reassure Francesa. To Elio, I state, "He is not walking out of here with her."

His hesitancy is visible for all present to see. This is life and death and he is terrified to make a decision. Holding his gaze for a few seconds, I realise his eyes are begging me for help. Elio is out of his depth.

"Killing her here will solve the problem just fine," Francesca's attacker snaps at me, picking up on my authority and Elio's deference.

"G, please," Massimo begs me, just loud enough for me to hear. Matty gives me a slight nod, telling me without words to take control because he has my back.

I'm going to kill this man, but I need to get my gun from my holster fast enough that he doesn't have time to slit her throat before I have even cocked it. He's using her as a shield and this won't be easy.

I step forward slowly. "Mate, I'm going to give you one chance to let her go and get the fuck out of here."

I let cold, hard, power ripple from me so no one has any doubt that I am in charge now. "If not? You will die here, in the middle of this deserted road." I'm lying. He's dying either way.

He scoffs. "Does your big sister fight all your battles for you?" He looks over to Elio, but not long enough for me to draw my weapon. I need the man to really look at him.

"Yes," I laugh, filling my voice with derision and arrogance. "He's fucking incapable of doing anything without me. Isn't that right, little brother? Can't even protect your own woman. Do you need me to carry her to your bed and make her cum for you too?"

His gaze is flicking between us as I spit out the cruel words that I know are hitting Elio's ego like darts to a board. I need Elio to play along, and hold his attention.

"Fuck you, Gio!' He shouts, picking up the strategy. "You're a fucking control freak. I had it handled!"

The man with the knife barks out a laugh and his diverted attention gives me the time I need to draw my weapon. When he next glances at me, he stares down the barrel of a gun.

"Last. Chance." I grit my teeth and warn him, but he's holding Francesca far too close for me to risk a shot. I step closer.

"Stop!" He shrieks. "Don't come any closer or I'll end her."

Francesca's attention is fixed on me. Everything in her is begging me to save her. If I get us all out of this unscathed, I'm never going to forget the memory of that look. The desperation, trust, and longing. She sees me as her saviour and protector and I'll die before I let her down.

"Darlin', you're going to be just fine," I soothe her. "I'm going to kill him, okay? Shut your eyes if you need."

She nods quickly, but leaves her wild eyes open and her attacker sneers over her shoulder at me. I just need him to move slightly out of line with her so I can

take the shot. I won't risk hitting her, but the longer we remain in this stand-off, the more likely she will be hurt.

"This got out of control, didn't it?" I say in a voice that is as calm as it is deadly and which masks the dread churning in my stomach. "You didn't picture it going like this. Were you meant to just kidnap her? Or is this a suicide mission?" As I speak, Elio gets Francesca's attention from where he stands off to the side a few metres from me. I see him subtly signalling to her to gently pull away from the man so that I have room for the shot.

"We're leaving now. Don't shoot unless you want her dead," the man announces and he begins to step backward in the direction of the car behind him, just as Francesca pulls forward as hard as she can, ducking to her right towards Elio. That is all I need, just a foot of separation.

My trigger finger contracts and I let the first shot go, hitting him in the face. His body falls as I step forward and pull the trigger again, hitting him again in the head. He hits the ground, yanking Francesca down with him, his hand only letting go of her arm when it bounces off the hardened earth.

Her horrified screams pierce through my focus, but I am not done. It isn't enough to take him down. The cold fury in me isn't satisfied with that.

Francesca rolls away from the now faceless body and I stride forwards with purpose, unloading a third shot into what is left of his head. Then swiftly covering the remaining ground between us, I stand over him and empty my clip into his chest.

The remaining gunmen scramble back into their cars, and the screech of tyres fills the now quiet air as they floor it out of there leaving us alone with the body of their comrade. Tyre marks on the road and ground sprinkled with shell casings the only obvious sign they were ever there.

Shoving my empty handgun back into my shoulder holster, I stare down in disgust at the man who dared to lay a hand on my girl. An unrecognisable mess of flesh, blood, and fabric. I appear emotionless on the outside, but inside my fury is only barely tempered by the knowledge that she is now safe.

An eerie quiet has descended on the street. We need to get out of here quickly, but with no sirens able to be detected, we can afford a couple of minutes to catch our breath. All I can hear are soft cries from Francesca, arms wrapped around her shins as she sits rocking side to side a metre or so from the corpse.

Coated in blood, she still looks like a work of art. Right now she is more like a monotone Jackson Pollock, but still utter perfection. There is something about her wearing the blood of our enemies that arouses me in a way it definitely shouldn't.

My knees hit the floor in front of her like I'm dropping before an altar to pray, to atone. I open my arms and she scrambles onto my lap, her arms encircling my neck.

"You're okay, little darling." I drop my chin and murmur against her forehead. "I've got you."

I hold her shaking body and look up to see no one has moved. They're all looking to me for instructions.

"Matty, get your guys in to get rid of him," I command. Wordlessly, he obeys. He slides straight into capo mode, pulling out his phone to call his crew.

"Bluey?" I ask, looking around.

"Here, boss," he answers weakly. Sweat coats his forehead with a film of dirt and blood and he grits his teeth against the pain of his gunshot wound.

Massimo is still crouching at his side, doing his best to stop the bleeding. I instruct him to get Bluey back to our house. No organs have been hit so we can handle his medical needs without involving the hospital. The fewer questions, the better.

I bark a few more orders and then look over at Elio. He too is waiting to be told what to do.

"Brother?" My voice is firm but affectionate. He will be hurting and embarrassed for many reasons, so I give him something to do to feel less useless. "Can you call Doc and get her to meet us back at home?"

Elio digs in his pocket for his phone. He looks emotionless, but I know my brother, and inside he will be torturing himself, feeling emasculated. He won't look me in the eye. He can't look at Francesca.

Readjusting her weight in my lap, and tucking an arm under her knees, I push to my feet. Francesca tightens her hold on me and presses her face, wet with tears, into my neck. I walk her over to the only one of our cars that is still drivable and go to sit her down on the bonnet, but she won't let go of my neck.

"Hey hey hey, I'm not going anywhere. I just need to set you down for a second so I can organise getting us out of here," I tell her softly and she reluctantly lets me sit her down.

She starts shivering almost immediately. Her beautiful emerald dress is now splattered with drying blood and is doing nothing to keep her warm.

Removing my suit jacket, I thread her slender arms into it and let it envelop her. I love how huge it looks on her delicate frame. I love it even more that I catch her pressing her nose into the collar to inhale my scent.

"You okay?" I ask her gently. Her eyes shift to the mess on the road that used to be a living and breathing human being. "Don't look at that, darlin'," I say firmly and she obeys, looking up at me instead.

She reaches out for me again and I step forward so she can slide her hands around my waist and pull me close so I'm standing between her legs. Her cheek presses into my chest and she holds me tight like she is afraid to let me go. She must be able to hear my thundering heart, still surging from all the adrenalin. It's going to be impossible to sleep tonight. I'm fucking wired.

I run my hands gently over her silky hair and press a kiss to her forehead. There is nothing I wouldn't do for this woman. I'll kill a hundred more men like I did tonight. Hell, I'd kill motherfuckers just to see her happy, let alone to save her life.

"I will never let anything happen to you," I can't help but whisper to her. "I promise you. You're safe with me, *la mia cara cucciolotta*." *My darling puppy.*

"I know." They're the first words she's spoken and they come out in a soft rasp. "Please don't let me go," she pleads.

CHAPTER THIRTY SIX
FRANCESCA

"Here you go," Giovanna says softly, depositing me on the large leather sofa in her office. "I'm just going to make you a sweet tea, okay?"

Alarm must show on my face because she crouches down in front of me and presses a kiss to my forehead. "I'll be just downstairs. Five minutes max. I promise."

I nod, not wanting to seem clingy or like a baby. But, dread seeps through me as she walks away. Being wrapped in her arms made me feel safe and held all the terrified pieces of me together. For the first time in a long time, I felt protected and like I was something to be treasured.

Notwithstanding my mafia heritage, I'm not a violent person. I have shied away from the violence rife in our *Famiglia* and community. But I can't deny that seeing Giovanna obliterate the man who held a knife to my throat felt reassuring. She didn't flinch as she shot him so many times I lost count.

The first shots made me feel saved, rescued, but the rest were delivered with the satisfying tang of retribution. 'Do not fuck with us', the shots said. *Do not fuck with our girl.*

I thought I knew what Giovanna looked like in mafia mode, but it turns out I didn't. Not until today. Until I saw her kill a man with all the confidence and calm of someone who does this kind of thing *a lot*.

Underneath my terror and horror at witnessing a body being blasted apart, her sheer dominance and power made me fall for her even more. Something in

her energy calls to me and her violence doesn't detract from it. If anything, I can't help but want her more because she has spilled blood for me.

Elio again proved why we shouldn't be marrying each other. He froze, seeming to lack the motivation to negotiate for my life, and if Giovanna hadn't stepped in, I wonder if I would have been the one to die, my throat cut wide open.

Thinking about our stupid engagement only frustrates me and I push it from my mind. It isn't something I need to think about right now. Elio is simply getting in the way of the magnetic pull I feel toward Giovanna. I'd rather bathe in that.

Giovanna has dropped her tightly controlled barbed-wire fence. The moment I had a knife to my throat, I saw the fear in her expression and then the resolve to save me.

Even in my state of shock, when she called me 'darling' and scooped me up my soul sighed in relief. Her tenderness and protectiveness are like a soothing balm and I'm dreading the moment when the barbed wire goes back up and she tries to palm me off to Elio again.

Wrapped in a blanket that smells like Giovanna's androgynous perfume and curled into the corner of the sofa, her absence has me feeling very alone and fragile all of a sudden. Everything in me aches for her to touch me again. *Please don't pull away.*

When she reappears with my cup of tea and some chocolate biscuits, I can't help but sit up expectantly. I know my eyes will be giving away my desperation for her to come back to me, but it isn't like I have been subtle with my feelings up to this point.

"Doc is about 15 minutes away. She'll have a look at your neck. Drink up and get some sugar in you for the shock." She carefully passes me the steaming mug and watches as I nibble on a *Tim Tam.*

"Will you stay with me?" I ask weakly.

"I'm not going anywhere," she looks me dead in the eye and whatever she sees there has her asking, "Do you want a cuddle?"

When I nod, she takes back the cup of tea and gets me to scoot over so she can sit in the corner of the sofa. "Come," she opens her arms and I crawl back into her lap and sip the tea.

One of her arms wraps across my body holding me to her while she strokes my back and hair with the other hand. My body melts into her, limbs relaxing and tension ebbing away. If I was a cat I would be purring as loud as a freight train.

"How's your neck?" she murmurs, pulling my hair away so she can look at it.

"I feel kinda numb. It should hurt, but it doesn't."

"Mmm, that'll be the shock."

Draining the last of my tea, I reach out and set it on the coffee table. I'm feeling less like I could faint at any second and the quiver in my hands is more to do with my proximity to Giovanna than shock.

I could have died. We all could have died. The entire future of the Marino *Famiglia* wiped out in one night.

What would any of the stupid mafia politics have mattered then?

The man I'm supposed to marry in order to consolidate his power nearly watched me have my throat slit this evening. As harsh as it may seem, if I am neither physically nor emotionally safe with Elio, what incentive is there beyond power and wealth for me to become his wife?

Until tonight I didn't realise how important it is to me to feel protected and like I am someone of value worth fighting for. I mean, I knew I liked those things and I knew I was hopelessly infatuated with Giovanna, but after tonight? My feelings for her have expanded at a meteoric pace like air filling a gigantic balloon. They feel too big for my body and I'm afraid they'll spill out or burst.

My childhood puppy-like obsession with Giovanna is joked about by the family and the two of us have shared plenty of moments lately that make me certain that she at the very least returns my physical attraction to her. But, I haven't expressed my feelings explicitly. I haven't told her the truth of the depth of them or that I would marry her, instead of her brother, in a heartbeat.

I want to kiss every single one of the scars that are scattered, innumerous, over her body. I want to trace the defined lines of each of her muscles. I want to go to sleep encased in her warm body, protected and safe. I want to wake up the same way. I want to learn how to make love with her. And I desperately, want her to fuck me, how ever she wants.

How do I get what I want? Tomorrow I can refuse to marry Elio for the thousandth time, but while the earth feels like it shifted for me tonight, nothing will have changed for those who are pushing our unhappy union.

I want her, not him. *What would happen if I said it?* Everyone accepts she's gay because she has always been *so* completely *gay*. A walking collection of lesbian stereotypes, no one has ever questioned her sexual orientation and if they did she would probably knock them the fuck out. But me? I'm a mafia princess. I'm feminine and dainty and exist solely to be married off. I dread to think what my father would do if I came out.

Came out. Come out as what? Obsessed with Giovanna? I can't exactly come out as a lesbian when I haven't so much as been kissed by another woman. Even though I feel in my soul that kissing Giovanna would be earth-shattering. Heavenly.

Besides, I'm not, not attracted to men. I find some men attractive and have had enjoyable sex with men. I guess that makes me bisexual. Ugh, I hate that.

The idea of 'coming out' as bisexual makes me cringe. Probably because of all the negative stereotypes of bi people as greedy, cheating, attention-seekers. I don't want a threesome or to show off to men. To be honest, spending time with Massi in gay clubs and parties hasn't helped with that perception. It seems lesbians and gays are as suspicious of bisexuals as heterosexuals can be.

It is wild that I am worrying about this shit mere hours after nearly being murdered on a deserted road next to a golf course, but this shit feels existential.

Imagine if I had died without knowing what Giovanna's lips felt like pressed against mine. Imagine if I never allowed myself even the chance to take what I want from her.

I breathe deeply and slowly exhale, turning slightly, I place my hands tentatively on Giovanna's chest. Our faces are only inches apart and I can't stop thinking about how she looked standing over my attacker's body. She killed a man in front of me, I repeat the thought over and over

"Thank you," I whisper, holding her gaze and filling it with as much emotion as I can.

"What for, beautiful?" She frowns a little and I'm struck again by how incredibly gorgeous her serious face is. Dark features tugged into a frown, that scar in her eyebrow just begging to be touched.

"Saving me. Protecting me. Holding me." I shrug, uncertainly. I'm going to need more than a cup of tea to stop my shaking hands and racing heart now.

Giovanna lifts a hand to my cheek and I lean into it, my eyes flutter shut briefly. She tucks a piece of hair behind my ear and then softly moves her hand to cup my chin. My heart races even faster as her gaze drops to my lips. I nervously bite my bottom lip. *God, please just kiss me.*

Painfully slowly, she pulls me closer by the chin until her lips hover above mine. I can practically hear her thinking. Second-guessing herself. Talking herself out of doing what she desperately wants to do.

When she finally closes the remaining distance and our lips come together, the electricity between us gives me a thrill like nothing I have felt before. Her tongue slides into my mouth and I can't help but moan against hers.

I'm no Virgin Mary and have been kissed many times before, but I have never felt like this. My whole body reacts to hers and I'm dizzy with how hot it is. How did I not know that kissing could feel like this? Just a few seconds of locking lips with Giovanna has eclipsed every kiss I've ever had.

Threading her fingers through my hair, she grasps the back of my head and tilts my head to the angle she wants. Giovanna is in complete control and I love it. I let my hands roam over her chest, shoulders, and neck, and she growls, our kiss vibrating, when I drag my nails through her undercut.

"You taste like chocolate biscuits," she mumbles against my lips with a small smile when she eventually relinquishes my mouth.

"There are worse things to taste like, I guess," I smile back shyly, already desperate for her to kiss me again.

She chuckles and gives me what I want. This time our kiss is deeper and hungrier. My insides are molten lava and I'm so absorbed in how good everything feels that I barely register that this is the first time I've kissed a woman. Does it always feel this good? Or is it just because it is Giovanna?

All we do is kiss for what feels like a long time. The tiny piece of lace between my legs grows so wet I am sure that Giovanna will be able to smell my arousal soon.

I am sitting on her lap sideways so all I can do is squeeze my thighs together in search of relief. I wish I was straddling her so I could find a point of contact and rock against her, creating friction between my legs.

Giovanna smiles when she feels my thighs clench. Her hand lazily roams to my thighs, pushing aside the satin fabric and running her fingertips from my knee to the crease of my hips over and over again as we kiss.

Desperate for more, I slowly peel my thighs apart. I need her to touch me between my legs like I need my next breath.

"Please," I whimper. Ordinarily, I would be embarrassed to be so needy and desperate, but with Giovanna, I don't care. My body calls for hers and I need her to know.

Her hand sweeps to the inside of my thighs and my whole body tenses in anticipation. I've dreamed of those long, tanned fingers sliding through my folds more times than I can count. I can hardly believe that in a second I will finally experience it for real.

Of course, just as Giovanna's beautiful hand, decorated with just the right amount of veins and big enough to envelop mine, delves tantalisingly close to my slick centre, there is a brisk knock on the door.

Giovanna yanks her hand from between my thighs and tosses the fabric of my dress back across to cover them.

"Come in," she calls out remarkably calmly and tucks my head under her chin in a tight cuddle.

A solid, short woman in her fifties strides into the room. Her short greying hair is sticking up all over the place and she looks like she has just been roused from sleep. She wears matching purple cotton tracksuit pants and sweater and rolls a suitcase, the size of carry-on luggage, behind her.

"Thanks for coming, Doc. Apologies for waking you," Giovanna greets her before introducing me. "Francesca, this is Dr. Margaret Hunter. She works for the *Famiglia.*"

"Call me Marg."

Despite her unorthodox attire, Marg is efficient and professional, if not particularly warm. She inspects the wound in my neck, cleaning it carefully to prevent infection.

"Hmmm, I'm going to need to chuck a few stitches in where it is a bit deeper just here," she points to a spot on my neck that I can't see, but Giovanna nods. I'm still sitting on her lap and Dr. Hunter instructs me to get up and lie down flat on the sofa.

"I'll stay right here by your feet," Giovanna kisses my temple seeing my reluctance to leave the safety of her embrace. She gets me up and helps me to lie on the sofa, treating me so gently I again get the deliciously warm feeling that I'm precious to her.

True to her word she perches at the end of the sofa and gently squeezes my bare feet while Doc injects me with some local anaesthetic.

It hurts a lot, the injections and then the stitches, but all I can think of is our kiss. I've been pining and fantasising about it for so long that as the minutes pass since our lips parted I start to wonder if this kiss too was merely a figment of my imagination.

It is like the impossible has happened, but at the same time, it is all entirely inevitable. That one kiss felt like fate; my destiny, our destiny.

It isn't the pain that has me willing Marg to hurry up and finish stitching my neck, it is my hunger to climb back into Giovanna's lap. If she'll let me. A worry that she will regret our kiss already niggles at me. She's stroking my feet and the bottoms of my legs and it is lovely, but what if she backs off as soon as the doctor has left?

What if she says it was a mistake and tries to foist me back onto her brother? My heart might just shatter.

I've wanted this for so long.

The head rush I got from her mouth devouring mine was like nothing I've ever experienced. It was so soft and languid. The most sensual thing ever and it was just a kiss.

We didn't even get to second base. Did she feel the power behind it like I did? Maybe it was just another kiss for her, like every other kiss I've had up until this point.

CHAPTER THIRTY SEVEN
FRANCESCA

16 Years Old

It feels dangerous like I shouldn't be here. I don't have permission and even if I pretend to myself that I'm just going to grab Massimo's phone charger, I know that I'm really satisfying my uncontrollable curiosity.

Desperation to learn more about her propels me. The desire to be in Giovanna's personal space and see where she sleeps, gets changed, and takes women to bed. The latter gives me a pang of jealousy.

She has a whole wing of the house to herself and I enter through the living area, it's minimally and tastefully furnished. The sofa is big and comfy-looking and I imagine what it would be like to snuggle up to Gio and watch TV. She's a lot taller than me and has lots of muscles. The thought of her enveloping me in her body has me wrapping my arms around myself tight.

My infatuation is entirely one-sided. Giovanna sees me as a child; her brother's best friend. The little girl she has babysat for years. But, I'm 16 and soon it won't matter that she is 14 years older than me. Look at Mum and Dad or Sandy and Peta. They have bigger age gaps than that.

Deep down I don't think she will ever want me though. I'm scrawny and awkward. I've seen the women she likes and they have curves, big boobs, and juicy bums. They ooze sex whereas I am a walking and talking example of inexperience and innocence. Like Bambi learning how to walk.

Massi said he left his charger in her bedroom so I head over to the door on the other side of the lounge, a thrill slithering up my spine. The door is open just a crack and as I approach it I hear voices from within. *Shit, Giovanna isn't out after all.*

'Just knock and ask for the charger, idiot' I think, but my hand stalls as I am about to rap my knuckles on the door.

"Good girl," I hear Giovanna growl and I hurry to align my eye with the crack in the door, desperate to see the lucky woman on the other end of her praise.

My heart stutters and I swear it stops for just a moment. Giovanna has her back to me. She is standing at the end of her bed and she is completely naked. Naked, except for straps that go around her hips, thighs, and bum. Her muscles strain against them and the sight triggers a throb between my legs.

She has an arm behind her head, her elbow pointing upwards, and it makes her upper back muscles ripple. My mouth waters and despite my sexual inexperience, my body tells me I want to dig my fingers into her toned back. Her other hand is gripping the hinge of the hip and thigh of a naked woman. She is on her hands and knees on the bed, bum in the air, face pressed into the bed.

With each thrust of her hips, Giovanna lets out a sexy grunt that has my vagina clenching in time with the slap of their connecting flesh. The woman on the bed is moaning like a cat in heat and I am overcome with thoughts of violence. I have never felt this degree of desperation to have something before. I gulp. I want her hands on *me*, moving *my* body, fucking me hard.

"Push back into me, babe," Giovanna instructs roughly and then rewards her with another low, "Good girl". How are those two words so hot? I want to be her good girl. I'd do anything to hear those words from her.

When Giovanna drops both hands to the woman's hips, lifting her so that her knees rise off the bed so she can plough into her harder, my insides turn to mush and I let out an involuntary whimper. I slap a hand over my mouth, but it is loud enough that Giovanna snaps her head around and her eyes meet mine.

My cheeks redden and I immediately want to cry with embarrassment. She stares back at me, eyes burning right into my soul, through the crack in the door, without breaking her rhythm. I am frozen, sick to my stomach, and yearning for a woman I can't have.

Slowly one corner of her mouth curls upward into a smirk and she winks before turning her back on me.

That wink will haunt me forever, I'm sure of it. It is torturously sexy and reminds me how entirely out of my reach she is.

CHAPTER THIRTY EIGHT
GIOVANNA

"Thanks, Doc," I say as I walk her toward the door. Francesca only needed a few stitches and her wound is now protected by a big white dressing.

"I'll just check back in on Bluey and then I'll be off," she responds briskly.

I close the door to my office slowly, I need time to think. Kissing Francesca was completely inappropriate. She is engaged to Elio for a start, plus she is only 24. I also feel bad for instigating it when she was fuckin' traumatised and in shock. I need to apologise.

It feels so wrong to apologise for something that felt so right, though. It was the sweetest, softest kiss I've ever had and god do I want more. It has been so hard to push away the attraction I feel for her, ever since she came back from the UK. Everything about her sings to me. She hits every one of my turn-ons and tonight the way she sought protection in my arms just felt so goddamn right.

Her big brown eyes widen slightly as I approach, full of expectation and a little bit of worry. I sit next to her, leaving a bit of distance so we aren't touching. Disappointment draws like curtains across her beautiful face and it hurts me to see the hurt in those expressive eyes.

"You okay?" I ask tentatively, running a hand through my hair.

She shrugs and leans away from me as if to start building a protective force around herself. "Mostly, I guess. I'm not looking forward to hearing you tell me you regret kissing me though." Tears well in her eyes and she swallows hard.

I swallow the lump in my own throat. "It's not that I regret it. It was fuckin' perfect, darlin'. I just need to apologise to you for laying it on when you've just been bloody traumatised. It was wrong of me -"

She interrupts me with uncharacteristic snappiness. "Don't apologise to me. I don't want to hear it. It was everything I wanted and wouldn't take it back. Don't ruin it for me."

"You're engaged to my brother," I whisper, reaching out for her hand. She lets me take it but doesn't respond to the thumb I stroke over her knuckles.

"I don't want to be and he doesn't want to marry me either. I've-I've wanted you, forever," her voice cracks and she won't meet my eye. "Ugh, why do I keep allowing myself to be humiliated by Marinos," she whispers more to herself than to me.

"There is nothing for you to be humiliated about, Francesca. This isn't about me not wanting you. I'm aching for you, honestly. Everything in me is screaming just to kiss you again, but I'm trying to do the right thing by you and by the *Famiglia.*"

She looks up and stares for a moment and then before I know it she has closed the distance between us and is climbing onto my lap to straddle me. I lean back and rest my head on the back of the sofa, looking up at her determined face. She places her hands on my chest and her hair slides over one of her shoulders to cascade over me. I can't help reaching out to touch it.

"I don't care about what we should or shouldn't do or what is best for the *Famiglia,*" she whispers fiercely. "I need you."

Fuck. Those three words. Her neediness speaks to my deep-set desire to protect and dominate. I groan and before I can second guess myself, I grasp the back of her head and pull her mouth down onto mine.

Our second kiss is more urgent than our first. It's needier, hungrier. My tongue sweeps around her sweet mouth, desperately exploring her taste. Her delicate fingers touch my face and she slides down my legs more so that our pelvises are pressed as closely together as possible.

She tugs my bottom lip into her mouth and nibbles at it, her hands cupping my jaw. I try to reason with myself to stop this, but I know I am too far gone. If I don't have her tonight, I feel like I'll combust.

But, I need to get her out of these bloody clothes, so I pull back and take her hands off my face. She frowns and it is the most adorably furious expression I've ever seen.

"No," she states. "Don't ruin it," she pulls a hand back and presses her index finger to my lips.

I chuckle. "I won't. I need you too," I admit. "But we need to get you cleaned up."

Scooting forward on the sofa, I wrap my arms around her and stand up. Her legs squeeze around my hips and her arms loop my neck. I carry her through the door that joins my office to my bedroom suite and she dots little kisses over my face and neck. Her sweetness will be the fucking death of me.

I set Francesca down on the counter in my en suite and get a bubble bath running. She watches my every move and unzips the side of her dress so she can tug it over her head. A groan escapes me at the sight of her tan slender body wearing only a matching black lace lingerie set.

The groan gives her confidence. She smiles sexily and reaches behind her to unclasp her bra. I'm frozen as her perfect handfuls spring out of their cups. I move to stand between her legs and immediately cup both of her breasts, running my thumbs over her little dark nipples. Lifting and squeezing them together, I drop my head to kiss each one. "Fuck," I rasp, pushing my face in between them. She giggles and drags me back up for a kiss.

"Are you going to get in with me?" she asks coyly.

"If I'm invited, yeah. But, we have to be careful not to get your bandage wet."

She starts unbuttoning my shirt. "Oh, you're definitely invited."

"Have you ever been with a woman before?" I ask not long later. We are in the bath and she is lying between my legs with her back to my chest.

"No," she whispers. Then after a few moments of silence she adds, "But I've thought about it a lot."

My hands are resting on her stomach, but I keep letting them wander up to cup her boobs because they are fucking insane and I think I'm obsessed with them. "What have you thought about?"

She clears her throat and lifts a leg to prop it up on the side of the bath. "Honestly? Well, mostly I just think about you fucking me. I don't know if you

remember, but I kinda accidentally saw you having sex not long before I left for England."

"I remember." Fuck. I try to suppress a laugh. The little pervert was spying on me. I thought it was hilarious at the time.

"I-I-I touched myself a lot thinking about that over the years," she confesses a little hesitantly. "I imagined you were fucking me like that."

"Like what?" I prod.

"Like from behind. With your, umm, strap-on."

My cunt is fuckin' throbbing at the thought of her making herself cum to fantasies of me. "You liked the look of that huh?"

"Yeah, I was so jealous when you told her she was a 'good girl'."

Interesting.

I kiss her neck and murmur into it, "Do you want to be my good girl, Francesca?"

"So much," she groans and leans her head back on my shoulder.

"Let's get out of here so you can show me what a good girl you are," my voice is low and gravelly. I am so turned on that I can barely speak.

Gently I dry her off and then myself. She stands expectantly as if waiting to be told what to do next. She's a fucking dream; so compliant and eager. Her sexual energy fits perfectly with mine.

"Take me to bed," she whispers and I don't need to be asked twice. I scoop her up in my arms and carry her into my room. Laying her gently in the middle of the bed, her hair fans out over my light grey bed covers.

I crawl over her and settle my naked body between her legs. Holding my weight on my forearms on either side of her head, I take her mouth in mine again and she wraps her legs around my hips, rocking her wetness against my stomach, searching for friction.

"You sure you want to do this, Francesca?" I double-check just to be sure.

She nods her head quickly. "I've wanted this for so long. But…um. I don't know how I'm supposed to do it…"

I look down at where her hips are grinding on me. "Your body knows what it wants, my darlin'. Don't stress. Just go with what feels good."

"This feels so good already," she sighs. "Teach me how to fuck, Gio."

Jesus Christ. If she gets any hotter, I will explode.

My hips start to rock in time with hers and I kiss her harder this time. She clings to me and our chests press together. The sensation of her breasts hard against mine drives me fucking insane and start fucking her mouth with my tongue.

Driven by pure desperation to be inside her, I slide a hand down her body and lift myself so it can dive between her legs. Her folds are slick and I let out a growl at how easily my fingers slip through them. My thumb circles over her hard clit and she gasps and arches her back into me.

Continuing to spread her wetness over her clit, I push my index and middle finger slowly inside her. Her warmth sucks my fingers in and my eyes roll back into my head with the mental pleasure the sensation provides. My tongue fucks her mouth while my fingers fuck her pussy and her little noises and reactions drive me wild.

The walls of her vagina start to tighten as the pressure builds and I curl my fingers to hit the most sensitive spot inside her. Her hips buck and she cries out. "Don't stop! Please!"

"Are you going to cum for me like a good girl?" I ask her.

"Yes! I'm…close!" She gasps.

"Who's name are you gonna say when you cum, darlin'?" I growl in her ear.

"Yours!"

My hand picking up the pace, I kiss her and then pull back to watch her cum as I say, "cum for me. You're such a good girl."

She shatters, clenching so tight around my fingers that I can't move them at all. "I'm -! Oh god, Giovanna!" she cries. She fucks my hand, riding out her orgasm, hips thrusting underneath me.

"You're so beautiful when you cum," I groan as she melts into a sated puddle. She blushes and hides her face in my neck.

"Gio?" She mumbles against my skin after a few minutes of being wrapped around each other.

"Yeah, baby?"

"How do I make you cum now?" She's so cute.

I kiss her forehead. "I'll show you. I'm going to do the work this time. I'll fuck your body until I see stars. Roll onto your tummy."

She looks like she doesn't understand what's going on, but does as she is told. Like most people, I think she assumes that the only two ways women can make each other cum is by oral sex or fingers. Well, I'm about to introduce her to the world of tribbing because I love it.

Kneeling behind where she lies face down on the bed, I gently tap both sides of her hips and say, "Up". She obeys immediately, lifting onto her knees. Seriously, if she keeps being so responsive and obedient, I'm never going to let her out of my bed.

I position myself directly behind her and press my hand into the centre of her upper back so that her tight bum is in the air, but her chest is pressed into the bed. She arches her back without being told and I give her another mumbled, "Good girl". She sighs happily.

I pull her thighs apart a little more and run my fingers through her soaking cunt again. Lining up my pussy against hers, I hold her hips and pull her back tight against me. My eyes roll back as our wetness mingles and my hard clit buries into her lips. I start to grind my hips and control hers in front of me.

"Oh, it feels good," Francesca looks up from where her head is resting sideways on her forearms.

"I fuckin' love it," I rasp back. "I'm going to cum so hard on your cunt."

She whimpers in pleasure in return. My words seem to have an acute impact on her. I like that.

"Touch yourself," I demand and she immediately slides an arm underneath her and begins teasing her clit. Her moans as she works herself back up to a climax are so hot and I can't help but fuck her faster and harder.

My fingers are going to leave bruises on the hinges of her hips that I'll be turned on by in the morning. I lift and hold her, grinding us together as the pressure builds in my lower tummy. I'm going to explode, I haven't been this turned on in ages, maybe ever. My clit is rock hard and every nerve ending sparks at the contact with Francesca's soaking wet pussy.

"I'm going to come again, baby," she moans underneath me. *Oh, I like her calling me that.*

"I'm nearly there too, beautiful. Oh fuck!" I become frenzied as my body climaxes, thrashing against her and lifting her off the bed like a rag doll.

She cums, calling out my name again and then it's my turn. "Ah! Fuck! Francesca!" I grind out through clenched teeth, dropping her hips and falling half on top of her.

My heart is going a million miles an hour, beating against Francesca's back. I kiss her shoulder and begin softly stroking her back and hips. She sighs and makes little noises of pleasure.

I can't believe this is happening. I was attracted to her before - crazy attracted - but now I'm bloody wild for her. It is like she was made for me. Her eagerness to please and her pliable submissiveness are the ideal mates for my need to dominate and control in bed.

My breathing and heart rate slow down and I'm already thinking of all the other ways we can fuck. Teaching her all the ways women can have sex would be my absolute pleasure.

She rolls over so we are lying on our sides facing each other. Her eyes are sex drunk and she looks devastatingly good post-orgasm. Practically glowing.

"Was that good for you?" she asks hopefully.

"Seriously?" I grab her chin and make her look at me. "It was incredible, my darling. You are incredible."

A big grin splits across her face and pulls at my heart. "Good because it blew my mind," she giggles. "I'm kinda speechless."

We fall into a slow, deliciously sloppy kiss before I prop myself up on my elbow and give her a wicked smile. "You don't think that's it, do you? That was just the warm-up, baby!"

Her eyes go wide as I kiss a path down her body, stopping to pay attention to each of her nipples. I tease and torture her with kisses all over her body before I finally take the swollen bundle of nerves between her legs into my mouth and give her the best head of her life.

~

I wake with a start before dawn to the distressed mumblings of sleeping Francesca in the throes of a nightmare. There is no making sense of what she is saying, but the tears that splash down her cheeks indicate the dream is not a nice one.

"Wake up, Francesca," I say softly, gently rubbing her arm to wake her. "It's just a bad dream."

Confused, her eyes flutter open, but she continues to sob.

"It's okay, darlin', you're safe." I open my arms and she wriggles over, tucking herself in under my chin. She quickly calms down and we remain silent, wrapped around each other in the dark. I've picked up that she loves any physical affection, so I lazily stroke her bare back.

A while later, when I assumed she has gone back to sleep, she suddenly speaks. "Giovanna?"

"Yeah?" I croak, pulled from the recent memories I'm indulging in. If only she knew I was reliving every moment of our earlier exploration of each other's bodies.

"Can we…Do you wanna have sex again?"

I choke on my laughter, not expecting the blunt proposal. I made her come four times before we went to sleep, but clearly, my little darlin' is insatiable. "If I ever answer that question with 'no', please take me out the back and shoot me," I laugh.

Not needing to be told twice, Francesca nudges me onto my back and climbs on top to straddle me. "That's cute," I tease her. "You think you're going to be in charge, baby?"

"Maybe," she retorts cheekily. She leans over me, breasts hovering temptingly over my face. I take them in my hands massaging them before I reach my mouth up to suck on one of her nipples. She giggles and I let her push me back down so she can kiss me. We kiss and kiss and I love it. Kissing her is heaven and she is an angel.

"Gio?" She lets my mouth go and sits up.

"Mmmm?" I'm drunk on her kisses. Fuck.

"Can you take charge again now?" She whispers, sounding just a little embarrassed.

That has me cracking up again. I'm usually the most serious, surly bitch but she somehow gets me laughing. It's not even that she's a comedian, it's just her and her quirks. I grab her by the waist and haul her up my body so she is kneeling a leg on either side of my head. With my hands on her bum, I yank

her down to sit on my face. "Ride me, baby," I instruct her and plunge my tongue inside her cunt.

Her cry of pleasure at the sudden sensation hits me like a bolt to my pussy. The needy way she immediately starts dragging her clit against my tongue and mouth is making me ridiculously wet. I look up and she is gripping her breasts, head tossed back, as she drags and thrusts. *Goddess.* How is this woman simultaneously the purest angel and a sex goddess?

My hands roam wherever they can reach; up her back, over her tummy, down her legs. I want all of her. I start to hum, sending vibrations over her pussy and causing her to cry out my name in surprise.

I don't take my eyes off her as she rides my mouth, demanding the pleasure I'm only too happy to provide her. "Baaaby," she whines and I know she's close. I zero in on her clit and grab her hips so I can control the speed and movement. She screams my name over and over as I draw another orgasm from her. With pleasure.

Before she can collapse, I lift her off me and lay her on her back. Lifting her slender legs, I position myself between them and let her ankles rest on my shoulders. My fingertips dance down the back of her thighs and I kiss the inside of each of her ankles. She sighs, satisfied.

I open the lips of my pussy with my fingers and press myself between Francesca's legs. I hiss out a harsh breath as our cunts make contact again. My clit is hard and I rub it against her wet folds slowly at first. My hands hold my weight on either side of her head and I push forward to see how flexible her legs are still hooked over my shoulders. Turns out they are pretty fuckin' flexible and I can get the perfect angle to glide against her.

"This is so good," she gasps. "I didn't expect it to be like this." Her eyes are wide and wild and she is almost delirious.

"You're so good," I drop her legs so she can wrap them around my hips and kiss her deeply, still grinding against her.

"I-I think I might come again," she says, shocked, and I smile against her mouth. Her hips are lifting to meet my grinding thrusts as she seeks out another high.

"My greedy girl," I growl in her ear and she drags her nails from my bum up my back in response. I'll have red tiger scratches, I'm sure.

My lower tummy sparks and I tell Francesca I'm going to come. She wraps around me even tighter and whispers in my ear telling me to come for her. When I do, she is just a moment behind me, crying out and then panting into my shoulder.

"Jesus Christ, Francesca. I'm nearly 40. You're going to kill me," I tease, rolling off her so I can spoon her.

"You don't fuck like an old lady," she quips, wiggling her bum against me.

"How do you know what old ladies fuck like, huh?" I tickle her ribs and she squeals.

"I know that this is the best sex I've ever had in my life," she sounds shy which is adorable. It has been the best of my life too, but I know I shouldn't make any declarations when in the morning we have to figure out what all of this means for our complicated lives.

Instead, I kiss her neck and tell her to get some sleep.

CHAPTER THIRTY NINE

FRANCESCA

Before I have even opened my eyes I can't stop a grin from splitting my face in half. I'm in Giovanna's bed! I'm in Giovanna's bed and I'm naked! Is this what it feels like to win a world cup? To finally have the thing you've dreamed and obsessed about come true?

I bury my nose in my pillow. It smells like her perfume; fresh, androgynous, jasmine, and patchouli. The sheets smell like our sex and I love that too.

I stretch out and try to keep the anxiety that threatens to steal my joy at bay. The bed is cold and Giovanna is nowhere to be seen. I wish I could have woken up in her arms. We could have had some lazy morning sex. Not that we didn't have plenty last night; I'm just pussy drunk I guess.

I should get up.

The longer I lie in bed, the further my thoughts descend from innocent and explainable reasons why Giovanna is gone to worst-case scenarios. Maybe she wants me to leave, but couldn't wake me up. Has she run from her own bedroom? Rapidly I'm destroying the memories of a perfect night of sex and intimacy with paranoia about what it all means this morning. Eventually, it feels like I've woken up the morning after the world cup win to find out there was a mistake and I didn't win after all.

Shower. I need to disrupt my spiralling mood. Turning the dial to the coldest setting, I take a deep breath and step under the stream. My body

immediately comes out in goosebumps and I shiver. The shock calms me and I take my time washing my hair and body in the freezing water. I hope Giovanna doesn't mind me using her stuff, but it's not like she is around for me to ask permission.

After changing the dressing on my neck, I twist my hair into a towel turban and steal a hoodie from Giovanna's wardrobe. It is super baggy and covers my bum so I don't bother stealing any underwear or shorts. I only need to get down the hall to the guest bedroom I'm using after all.

I make the bed, even though the sheets need changing. I just don't want to leave it messy and have her think I'm rude. What should I do with my blood-soaked dress? Can I just chuck it in the bin or do I need to dispose of it more…thoroughly? I leave it next to her laundry hamper; she'll know what to do.

With nothing else left to do, I slowly open the door that leads to Giovanna's office and poke my head, damp and unbrushed hair and all, around it.

She's sitting at her desk, reclining slightly in her chair and she looks up at the sound of the door opening. My heart skips a beat. She's even sexier now I know how it feels to be fucked by her. She raises her eyebrows, but she is distracted by the phone.

Closing the door behind me, I lean back against it, suddenly nervous and awkward. I wait for a few minutes, but it is obvious that the conversation is an important one. She's talking to someone about what happened last night. I'm just contemplating whether I should just give her a wave and leave when she beckons me over and pats her lap.

A small trickle of relief soothes my anxiety. She wouldn't want me to sit in her lap if she was trying to run away from me.

"Hold up a sec, Matty. Just getting my earpods." She quickly pops them in and leaves her phone on the desk so she has both arms free.

Back in her arms, the trickle of relief becomes a tsunami. She cradles me against her chest and kisses my forehead. Her conversation with Matty resumes, but I'm not paying attention. I'm distracted by the hand she's running up and down the outside of my thigh.

When she finally hangs up, I get nervous all over again about talking to her. She is back in boss mode, and I'm scared the woman I spent last night with is gone.

"We don't know who they were exactly. But we know they're bikies. Affiliated at least. We need to find out who paid them though," she talks into the top of my head and it takes me a moment to realise we are talking about the guy who had a knife to my neck last night. It's like anything that happened before Giovanna kissed me doesn't matter anymore.

"Oh...okay, do you think this was like a one-off? Or...should I be scared?" I ask.

She sighs. "Honestly don't know at this point, hon. My guess is that there are others involved so we are upping your security."

Hon. I've heard her call her friends that. Last night I was '*baby*'. I love it when she calls me *darlin'* too because she always has and she doesn't call anyone else that. But 'hon'' sounds like she is talking to a friend and after last night I don't want her to see me like that.

She continues talking to me about my security for a while and it's obvious she would rather talk about this than deal with what has happened between us. Finally, I just interrupt her quietly, "you regret it," I say, barely above a whisper. It is a statement, not a question.

There's silence and she goes completely still. I'm not sure that she is even still breathing. I move to get off her lap, but she holds on to me. "Hey, where are you going?" she asks softly.

"Pull the bandaid off, Giovanna. Just don't lie to me," my stupid fucking voice cracks and ruins the facade of stoicism I was trying to cultivate.

"Francesca," she lowers her voice and it sounds like a warning. "Stop it."

"I'm not wrong though. Am I? Tell me I'm wrong."

"I don't fucking regret it," she hisses. "But, -"

"Here we go. There's always a 'but'," I interrupt.

She fists my damp hair in a bunch at the back of my neck and turns my head so we are staring directly at each other. "I don't regret a single fucking thing about what we did last night. But yes, there is a fucking 'but' because I have the entire *Famiglia* to think about. You are engaged to my brother, Francesca, and the politics around that are fuckin' complicated."

"You still want me to marry him?" I gasp, the sharp pain of betrayal stabs my gut and a weight settles on my chest.

"Of course, I don't *want* you to marry him."

"But you'll stand by and let them force me to anyway?" My voice raises. I am so stupid. What a naive little girl. *La cucciolotta.* Always the pathetic puppy.

This time when I stand she doesn't stop me. "There is a lot more going on than you're aware of," she barks and runs a hand through her hair.

"I'm sure there is," I reply coolly. "I shouldn't have assumed that this would change anything. I'll leave you to it then."

I manage to hold onto my childish tears until after I've marched my bare arse out of there, but the minute I slam the door shut they fall.

CHAPTER FORTY
FRANCESCA

Massimo decides that after my traumatising experience last night - the knife incident, not the utter railing his sister gave me - we need to have a day by the pool. I haven't told him about the night of perfect sex at all, yet. I don't know if I can talk about it without getting upset.

So I act as if my morose mood is entirely down to the fact that a madman held a knife to my neck and threatened to kill me.

I choose to do my moping in the skimpiest bikini I own, purely in the hope that Giovanna has to walk past the pool at some point and is tortured at the sight of the body she will never touch again. Because she won't.

Just like I cut off Elio after that first time, it looks like I'm doomed to only bang Marinos once. Not that what we did last night feels like 'once'.

What hurts the most is that the intensity that I have always craved and never experienced was there last night. It's not just that I have wanted her for so long, it is that we burn so bright and hot together. I've never wanted a middle-of-the-road relationship, but that is all I have had until now. If I were allowed to choose my husband or wife I would settle for nothing less than searing passion and utter obsession.

If I have to suffer then so does Giovanna. She may not feel our emotional connection, but I know she's insanely physically attracted to me and this turquoise string bikini with g-string bottoms will punish her.

Massimo and I are playing the gimme-a-song game, but we are choosing for each other rather than for our own emotional state. He is making me laugh at least with his silly choices.

Pointing theatrically at me, Massimo hits play on *GAY 4 ME* by G Flip & Lauren Sanderson thinking he is torturing me about my crush on his sister and not my now-established unrequited feelings. We're jumping on the outdoor furniture screaming out of tune and to be honest it is a bit cathartic.

"Take the verse, Cheska!" Massi bellows and I butcher all the lyrics except for the most relatable bit. The bit he naturally wants me to sing.

He roars with laughter as I rub my hands down my body, swivel my hips, and shout about how I know 'she' masturbates to thoughts of me.

I curtsey to his round of applause and he sings the chorus into his invisible microphone.

"Massimo! *Porca puttana*! Pull your fuckin' head in," Giovanna shouts from somewhere behind me and he quickly turns off the music.

I widen my eyes at him and whisper, "Ooooh you're in trouble".

"Francesca! A word please," she marches inside without checking to see if I'm following.

"I think *you're* in trouble, actually," Massi says in an exaggeratedly camp voice flicking his wrist.

Giovanna is waiting in the kitchen, leaning against the bench. Her fingers are drumming against the cabinet and she has a furious scowl on her face.

I feel a bit like a lamb going to the slaughter, except that for her I'd roast myself and slather my body in mint sauce.

"What are you wearing?" She snaps at me. *Ding, ding, ding*. Victory to me.

I look down at my bathers, turn to look at the pool, and then look back at her with an innocent expression. "A bikini?"

She narrows her eyes at me and the anger in them makes me regret playing this game. I've just set myself up to be reminded of how insignificant I am. She shakes her head and looks at the floor. "What are you doing, darlin'?"

"Don't call me that," I bite out before I can stop myself.

"Why? I always call you that?" she frowns.

"Yeah, well it hurts now, so stop it." The game is well and truly over now. If I can get out of this conversation without crying it'll be a miracle.

She pinches the bridge of her nose with her index and middle fingers as if to try to squeeze out the tension.

"Sorry for stressing you out. Last night was just…I'll pretend it didn't happen, okay? But can you leave me alone because I can't - " and my voice breaks. I shake my head, turning away before the tears fall, and get the hell out of there.

I'm nearly at the door when I hear a wolf whistle and Bluey's voice calls out from the garage stairs, "damn Cheska! Elio's a fuckin' moron."

"Shut the fuck up, Bluey! Never let me hear you talk about her like that again." I've never heard Giovanna so angry. But I don't turn around. I walk outside and tumble deliberately face-first into the swimming pool.

CHAPTER FORTY ONE
GIOVANNA

The past forty-eight hours have been a fucking rollercoaster. You'd think having to kill someone would be rock bottom, but seeing the hurt and fury in that beautiful face and sexy little body kills me.

I wasn't born yesterday. That piece of blue floss she called a bikini was all for me and *fuck me* it was hot, but we have soldiers in and out of the house all day and I don't want them ogling her or getting any ideas. Fucking Bluey pushed his luck in front of me even. Not that he would have any idea about how I feel about her.

She's got it into her head that I saw last night as a one-night stand, that it was purely sex. That I see her just like any woman I could have picked up from a club. She assumes I didn't feel our electric connection and insane chemistry. The opposite is true, but I am juggling a million balls in the air right now and I can't figure out how to get her out of this marriage with Elio.

Technically I could just say it isn't happening, but the arrangement was Dad's last move as Don and he wants it to be seen through. Even in retirement, he holds significant power over us all. He can ease the transition in leadership or make our lives very difficult.

My body physically aches with the need to go to Francesca and comfort her, but I need time to sort out this mess. I don't want to make promises I can't keep or fuck things up for the entire Famiglia.

Her tears affect me. I'm cold, calculated, and disaffected usually, but when it comes to her everything crumbles and I would sell a fuckin' kidney to put a

smile on her face. She makes me weak and that is very, very dangerous for someone like me.

Fuck. Right now I need to find Elio. He's been missing in action since last night and I need to bring him in for damage assessment. I quickly type out a text to Massimo and then force myself to focus on the task at hand.

Me: Look after Francesca, please. Don't leave her side.

I'm in a foul mood and Bluey is copping an arctic blast from me as he drives us into the city.

Last night was one of the most incredible nights of my life and yet I managed to fuck it up so thoroughly this morning. I allow myself a moment of self-pity; to wallow in the unfairness of a life that means I have to watch my brother in the role that should be mine and set to marry the girl who brings me to my knees. And he's fucking both up. He doesn't even want them.

If it weren't for all this shit with Stefan and the Rossis and needing Elio to fucking hold this shit together, I would have spent the morning in bed with Francesca. I would throw myself head first, for the first time in my life, and tell the world that she is mine. Instead, I have to push her away and hurt us both in the process.

My gut is churning and I'm not used to the distracting physiological responses to my emotions. I can't afford the distraction, but I am plagued by it regardless.

My phone rings as I take the elevator up to our offices.

"Tell me you've found him," I sigh to Matty.

"Yeah, I've got him," Matty drawls. "He's been shagging up a storm at some socialite's house."

Of course, he has. "Bring him into the office. Work, not home."

Elio looks defiant despite the bags under his eyes, his crumpled suit, and a massive hickey visible on his neck. He sits on the other side of my desk, legs spread wide as he reclines and looks down his nose at me. Defiant. Matty is leaning against the wall next to us, regarding the tension with his usual dispassionate silence.

"Last night was…full on," I began and Elio snorts. "Yeah, understatement, right?" I joke.

"We will talk later about what caused…your inaction. We need to be able to rely on you in those situations and Francesca could easily have been killed."

"Thought you just said we were talking about this later," he snaps.

I pause, staring at my angry younger brother. A man at 36, but still the cheeky kid who was always getting into trouble and then smiling his way out of it.

I feel like I'm watching his self-destruction in double time and can't do anything to stop it. A train crash in slow motion. Elio has always been the fun-loving, good-time guy. The optimistic, pleasure seeker where Matty and I are in our element in the darkness. I don't like the man who sits in front of me fuming and bitter. He bears no resemblance to our Elio.

"It's fair to say things are escalating," I continue. "We need to know who ordered the ambush. If Stefan had a hand in it, we need to make an example of him."

"On it," Matty mutters.

"Elio, I know you're angry, but if we don't show a united, stable front, Stefan and, by proxy, Romano will walk in and take everything," I need to make him understand how precarious things are. "For the love of god can you give chasing pussy a rest for, I duno… a month? We don't need the side drama."

"One month?" he raises an eyebrow. "Does that include chasing my wife-to-be's pussy?"

His words hit me hard and I feel like I've been winded. Every fibre in my body wants to reach across and slug him in the face.

Mine. Mine. Mine.

My brain tortures me with images of the pussy being discussed, shiny and wet for me. I know how it smells and tastes and the thought of anyone touching her again makes me feral. But the *Famiglia* needs this marriage and I swallow my pride and say, "No, but you'll need to start treating her with respect if you think she's going to let you back between her legs."

This is so fucked up. If I didn't know he'd been whoring around last night, I'd feel guilty about sleeping with his fiancee.

I turn my attention to Matty, "Have we still got eyes on David Rossi too?"

"You think he's involved?" he responds.

"It's the type of shit he loves and he is hanging around like a bad smell even though I gave him his marching orders."

He nods, "I'll make sure we have him tailed."

"It's all on us now, brothers," I stare at them both and the hollowness I get back worries me.

CHAPTER FORTY TWO
FRANCESCA

Sixty-six days to go and this morning I lay in bed wondering if I should just stop fighting it. Just switch off my brain and allow the Marino Famiglia and my parents to push my shell of a body around their chessboard.

Now that I know that Giovanna doesn't want me beyond the night of sex we had, there isn't much point in resisting the marriage to Elio. Whether I marry him or anyone else I will be miserable because it won't be her.

I may as well give up on my dreams of a loving marriage and focus on the second part of my dream - motherhood. All I have to do is lie there and let him fuck me without birth control for a few months, maybe more, and then I can focus the rest of my life on my children.

Elio will have his mistresses, but so long as I don't know about them and he doesn't knock them up, it won't matter.

Massimo drives me to my wedding dress fitting. We pick up Sammy on the way and the pair of them try their best to lift my mood, but even though I'm not putting up a fight, I feel like today is all an elaborate sham designed to make me choose the outfit I'll be buried in.

Mum and Peta are already waiting at the boutique, each holding a glass of champagne. Their heads are huddled together and they're talking in hushed tones, but I'm a robot now and no longer have any curiosity about what they could be talking about.

Eyes straight ahead, I walk stiffly into the exclusive establishment and take a seat on the ornate pale pink lounge seat situated facing the grand changing room and modelling platform.

Sammy follows me immediately like the good friend she is. She sits next to me, as close as she can, and picks up my hand, squeezing it tight.

Behind us, Massimo kisses his mother and I hear mine ask him if I'm in a 'mood'. *Well, if you consider deleting all your feelings and becoming an ice queen a 'mood', then yes, I'm in a mood.*

"Good morning, you beautiful people!"

Great. An over-exuberant retail assistant is exactly what we need.

"I'm Penny," she gushes as she sashays towards us in a pale pink suit jacket and skirt. The skirt is tight and I'm not sure how she is going to bend down and fluff my skirts and whatnot.

With a flick of her Bondi blonde hair that sends her liberally applied perfume wafting toward us, Penny stops with her hands on her hips. "Now which one of you lucky ladies is our bride?"

"Me," I state with no emotion and barely a flicker of expression.

"Oh," she is taken aback. I guess she was expecting squealing and for me to jump up and show her my engagement ring.

"It's an arranged marriage," I tell her matter of fact and my mother hisses at me. "What? It's the truth?"

"Let's just get going shall we?" Penny thankfully leads me through to another room where she has hung up a selection of dresses in roughly my size. I indicate for everyone else to stay behind and wait.

Silk, satin, lace, organza. I trail my fingers through the hanging white garments. They're beautiful. All of them. Dresses I would love to wear in different circumstances.

I think back to my Pinterest board. For years I collected photos of dresses, venues, party favours, cakes, and floral arrangements. Before Pinterest, I had my notebooks full of carefully cut-out pictures and badly drawn designs. I know exactly what I want.

My dream dress is pure white flowing silk. Sleeveless with a high subtly-draped neckline and a low scooped back. So low it is bare until just above my bum. It flows to the floor, molding to my curves like water.

Classic. Classy. Timeless.

But as much as I have dreamt of this dress, I cannot bear to wear anything like it. It will stay in my precious dreams where I can still imagine that it will be Giovanna waiting for me at the end of the aisle.

I pick out three dresses that are as different from my dream dress as I can find. One is a long-sleeved lace number a la Kate Middleton at her wedding to Prince William. Beautiful, but not what I dreamed of.

The next is less modern princess and more Disney princess. The skirt is big and voluminous with lots of organza. I hate it. I choose it because I know Mum will too.

And the third is a Grecian-style dress with a plunging neckline and lots of drapery. I like the first and third dresses, but I don't care which I end up wearing.

"Are you okay?" I'm pulling on the first dress with Penny's assistance when she pauses and whispers to me.

"Yes," I sigh, but I'm touched that someone, even this over-the-top stranger, has cared enough to ask. "I'm not happy about getting married, but that's what divorce is for right?"

She gives me an uncertain smile. "They can't make you get married though can they? That's like…not legal, right?" *Oh yes, they can. They don't care about legal.*

"Of course not," I giggle, lying through my teeth. "Thanks for your concern, but I'm fine. Truth be told, I had a fight with my fiance last night and it has just put me in a mood."

Happy to be absolved of any responsibility for assisting in the forced marriage of a distressed young woman, Penny goes back to chirping about the dress. She lists all the pros and cons of wearing such a design and primps and preens me.

After much discussion, mostly between Mum and Peta, the Kate Middleton style dress is purchased and taken away to be adjusted to my size.

I look lovely in it and I'm sure everyone will ooh and aah over me as I trudge down the aisle. It is elegant and suits me, but I'm fantasising about the moment I can take it off and burn it.

CHAPTER FORTY THREE
GIOVANNA

"Where's Francesca?" I've waited fifteen minutes to ask Massimo this question so that it seems casual and not something I have been desperate to know since I walked in the door.

Stretched out on the massive sofa in the TV room, Massi doesn't take his eyes off the rugby league match on the big screen. "Staying at her parents' tonight," he says.

"Is everything okay?" It is no secret that there is little love lost between Francesca and her dad and her mum is a self-absorbed moll who didn't deserve the daughter she packed off at 16. It seems unlikely that Francesca would choose to stay at their house when, despite the dramas with Elio, she had been relieved to have an escape from her parents.

"Yeah, why?" he frowns, irritated that I'm asking him questions when there are eight minutes left on the clock and his team is down by six points.

"No reason," I ruffle his chestnut mop of hair and turn to leave him to watch the remainder of the game in peace.

I'm nearly at the door when he speaks, just loud enough for me to hear. "Don't mess with her head, G. She's been through a lot."

For a split second, I consider responding. Instead, I just keep walking. I'm surprised that Francesca has told him about us, but then maybe she hasn't and he has just picked up on a vibe. Sigh. He's right though. I should never have

dipped my toe in the water. She needs to be encouraged to build a life with Elio, not fuck his sister.

Thankfully, I don't have much chance to dwell on Massi's comments as just as I have made myself a peppermint tea, Bluey appears in the kitchen.

"Boss, Stefan's at the door…" he says.

My head jerks up from blowing on the hot tea. *What the fuck is he doing here? Has he come to gloat about the ambush or to deny involvement?*

Bluey continues. "Says he wants to speak to you."

Tapping my fingers against my lips, I think for a second. I don't want to look like I'm afraid, but I don't want to roll out the red carpet for someone who is plotting to take everything my family has worked for.

"Righto. Bring him up to my office. Get Massi to go with you." I head upstairs to my office and clear anything confidential off my desk, sitting down and puffing on my e-cigarette as I wait for Stefan Rossi.

"Knock knock," Stefan says, poking his head around the door. His expression is friendly and open, but I wouldn't trust the bastard as far as I could throw him.

"Stefan. What can I help you with?" My clipped tone carries no hospitality or desire to make him feel welcome.

He sidles into the room despite never receiving an invitation. He is wearing an immaculate Italian suit, tapered to his lean body. He is sinewy, tough. Like an old goat despite being just a little older than I am. It is difficult to believe that he shares half his DNA with Francesca. Her features are soft and feminine to the extreme. Stefan is all angles and harshness.

"I just came by to see how everyone is doing after the crash. Sounds like it was a lucky escape for you guys," he answers with sickly smooth faux concern.

Yeah, I bet you're really bloody concerned, mate. Snake. Lower than a snake's belly.

"The 'crash' was intentional, as was the clip that I emptied into the guy holding a knife to your sister's neck," my words practically gather frost as I spit them. "How is Francesca? I'm sure you've been to see her first?"

"She lives here doesn't she?" Stefan seems genuinely concerned that he has picked up a piece of dodgy intel somewhere along the way.

"She's with her parents tonight. It has been a traumatic experience for her." And she is likely to be further traumatised by having to spend time in close proximity to her heartless parents.

We stare at each other, him standing awkwardly in front of my desk, toeing the edge of the rug under his feet. While I'm showing nothing but cold, hard composure, the knowledge that Stefan may have been willing to put a hit on his own sister to destabilise our *Famiglia* has me on edge. Assuming it was his hit. He seems the obvious candidate.

"I wonder, Stefan, who do you think has a reason to take out your sister?" I don't blink and he meets my gaze without a quiver.

Something clicks into place in his brain and Stefan suddenly exudes confidence. He drops into one of my chairs and sits as if he is relaxing in his own lounge. "Let's speak honestly, yeah?"

I raise an eyebrow. "I assumed we already were."

"We both know Elio is in over his head," he pauses for dramatic effect which I don't acknowledge. "He's on thin ice with the capos already. The Rossis aren't happy."

"You seem to have an ear for all sorts of gossip," I yawn and look at my watch.

"Come on, G. Don't give me that shit. Don't be coy," his smirk is irritating. Almost as irritating as him calling me G. We may have known each other as kids, but he has been in Melbourne for about 15 years. Francesca barely knows the guy and he's her brother.

"Have you got anything to say, mate? I've got shit to do," he doesn't need to know that I'll probably just go to bed and mope over his sister all night.

"Shit is going to get messy. Elio will lose control and the capos will look for leadership elsewhere. Save us all the trouble and support me to step in. I'll keep you as *consigliere*, right hand. We're family. It has always been Rossis and Marinos. Elio doesn't want this. Are you going to stand there and watch him fuck everything up?"

Finally, some honesty from the man.

I stand and place two hands on my desk, leaning forward. "Listen very carefully. Sydney Cosa Nostra *is* the Marino Family. You say things will get messy… If you threaten my family again, I will put a bullet in your brain. If you

even think about harming Francesca again, I will make sure your death is slow and fuckin' excruciating."

Stefan stares, a muscle in his cheek pulses, and rage blackens his expression. He opens his mouth to speak but I don't want to hear it. I hold a hand up. "Get out, Stefan. Now."

CHAPTER FORTY FOUR
FRANCESCA

There is no way I would have gone to my parents' house if they had actually been there. Luckily for me, they are away on a skiing trip in Queenstown. My mother doesn't even ski, but she likes all the pageantry around it. The outfits, the cosy fires, mulled wine, and photos in front of beautiful scenery.

Performance. So much performance. I'm sick of it. The only person who has ever been real with me is Massimo, but now I don't know how much of that was pretence too. I used to think Giovanna was real, but she is just a fantasy of my own making. I built her up into this impossibly perfect human and projected all of my desperate feelings onto her.

What I experienced with her when we had sex is entirely different from what she experienced. It was just fucking for her. For me, it was the realisation of everything I ever desired. I have fantasised and dreamt about being with her for years and it was finally real. All the men I've slept with were fine, I mean I enjoyed sex with most of them, but being with her was like what I imagine taking a first hit of heroin is like. Pure ecstasy, a surge of glorious pleasure followed by peace.

The withdrawals are bad. It hurts now. Like my heart has been ripped out of my chest and shoved into a blender. Eventually, maybe I will be glad that I had that one night with her. I won't die wondering what it would be like to be with the only person I've truly yearned for.

Now I need to protect myself. Set up some defences. But I can only do that if I stay away from Giovanna. I need to stay away from all of the Marinos and give myself room to think.

I go to work and hang out with Sammy. I envy her strength and the way she simply refuses to take any shit. She is independent in a way that I can only wish to be.

She is the only person outside of the Famiglia who I have told about the Elio situation and the only one other than Massimo who knows about Giovanna. She doesn't judge me outwardly, but I am still embarrassed because I know she would never allow herself to be married off to a man she didn't love.

"Why can't you just marry Giovanna?" she asks as we lie next to my parents' swimming pool.

"Well, for a start she would have to *want* to marry me. But also I'm supposed to be making Elio settle down and be a stable boss. Not sure that is possible, to be honest. He needs a wife who is less of a pushover."

"This shit is totally archaic, babe," she sighs sympathetically. "At least Elio is hot though."

It is the first time I have heard her express attraction to anyone. I thought she might be gay at first. She is a total tomboy. A beautiful tomboy, but I'm pretty sure she doesn't even own a dress. "You think he's hot? Never seen you drool over anyone!"

"You'd have to be blind not to be attracted to him. Or a lesbian I guess. But I'd rather eat glass than ever go there. He's a soulless manwhore…oh shit, sorry! I forgot you have to marry him for a second!"

Unphased, because her statement is accurate, I just chuckle. "Lucky me!"

It takes a week for Giovanna to call me, wondering where I am. I don't answer. Then Elio starts calling and I ignore his calls too. Giovanna will have told him to call me anyway.

Sammy and I hang out every day and I enjoy the normalcy of working and having a friend who isn't a member of the Italian mafia.

I miss living down the hall from Massimo, but we are still figuring out how to navigate this new phase in our friendship where for the first time we have to reestablish trust. Things are a bit awkward and he can't seem to look at me without a face riddled with guilt.

I think about Giovanna constantly. I dream of what it would be like if she wanted me like I want her and we could be together. At night I make myself come to the memory of being in her bed. I wonder if she is thinking about me at all.

Anyway, my parents get back tomorrow and there is no way I will be staying here with them. It is time to leave limbo. Time to decide if I will allow my life to be driven by others or if I will forge my own path.

The Uber pulls up outside Stefan and Allegra's house and I hesitate before getting out. It isn't too late for me to turn around and go back to my car where it is parked outside my work. No one need know that I even considered running from my fate.

The driver looks over his shoulder expectantly, his face communicating that I should hurry up and get out of his car.

Apologising, I quickly exit the vehicle and stand clutching the sports bag that contains the essentials I might need. Sadly this isn't a lot. Just my passport and some clothes.

I feel small standing outside my brother's house so uncertain and alone. Am I being petulant? Petty? Like a child who throws a tantrum and declares they are running away?

Being amicable and obedient my whole life has ultimately led me to being traded like property and unable to trust anyone. Just the thought of Massimo arriving in London - me so excited and relieved to see him - when he was there on an assignment makes me want to cry. He was there to manipulate my life as instructed by our fathers.

I should have left earlier. The moment I found out I was to be married to Elio. But like so many women stuck in circumstances they cannot stand, it felt impossible. My family is very wealthy, but I have next to nothing to my name. Not enough to buy a plane ticket back to the U.K. Not even enough to set myself up in some sleepy beachside town hours from Sydney.

Trying to escape the control of my father and future husband has led me here, instead, to my brother's door where I will put myself at his mercy as I beg

for help. I am a mouse stuck in a maze. I keep hitting dead ends and running in circles. I just need to get out.

Hurried footsteps approach the door a few moments after I have knocked. My heart races and push down feelings of embarrassment. There is no shame in asking for help, I tell myself.

"Francesca," Allegra answers the door and her eyes widen in surprise. "Come in, come in. Are you alright?"

Her question is like the pin that pops the water balloon and I dissolve into tears. Hurrying me inside she leads me to the austere living room where we perch on uncomfortable oversized chairs.

Handing me a tissue, Allegra sits quietly and waits for my tears to subside. "What's going on? Do you need me to ask Stefan to come home? He should be home in a few hours anyway," she says softly. She never seems to speak louder than a whisper.

I shake my head. "I can wait for him. If you don't mind? I just need to talk to him. I need his help."

Stefan returns home a few hours later just as Allegra said. She must have spoken to him at some point as he isn't surprised to find me in his house.

He pulls me into a hug and I want to feel comforted, but it is stiff and unfamiliar. If anything I feel more isolated afterward, but I appreciate that he was trying to show support and affection.

"Allegra says you need my help," he states, sitting down opposite me at his monstrosity of a dining table.

I bob my head and drag my gaze from the tabletop to find his eyes. "I can't marry Elio, Stefan. Please help me. I need to get away, but I have nothing."

The tears start again and Stefan's brow crinkles into a concertina of concern, but a strange lightness comes over him. He pauses, running his eyes over my face. Lost in his thoughts he doesn't respond for several moments and my breath catches in my chest. He is my last resort. I have no one else to go to.

"Of course, I'll help. You're my baby sister," he finally says. "Who knows you're here?"

"No one," I reply honestly.

"Good. That gives us more time to figure this out," his mouth sets in a satisfied line and he looks at his watch. "It is getting late. Allegra has made up the spare room. Get some sleep and we will talk about it all tomorrow."

After a long shower in which I shed many more tears, I tug on some cotton sleep shorts and a singlet and slide into bed. It isn't that late. It's just after 9 pm and I'm wide awake.

The sheets are crisp and cool and usually, I would relish sliding into them after a warm day, but there is something about them that feels clinical and cold. The room is sparse and the lack of homeliness makes my misery even more pronounced.

Stefan has said he will help me, but our interactions are just so stilted. I can't seem to relax in his company. I wish I felt more certain about our relationship. Though given the people I have felt comfortable and safe around have sold me out I guess that doesn't matter.

Tomorrow I will ask him if he can lend me some money to set myself up far from here. I can pay him back once I have a job. I just need to leave.

CHAPTER FORTY FIVE

SANDY

The upstairs room at *La Fazenda* is even more crowded than usual and it isn't doing the headache I'm currently nursing any favours. Sarah has brought in two freestanding fans to try to get the muggy air circulating, creating the perception that the room isn't hotter than Hades' arsehole.

For the first time, I don't sit in the boss' chair and I can't deny it is strange. Elio sits on the old throne now, his sister on his right and Matteo on his left. I'm proud of them. All three of them.

But something isn't quite right. Elio is the square peg I have been trying to ram into the round hole for over thirty years. He isn't comfortable and he doesn't have the respect of the men.

Dread, regret, and guilt swirl around my gut tormenting me with the question of whether I have done the right thing. Would it have been better to break a rule, ignore tradition and give the role to my eldest? Would these men have respected a woman, albeit a far more capable one, more than they do my son?

They all know by now that he froze when his fiancee was held at knifepoint in front of him. The gossip mill has well and truly digested the news that Giovanna had to step in and make the kill for him. That one incident alone makes him look weak.

The meeting begins with a blow-by-blow account of the ambush after Sarah and Tiny's wedding.

Feet shuffle nervously and meaningful glances shoot across the table like a pinball. As we use the process of deduction to narrow down which of our enemies could be responsible for such an attack it is difficult to conclude that anyone but Stefan Rossi and the Romano *Famiglia* are responsible. An uncomfortable reality for the many members of the Rossi family who are present.

"There is no proof that Stefan ordered the attack," Baz Rossi begins, but he is cut off by Paul.

"Who here has been in contact with my son?" he demands and slowly all of the Rossis including Champ Brown raise their hands.

"He approached me," Joseph Rossi explains at the same time as Champ says, "We spoke but I never entertained the idea of him taking over things in Sydney."

More voices join the fray and suddenly everyone is talking over each other, making excuses and denying collusion with Stefan. Struggling to make heads or tails of what everyone is saying, I remain silent and swallow the urge to tell everyone to shut the fuck up.

"Enough," Elio yells after Giovanna elbows him in the ribs. "Quiet, all of you."

As the room settles and everyone turns their attention to Elio, he turns to his right and indicates for Giovanna to speak.

I can tell she is smothering irritation that he isn't taking the chance to assert leadership, but she backs him up nonetheless.

"It's not a crime for any of you to be in touch with Stefan. Many of you are relatives of his. But, there are some of you in this room who have bolstered him, given him confidence, by promoting him as an alternative to Elio," she speaks calmly and with authority and holds the attention of every man in the room.

"You're all fuckin' lucky that you don't have Francesca's blood on your hands. Instead, the blood is of the hired bikie who held a knife to her throat. Let me be very clear, we - Elio - will not hesitate to cut the throat of any man at this table who took part in plotting the attack. We will find out so speak up now and die with whatever honour you have remaining," she stares into the eyes of everyone present at least once as she speaks.

The room is silent as no one volunteers that they were involved. Eyes are cast down and I can almost hear the rapid heartbeats of the Rossi men.

"Francesca will be married to Elio in under two months," my voice slurs slightly as I contribute to the conversation for the first time. "Elio's heirs will be your kin. But not if Stefan succeeds in knocking off his sister. Pick a side, gentlemen. You're either with the Marino *Famiglia* defending Francesca or you're on the side that aims to kill her."

Confused, I examine the glass of red in my hand. It is half full and my first drink, yet my tongue feels heavy in my mouth. I toss back a glass of water and shake my head vigorously.

Elio nods at me and then Giovanna and she continues. "Anyone who still thinks that Stefan is an alternative option should get up and leave now. Get the fuck out of Sydney and do it quickly. We'll give you twenty-four hours headstart. You know what happens when you betray the *Famiglia*."

Again no one moves for several seconds until Champ breaks through the quiet. "We may be Rossis, but we are made men of the Sydney Mafia and the Marino Famligia first. My loyalty is with you." He nods toward my three adult children.

Murmurs of agreement follow his statement and each of the other capos speak up with similar sentiments. Pledging their allegiance.

The whole charade leaves a bitter taste in my mouth. I can't keep the displeasure from my expression as I watch on, sure that at least one of these men is a liar.

My annoyance is only compounded by the discombobulation I'm feeling physically. Raising my wine glass to my mouth my hand quivers and a numbness seeps from shoulder to wrist. Before I can even register the loss of control, the glass tumbles from my hand spilling the burgundy liquid across the tablecloth.

"Dad?" Elio's voice echoes and sounds like he is speaking to me through water.

I open my mouth to respond, but all that comes out is a garbled collection of noises. Is my mouth moving? Fear grips me. Am I dying? Is this it? I'm not ready to go yet.

Chairs scrape against the scuffed wooden floor as all three of my kids rush over to where I sit. Paul's face is there too and even he has managed to show some emotion and concern.

"Dad, are you okay?" it's Elio again. I want to tell him I'm sorry. He wasn't made for this life and I have pushed him and pushed him. All he hears is how incapable he is and that no one respects him, but he was always a good kid. Funny, smart, and caring.

I look down and watch my hand trying to grasp a forearm, but I'm fumbling. Another hand comes down on top of it. Matteo is holding my hand. He rubs it before pressing kisses to my knuckles.

"I think he's having a stroke," I want to smile at how calm my daughter sounds. She is barking instructions, but no one is in any doubt that she is in control. I have the weirdest thought that I know she won't let me die here. She just won't. She'll drive the fucking ambulance herself and have the doctors standing at attention.

'It would be a real fucking inconvenience to die now,' I think as I drift away from the noise of the Famiglia, the faces of my children, and the uncertainty of our future.

CHAPTER FORTY SIX

FRANCESCA

"Yeah, yeah. Of course, it's fuckin' fantastic. Too easy, but where do you think they'll look first, mate?" I hear Stefan hissing excitedly.

I pause on the set of cold industrial-chic stairs linking the first floor to the second. Hearing his voice drifting through the ajar door to his office, stops me in my tracks and has me straining to eavesdrop on my way down to breakfast.

Stefan continues, "The minute Giovanna realises she is missing every Marino soldier in the state will be beating down my door!"

Who is he talking to?

The silence that follows his statements tells me he must be speaking on the phone. I wait.

"Yeah, I know that," he suddenly snaps. "Right well, we have to move her. She can't stay here."

There is no way they aren't talking about me. I mean, how many people that Giovanna gives a shit about (well, kinda) could he have hiding in his house?

I don't like the sound of Stefan making plans to "move" me. Not one bit. Running away from getting married was about being free and making decisions for myself. I will not be ordered around and kept captive by another family member.

"I don't care. Do with her what you want. Just make sure she isn't around to be married off. Righto, see you soon." He hangs up and I sit with my hands clasped over my mouth. Taking slow breaths I try to quiet my panic and creep slowly back up the stairs to the spare bedroom.

If he doesn't care what happens to me, why does he care if I get married? It doesn't make sense. All I know is that I am not safe here. In my gut, the churn tells me I have made a very bad mistake in turning to my brother.

A few minutes later, I am packing my bag with urgency, having decided that I need to leave immediately. Sounds of my nephews playing come from the floor above and I feel a twinge of sadness that I'll be leaving them without saying goodbye, but I can't risk a detour just to give them a hug.

"Are you going somewhere?" Stefan's voice says from the doorway and I whip my head around to see him force a cold gaze into an uncomfortable smile.

Plastering what I hope is a more casual and less uncomfortable smile on my face, I shrug and say, "I've decided to go home and talk it through with everyone."

"They won't listen to you," he snaps and I freeze at the sharp impatience in his voice.

"Worth a try though, right?" I coach myself to keep smiling and acting like I'm not becoming more and more afraid.

He frowns. "I can't let you go, I'm afraid. I can't take that risk with your safety."

"Oh, they would never hurt me! I'll be fine!" I swing my bag over my shoulder and take a few steps toward the door.

Placing a hand on each side of the door frame, Stefan fills the space, blocking my path. He may be lean, but he is taller than me and uses his size advantage to show me that I won't be getting around him.

"Honestly, Stefan, I know you're being an overprotective big brother," I don't know this at all. I am doubting very much if his attempts to forge a relationship with me have anything to do with family or love at all. "But you don't need to worry. Thank you so much for letting me stay last night."

He doesn't budge. "Stefan?"

"You aren't leaving!" he roars, stepping back and slamming the door with so much force I swear the walls shake.

I hurry over and yank on the door handle, but he has locked it. I didn't even notice there was a lock until now. *Fuck!* My palm stings as I slap it against the door in frustration.

"You just need some time to calm down. We'll talk when you're being reasonable," he shouts through the door before stomping off down the hall.

The single, albeit large, window in the room is heavy and hard to push open. I could fit my body through it but there is nothing for me to hang onto or stand on the other side. The drop is two storeys and I'll be certain to break my legs if I try to land it.

All of my senses are heightened; adrenaline and fear are in the driver's seat as I strain to hear anything that will inform me of what my brother is up to and what my fate might be. I begin to pace, searching for the confidence to know how to get myself out of this. I'm mid-stride when I'm struck with the realisation that somehow both Stefan and I have forgotten that I still have my phone in my bag.

My hands shake as I rush to tear open my bag and pull out my phone. I hold it up to my face, but it must have updated itself or something because it is requiring I enter my passcode instead. I tap it in, but my unsteady fingers press the wrong buttons. I try again and still get it wrong.

For fucksake, I type this in multiple times a day every single day! A pop-up message tells me that if I get the passcode wrong for a third time I will be locked out for ten minutes.

My hands are now shaking with so much ferocity that I can barely read the screen. Sweat pools at my temples and under my arms. I blow a slow breath out of my nose. And another one.

With my phone lying flat on the bed, I slowly and deliberately enter my code and my home screen flashes up just as I hear footsteps coming up the stairs. Fuck fuck fuck.

I quickly type messages to Massimo, sending them as I go:

Francesca: Help
Francesca: At stefan
Francesca: He locked me in
Francesca: Someone is coming to get me
Francesca: Help please

The footsteps stop outside the door and I just manage to shove my phone under a pillow before the lock turns and Stefan's head pokes around the door.

"Allegra made you a smoothie," he states as he places a tall glass full of thick light mauve liquid just inside the door and throws a water bottle in my direction.

I say nothing, just watch his every move, holding my breath and willing him to leave.

He turns and pulls the door closed and I breathe out, but my relief is premature. Before Stefan can turn the lock, a loud ping sounds from behind me on the bed and I cringe. The door is flung back open and Stefan steps back into the room with panic and fury competing for space in his expression.

"GIVE IT TO ME!" he bellows and I scoot backward on the bed putting distance between us. My back hits the headboard and my bum vibrates as my phone sounds again underneath me.

Not bothering with words any longer, my big brother grabs me by one of my biceps, his long boney fingers wrapping all the way around it. A gasp followed by a cry escapes my lips as his grip digs in, sure to leave bruises.

He drags me off the bed in one fluid movement, casting me aside so I go flying into the wall by the door. From there I watch him manically digging around in the bedding for my phone. Her curses in English and Italian until finding it, he holds it aloft in victory.

"Who have you been texting, Francesca?" he demands, but I remain silent. "Tell me your passcode."

Breathing heavily through my nose I glare at him, only now realising that I'm covered in berry smoothie having kicked over the glass over as I was so aggressively thrown from the bed.

When I continue to keep my mouth shut, he launches himself off the bed, and grabs me by the back of my head, wrapping my hair around his hand. He holds my head up and the phone in front of my face, but I close my eyes and grimace.

I don't see him wind his arm back so the slap comes as a shock. My head snaps to the side and my cheek stings where his hand collides with it.

"What are you doing?" I cry out, trying to clutch at my burning cheek. "I don't understand!"

"Let me unlock your phone or I'll do a lot more than slap you," he threatens and holds the phone in my face again.

This time it unlocks and he quickly goes to my recently sent messages. I can see Massimo has responded, but not what he said.

"FUCK!" Stefan screams and a bubble of hope grows in my chest. Massimo has seen my messages. He will save me. Despite how angry I have been with him, I know he will come for me.

Stefan staggers from the room, almost forgetting to lock it behind him. He thunders down the stairs still shouting and swearing to himself. Frustration at my naivety has me banging the heel of my palm against my head. Like a complete moron, I have leapt from the frying pan into the fire and now my options are exhausted.

Massi will come.

Outside the sky turns from pink to purple as darkness falls. There is a loud knock on the front door and my heart leaps into my throat. *Is it him?*

But Massimo wouldn't knock if he was trying to rescue me, right?

Allegra's light footsteps shuffle down the hallway to answer the door.

"Oh hello," I hear her say nervously.

A muffled man's voice says something in response and I press my ear to the floor, desperate to learn who has arrived. Footsteps approach the door, muffling any sounds coming from downstairs and I scramble backward, my back hitting the side of the bed.

"Up!" Stefan bursts into the room and barks at me. When I am not quick enough to stand, he grabs me and yanks me up, adding more fingerprint-shaped bruises to my upper arm.

He thrusts me forwards and I stumble on the first few steps, kept on my feet only by Stefan's vice-like grip.

"Where are we going?" I ask meekly and hate myself for not sounding stronger.

"*You* are going with Billy," he snaps. *Who the fuck is Billy?*

I look down at my bare feet, sports leggings, and white t-shirt. "I-I-I need a jumper and my sh-shoes."

"You'll be fine," he replies instantly, clearly not caring. His other hand plants firmly on the small of my back and he thrusts me into the hallway.

Standing on the front doorstep is a huge man. Young. Maybe my age. He is dressed in black jeans, motorcycle boots, a leather jacket, and a motorcycle club cut. He is an imposing figure, oozing aggression, and danger.

We take a few more steps toward the front door and the biker's face is suddenly lit up by a motion-activated outdoor light. *I know him.*

Recognition must show on my face because his face breaks into a smile that sends shivers up my spine. It is menacing, laden with arrogance, and lecherous.

"Good to see you again, princess," he sneers.

My hand goes to my throat and I swallow. He is one of the bikers who threatened and choked me at the gym.

CHAPTER FORTY SEVEN
GIOVANNA

"FUCK!" Massimo shouts, startling the two nurses quietly discussing a chart behind their station.

We're sitting in a stark white and blue hospital waiting room, all four of us siblings. Massimo met us here after we tailed the ambulance that picked Dad up from *La Fazenda*.

He wasn't conscious when he arrived and has been carted off to surgery. Things aren't looking very positive.

"G," Massimo is the picture of panic. He can barely get my single-letter nickname out of his mouth. "G. Stefan's got Francesca!"

"What? What do you mean?" I haven't seen Francesca since we argued about her bikini the day after I slept with her. I thought she was cooling off at her parents' house.

Massimo shows me his phone and Francesca's stilted texts begging for help. Immediately I get to my feet as Elio and Matteo huddle over the phone to read the messages too.

"Reply to her," Matteo says and I grab the phone out of his hands.

Massimo: are you at Stefan's house?
Massimo: we are coming
Massimo: don't panic darling

"Try calling her," Elio suggests.

It goes straight to voicemail. *Fuck.*

"Get me Stefan's address!" I shout at my brothers and take off at a run towards the exit.

"I'm coming with you!" Massimo calls out and quickly catches me up.

We have just burst into the dark hospital carpark and climbed into my car when a text comes through to our sibling group chat from Elio. It's Stefan's address.

"You gotta breathe, G," Massimo mutters from the passenger seat. He seems to have got a hold of his emotions and is now worried about mine.

"Fuck, Massi. If anything has happened to her - " I clear my throat as my voice cracks and then shake my head vigorously. *Focus. I need to focus.*

"I know. Trust me, I know," he responds.

It takes about half an hour with me driving like a goddamn maniac for us to arrive outside the address. Giving zero fucks about the garden, I drive my SUV into their driveway, across the perfectly manicured lawn, and come to a stop in the flowerbeds next to the front door.

My Doc Martin boots trample on what is left of the colourful floral display and I release my handgun from my shoulder holster just as Massimo pounds on the front door. It swings open, unlocked, and phantom fingers of panic claw at my neck.

"Lights are all off," I mutter. It isn't that late. About 9.30 pm. People should still be up.

Broken glass crunches under my boots as I step over the threshold. It comes from a large picture frame that lies broken against the wall. The hallway table is empty, the floor around it littered with letters, knick-knacks, and the debris of a tipped-over vase of flowers.

We quickly move from room to room methodically and discover no one is here. On the second floor, Massi finds some of Francesca's clothes and a bizarre purple coloured liquid smeared across the floor. It looks like there has been a struggle.

My heart sinks. I thought I was doing the right thing by giving her some space. Massi said she was hanging out with Sammy and going to work. I should never have let her stay by herself at her parents' house. She was a sitting duck.

"Nah she's not here," Massimo is on the phone with Elio and Matteo, pacing in the hallway as I assess the spare bedroom where we found Francesca's things. "Looks like there's been a struggle."

Where would he have taken her? He doesn't have any other properties in his name or Allegra's in Sydney. We have been keeping an eye out for him buying up assets since he moved his family here.

Would he take her back to Melbourne?

That would stop her from marrying Elio and he knows that means the capos will look elsewhere for a Rossi to step in. But, kidnapping her has made it impossible for him to return to Sydney without staring down the barrel of one of our guns.

It's like none of this was planned out and that makes it very difficult to make guesses as to where he has gone and what his endgame is.

"Matteo and Elio are going to swing by some of Stefan's known associates and see what they know," Massimo informs me.

"How's Dad doing?" I ask, looking up at him from my perch on the end of the bed.

"No word yet. Still in surgery." His mouth flattens into a grim line.

After a moment he opens his mouth again. "Something I can't stop thinking about…Cheska's text said *'Someone is coming to get me'*. Maybe Stefan is working with someone"

"But who?" I frown. He does have a point though. It is a strange thing to text if she was just dealing with Stefan. *Someone.*

"Baz? Azarro?" Massi names a couple of the capos we know Stefan has spent time with.

"They both made a big show of swearing loyalty to us at the meeting. Would they have left *La Fazenda* and gone straight to Stefan's house to partake in kidnapping the future Mrs. Marino?"

"Maybe?" Massi shrugs. "Who else then?"

"The bikies?" I suggest. "They threatened her at her work."

"But you dealt with them didn't you?"

"We got hold of two of the three, but Billy the Kid has been hard to pin down. No sign of him since the ambush."

"But why would they be involved?" he asks. It is a fair question because on the surface it would appear they have no shared interests here.

"They're being paid and gambling that when Stefan takes over they will have the means to take over Billy's Uncle Ned. Stefan and Billy are both trying to knife their family members to gain power."

It has to be the bikies. Stefan's mercenaries.

"Fancy a visit to the Rusty Clutch?" I raise my eyebrow grimly.

"Can I shove my nuts in a jar of fire ants instead?" Massi shoots over his shoulder as he heads out the front door.

~

About fifty motorcycles are lining the street outside the shabby standalone building set off the road and surrounded by heavy gravel. Rock music blares through the open double doors and several windows and a large verandah attached to the front of the building is full of men and women wearing leather and smoking cigarettes.

We idle on the other side of the road watching the door through tinted windows. There is no sign of Billy or his one-handed buddies outside. Would've been a massive stroke of luck if they had been lounging around out the front, but we are going to have to brave the bourbon fumes to check if they're inside.

"Let's get this over with," I grumble to Massi who is shoving a handgun into the back of his pants. He nods and we step out of the car at the same time.

We have barely taken two steps across the road when the attention of everyone hanging out the front of the bar zeroes in on us.

"Did the temperature just drop by like 20 degrees?" Massi murmurs.

The hostility is palpable. Frosty is an understatement.

The crowd is shifting; men in Satan's Sons cuts move forward to create a barrier between us and the entrance to the bar.

"What brings a pair of Marinos to our neck of the woods," a short, stocky biker asks, his tone leaving us under no illusions about how unwelcome we are.

"Looking for Billy," I bark. My stance is wide and confident. I stare each of the bikers down without a flicker of doubt in my expression.

Looks are exchanged between the leather-clad men and whispers ripple through the gathered crowd.

"He ain't here," the stocky spokesman replies.

"You know where I can find him?"

"Nope," he pronounces the word with a pop. "If you see him, remind him he is on borrowed time."

"He's not a Son anymore?"

"He's a traitor!" a man shouts from somewhere in the crowd.

So he has gone rogue. Him and his little posse.

This doesn't get us any closer to finding Francesca though. We need to find out where he would take her. If it is even him.

"Ned here?"

"Nah, but I am," a deep, raspy voice replies. It comes from a tall lean biker, his blonde hair pulled back into a bun, tattoos creeping up his muscular neck. "I'm Billy's brother."

"Giovanna, Massimo," I introduce us. "Your name is?"

"Dutch."

"Reckon we can have a chat without the audience?" I look pointedly at the rubberneckers.

"Fuck off back inside," Dutch rasps and immediately everyone moves back inside or onto the verandah.

"What does the mafia want with my brother?" he asks once the three of us stand alone on the gravel path.

I pause. It isn't in my nature to disclose weakness to anyone. Telling bikers that one of our women has been taken is an admission of utter failure. But I will swallow my pride if it means getting a step closer to finding Francesca.

"My brother's fiance has been taken. We think Billy might know where she is."

He frowns. "What would he want with her?"

"He and two other bikers threatened her at work a while ago. They said they were paid to rough her up. We figure that he may have been paid to take her too."

"Hmmm," Dutch runs a hand over his stubbled jaw, contemplating his next words carefully. "I know you catch up with Uncle Ned and he considers you an ally…Billy… he and a few of his mates…they've gone rogue. Not surprised they've been acting as mercenaries."

"The guy we think he is with doesn't have any properties he could take her to. Is there anywhere Billy would use?" Massimo asks.

Elio has already tracked down two properties linked to Billy. His mother's house in Cronulla and an apartment in the city.

"Nah, I mean he rents an apartment, but about a hundred people would see him if he tried to drag a girl in there. He crashes at our mum's house…or he used to. She's Satan's Sons through and through."

"What about his mates?"

"Doubt they have anywhere. These are kids, you know. Early twenties. Fuckin' young, dumb, and full of come. They'll be picking up gigs to pay for booze. No way they can afford property."

Fuck. This is going nowhere. We are no closer to knowing where Francesca could be.

I shove my fingers into my hair and swear profusely under my breath. Dutch looks at me with pity.

"Sorry, I can't be of more help. Can't even try to understand what is going on in that kid's head at the moment…"

We nod and say our goodbyes, dejected. What now? I want to tear up the city looking for her. I'll knock down every door, but we just need to know where to start.

We reach the car and I am just pulling my door open when Dutch's voice calls across the road to us. "Hey! Hang on a minute!"

He jogs across the road as I shut the door again and lean against it.

"Look, I duno if this is helpful at all, but I just remembered…when Billy first left we had some of the guys follow him for a bit. They trailed him to a storage facility out west. He was storing all his motorbike gear there. Nothing interesting, but yeah, do with that information what you will," he shrugs.

"Text me the details?" I give him my number and when his text comes through a minute later we are already tearing down the road away from the Rusty Clutch and the surprisingly friendly biker.

We send Fat Tony and Tiny to Billy and Dutch's mother's house, just to be sure, but they quickly report back that there is no sign of him there and his mother is so furious with him that she wouldn't open the door to him anyway.

Joseph Rossi and Frank Ambrosino cover the apartment, but that too is a dead end.

With the storage facility our only lead, Massimo and I break all traffic laws to meet Elio and Matteo there. They arrive minutes after us and we all rush towards the dark monstrous building, with no semblance of a plan, drawing our weapons as we go.

A security guard moves to stop us at the front door, but after looking all four of us up and down and noting we are armed, he makes the wise decision to open the door for us.

We vault one at a time over the security barrier that requires some kind of swipe card and push through a heavy glass door into a concrete maze. The reality of our situation sinks in. We don't know which of the units is Billy's. We could spend all night going from unit to unit while she is being tortured somewhere else.

"This is fuckin' impossible," Elio growls under his breath. "We don't even know if she's here."

"I'm going back to talk to the security guard," Matty announces quietly and heads back the way we came.

We're all whispering and moving carefully as if by instinct. The empty carpark outside indicates that the building should be empty at this late hour, but something feels off. Maybe it's just wishful thinking that we will find her here.

The door we came through seems to have led us to about the halfway point in the long building. On either side of us, stretches the beginnings of rows and rows of storage units. To our right, they are closer together, and more compact. To our left, the rows contain larger units with roller doors.

The cavernous space is only dimly lit. Power saving, I suppose. It makes for a spooky atmosphere. Full lighting only switches on in rows that are currently being accessed by users. Not a single row is lit up.

A wind whistles through the warehouse and a chill creeps up my spine. It makes me grip the gun in my hand slightly tighter. My gut is telling me this is the calm before the storm.

"We're in the right place," Matty whispers as he rejoins us. "The security guard is dead."

"What?" I hiss. "The one who just let us in?"

Matty nods. "Yeap. Throat slit."

"Fuck! Okay, odds are to fit bike equipment he will have needed to hire a large unit, yeah? So let's start clearing row by -"

My instructions are interrupted by a high-pitched scream coming from somewhere far away to our left. It echoes through the open air and we all freeze. It was a female scream, but I couldn't say if it was Francesca.

"Must have come from right down the end," Matty's lips barely move.

Nodding I break into a soft jog and my brothers follow close behind. Even though we are doing our best to be stealthy, our footsteps and breathing sound like a herd of elephants to my acutely on-edge senses.

From the general area of the scream a minute or so earlier, a light suddenly illuminates an area in the centre of a row.

"Gotcha," Elio grins briefly, but our small triumph is short-lived when three men come hurtling out of the row we have just passed, one of them barrelling into Massi.

The other two have guns drawn, but before they can get off a shot Matty spins and puts a bullet between the eyes of one before screaming at the other to drop his weapon.

The men are in all black with ski masks over their faces. Faceless goons doing the bidding of a useless would-be usurper.

"Where is Francesca?" I ask him urgently and with more than a little menace in my tone.

A couple of metres away Massi is still wrestling with his attacker. He pins him to the ground and rains punch after punch down on his head and chest.

"Finish him," Matty orders our youngest brother flippantly and he obeys immediately, fixing his hands around the man's neck and snapping it efficiently.

"Answer me!" I point my gun at the last remaining assailant's head.

After a short pause, the man seems to realise his time is up and he nods toward the spotlight that came on not long ago.

"Who has her?"

"Stefan Rossi," he mutters and a split second later Matty puts a bullet through his skull as well.

Without so much as a backward glance, I turn and sprint toward the light. It takes me less than a minute to reach the right row and I practically skid on the rough slightly dusty floor as I round the corner.

Grey roller doors flank the concrete walkway on either side and as we continue to run toward the spotlight ahead, we hear the rattling of one of the units being closed in a rush.

A tall blonde figure in a leather jacket takes off running and Elio sprints past me calling out, "On him" as he chases after him. It was Billy, I'm sure of it.

All is quiet as we finally come to a stop under the bright light except for the slight rattling of the roller door as it recovers from being slammed shut.

A chunky padlock secures the door to the ground and I crouch to examine it. Billy managed to ram the lock back on before he left. Dammit.

"Gonna have to shoot it off," Matteo suggests and at the sound of his voice, a smothered scream comes from inside the unit.

"She's in there!" Massimo shouts. "We've got you, Ches! Hold tight!"

I raise my eyebrow at Matteo and we all step back as he points his gun at the lock. It is blown apart, pieces ricocheting around our feet. He bends and pulls the last piece off the door and hauls the unit open.

It is an almost-empty space, floors concrete and walls of unpainted GIB board. An old motorbike is propped up against one wall with various parts and boxes nearby. But in the centre of the four metre by four metre space is Francesca tied to a chair.

A large bony hand is clasped over her mouth and Stefan stands behind her, a gun in his other hand pointed at her temple.

Francesca's pupils are blown wide and she is in full panic, straining against the ropes that restrain her.

"Woah woah woah, Stefan. What's all this about man?" I try to sound casual and like I want to de-escalate the situation.

The man looks wild. He is panicked too. It is clear that nothing has gone to plan for him and two years of destabilising our *Famiglia* is sliding down the drain. He knows he has lost, but it is in this last moment of desperation that he is the most dangerous. The most likely to be reckless and harm his little sister.

"Handover the *Famiglia* to me and Francesca can live," he snarls.

"Not really in a strong negotiating position, mate. You think you'll get support from more than a few of your pals after they hear what you've been up to?" I tilt my head at him. Pretending nonchalance is taking a lot of energy.

"See Francesca," he leans down to her ear. "They don't give a fuck about you. They'd sacrifice you to hold on to power."

Her eyes are already full of tears and I can't tell if she is buying his shit or not. I fuckin' hope not.

"As opposed to you, her brother, who currently has a gun to her head?" I snap.

"Put the gun down, Stefan," Matty says calmly from my right side.

"No! You need me. The *Famiglia* needs someone to respect and you know it!"

Delusion is strong in this one.

"Not gonna happen, mate. We all know this ends tonight with you off to meet your maker," as Matty talks to him, I mouth to Francesca that it'll all be okay and the trust that gleams in her eyes nearly brings me to my knees.

"...Unless you put down that gun now. You do that and we'll leave you to get out of the city so long as you never come back," Matty continues.

Stefan shuffles his feet. He's contemplating it. *Come on, man. Cut your losses.*

"Gun down now and you walk out of here," Matty repeats.

Finally, dropping his head in defeat, Stefan tosses his gun to the ground and puts his hands in the air. Massi dashes forward and picks it up, emptying the clip and tossing it to the side.

"Okay, I did what you asked..." Stefan whines nervously as Matty prowls towards him.

Matty has Stefan's face pressed into the concrete in no time, arms twisted up behind his back.

"Stand up, dickhead," he orders and Stefan staggers to his feet with assistance.

My favourite eyes in the entire world haven't left mine the entire time and the moment Matty has the man incapacitated, I rush forward and press a brief kiss to her forehead before making quick work of untying her bounds.

Massimo kneels to untie her feet and slowly and I gently peel the masking tape from Francesca's poor chapped mouth. Swallowing the urge to kiss them better, I run my thumb lightly over her sore red lips and she whimpers slightly.

"Hey," is all I can manage to say, the lump in my throat threatening to set off emotions I didn't even know I had.

"Hello," she rasps back, her voice barely a whisper.

"Are you hurt?" I run my eyes over her and spot some bruises and scrapes, but no obvious signs of major trauma.

She shakes her head. "Just cold and a bit bruised."

The relief at finding her relatively unharmed has washed over me like a drug hitting my bloodstream. I feel euphoric, but also really weak as if I could collapse to my knees.

Once she is completely free to move, Massimo gently lifts her into a big bear hug and she softly begins to cry against his chest. My chest aches and I itch to take her in my arms, even though I shouldn't.

"Bastard got away," Elio pants as he returns from chasing Billy. He takes in the scene in front of him and nods in approval. "Glad you're okay, sweetheart," he says, stepping forward to pull her into a hug and resting a hand gently on the back of her head.

Jealousy surges through my relief, green and toxic, but when I look up she has her gaze firmly on me even as he embraces her. Even Elio's use of the name 'sweetheart' feels familial rather than romantic. Not that this gets my jealousy under control.

Francesca's tears suddenly intensify and she cries out, "I'm so sorry!" She repeats it over and over as Elio lets her go.

"What are you sorry for?" he asks her, confused.

"I-I-I wasn't k-kidnapped," she stutters. "N-not really."

The four of us trade frowns before Massimo pushes her for more information.

"I r-r-ran…I ran away…I didn't want to get married," she sobs. "I thought…he would help me. He's m-my brother!"

"I told you I didn't kidnap her!" Stefan spits furiously but shuts his mouth quickly after taking in Matty's death stare.

"Jesus Christ," Elio mutters, stepping away and resting his hands on top of his head. I just shake my head sadly.

"Don't apologise, babe," Massimo says sympathetically. "I would have run away too."

And he's right. Any one of us would run away from a forced marriage. Elio has essentially been doing just that this entire time. The poor girl was desperate. She would have to be to turn to that fuckin' weasel brother of hers for help.

"Massi is right," I sigh reluctantly. "You have nothing to apologise for, but we can talk about this later, okay? Matty, can you call some guys to come do the clean-up? We need to get out of here and back to the hospital -"

"Hospital?" Francesca looks down at her uninjured body assuming I am suggesting we take her for treatment.

"Dad has had a stroke," I explain. "Look, darlin' we are just relieved you're okay. We can talk about the rest of it later. Don't stress."

She nods and steps forward into the arms I didn't even realise I had opened for her.

It takes us some time to get back to the cars with me helping Francesca and Matty dragging Stefan along. He hasn't said much since we left the storage unit, but his scowl tells its own story.

"Why are we bringing him with us?" Massimo asks, nodding towards Francesca's brother with a look of distaste.

"The unit would've been too hard to clean up. The guys already have to get rid of the guys in the corridor…" Matty responds and alarm explodes in Stefan's eyes. He begins to drag his feet and pull away from the firm hands on the rope used to bind him.

"I'm on camera! I'm on camera! They're all over the building!" Stefan screams, his body thrashing so wildly that Elio steps in to help Matty and Massimo drag him past the dead security guard and into the dark carpark.

"Do you think we would all be here if their security system hadn't mysteriously crashed tonight?" I reply. My arm is wrapped around Francesca and the fact that Stefan continues to draw breath after what he has done is making my thoughts very dark.

"I'll leave! Never come back! I'll leave Australia!" His desperation is just irritating.

"Mate, you aren't in a position to negotiate or beg," I tell him. "You sealed your fate the moment you tried to undermine us. You sped up the process when you decided to fuck with Francesca."

"It was David!" He twists to try to catch my gaze as he rolls the dice again.

"Don't you worry," I mutter darkly. "David is right at the top of my shitlist too."

His futile begging and bargaining continue across the empty carpark and I simply stop responding. He isn't worth the breath.

"Massimo, take Francesca to the car," I command as we reach Elio and Matty's SUV.

Elio rams Stefan's head into the side of the vehicle and holds him while Matty makes quick work of laying plastic drop sheets inside the trunk. Together they drag the skinny man kicking and screaming around the back of the car.

"Cameras are out. Just do it," I bark impatiently. "He's making too much fucking noise. Get it done and get rid of him."

They toss him in the trunk and in one fluid movement Matty bends to swipe a knife from the inside of his boot and lunges at Stefan allowing Elio to quickly step away and avoid the mess. It is over in an instant. Dark steel slices through Stefan's throat and a crimson spray hits Matty in the face before he has the chance to direct the blood flow into the plastic.

All of a sudden there is silence.

Matty straightens and turns to meet my gaze. His eyes are slightly wild and unfocused and the splatter of blood across his face only adds to his appearance of a feral madman.

I nod once at him and we stare at each other for a minute or so as he battles to slow his heart rate and centre himself. Finally, he swipes the back of his hand across his forehead, smearing blood into his skin, and nods back at me.

"See you back at the hospital when you're done," I look from Matty to Elio as I walk back towards my car.

CHAPTER FORTY EIGHT

FRANCESCA

After a quick shower, I tug on clean sports leggings, a cropped lightweight sweater, and Nikes. With wet hair and no makeup, I rush to Sydney Hospital with Massimo and Giovanna.

It is the middle of the night now so traffic doesn't slow us down. We drive without talking, cranking one of Massimo's playlists, and I ruminate, torturing myself with thoughts unable to be drowned out.

Even pushing aside the guilt that has been curdling in my stomach since seeing the relief on all four Marino faces when they found me, Sandy's stroke has thrown a whole lot of other emotions into the mix.

The sad truth is that I am more worried about Sandy than I would be if it were my father in the hospital.

Sandy has done bad things, without a doubt, and he was involved in sending me away, but he redeems himself as a father. He loves his children and has done his best to equip them with everything they need to take over from him. He has shown his children affection and treats them as if they are of value.

Paul Rossi, on the other hand, has never made me feel loved. The only time he has taken interest in my life is when it has benefited him.

Stefan hates our Dad - *hated* - but it seems to me they are more alike than either would like to admit. The only difference is Dad has always been content to wield his power as Sandy's right-hand man. Stefan wanted the top job and he has now shown he would do pretty much anything to get it.

A few circuits around the hospital car park later, we are running into the emergency department. I pull my wet hair into a messy bun on top of my head as I go.

"Alessandro Marino?" Giovanna's deep voice asks as soon as we reach the busy reception desk.

We follow the directions of the flustered woman trying to manage the inflow of patients, many of them drunk and difficult to deal with. We round the corner of the ward we're looking for and see a cluster of expensively dressed Italians.

Matteo and Elio are already here and they stand with several men I know are Sandy's capos, all in suits, talking quietly. Next to them, Fat Tony has an arm around Peta and Bluey is a few metres away uncharacteristically aggressively barking into his phone.

Peta shrugs as we near and Fat Tony says, "No news yet."

Giovanna places a hand softly on my lower back as we stand aimlessly, waiting. She catches my eye as I look up at her and I see emotion and vulnerability that I'm not used to being there. Without thinking, I take her hand and tow her out of the waiting area and around the corner.

There's no one around in the empty service corridor and as I turn to her she wraps her arms tight around my lower back. My arms go up over her shoulders and she buries her face in my neck for just a moment before she regains her composure.

"I'm so sorry, Gio," I whisper, gently rubbing her back. "Are you okay?"

She nods against me. "I missed you," she says so quietly I only just make out the words, but they make my heart soar.

"I missed you too," I murmur back and she squeezes me just a little bit tighter. Not seeing her, even just from afar, and not talking to her has been hard.

"Fuck I was so scared when we got your messages and then to see you with another weapon to your head…" She lifts her head from the crook of my neck to look me in the eye. Her gaze drifts down to my lips and I can't help but wet mine.

Is she going to kiss me? I want nothing more right now than to feel her press her lips to mine. To kiss away all the shit we are dealing with.

We may have only just slept together, but our late-night chats with peppermint tea or a bottle of wine have become my favourite part of my week. She is the only one who can calm me when I'm spiralling into a panic attack. The only one that makes me feel safe.

"We better get back," she murmurs and presses a kiss to my temple.

Reluctantly, I extract myself from her and we walk back to the waiting room as if we didn't just bleed our souls into each other just a little bit more.

CHAPTER FORTY NINE
GIOVANNA

He can't die. Not just because I'll miss the grumpy bastard and want him to be around for the next generation of Marinos, but because things are so fucking precarious in the *Famiglia* at the moment.

We need Dad to reassure the capos and hold together the old allegiances, especially once the news of Stefan's death becomes public knowledge.

The reality is that they don't respect Elio. Most of them like him, but they don't trust that he has the discipline to put the *Famiglia* above all else. "He is a slave to every vice known to man! No discipline," Champ told me just the other day.

I should feel guilty about thinking about politics while Dad is fighting for his life a few rooms away. But, I'm doing exactly what Dad would expect me to do. Exactly what he would be doing. Assessing the situation for threats and planning a strategy. Ensuring the future of the Marino *Famiglia* has always been his number one priority.

Down the corridor, Francesca carefully makes her way towards us with a tray of coffees in each hand. She is a goddamn angel and it kills me that she felt she had to run away from us. She ran to that psychopath thinking she would be better off with him.

I watch her shamelessly as she grows nearer, assessing her for any signs of pain or injury. Her big eyes - those fucking eyes - are framed by thick black lashes, voluminous even without a jot of makeup. Her face is earnest and

worried; she is the goodness I need in my life. Without makeup, she looks younger, more innocent somehow.

My mind drifts, recalling her looking up at me, her body beneath mine. Dishevelled, smiling shyly, eyes drunk from multiple orgasms. Perfection.

Staying away from her has been torture. I hated every day. Going to bed alone was never something that bothered me and yet after one night with her, it feels wrong.

Every phone call she rejected stung like a slap across my face. It took every bit of my self-control not to storm over to her parents' house and drag her back to my bed. I drove over there a couple of times and sat outside until I got my emotions under control enough to drive home.

I should have gotten out of the damn car. I should have listened to her.

When she pulled me around the corner when we first arrived at the hospital, every sensible thought and bit of self-control I had went out the bloody window. All I cared about was her body pressed against mine and the smell of her shampoo and moisturiser on her skin. I inhaled her and calm descended over me like a soft cloak.

The sun is rising now and she is handing out coffees to everyone, bestowing each of them with a kind smile. She would make a perfect mafia queen, I just wish she was mine.

She leaves me to last, coming to stand between my spread legs as I recline in the hard plastic seat.

"For you," she says softly, passing me the cup.

"Thank you, my darlin'," her face lights up at my words and I pull her onto my lap. There are no more seats available and that's excuse enough for me.

Francesca sits on my lap, arm around my shoulders, as various capos, soldiers, and family members come to speak to me. I'm being reckless. I shouldn't be letting them see that there is anything between us.

Elio's stormy face a few seats away tells me that he is not happy with the situation. A part of me thinks he has no one to blame but himself. But, I understand that even if he doesn't want the leadership or Francesca, he is embarrassed by me seeming to take them both in front of everyone.

The capos have all gone home and Peta isn't talking to anyone. She just sits watching the door that he was taken through so many hours ago.

Heartbroken and afraid that the inevitable time she will have to live without him is about to begin.

"Massi," I beckon him over. "Take Francesca home. I'll call you as soon as we hear anything."

Francesca has drifted off to sleep with her head tucked into my neck. I kiss her forehead and gently wake her up.

"Come on, Ches," Massimo holds out his hand to her. She looks at me, unsure if she should go.

"Go home, baby," I call her 'baby' quietly to see the spark in her eyes again.

"Will you be okay?" She whispers to me and I nod, my heart melting at how sweet she is.

She pauses, looking into my eyes and then down at my lips. I know she wants to kiss me, but that would be pushing everyone a bit far at this point. I shake my head just slightly and press a kiss on her cheek instead.

When she walks away with my little brother my heart feels like it splits in two. Like I am watching part of it walk down that corridor. I'm in uncharted territory.

Elio is sitting on the opposite side of the corridor, a few metres away, facing me. His thunderous expression is quite clearly aimed at me and I sigh, knowing I need to deal with this.

"How's it going, Elio?" I ask.

"Oh just fine. All fucking good, G. My Dad had a stroke, we took out four men tonight, my sister is cracking on to my fiancee, and everyone thinks I'm a fuckin' joke," he hisses at me, anger etching ugly lines in his handsome face. But it's more than that; he's sad. The misery is oozing off him like he has dropped the charm curtain and exposed the raw hurt behind it.

"Well, when you put it like that…" I joke, misreading the moment. "Sorry, not the time," I mutter. He just directs his deadened gaze to a spot just above my head.

I try again. "Eli…I love you. You know that. You three dickheads have always been the most important people in my life. You gotta know I'm never not on your team."

"Except when you're taking everything from me?" he snarls.

"I'm not going to let you get away with that, brother. You don't *want* to lead this family - behind the scenes or in front. I can see you hate it. And, you've not been able to shut up about not wanting to marry Francesca. I don't know what is happening with us, but I do know she deserves a fuck load more respect than what you've shown her."

He knows. He doesn't want this life. Just like I don't like the one laid out for me. But it is the hand Dad has dealt us. For whatever reason. I'm increasingly questioning his judgement on this one.

"Get fucked," Elio replies under his breath and that is how I know I've won the argument.

"Here's hoping," I say with a wink and he can't help but snort. He isn't ready to concede though. He's hurting and I'll give him room to hurt.

Our tense cross-corridor conversation is interrupted when a nurse appears through the door Peta has been staring at.

"Family of Alessandro Marino?" she asks us even though we are the only ones here and probably the only ones in the hospital dressed like mob bosses.

"That's us," I stand and brush the creases out of my pants.

"Alessandro is doing well. He is awake, but very fragile. I'll take one of you in now, but we don't want to overwhelm him," she gives us the good news in one rushed breath.

Everyone looks at Peta. "You go, Pete," Matty pipes up and I give her a small smile of encouragement.

Elio and I are next to go in. We both inhale sharply when we see the frail old man in the hospital bed. This is the bloke who we never doubted could move mountains. The pillar of strength and infallibility in our lives. Age is catching up with him rapidly and even though it looks like he will pull through this time, this wise old cat is running out of lives.

"I'm not dead yet," a quiet bark is directed at us. "Don't fuckin' walk in here like you're paying respects to my corpse."

"Thank goodness the stroke hasn't robbed you of your sunny disposition," I remark wryly.

He hacks out a laugh at that. "You know me, box of fuckin' birds. Now, do we still have unhappy capos?"

We look at each other. We may have been scrapping a few minutes earlier, but in the face of our father's disappointment and disapproval, we find solidarity.

"We took out Stefan tonight, Dad. He kidnapped Francesca..." I speak slowly and in a low voice.

Dad's face registers shock, before he simply asks, "You clean up properly?"

I nod. "Clean up in progress. Dealing with the Rossis will be the most complicated thing."

Dad gives us a little taste of approval before drawing his brows into a frown and making his voice gruff. "Elio, pull your finger outta your arse and show the Rossis what they need to see to feel safe. For God's sake keep your dick in your pants unless you're wooing Rossi's girl."

His attention shifts to me. "And you, Giovanna. Stop being a pussy and pull your brother into line. You've gotta get tougher."

Neither of us is impressed with how quickly Dad has slipped into barking orders. Though it does reassure us that he's going to be okay.

CHAPTER FIFTY

FRANCESCA

I'm wrestling a huge dish of lasagne from the oven when my brand-new iPhone starts ringing on the other side of the kitchen. My old phone is probably floating in Sydney Harbour with my big brother, so Massimo picked me up a new one while I napped today.

Letting the dish clatter onto the top of the stove, I slam the oven door shut and answer the call in a fluster.

"Francesca," Giovanna's tired voice rasps on the other end.

"Oh! Uh hi," I stammer.

"You okay? Sounds like you're in the middle of something?"

"I'm fine. I was just getting lasagne out of the oven. How are you doing?"

She sighs and there is a slight pause before she answers. "Are you staying at your parents tonight?"

I'm not. I brought my stuff home when I got back from the hospital. *Home.* I guess the Marino house is home.

"Why's that?" I ask softly, hoping she wants me to be here, in her home.

Again there is a pause. I hear traffic. She must be in her car. "Giovanna?"

"Come home, yeah?" She finally answers.

"Your house, you mean?" I cringe at the hope I hear in my voice. Always the pining puppy.

"Yeah," her answer is quiet, but she drops her voice even lower to say, "I need you."

My heart flutters and I smile into the phone. *She needs me!* And it doesn't sound like she needs to see me about family business. At least that isn't what I hear in her voice.

"I'm here already, Gio. I've made you guys some dinner. Sorry, it is full of carbs and cheese, but I thought comfort food was appropriate. I made you salad to go with it though," I ramble hoping she will eat my calorie-laden dinner.

"Sounds perfect," there is a slight smile in her voice now; she sounds lighter. "You're an angel."

Just then Massimo saunters into the kitchen in grey sweatpants and a hoodie. He's singing quietly to himself with AirPods in his ears. "Fuck yes! Lasagne!" He shouts, eyeing up the deep dish sitting on the stove, sauce crusted down the sides.

Giovanna snorts. "I better get home before Massi eats it all. See you soon, darlin'."

"Bye," I reply, hanging up before I call her 'baby'.

Massimo's singing grows louder as he dishes himself up a huge slice of lasagne. His movements are angry and the lyrics talk of booty calls and feeling used.

Recognising the song as *Why'd you only call me when you're high?* I join in with him.

He dances his way over to the huge dining table in time to the beat of the song and points to me as we both shout the question central to the song.

We're grinning at each other like idiots when we notice Matty and Bluey have appeared from the internal garage stairs. Matty shakes his head at us.

"Something smells, unreal in here," he says sniffing the air.

"Cheska made lasagne," Massimo says with a mouthful of hot pasta. He swallows it and continues humming the *Arctic Monkeys.* He repeats the line from the chorus quietly, his eyes following Bluey who is fetching himself a plate from the cupboard.

I'm starting to think Massimo might have a thing for him. My poor bestie. Bluey is second only to Elio in being a giant friggin' manwhore. He is a ranga lothario.

The guys are just depositing their empty plates in the dishwasher when Giovanna trudges up the stairs from the garage, her footsteps heavy and tired.

She stops at the top and raises her eyebrows at them before her eyes sweep the room to settle on me sitting at the dining table nursing a glass of red wine in one of her hoodies and some sleep shorts.

"Smells good, Ches," she says, stepping out of her shoes and kicking them out of the way.

"Tastes fuckin' unreal too, boss," booms Bluey over his shoulder as he grabs a couple of glasses and a bottle of whiskey from a cabinet. "League kicks off in ten minutes," he says to Massi and heads off to the TV room. They'll be preoccupied with rugby league for the rest of the night.

Giovanna sits down opposite me with a healthy portion of lasagne and salad. She takes a bite and groans exaggeratedly. "Yummmmmm. Darlin', this is delicious."

I can't explain what makes me respond the way I do, but I guess it is reflexive. "*You're* delicious," I shoot back cheekily, shocking myself with my brazen flirting.

Her fork stops mid-air on the way to her mouth.

"Francesca," she warns, shaking her head.

"I don't know why I said that," I tell her honestly, my cheeks growing warm and pink.

"We can't, Francesca," she says with a pained expression on her face.

"We already have though."

She chuckles softly. "Yeah we have, darlin' and it doesn't mean I don't want to do it again. We just...can't."

"You said you need me," I whisper, embarrassed.

She groans. The look she gives me is full of heat. Her eyes darken and I can almost see the battle playing out behind them. When she doesn't say anything, I stand quickly and take my plate to the dishwasher. My cheeks are burning and the sting of rejection bites.

Sitting at the table, Giovanna's back is to the kitchen and I take a moment to run my eyes over her broad body. Her dark hair is pulled up into a small bun at the back of her head and I appreciate the sexiness of the buzzed undercut she maintains. It just makes her look so fucking gay and that is a serious turn-on. Her strong jaw moves as she chews and I'm mesmerised by the muscles in her neck flexing slightly.

I wish I understood my obsession with this woman. It is as old as I am. I can't remember ever not thinking she was the most amazing human on earth. She is under my skin. Even eight years on the opposite side of the world did nothing to dull it.

Ugh. I've made a complete tit of myself.

My hands are wrinkling in water that is almost too hot and I use a scouring pad to scrape at the empty lasagne pan. The leftovers have been cut into even portions and popped in the fridge for my family of hungry mobsters to reheat later.

I feel like one of those perfectly put-together 'Pinterest Moms' who labels everything and only feeds her children organic food. I wouldn't mind that, to be honest. Perhaps because of how loveless my relationship is with my parents, I have always craved a family of my own making. I dream of showering my children with love, and security, and being the parent that I so desperately needed.

Foolish dreams for a woman who is engaged to a man who can't manage even the pretence of monogamy and is in love with a woman who is committed to ensuring she marries the aforementioned man.

But it does get me thinking that if I want to feel more in control of my life maybe I should start carving my own role in this family. My own place. Rather than sitting and waiting for everything to happen to me, I can contribute in ways I want to. Create my own power. Running away proved to be a pointless and painful endeavour.

Deep in thought about enacting my Pinterest fantasies, I jump when a warm hand slides under my hoodie and along my stomach just above the waistband of my sleep shorts. The warmth of Giovanna's body, as it crowds my back, sends my pulse racing and my breath hitches as hers tickles the skin behind my ear.

"Thank you for dinner," she murmurs and kisses the side of my neck gently. It sends a shiver up my spine and the hand against my stomach pushes me back against the muscular body behind me.

A smile creeps across my face. Looks like she's changed her mind.

"No problem," I long to call her by the affectionate names I use in my head, but I feel like the moment I do she will snap out of her indulgence of me and push me back to Elio.

Remaining behind me, Giovanna dries my hands off with a tea towel and then turns me around. My back presses against the sink and I look up into her serious face. I trace a finger lightly over the scar in her left eyebrow. I like it. It makes her look sexier, and badass. As the saying goes, 'bitches love scars.'

She closes her eyes as I lift my other hand and trail my fingertips down her jawline. Feeling brave, I follow the path of my fingertips with my lips. Little kisses, soft and slow. Her head falls back a little and she begins to hum. Her hands grasp my hips and keep my pelvis pressed against hers.

I slide a hand behind her neck and up into her undercut. Her eyes darken as I scrape my nails over her short hair and her scalp.

"I like it when you do that," she rasps and I smile at her. I'm drowning in the heat from her gaze. No, I'm bathing in it.

One of her hands goes to the side of my neck and she tilts my head up. I know her kiss is coming and I'm in agony with each second I have to wait. I'm desperate. On fire. I need her.

The way she bears down on me is so perfectly dominant. She is in control and she wants to use her power to get lost in me. Her firm lips capture my soft ones and our kiss begins slowly. Then both of Giovanna's hands are on my neck, moving me exactly as she wants and I put up no resistance.

I melt into her and she deepens the kiss. The butterflies in my tummy are multiplying and her tongue moving with mine. Everything feels so acute. Every touch is a spark.

"I need you," I whisper against her lips.

"Tell me what you need, baby," she replies, planting more kisses on my lips and chin.

"I-I need your fingers inside me," I gasp. "And, I want to taste you this time." I'm nervous, but I am desperate to taste her for the first time.

The look she gives me is pure fire and she steps back throwing her hands behind her head and groaning. "Fuck, Francesca. You're killing me."

I wait, watching her, worried that I said something wrong and she is going to walk away. But instead, she grabs the nape of my neck a little roughly and plants a kiss on my forehead.

"Bedtime, baby," she growls, taking me by the hand and leading me upstairs to her bedroom.

As soon as the bedroom door shuts behind us, I leap into her arms, my legs wrapping around her hips. Our mouths crash together urgently and we devour each other like we are each the other's last meal.

She slams me up against the closed door and pulls back to look at me. "I…I can't promise you anything, darlin'. Just tonight. Leave now if that ain't enough."

'This is going to hurt in the morning,' I think as I pull her head back towards me and slam my mouth against hers.

"God, I want you so bad it hurts," I groan into her mouth as she steps back from the door and turns to drop me down onto her bed gently.

"As much as it gets me wet to see you in my hoodie, I'm going to need you to take it off now," she growls standing next to the bed.

I give her a slight smile and my most innocent wide-eyed expression as I tug the oversized hoodie over my head revealing I'm wearing nothing underneath.

"And the shorts," Giovanna says darkly. Her teeth are clenched and knowing how much she wants me makes me even wetter.

I give her the same smile and innocent expression and slowly lift my hips, tugging the little cotton shorts down. I'm wearing nothing under the shorts either.

"Open," Giovanna commands, gently tapping the inside of one of my knees. I let my legs fall apart and my eyes roll back into my head at the hiss she makes when she sees how glistening wet I am.

I keep my eyes on Giovanna's face. Watching her appreciate my body as if it were the most incredible piece of art. A piece of art, but one she wants to devour, tear apart, and put back together.

Giovanna runs her hands over my body and there is something erotic about lying naked for her while she explores me fully clothed. Her palms follow the curves of my body, skimming over my skin, and leaving me covered in goosebumps. It feels like no part of my body is unexplored by her gentle hands and I feel worshipped.

"You sure?" she rasps.

"Yes, just fuck me. Please," I beg.

Sliding her hands underneath my bum, Giovanna tugs me to the side of the bed. My pussy hovers over the edge and she places my feet wide on the edge too so that my legs are splayed open. Standing between my legs, she leans over me, a palm on either side of my head. She kisses me deeply and my exposed pussy aches for contact, but she makes sure her body doesn't provide any friction for it.

"I can smell how wet you are for me, my darlin'. Do you know how hot that is?" Giovanna groans against my mouth before dragging her lips down my body in a series of kisses, licks, sucks, and bites.

She doesn't stop until she reaches my slick cunt. It is throbbing for her; my whole body quivering. She drops to her knees next to the bed, still wearing her suit, and slides her tongue deep into my wet folds, dragging it from my vagina to my clitoris. I cry out in shock and pleasure.

Her hot mouth covers me and she eats me out with reverence. My tummy muscles contract and shake at the assault on my senses. Sinking my nails into her hair, I claw at her head as my hips buck involuntarily under her mouth.

I have never felt so good in my life, but it is almost too much to handle. My body is on a knife's edge, jumping at the slightest touch.

The pressure building inside me grows and pulses. "Baby, I'm going to come," I whine, slightly embarrassed at how little time it has taken.

In response, Giovanna gently presses her fingers into my entrance while her mouth focuses on my clit.

"*Giovanna,*" I breathe. "I'm coming!"

She thrusts her fingers into me as I come, dragging against the spot inside me that makes me see stars. I'm crying her name louder and louder as I'm rocked by the waves of the most intense orgasm of my life.

"Good grief," I exhale as the pleasure waves subside. Giovanna chuckles and stands, looking over my flushed panting body.

"Good grief?" she teases.

"Good fuckin' grief," I nod. "When are you getting naked?"

"If you wanted me naked all you had to do was ask, little darlin'," she winks and begins peeling her clothes off.

I watch eagerly, taking in my private strip show. Each piece of clothing is discarded over her shoulder while her eyes never leave mine. She doesn't do anything overtly sexual; doesn't dance or gyrate. But it is so sexy nonetheless.

My mouth waters when she is completely naked. The pull to fuck her is so intense I can hardly express it. But I'm nervous to the point of paralysis. My inexperience is obvious and I don't want to turn her off by bumbling around clumsily.

"Can I taste you?" I whisper, shy and tentative.

Giovanna grins tilting her head to regard me with humour in her eyes. "Are you sure you want to, sweetheart? You look terrified."

I cringe and push up on my elbows to sit on the edge of the bed. She stands, gloriously naked, right in front of me waiting for my response and watching the rise and fall of my breasts.

"I'm just…nervous. But, I want to. If you help me…tell me what to do…" my voice trails off and my cheeks flush in embarrassment.

Giovanna reaches a hand to softly tuck my hair behind each of my ears. Her smile has faded and as she tilts my chin up to force me to meet her gaze I see only heat, serious heat, in her expression.

"Come here," she points to the carpet at her feet. "Get on your knees."

I shudder as her words send an unexpected bolt of attraction and arousal from my head to my toes. Her commanding tone and dominating stance have me quivering with anticipation all over again.

Scrambling off the bed, my knees hit the carpet with an inelegant thud and I instinctively get into position kneeling with my bum resting on my heels. My hands rest on the front of my thighs and the simple act of being at her feet waiting to be told what to do has my core clenching.

"Eyes on me, Francesca," she commands and I obey in an instant.

Wetting my lips, I await instruction, but she just watches me for several moments. The tension is indescribable. The air between us crackles as if our sparks might catch on something and set the whole room ablaze.

Her face is dark and the dim lighting casts shadows over her muscular form. The light catches her bold cheekbones and looks like streaks of light warpaint on her dark olive skin. From my place at her feet, she looks like some

kind of warrior. An avenging angel. The scar in her eyebrow adds to the image of an anti-hero who will save your life only to ruin it.

Slowly she reaches down to run a finger through her own pussy separating her folds and showing me how wet she is. My eyes widen and I swear I feel them dilate with arousal.

I gulp and wet my lips again.

"Taste," she presses the wetness to my lips and I open my mouth to suck her from the base to the tip of her finger.

"Do I taste good?" She teases and I nod eagerly, allowing her to slip her finger out of my mouth.

Her hand cups my chin firmly. It is grounding and reassuring, but she increases the pinch in her grasp to offer more dominance if I'll take it. "You want more, baby?"

"Yes," I whisper, biting my lower lip.

"Yes, what?"

Please? Ma'am? Daddy? What am I supposed to say?

"Um…yes, I want more. I want to…" I look pointedly at the glistening lips sitting below the tidy triangle of dark hair between her legs.

With no more encouragement required, Giovanna throws one of her legs over my shoulder, propping her foot on the bed behind me, and I scoot a little closer so I'm kneeling with my face just centimetres from her pussy.

Pressing my nose into the very top of her inner thigh I relish her earthy smell and groan. I'm terrified that I'll do the wrong thing and don't know where to start. Sure I've received oral sex many times in my life, but I feel utterly clueless as to what I should do in the role of giver.

Tentatively, I let my tongue dart out to lick her clit. It's hardening and covered in her arousal. She hisses and her hips jump a little. I feel her reach out and grab the post of the bed to steady herself.

"That's it, darlin'. Just do what feels right," she rasps in that low, gravelly voice that drives me wild.

Confidence growing, I lap gently at Giovanna's pussy. My strokes grow longer and more languid, sliding through her slick lips. My core is throbbing again and I can't believe how turned on I'm getting just from eating her out.

One of her hands is in my hair and I look up to see she has thrown her head back. "You're doing so good," she praises me.

Both of her hands go to cup my face as she balances on one leg. She grinds her pussy against my face and can't resist taking control of me bit by bit. Soon she is fucking me, not the other way around, and the way she takes ownership of my body when she fucks me taps into sexual needs I didn't even know I had.

My tongue delves boldly inside her thrusting, seeking as much depth as possible and I groan as she grinds against my mouth to assist me.

"Suck on my clit," she commands and I obey in an instant.

"Good. Girl," she groans. "I'm going to come on your pretty little face."

Nothing prepares me for how hot it is when she comes, shuddering against my face, crying out my name. Her fingers are tangled in my hair and I'm gasping for air from the intensity of it all. The power I feel in being able to bring her such pleasure and the connection with her are intoxicating.

She doesn't stop touching me. We lie in her bed talking in sleepy hushed voices. She tells me about what the gay scene was like in Sydney when she was my age and I tell her about the time Massi and I met some insane Italians at a club in Soho who invited us back to their small village in Italy. We left that same day and spent a month staying with various nonnas and relatives. I had to find a new job when we got back because my employer was less than impressed with my sudden absence.

It is refreshingly normal to talk about things that don't matter and to share memories from the past that aren't painful.

Her hands skim over my bare skin absentmindedly. Every so often she leans over to kiss me softly. On my lips or my shoulder or my boob. I stretch and practically purr at all the attention and physical touch. It is pure pleasure.

"I don't think Elio wants this life," I find the courage to raise the elephant in the room after we have been lying in companionable silence for several minutes.

She is unsurprised by the comment, but still asks, "What makes you say that?"

"This. It just doesn't feel like his destiny. That sounds silly, but what I mean is that he finds joy in ways that aren't compatible with being in charge of Sydney's mafia. I don't mean fucking either. He's too…frivolous…wait, no that

sounds too negative. He's…this is going to sound strange since he has been such an arsehole to me, but he's too sweet and self-indulgent. He is made for a job that he can clock off from and party to his heart's content."

I cut myself off and look over at her pensive face. She is considering my rambling as if I have said something worthwhile. It is nice to feel like what I say is worth being heard.

When she doesn't say anything, I push my luck some more. "But you, you were made for this world," I whisper.

"Because I'm not sweet? Or good? I'm not afraid of violence?" She sounds a little bitter and I cautiously reach out and cup her cheek. My thumb gently strokes her stunning high cheekbones.

"No, because you're not afraid full stop. You're a born leader. People naturally look to you. You're serious, a deep thinker. And yes, you were willing to kill a man to save me."

Emotion dances behind her eyes in the dim light and I wonder if I should have just shut up. But she reaches out and drags me closer to fit me under her chin, tangling our legs together.

"I am afraid sometimes," she murmurs into my hair. "I'm afraid of failure. Of something happening to my brothers; to you. I just know how to hide it."

I shift my face so I can access her neck properly and begin to kiss my way up to her sharp jawline. She emits a quiet groan as my kisses become more sensual and my hand, resting on her back, starts to stroke her tight muscles.

"I want you," I whine, needy and desperate.

She responds by grabbing me under my chin and kissing me hard. My pussy aches for her touch again and I begin to rub myself back and forth on the leg that is pressed between mine. I'm almost embarrassed by how horny I am. Almost. I have never wanted sex like this in my life.

"Again?" she murmurs in quiet amusement. "You're a horny wee baby lesbian, aren't you?"

Pushing me onto my back, Giovanna lays her naked body over mine, between my splayed legs. She kisses me hungrily for what feels like hours, savouring me, not wanting to rush.

Eventually, she allows one of her hands to stroke down the side of my body and across my pubic bone. Her fingers stroke the bare skin just above my pussy.

"I'm going to fuck you now, baby," she growls against my mouth.

"Oh god, please," I moan, trying to spread my legs for her even more.

I'm so slick that when her fingers find my centre they slide through my folds with ease. She groans as she pushes two fingers inside of me and my heat sucks them in. The heel of her palm creates friction for my clit as she slowly slides in and out of me.

I claw at her back as she curls her fingers to hit the rough spot inside me that makes me shudder.

"Good girl," she praises me again. "Take it."

She speeds up, her biceps and forearms straining as she ploughs her fingers into me. The orgasm builds deep inside me. I can feel it in my spine and pooling in my stomach.

"*Giovanna*," I moan, elongating each syllable of her name. "Please don't stop."

"Oh I won't," she promises, keeping steady pressure on my hard clit and I fall apart, my body spasming. I cry out her name as the waves of pleasure wash through me.

I'm still shuddering when she pushes up onto her knees and peeling her folds back, layers her wet pussy over mine. Her hands go under my bum and she undulates her hips sliding us along each other.

"*Fuck,*" she hisses, finding a spot she likes and increasing the pressure. My eyes roll back in my head. This feels so primal. I never knew sex with a woman could be like this. My imagination, my fantasies about Giovanna fucking me all these years have been well short of the mark.

I tell her. "You fuck so good," I rasp.

"You're fuckin' beautiful like this. So perfect," she grinds out, rocking faster. Her fingers dig into my hips, moving me in sync with her. Then she moans my name, the sound hitting me right in my core. She comes hard, pressing our clits together and rubbing ferociously.

Collapsing between my legs, her head rests on my chest and my arms wrap around her, holding her tight. Her heart rate is rocketing against my stomach and I love that my body did that to her.

We lay like this for ages. So long that the satisfaction and inner peace I feel gradually begin to give way to the usual panic and anxiety.

How can I ever go back to Elio, to anyone, after this? Nothing will ever compare. She said she can only give me tonight. But, maybe she will keep me as her dirty little secret?

I hate myself for even wanting to be her illicit affair. Her dirty laundry.

But I never want to let her go. My body and mind have craved her for so long and now that I have her and she is so much more than I ever expected, I feel empty at the prospect of not doing this night after night.

"I can feel you thinking," she says sleepily. I thought she was asleep.

"Can't help it," I say, attempting to sound lighthearted.

"Darlin', don't. Just live in this moment. Reality will be there in the morning."

She knows.

Something squeezes my heart, reading the inevitability in her words. When morning comes she won't be mine. She'll be gone with the darkness.

CHAPTER FIFTY ONE
GIOVANNA

I'm ruined. She has ruined me and I willingly walked into self-destruction. She makes the sweetest noises as she sleeps, her chest rising and falling softly. Her slightly pouty lips are both angelic and pornographic, and I have to restrain myself from stealing one more kiss before I force myself to be a complete arsehole. Again.

I have to get out of here. As I shower I simultaneously hope she'll wake and come join me while praying she won't.

Morning has come and so has reality, just as I promised her it would. Only I'm the one running from it now.

Dressing at speed, but as quietly as I can, I feel the shame gathering inside me like bile. She told me last night that she thinks I'm afraid of nothing and here I am proving her so completely wrong. I'm a coward.

I slip out of my room, leaving the most beautiful woman I've ever been lucky enough to get my hands on, sleeping. Unaware that she is about to be ghosted. Well, as much as someone can ghost their sister-in-law. *Fuck, that makes it sound way worse.*

Why did I have to give in to temptation last night?

I was feeling so wrecked from tracking Francesca down and being at the hospital with Dad and all I wanted was the respite I knew I would find in her arms. I was selfish. A complete fucking arsehole.

I'm in such a hurry to put distance between me and the angel in bed, that I forgo my usual breakfast routine and stop to grab a coffee and a protein shake on the way into the city.

The view from our offices usually centres me. The panoramic views of Sydney are breathtaking on a clear day. Strolling along the vast floor-to-ceiling windows, atop the city I love, is where I do some of my best thinking. Today, however, the bitter coffee I sip as I pace my office is nowhere near as bitter as I feel.

"Hey, G," Matty's gravelly voice announces his arrival and I hear him deposit himself in one of the chairs facing my desk.

"Hey, mate," I sigh without turning around. "Peta said Dad had a good night and is already telling the doctors how to do their job."

He chuckles softly. "Yeah, he'll be fine…hospital staff might need counselling by the time he's discharged though."

I look at my watch and Matty reassures me, "Massi is on his way. I think he has Bluey with him. Shouldn't be long."

"I didn't ask for Bluey," I snap. "I need to speak with you and Massi. Fucksake, those two are attached at the hip these days."

Unphased by my sharp tone and grumpiness, Matty shrugs.

Just a few minutes later the pair of them amble down the hallway in fits of raucous laughter. I eye them jealously thinking how nice it would be to be young, carefree, and not fuckin' tired all the time.

"Massimo! I said 9 am! Don't piss me about!" I bark through my open office door and the laughter stops. Sheepishly my massive littlest brother folds himself into the chair next to Matty.

"You need me, boss?" Bluey's shaggy head pops around the door.

"No. We'll be about half an hour. Then you can take me to the warehouse."

The door shuts. "Well, go on then. What's up your arse today?" Massimo is playing with fire.

Leaning on the back of my chair I hit him with a stare that would chill the Red Centre of Australia.

"Massimo," my voice is low. "You are lucky that door is shut and it is just us here. You speak to me like that in front of others and I will have no choice

but to make an example of you. I am your sister and I love you, but I am also your boss. Well, kind of. Fuck!"

He gulps and nods quickly.

"As to what's up my arse," I continue. "I fucked up and I need your help."

"Did you fuck Francesca again?" Matty enquires gently.

My exhale is aggressive and I drop my head back to rest on the back of my chair with a groan.

"Yeah," I concede.

"WHAT!" Massimo explodes. "I mean...*with all due respect,* sister boss... but what the fuck? She's in love with you! This is going to mess her head up, for real."

"I know. I know. Trust me, I'm beating myself up. I'm always in fuckin' control. Always. But with her, I just can't stop myself," I'm second guessing how vulnerable I'm being in front of them, but I need help. I need them to look out for her. I have to stay away.

"This is fucked. She's been obsessed with you since she was a kid and you're into her...why can't you be with her, again?" Matty asks.

"Because she has to marry our brother, for fucksake!" I snap, looking at him like he is a goddamn moron because he would have to be to forget the arranged marriage that is fucking up all our lives.

He looks thoughtful for a second and then asks, "Why?"

"Are you kidding? Do I seriously need to remind you? We need to connect the Marinos and the Rossis and show Elio is settling down. This is about stability. Even without Stefan Rossi trying to force wedges everywhere." Frustration spills over as I have to explain the set of circumstances when he knows this all too well.

He nods. "You're right. We need her to marry Elio, but he's going to keep on shagging other women so why don't you just set up an arrangement. A marriage of convenience, but she's yours behind the scenes?"

Behind the scenes. Just like I run the fucking Famiglia behind the scenes. I can't say I haven't considered it. Having her in bed each night would be heaven, but seeing them play husband and wife, and have children, would be unbearable. No way.

"That won't work," I admit to myself and my brothers. "She wants to be a mother more than anything else. I'd be a distraction, a barrier to her happiness. No, she needs to marry him and learn to love him. Have his babies. That's why I need your help. Matty, I need you to talk to Elio and get him to understand that for this to work he needs to work on his relationship with her. He needs to build trust. Massimo, you need to be there for Francesca. She will be hurt. Comfort her, agree that I'm an arsehole. Push her towards Elio."

Matty nods, but Massimo glares at me. "You're going to break her fucking heart. I'll agree that you're an arsehole all right. You don't understand what you've done! It's always been you for her. She has adored you since she was a kid. You should have stayed the fuck away because this is going to kill her."

My own heart feels like it is shattering. Even though my feelings for her were purely platonic before she returned from England, I've cared about her for her entire life. My little darlin'. And now? I'll kill anyone who harms a hair on her head and worshipping her body feels as vital as breathing.

But this way is best for the *Famiglia*. It is best for her. I just have to find a way to survive.

CHAPTER FIFTY TWO
FRANCESCA

I thought the way Elio treated me was bad, but it was nothing compared to what his sister has done. From him I expect nothing less than selfishness and disloyalty, but her? No.

It has been a week since we slept together for the second time and I awoke in her room alone again. I was disappointed and wished that she would have woken me to say goodbye, but I didn't for a second doubt that we would talk later in the day.

The rose-tinted glasses I have worn since I was old enough to think Giovanna Marino was a mixture of superhero and goddess, have left me vulnerable to the fact that she is as capable as her brother of using and discarding women.

At least Elio never pretended to be anything different. He told me explicitly that he didn't love me right before we had sex. Giovanna sucked me in. She gave me a taste of what I have craved for so long. I felt safe with her, protected.

My eyes roll every time I think of the warmth I felt when she called me baby or my darlin'. How naive and stupid was I that I thought that meant she cared at all for me?

Wherever she has been sleeping this week, she has probably been whispering the same sweet words into another woman's ear.

My cheeks redden with the humiliation I can't shake. The feeling that I am pathetic. All I am worth is a political marriage. My mother can't see me past

her self-obsession and he sees me as a pawn in his miniature game of thrones. My half-brother fucking kidnapped me, for goodness sake.

The fact remains that the only person who I have ever truly felt loved by is Massimo and he has been lying to me too. He spends more time with Bluey than he does with me now anyway and I feel our special bond slipping away.

I'm glad I have Sammy, but our friendship is still new. We bond over work dramas, the gym members who hit on us, and all the normal bullshit. We hang out, but she doesn't know all the inner workings of my complicated life.

The past week I have been a zombie. I don't want to speak with anyone. I have stayed at the Marino house because being near my parents would only make me more miserable, but I haven't seen Giovanna.

I snuck into her room the first night in the wee hours of the morning and she wasn't there. Her bed was still as I had made it that morning.

The second day I text her.

Francesca: Hey? Is everything ok?

But I didn't get a response. That was when I knew that she was avoiding me. There was no alarm in the rest of the family that she was missing or out of touch. It was just me she avoided.

Massi tried to comfort me. He called his sister all sorts of names and was on my side. But he kept pushing me back towards Elio. His solution to my heartbreak was for me to throw myself into my sham marriage.

"You're only saying that because it's what the *Famiglia* wants!" I screamed at him. "When did you stop giving a shit about me!"

The guilt on his face told me I was right. He was working toward an agenda, not caring about his oldest friend.

Interestingly, Elio has been nice this week. His cheerfulness has been a reprieve from all the angst. He took me out for brunch on the third day and although it was nice, his hand on my lower back as we walked through the cafe felt wrong.

He is the only one who seems to get how shit it is to have your life at total mercy to what the *Famiglia* dictates. We have bonded over our mutual hatred of the control being exerted over us.

Now, it's six nights since I last saw Giovanna and I've sent several texts which have all received no response. Miserable, I sneak into her room again. I can't sleep and pathetically, I think maybe if she still isn't there, I could just sleep in her bed. Maybe her scent on her pillows will help me drift off.

I pad barefoot down the hallway wearing one of Massimo's massive t-shirts and slip into Giovanna's room. I pause, allowing my eyes to adjust to the dark room before tip-toeing toward the bed.

A dark form lies entangled in the blankets. She is home. She's here and she didn't reply to a single text or check I am ok.

I want to throw things at her sleeping body. Wake her up with my hurt screams. But instead, I walk around to the other side of the bed and slip under the covers. I crawl over to her and turn around so my back is to her. I rest my head gently on the bicep of her outstretched arm and she instinctively pulls me in close, curling her body around mine. I loathe how good it feels. My eyes fill with tears and my heart with self-hatred.

"Francesca," Giovanna groans, sleepy and exasperated, a few moments later.

"I hate you," I reply, my voice thick as I battle the tears threatening to fall.

She is silent for a moment and then sighs. "I know, baby. I hate myself too. Go to sleep."

And I do. In her arms, I slip into the easiest sleep I have had all week. I know that the morning will bring with it more heartache. She will push me away again. But for now, I feel safe and exactly where I'm meant to be.

I wake before Giovanna. She is still wrapped around me and every fibre of my being cries out for me to burrow deeper into her arms and go back to sleep. Thankfully I have a tiny bit of self-preservation left and instead, I gently peel her off me and creep back to my own bed.

Sliding into the cold sheets feels like salt in the wounds of the past week, but I do it because I can't bear the thought of waking alone in her bed again.

CHAPTER FIFTY THREE
FRANCESCA

18 Years Old

Everything is grey and cold here. The buildings are old and hardly anyone has gardens unless you drive far out of the city. And yet, this dreary place now feels like home. My grandparents are nice. They aren't what I expected. I mean, they don't even have devil's horns. Though if they were really that bad it would be pretty messed up for Mum to send me here.

Two years on and there still isn't much about this situation that isn't completely messed up. I go to therapy and talk about my feelings, but I still feel defective.

Maybe if I was stupid enough to think that I matter at all to my parents I'd be able to conjure up more outrage at what has been done to me. As it stands, I am under no illusions that my existence is viewed as anything more than a set of political opportunities for my father.

He once told me that if I were ugly he wouldn't know what to do with me. For a moment I considered if that might be preferable. He might let me have control of my own life if I were unattractive. Maybe none of this would have even happened. Uncle David would have ignored me and I wouldn't be a world away from Massimo. A world away from *her*.

I know I'll be here for a long time. Maybe I'll never go back to Australia. Massi promises me he will move here as soon as he can, but I'm not holding my breath.

If I were to return to Australia, the thought of finding Giovanna in love with some woman makes me want to be sick. I am now finally old enough, and my body filling out enough, that she might notice me in the way I want, but I'll never get a chance with her.

Is it possible that I love her? The obsession has always been there. The adoration and idolising like she is a celebrity I know in real life. But, the way I burn for her feels more intense than all that. I've known her forever and am not just blinded by the very best parts of her. Her constant seriousness, often grumpiness, isn't something I have to overlook. Her broody and dark personality is part of the appeal. I want to be enveloped in her darkness. I want to be her light.

Maybe it's my hormones, but I swear since I walked in on her having sex just before I left, I've thought about it every single day. It is branded in my brain and I relive all the little details of it. I'm utterly consumed with thoughts of her rippling back muscles and contracting bum as she thrust the strap-on in and out of the woman. A sheen of sweat coated her body and I imagine sliding my hands over it.

Most of all, I remember the way she stared at me over her shoulder. She didn't stop fucking. I see the combination of all my favourite parts of her face. The scar in her eyebrow was pronounced as she arched it at me, the dimple deep in her cheek as her lip curled up, and that jawline. That strong jawline that somehow speaks of dominance.

If I wasn't such a broken, sexually inept mess, I'd like to experience it all with someone. I'll never have her and I need to get it out of my system, but how can I do that when I haven't even been able to make myself come?

Lying in my bedroom at my grandparents' house, I can feel the dampness in my cotton knickers growing. I've touched myself before a little bit, trying to chase the experiences that girls at school have described. But at eighteen, I am the only one who hasn't had an orgasm.

Most of them have even had sex, but it seems the orgasms are usually achieved solo.

I've been scared to touch myself properly after what happened to me. I start, but always end up stopping before I reach my goal.

There is a throbbing between my legs. It's like thinking about Giovanna creates a physically painful response, but it is only painful in that it feels like a desperate ache that needs to be relieved.

Some of the girls at school have been eaten out by their boyfriends and even though I've never tried it, I can't help thinking about how Giovanna's hot, wet mouth would be the most perfect release.

I try to imagine how her tongue would feel sliding through the lips of my pussy. The idea makes me writhe in my bed. I trail a finger slowly down my wet underwear. My nail gently scratches over my clit, down to where I open. A shiver runs down my spine and I do it again.

My legs are splayed, the outer sides of my knees on the mattress, and the soles of my feet pressed together. My back arches a little as I continue to stroke myself through the outside of my knickers.

My other hand grasps one of my boobs. They're only small, but they fill my hands. Would Giovanna like them? What if she likes big ones?

I play with my nipple, rolling it between my finger and thumb, sending little bolts of sensation down to my pussy. But it's not enough. I yank down my knickers, kicking them down to the foot of the bed.

It feels bad to be so exposed. The feeling of the top sheet settling on my wet pussy makes me jump. The throbbing is intensifying. I gently run one finger through my slick folds and gasp at how good it feels. I spread my wetness around, generously covering my clit in my juices.

As soon as I start making little circles over my slippery clit I start to feel it. The feeling starts deep inside my tummy and builds like a kind of pressure. It feels so wonderful you just want to chase it and let it take over your whole body.

But, like always, I stop.

Frustrated with myself and desperate for some relief from the intense need I feel, I tell myself that this is happening. Tonight is the night. I'm going to come, even if it takes me hours.

Usually, when I touch myself I lay on my back as I am doing now, but I get the idea to try positioning myself in the same way as the woman I saw Giovanna fucking. I want to lose myself in the fantasy that it is her touching me.

I throw my blankets off and get on my hands and knees. Dropping to my elbows, I arch my back and relish the cold air on my exposed pussy. I reach

underneath my body and resume the circles on my clit, moving my hips back and forward as if Giovanna was thrusting in and out of me from behind with her black strap-on.

My pussy is clenching like it wants to be filled and the pressure is growing, moving from deep inside me to flood my cunt. As it builds I push down the panic and try to relax my body.

My movements become more frantic as I chase the feeling, pursuing the high that I know is just beyond my reach. Then I'm exploding, a sensation overload. I moan, "Giovanna" and collapse forwards onto the bed, my hand still trapped between my thighs.

Embarrassment cloaks me once my heart rate has slowed down. I'm relieved and excited that I finally did it, but it is pretty weird to say someone's name when you make yourself come. The thought of Giovanna knowing that I think about her like that let alone that I have called her name while thinking about her is mortifying. I swear to never do that again. But I do. Many, many times.

CHAPTER FIFTY FOUR
FRANCESCA

Peta wheels Sandy into the back door of the Marino house. His face is like thunder and he is beyond unimpressed to be sitting in a wheelchair.

Peta has barely left his side and is reluctant to let anyone else care for him. She was like a lioness at the hospital, always protecting her mate. The poor nurses will be pleased to see the back of us all.

"The doctors have given him a whole lot of exercises he needs to do to help get his left side working as strongly as his right. When he's up to it, walking up and down the pool is good too, they said. But he has to take it easy," Peta explains to Massi, Bluey, and me. We are sitting at the dining table eating the steak and salad I made for dinner.

"I'm right here!" Sandy barks. "Got full use of my ears and fuckin' mouth too!"

Peta shushes him like she is soothing a baby and he bristles but doesn't protest.

"Back in London, I helped a few clients at the gym who were recovering from strokes," I say. "I'd be happy to take you through your exercises each day if you want, Sandy?"

He is about to reject my offer, but something stops him. He hates being an invalid and ultimately he will do what he is told if he thinks it'll get him back to normal.

"Righto. Sounds like a plan," he says begrudgingly.

"It'll be nice to do some proper work again," I muse to Massi and Bluey. "These days I just wipe down equipment and pretend I can't hear men with roid rage talking about my ass."

Massi frowns. "You know you don't have to work there, right? You don't need a job."

"Yeah. I just want at least one part of my life to be under my control…mostly. Plus I have Sammy there now and I like hanging out with her."

Despite instructions to take it easy, Sandy wants to get into his rehab straight away. Each day I take him through the basic exercises his doctors provided, plus I do some research and add more variety to his routine.

He's a grumpy, cantankerous old bastard, but I make it my goal to make him at least snort in amusement once per session.

At first Sandy and I only discuss things that revolve around stroke recovery and exercise, but after a handful of sessions, we relax a bit. I know Peta has been making him watch *Love Island* with her and I've been having a lot of fun trapping him into talking about it as if he is properly invested in the reality TV show. If only everyone could see the big bad ex-don of Sydney pontificating about the latest coupling-up ceremony.

After just over a week, Sandy demands that we do a pool session so Peta helps him into his boardies and I put on a sports bra and lycra gym shorts - they seem more appropriate than a bikini - and we head down to the pool.

I'm walking backward down the pool steps with Sandy's hands in mine when I hear Giovanna's voice inside. My head snaps towards where the glass doors have folded to the side like a concertina, leaving the house open to the back garden.

She stands in the middle of the living area with a hand on her hip. She's laying into someone through the phone and even though I haven't seen her in a week and the last thing I said to her was that I hate her, my heart races.

Sandy clears his throat and I apologise for the lapse in concentration. Surprisingly he smiles kindly, almost sympathetically. We continue our descent into the water.

"How are things going with Elio?" he surprises me by asking.

"Um…well…" I'm not sure how honest to be with him at this point and he senses it.

"Don't be afraid to be honest with me, Francesca."

"Okay…well, I don't think love is on the cards for us. He's funny and charming, but he doesn't want to be married to me any more than I want to be married to him. He um…doesn't do monogamy and I'm quite keen on it."

Sandy takes it in and thinks quietly for a few minutes. "You're in love with someone else," he states.

Shit. What if he asks me who it is? I exhale. "Yes. But they don't feel the same way so it doesn't matter."

"I'll have a word to Elio about monogamy," he states.

"Um, thanks. But I won't hold out too much hope," I shrug.

I get Sandy out of the pool and onto the outdoor lounge suite. He rests his head back and soaks in the sun's rays.

"Can I get you anything?" I ask.

"Just a cold glass of water, thanks, *bella*."

Fuck. I was hoping he would say he didn't need anything. Now I'm going to have to go into the house and see Giovanna.

I wrap myself in a towel, cross the patio, and jog up the few stairs toward the house. I'm nearly at the wide open threshold, but obscured by a potted palm tree, when I hear my name mentioned.

"Why the fuck do you care how Francesca is? You said it was just sex." Massimo's voice is angry and defensive.

I pause, remaining behind the palm fronds.

"It isn't for you to ask why, little brother! If I ask you a question just fucking answer it," Giovanna is even angrier.

"Okay, You wanna know? She's barely sleeping and eating. She won't talk to anyone except Dad when she's doing his rehab. She's like a scared fuckin' animal who thinks everyone is going to hurt her. So stay the fuck away from her because I swear to God if one more of my dickhead siblings hurts her I'm going to lose it."

Huh. I thought I was doing a good job of concealing how much pain I am in. Apparently not.

An awkward silence descends over the room and I emerge from behind the palm to enter the house just as Giovanna decides to respond. "Jesus Christ, Massimo. We just fucked. It's not my fault that she's a stage 5 clinger. She means nothing to me beyond needing to get her and Elio down the aisle."

Massimo and Bluey are staring horrified at me. I'm a few steps inside the house and I've frozen. Every one of her words has sliced through me and buried its way into my heart. My knees want to give out, but I force myself to stand up straight.

I rush past them into the kitchen and grab a glass. I'm vaguely aware of Giovanna saying my name, but I just shut her out. I'm dead inside. She has killed me.

I carry the glass out to Sandy and then with as much dignity as I can manage I walk past them all to go upstairs pausing only to ask Massimo to tell his mum that Sandy is finished in the pool.

Tucked into a ball on the floor of my shower, I finally allow myself to cry. I've never been hurt by words so much in my life. I'm so pathetically desperate to be loved by her that I've left myself raw and exposed to being hurt.

The door creaks open and Massimo crouches down next to the shower.

"Oh Ches," he sighs. "I wish you didn't hear that.

I shake my head. "Better to know the truth."

He takes a deep breath and looks like he is battling himself over what he should say. "It's not the truth though. Not even close. You know that."

"No, I don't. She's been more cruel to me than Elio ever has. The difference is that I'm not in love with Elio." A new wave of sobs wracks my body and I'm too distraught to even think about the fact that I'm naked and crying on the floor of the shower in front of Massi.

He rubs a massive hand over his face. "What a mother fuckin' shambles. Come on, babe. Let's get you out of there."

He turns off the shower and holds up a fluffy white towel. After gathering me up off the floor, he flicks the toilet lid down and sits on it, pulling me between his legs so he can dry me off.

"Lucky I'm gay. Imagine the dramas if you had to deal with me as well," he teases.

"It would be easy if you weren't gay. I'd have married you already and avoided all this bullshit," I murmur.

"True," he agrees softly.

We are silent as he dries me off and helps me into some clean comfy clothes. He plants a kiss on my forehead and I snort, "Should I be offended that Matty isn't trying to ruin my life as well?"

He chuckles. "To be honest, sometimes I think Matty is the best of all of us. Whoever he ends up with will be worshipped."

CHAPTER FIFTY FIVE
FRANCESCA

Giovanna is blowing up my phone and leaving me messages that I don't answer. Pathetic half apologies. The kind that says 'I'm sorry, but…' Thanks, but I'd rather shave my head than put myself through any more of her shit.

She even came into my room late last night. I pretended to be asleep and she watched me for a while. She was close enough that I could smell her fresh perfume. I wish it didn't make butterflies take off in my tummy and my heart weep. After a while, she just left.

Apart from my sessions with Sandy, I keep to my room. It isn't like I am eating much anyway. Going to work is my main reprieve and Sammy doesn't mind when I ask if we can hang out at her studio apartment. I feel bad since at the Marino house we can hang out by the pool and I know she likes that, but she says she doesn't mind.

I know that Giovanna has soldiers following me. After they rescued me from the storage unit I noticed my protective shadows eased off a bit. I guess they're still supposed to jump out if someone tries to kill me. Or if I try to run for it again. At this point, I'm considering paying them to let the assassins finish the job.

Sammy and I work the late shift at the gym today and head to her apartment afterward with a detour to the bottle-o for a few bottles of Pinot Gris.

We sit on the floor, leaning against the sofa still in our gym leggings and sweatshirts. We've already smashed one bottle in record time and are making our way through a second.

Sammy is good company. We gossip about people at work, debrief on the latest *Love Island* episodes - her hot takes are remarkably similar to Sandy's - and she tells me about her family back in New Zealand. I can tell she notices my reluctance to talk about my own family dynamics and history and bless her she doesn't push me too much. But, I do wish I had someone outside of our fucked up world to talk to about all the shit.

"Are you going to tell me why you're marrying Elio? The guy is an utter cunt," she eventually asks.

"It's kinda embarrassing, but the *Famiglia* is…old-fashioned. Sandy has just stepped back from…all of the family businesses and Elio is taking over. It should be Giovanna, but she has a vagina, so…anyway. The guy who runs the family businesses in Melbourne wants to, like, bring Sydney under his erm, management? So he sent his son-in-law to Sydney to try to take us over. His son-in-law is also my half-brother; just to complicate things a bit more. The ummm… business investors in Sydney are all nervous about Elio taking over because he is the city's most notorious playboy. Some of them were starting to say that maybe Stefan - my half-brother - should step in. So Sandy and my father came up with the grand old plan of marrying me to Elio and showing the investors that he is settling down. Except he isn't. He's still fucking like it's going out of fashion. So we are engaged, but it hasn't made anything better. Plus, my brother tried to kill me and then another time he kidnapped me... and now he's…missing."

It's hard to explain it in terms that aren't explicit that I'm talking about the mafia. I know she has put two and two together and figured out that we are involved in illegal shit, but it is ingrained in me not to ever speak about *Famiglia* business like that.

She lets me get it all out, but her mouth keeps falling open. "Okay, so the goons following you around everywhere make more sense now."

"Yeah, it's a hot mess."

"Why isn't Elio playing ball? Like fuck dude, just lay off the pussy for like a few months and make the problem go away." She rolls her eyes. "But you guys did fuck, right?"

"Once," I cringe. "When we first got engaged. I thought I better try to make it work. It wasn't bad, but he just saw me as another root. Not like his future wife."

"Where does Giovanna fit in all of this?"

"She should be in charge. She kinda is in a way. She's smarter and more ruthless. She saved my life when Elio froze..."

Sammy shakes her head as she takes a big gulp of wine. "No, no. I mean where does Giovanna fit in your life like romantically." When my cheeks redden and I go silent she prods, "Come on, Francesca. You're in love with her! Are you embarrassed about being gay or bi or whatever?"

"I don't know what I am. I've enjoyed sex with men, but they just aren't...just nothing compares to her. But I have never been with another woman so I don't know if it is her or women in general."

"So you and Giovanna...?"

"No," my voice breaks and a few tears trickle down my cheeks. "We've been together a couple of times, but she's made it clear that it meant nothing. She's as bad as Elio."

"Fuck. I'm sorry, love. That family is a fucking nightmare."

"Utter nightmare," I agree. "Except Massimo. We've been best friends since we were babies. He's just getting busy with family business stuff and hanging out with Bluey."

Sammy smiles sympathetically. "Well, you've got me, girl. And don't worry, I won't make you marry one of my brothers. They're both smelly teenagers who smoke too much pot."

It's after midnight when I stagger from Sammy's apartment building. I'm way too drunk to drive. Even walking straight is proving impossible. Luckily, I know my permanent shadows will be lurking in a car somewhere out the front here.

"Hello?!" I shout down the quiet street. "If there are some gentlemen around here being paid to follow me, could they kindly give me a lift home?"

Almost immediately a guy about my age who I have seen around the Marino house before hurries over. "Ms. Rossi, you shouldn't be out here alone. You're bloody wasted," he scolds me.

"I'm not alone. You're here. Now are you going to give me a lift home or should I hitch-hike?" I stagger towards the road with my thumb stuck out.

"Jesus Christ," the Marino soldier mutters, pulling my arm down and leading me toward his SUV. "I'll take you home."

He has to practically lift me into the passenger seat before he belts me in and hurries around to the driver's side. "What's your name, young man?" I slur.

He raises his eyebrows. "I'm older than you, Ms. Rossi…and my name is Dylan."

"You're very beautiful, Dylan…" I sigh. He is, but he has nothing on the Marino siblings. That family is designed by gods and programmed by the devil.

Dylan shoots me a look of pure terror. "I'd prefer if you didn't get me killed tonight."

"Pffft. As if. No one gives a shit what I do so long as I make it down the aisle to Elio when I'm told to."

He doesn't answer me. Just shakes his head as if I'm a complete moron. Maybe he's right.

Dylan parks the car and escorts up to the back of the house. "You okay to get yourself off to bed? I'll text Ms. Marino to let her know I've brought you home."

Hmmm, interesting. He doesn't report to my husband-to-be or my father, he reports to Giovanna.

"Thanks for the ride, Dylan," I gently tap his cheek twice and he disappears to no doubt sit in his SUV all night in case I decide to go out.

Fumbling with the torchlight on my phone, I bump into the dining table. There'll be a bruise on my hip in the morning. I seem to be collecting a lot of them lately.

Hands splayed, I feel my way along the wall searching for the light switches like a blind woman who has lost her bearings.

"Success!" I whisper-shout to myself when I hit the right switch to bathe the kitchen in light.

I'm humming and singing my drunk version of Montell Fish's song *Fall In Love With You.* I'm trying to be poetically morose, but the result is probably akin to a drowning cat.

I mumble-sing, about things not working out because it's what I deserve, into the refrigerator as I scavenge for something to soak up all the wine sloshing around in my stomach.

"Ooooh!" my eyes light up as they hone in on a container of cannoli from *La Fazenda*.

"Hope no one was saving this," I snigger to myself as I sit at the dining table with a fork and the entire container of sweet goodness.

"Good to see you eating something. You're way too scrawny," the hair on the back of my neck stands up and I swallow the mouthful of cannoli along with the ball of dread that instantly forms in my throat.

That voice.

It is snake-like; dangerous, creepy, and with enough venom to kill a grown man dead in a few minutes.

Feigning nonchalance, I continue eating and respond with a mouthful of flaky pastry. "What are you doing here, David? Pretty sure you were given your marching orders."

"Visiting Sandy, of course," he says entirely too smoothly.

I stare pointedly at the clock on the wall oven. "At 2.46 in the morning?"

"You know how it is catching up over a few whiskeys. Time gets away from you." His smile makes me want to vomit, but I keep eating so as not to show him he has any effect on me.

"Hmmm, well you should probably get going then."

David tuts and steps closer so he looms over me in my seat. His hand shoots out and he grabs my ponytail, yanking my head back to expose my neck.

"Let me go now!" I shout with confidence I don't feel. "You think Giovanna won't break your fingers again if she knows you touched me?"

He shoves my head hard into the table and snarls into my ear. "Giovanna isn't always going to be there to save you, princess."

The tears I've done so well to keep in begin to trickle across my nose and onto the table. The panic is setting in and I've only just opened my mouth to scream at the top of my lungs when we both go still at the sound of a gun being cocked.

David keeps his weight on me, trapping me so I have no idea who has walked armed with a gun.

"I'm here this time, David," Giovanna's voice spits and my whole body relaxes in relief.

My creep of an uncle jumps back, leaving me free to sit up. I'm a mess of tears, smudged makeup, pastry, and snot and I can't even look at Giovanna.

"She's right," Giovanna says, moving towards David. "I will break every single one of your fingers, again, if you so much as think about touching her. The only reason you'll be walking out of here in a sec is because I won't be goaded into a turf war over you."

Now it's his turn to sag in relief at the news that he won't be getting a bullet in his brain tonight.

"Get. Out." she grinds out between gritted teeth. "Now."

His pride has him pause for a split second, but when Giovanna raises her gun again, he briskly moves to squeeze past her where she stands between the kitchen and the dining table.

He is almost past her when she whips her gun over her shoulder and then back across his face. A large crack indicates she has broken his nose and he staggers away, blood pouring through his hands as he tries to catch it.

"Get. Out." Giovanna repeats quietly and he scurries out the back door without a backward glance.

She flicks the safety back on and shoves the gun into the back of her pyjama pants. I sit unmoving as she grabs some kitchen roll from the bench and gently wipes the muck off my face.

"I hope you enjoyed my cannoli," she teases gently, but I remain silent. I won't allow myself to soften just because she saved me again.

She packs what is left of it into the fridge and leans on the bench assessing me.

"You got Dylan to bring you home?" She asks, serious now. I nod once.

"Good. I'll take you to get your car in the morning."

"No need. I'll ask Massi or Bluey," my tone is clipped and I suddenly feel a lot more sober than I did when I staggered in the door not long ago.

Using every bit of self-control I possess, I stand and walk out. I say nothing else. I don't look back when I reach the stairs. I just take myself to my room for another session of crying on the shower floor.

CHAPTER FIFTY SIX
FRANCESCA

"Ugh I feel like death," I whinge to Sammy. We're lounging on the reception desk at work, half-heartedly greeting gym goers as they enter and leave.

"Bitch please, you didn't have to start at 6 am this morning! I only forgive you because you brought coffee," she groans, taking a sip from the large takeaway coffee I brought with me when my shift started at 10 am.

As far as Sammy knows, I caught a ride home last night with my '*paid stalkers'*, as she calls them, and went straight to bed. I haven't decided if I'm up to sharing the events of the rest of the evening with her yet.

I battled Bluey and Massimo to let me go to work without my paid stalkers today. Of course, the matter was escalated to Giovanna who relented only because I agreed to Massi dropping me off and picking me up. Plus she knows Stefan is too busy feeding whatever lurks at the bottom of Sydney Harbour to be a threat to me any longer.

It is freeing to not have bored, brooding men in Italian suits lurking in my line of sight all day. I'm not sure how much of my conversations with Sammy they have picked up while on duty, but I heard one of them snort when Sammy called Elio "Rumpleforeskin" the other day.

"Ugh Noodles is here," Sammy nods at the guy sauntering into the gym. He isn't bad looking but has major tickets on himself.

Ignoring me, he shoots a cheeky grin at my friend. "Hey Sammy, about time we catch up. Text me."

The smile she gives him is entirely fake and screams 'I'm only smiling because I'm on the clock'.

"Why do you call him Noodles?" I ask quietly. The name on the screen, when he swiped in, said 'Todd'.

She grimaces. "He's done in 2 minutes."

Coffee sprays out of my nose and from between my pursed lips. I laugh harder than I've laughed in ages. "Girl," I wheeze. "You're hilarious."

The roar of motorcycles pulls our attention to the front of the gym. We don't have many bikies who go to the gym here so it's unusual to see so many of them parked out the front. They dismount in almost perfect synchronisation and walk as a pack towards the glass doors of the building.

After my recent encounter with the biker Stefan was working with - Billy the Kid - the sight of big hulking men dressed in leather and cuts sets off an instant attack of anxiety. The panic only intensifies when a few seconds later I recognise the patch they're all wearing, featuring a flaming skeletal devil, as the one Billy wore.

"What weirdos walk around with their helmets on?" Sammy observes flippantly, completely unaware of the internal meltdown I'm experiencing next to her.

Strutting in a pack across the carpark, none of them have removed their helmets. It makes for an imposing scene; they look bigger, less human. The helmets are their masks. They don't want their faces to be seen. They don't want witnesses to be able to identify them.

Something very bad is about to happen. Something that I know will centre around me.

Seconds later and mere metres from the front door, the men pull their weapons out. I scream for Sammy to get behind the desk.

A few of the braver guys in the gym come running to see what's going on. Three of them are shot down immediately and the screaming begins. First, only terrified screams of alarm, but then agonised screams of pain join the horrifying soundtrack.

In these seconds that feel like hours, I realise that Uncle David was right last night. Giovanna isn't always going to be there to save me. She isn't here now. I can't rely on her stepping in front of me and shooting dead my attackers.

No. If I am going to make it out of this alive and make sure that my friend does as well, I'm going to have to save myself.

First things first, we have to get away from the front desk. We are sitting ducks. I grab Sammy's wrist and yank her towards me. "We need to find somewhere to hide. We're dead if we stay here," I whisper to her.

She nods, her striking green eyes wide in terror. I feel a pang of guilt that my world has bled into her bright carefree life. There is no doubt in my mind that these men come from my world. They're here for me. I owe it to my friend, this ray of sunshine in my darkness, to protect her.

Pointing to a wall of shelves displaying uniformly folded towels and stacks of branded drink bottles, I tell Sammy to follow me and set off bear crawling on my hands and feet.

Plastering my back against the wall on the other side of the shelves, I pull Sammy around after me and a bullet whizzes past a second later. She gulps knowing it was meant for her. We stare at each other for a moment with matching round-eyed expressions that say, 'Holy shit that was close'.

It seems like the gunmen are shooting pretty indiscriminately. They're destroying equipment and making as much noise and creating as much damage as possible. If they hadn't already killed at least three guys I would think this was an intimidation mission rather than an execution.

"We've got to keep moving," I hiss.

She follows me as we duck between the rows of machines. Great big contraptions that you would think would be useful for hiding behind, prove to be useless with too many gaps that would leave us visible. The space is cluttered with gym equipment and yet totally exposed.

We keep moving and all the most obvious hiding places are already occupied by terrified gym members whose apologetic expressions tell us there is no room for us to hide with them, so we keep weaving our way toward the rear of the gym.

The bullets follow us as the bikers move further into the gym. They shout instructions out to each other and I swear one of the voices belongs to Billy. Their heavy black boots crunch over the piles of gym shrapnel they have created and their bursts of cruel laughter sound like pure evil to my ears.

The women's changing room is up ahead of us, but my gut tells me allowing ourselves to be cornered in there is a bad idea. Fuck. We don't have a lot of options, but once we enter the bathroom there will be only a few, very obvious, places to hide. No. That is not a good idea. We run past the tempting door.

"Francesca!" Billy barks out, confirming what I already know; I am the target.

Sammy falters and her hand squeezes tightly around mine. Realisation dawns on her frightened face and it is sinking in for her that these men are here for me. She's remembering all the cryptic conversations we've had and the bits and pieces she has put together about the Famiglia from being at the Marino house. The idea that I am from a mafia family has always been there, but here is the brutal reality.

"Here, Sammy!" I whisper, pushing her behind a large, long rectangular stand that carries at least thirty big round 20kg plates. It is propped against the wall on an angle leaving a small cavity for hiding in, but there is only room for one of us so I shove her in and hiss, "Do not move!"

Still exposed and now totally on my own, I frantically look around for somewhere else and a feeling of inevitability comes over me. If I hand myself over they won't hurt anyone else. They'll kill me, I know, but then maybe they'll leave without hurting anyone else.

I crouch behind a leg press machine, giving myself some time to think. More voices are calling my name now. All menacing, masculine, and deadly.

Time's up for me, I think.

Even though I'm mad at Giovanna for how she has treated me, I am suddenly full of regret that the last thing she will remember me by is me walking out of the kitchen last night. Maybe things will be simpler for everyone without me there though. Maybe it will be a relief for her to be rid of her 'stage 5 clinger'.

Sirens sound in the distance bringing with them a flicker of hope. If I only last a few more minutes until the police arrive I can survive. The gunmen are going to have to run for it before the cops pull up. Staying alive for a few minutes should be simple, right?

Adjusting my crouching stance so I don't cramp up, I press my face against the cool steel of the machine I'm behind and peer through a narrow gap. The

bikers seem to have dropped back and are prowling around the front desk, but I see a pair of black suit pants and leather dress shoes approaching.

The legs don't appear to belong to the bikies I saw charge through the doors. If anything, the male figure is dressed in standard mafia attire. The angle won't let me get a glimpse of his face, but somehow I just know that this is the man who wants me dead. The bikers are just hired muscle.

The mafia man draws nearer. If I don't move I'm dead. If I do move, I'm probably still dead. Neither are great options, but it takes no time at all for me to decide that I'd rather move than sit here and wait to die.

Sticking my head down, I sprint as fast as I can diagonally and backward toward the shelter of a cluster of bulky machines. They're just a few more metres away. The sirens are close now. Help is coming.

Pumping my legs as fast as I can, I swear I hear the bullet leave the gun and know it will hit me.

It's true what they say, time does stand still.

The streamlined metal nugget rips through my back and out through my chest. My body collapses to the ground. The bullet's path through my body burns, searing a tunnel through flesh, and crimson liquid flows from it in an instant.

I stay completely still, facedown on the gym floor. *Don't move*, I tell myself.

The sirens are getting louder. I play dead, praying that my shooter won't fire another round into me. His initial shot may well still kill me, but I don't want to take my chances with a second.

"Got her," a snarl sounds from a few metres away and I recognise it. "Move out now. Go, go, go."

Rapid footsteps retreat and the whimpers of frightened gymgoers become audible. The sirens are louder still and I hear the screeching of tyres outside replacing the thunderous departure of motorbikes just moments earlier.

I manage to roll myself onto my back, but the sheer amount of blood I leave behind on the floor sends me into a panic. *I'm going to die.*

"Francesca! Francesca!" I open my eyes with some effort, not sure how much time has passed since I lost consciousness if any at all. I'm still bleeding out on the gym floor, but Sammy is desperately putting pressure on my wound with her sweatshirt. The fabric is turning red pretty quickly.

"Don't close your eyes! Don't you dare!" She screams at me.

"It's okay," I mumble and smile at her. My body suddenly feels really warm where I had been shivering a few seconds ago. It's okay, I tell myself and let my eyes flutter shut.

CHAPTER FIFTY SEVEN
GIOVANNA

I spent all night trying to find a way to fix it. To make things right so she can be with me now that Stefan is gone, but the thing about the Rossis is that there are so bloody many of them that the capos will no doubt just suggest another of their family could step forward.

There are only two things I have truly wanted in my life. One is to work for the *Famiglia* and the second is her.

I swear to myself and her that I will figure it out, but first I have to get through this meeting with the Police Commissioner. I knew he'd have questions about the car ambush after Tiny and Sarah's wedding eventually.

He is waiting for me at the Famiglia Table down in the back right-hand corner of *La Fazenda.* I swear the fat fuck only meets with me so often so he can eat here on the house.

"Commissioner," I shake his hand and sit opposite him.

"Giovanna Marino!" He says jovially and I raise an eyebrow. Too much enthusiasm always makes me suspicious.

"That's me. Have you ordered? Let's get some tucker on the table before we talk shop, yeah?" I wave to Sarah and she hurries over.

"Go on then," he grins. "Twist my arm!"

I order a few of his favourite dishes and then wait for him to initiate conversation. He clears his throat, scratches his nose, and readjusts tie before opening his mouth.

"Our last meeting…I apologise," he grimaces.

"You wanted to get outta there pretty quick, didn't you?" I shrug.

"Mmm. These aren't conversations I thought I'd ever have. You don't think you'll be the guy sitting in front of the mob asking them to take the law in their own hands."

His voice is a whisper and he hunches over the table toward me. Sweat has gathered on his upper lip and hairline. I remain silent. Watching and waiting for him to continue.

"The bikies," he finally breathes. "I've…I…They've gotta…go."

I raise an eyebrow and nod for him to continue speaking.

"I don't want to know how. Don't tell me anything. Just…can you do it?"

His phone vibrates on the table next to his hand and frowning he answers it, "Yes?"

"Christ. How many dead? Fuckin' hell. Text me the address and, Morrow, media blackout until I get there."

My interest is piqued. It sounds like something is going down.

"What's up?" I ask.

"Mass shooting," he grimaces. "At one of those Strive gyms."

My blood runs cold.

"Which one?" I demand.

"Ah," he reads from his phone. "The one opposite St Catherine's Shopping Plaza. In your neck of the woods actually. Anyway, I need to get down there. I'll, ah, I'll be in touch."

He stands pulling his jacket back on, managing to look reluctant and urgent at the same time.

Francesca. I should never have agreed to drop her security detail.

What time did her shift start?

I curse myself for not knowing her schedule. I call her as I sprint to the car without saying goodbye to the Commissioner. No answer.

Fuck. Next, I try Massimo.

"Yo, sister boss," he answers.

"Where's Francesca?" I bark.

"At work. Geez."

"FUCK!" I scream, pulling out into the road and forcing traffic to stop for me to the soundtrack of several horns. "There's been a shooting at her gym. Mass casualties. Get down there. I'm on my way."

I hear him roar just before I disconnect the call and focus on getting back across town to my angel.

I've been battling traffic and my own chaotic emotions for about ten minutes when Massimo calls me back.

"She's been hit, G," his voice cracks and I can hear he is crying. "She's holding on, but it isn't looking good. I'm following the ambulance with Sammy now."

"Text me which hospital. I'll meet you there." My voice is calm, but I feel like my entire world has split open like a black hole forming in space. This is hell.

I get a small dose of *deja vu* as I rush into the same hospital Dad was in not so long ago, but this time the panic and desperation are amplified by a million times. I don't even recognise the woman in the mirror in the elevator. She's terrified and out of control. That's not me.

Massimo stands with his hands on his head in the middle of a small waiting area in the surgical ward. Sammy is a few steps away, dried blood on her white sports bra and staining the skin on her arms and bare torso. They're both frozen in shock.

"They've taken her in for surgery. Can't get anyone to give us an indication of what her odds are," he wraps his arms around me and we stand like that for a few minutes.

For the first time in many, many years, I cry and Massimo is as shocked as I am. He lets me bury my face in his chest to hide my tears and holds me tight until I regain my composure.

Elio and Matteo arrive not long after and the five of us sit and wait for news.

I'm struck by the stupidity of it all that now we are sitting outside an operating theatre, waiting to hear if Francesca will survive, my three brothers behave as if she is mine. They comfort me, reassure me. But, when things were fine and she wasn't marred by a bullet hole we all pretended that wasn't the case.

"You're shaking," I raise my head to see Elio crouching in front of Sammy speaking gently. "Come on, you're still covered in blood. Let's get you cleaned up."

She scowls at him and continues shivering.

Elio looks over at the rest of us for help, but I'm pretty sure at this point she has an even poorer opinion of me than she does of him.

She regards us all with cold suspicion. I can only imagine what Francesca has told her about us all. Well, about me and Elio.

She's a loyal friend and I'm glad Francesca has her. God knows she needs someone on her team.

Elio stands and holds out his hand to Sammy. "Come on. Let me help you and you can go back to hissing like a house cat when we're done. Promise you don't have to dock any arsehole points off my tally."

She rolls her eyes but lets him pull her up. He leads her over to a unisex toilet a few metres away and holds the door open for her. She stops in her tracks and eyes him like he is a predator.

"I'll leave the door open," Elio sighs. I'm impressed with how patient he is, but he knows as well as I do that anything Francesca has told her friend about us is probably fair enough. We are guilty as charged.

Apart from one exclamation of "Well, you do it then!" all is quiet until they emerge ten minutes later. Sammy is wearing Elio's hoodie and it nearly reaches her knees. Good deed done for the day, Elio slouches down in the chair to my right, as far away from the angry little Kiwi as possible.

A couple of hours later Paul and Vanessa Rossi arrive demanding answers. Fuck knows what they have been doing that it has taken them this bloody long to get here.

I can't even bring myself to acknowledge them and leave my brothers to fill them in. They aren't worthy of calling themselves her parents after how they've treated her. But, then I'm not worthy of anything from her either.

"Your father is insisting on coming down so Peta is bringing him in," Paul announces looking up from his phone.

I grunt and then add, "Make sure you tell that fuckin' sexpest brother of yours to stay the fuck away."

My brothers look quizzically at me. "He was at the house last night. I walked in on him with her head slammed into the dining table."

"What the fuck?" Massimo shouts.

"I pistol whipped him, but if I find out he had anything to do with this I'll kill him."

Paul and Vanessa share concerned glances but don't say anything. Most useless fuckin' parents ever. Sammy's expression, on the other hand, has shifted to one of begrudging respect.

Hours later, a dishevelled woman in blood-splattered scrubs walks down the corridor toward us. She looks dejected, but that could just be exhaustion. I stand, my heart racing.

If Francesca is dead…I don't know how I will survive that. I've spent the last few hours self-flagellating, beating myself up, and asking myself why I didn't just take her and run. We could be living in a beach hut somewhere tropical right now. No mafia. No arranged marriage.

Watching the doctor walk towards us is like walking on a tightrope. We are on a precipice. Whatever comes out of her mouth will change the course of our lives irreparably. It feels like I'm waiting to find out if I've been given the death sentence or not.

"Francesca Rossi's family?" the doctor asks, stopping in front of us.

"Yes," I croak. I'm the only one standing.

"She's in recovery now," she says with a small tired smile and I feel like I can breathe for the first time in hours. Like I've broken the surface after drowning. "She's very lucky to be alive."

Oxygen thunders into my blood and I suddenly feel like I can see and hear properly for the first time since I learned of the shooting. I suck in huge breaths and drag my focus back to the fucking heroine in front of me.

"Thank you, doc," I whisper, tears beginning to roll down my face.

Dad is watching me with interest, no doubt putting two and two together.

"Two of you can go in now, but just know she is still out of it," and with that, the doctor continues down the corridor, for her sake I hope it is towards a shower and a bed.

Paul and Vanessa move to go see their daughter and I see fucking red. Do they seriously think she wants to see them? A snarky voice in my head reminds

me she probably doesn't want to see me either, but I push the thought aside. She's unconscious so I can love her quietly for a bit before facing whatever she has in store for me.

Luckily, Elio speaks up so I don't have to throw hands. More violence is not what we need.

"Yeah, I don't think so. You two can wait. Massimo and Giovanna, you go first," he says, shaking his head at the audacity of the Rossis.

Paul opens his mouth to complain, but Dad pipes up from his wheelchair, "Don't be a dickhead Paul."

I follow Massimo into the recovery room, suddenly nervous to see Francesca. She'll be asleep, but what if she wakes up and tells me to fuck right off. She'd be within her rights.

My heart feels like it'll give out when I see her. She looks so tiny and pale, wires and tubes poking out of her at all angles. So fragile. My angel.

Massimo kisses her forehead and tells her he loves her and then he squeezes my shoulder and tells me he'll be just outside.

Taking a deep breath, I go to her. I drop my forehead to hers gently and tell her how sorry I am. Over and over again. The tears return and I brush them off as they land on her face.

"I'm so sorry, little darlin'," I whisper, kissing her softly all over her face. "*Sei il mio mondo,* you are my world."

I stand by her bed, grasp her hand, and whisper promises to her. Promises that I will make everything right and do anything, everything, to make her mine.

CHAPTER FIFTY EIGHT
GIOVANNA

I join the depressing coalition of smokers gathered outside the hospital sucking on cigarettes and vapes in quiet desperation.

Perching on a low concrete wall, I rest my elbows on my knees and let my head hang. My vape is a pacifier for all my current anxieties.

"She's here! Lena is her name! Thanks, brother. Yeah yeah, 7 pounds 4 ounces. Julia was a champ. Fuck man. Until you see it for yourself…gives you a whole new appreciation, ya know." I almost smile at the excitement in the man's voice.

How can he be having one of the best days of his life when the bloke he borrowed a lighter from probably just got a cancer diagnosis and Francesca was just shot?

An expensive pair of Italian loafers come to a stop in front of me and a huge hand reaches out for my vape. Sighing, I hand it over and Elio takes a seat next to me after dusting the wall for excess dirt.

"You know," Elio says, sucking on the e-cigarette, "I don't have a monopoly on being a shit cunt. You've been just as bad."

"Can't say I disagree, Eli," I wince, but he's right.

"It's one thing to force me to get married, but then to go and root the girl? That's twisted."

"You don't want her," I half-heartedly protest.

"That wasn't stopping you from forcing us to get married. My life isn't mine anymore, G. Yeah I've been a dickhead, but I'm fuckin' miserable. I just

wanted to be a black-hearted lawyer with a killer wardrobe and a shit tonne of pussy. I'm living someone else's life....I'm living your life."

I listen. I let him get his frustrations off his chest.

"We're not a normal family. Our lives were never going to be simple. You think I'm happy with how things have turned out?" My words sound hollow even to my own ears.

He turns and looks at me, forcing sustained eye contact. "What do you want, G? Forget what Dad says or what you think you're supposed to say. What do you want?"

"Francesca," I answer straight away, "and I want to lead this family. I'm the oldest and having a vagina has never held me back from anything else. I was born for it."

He nods. "So take it. Take Francesca. Take the reins. Take all the expectations and bullshit that have been dumped on me."

"It's not that simple," I begin, but Elio cuts across me.

"Who's in charge, G? Who says you can't be our don?" He presses.

Therein lies the problem. I'm a bit in charge, Elio is a bit in charge, and Dad is still a bit in charge.

He continues: "If me and you say you're in charge, then you're in charge. That frail fucker in there in the wheelchair chose to step down. It's not up to him anymore."

"What are you saying, Elio?"

"I'm saying, you're in charge. No more unstable party boy to worry about. You're respected, experienced, ruthless...and you get the girl. You marry Francesca. I'm much better suited to being yourconsigliere."

I'm speechless. When he sat down I thought he was going to get up my arse about Francesca, not hand over everything that should be mine but isn't.

"What's the catch, bro?" I'm back sucking on my nicotine pacifier. "What do you get out of this plan?"

He grins, his eyes roaming over an attractive young woman who has lit up a menthol a few metres away. "Freedom," he laughs. "Let me run legal. I'll work hard, but the big decisions are on you. No one looking to me to be a fuckin' leader or paragon of questionable virtue. And I don't have to get married."

"You really wanna sacrifice the prestige of being the boss so you can keep chasing pussy?" I tease.

"Well, I wouldn't put it like that," he nudges me gently and smirks.

"Are you sure about this? There's no going back once it is done..."

"One hundred percent. Tell me this doesn't make sense."

It does make sense and not just because it is exactly the outcome that I want. It plays to Elio's strengths and mine. The only issue is that Dad and the capos might kick up a stink. But Elio is right, he retired and this is our show now.

"Not sure Francesca will be any happier about marrying me though," I grumble. I'm irritated by the vulnerability I hear in my voice,

"You are fuckin' joking right? The girl has been obsessed with you forever. You've pissed her off, but marrying you is her dream come true," he sounds sincere.

I'm not so sure I haven't ruined all my chances. "Well, we will see when she wakes up. My bet is on her kicking me out of the room."

CHAPTER FIFTY NINE

FRANCESCA

Like swimming through lukewarm soup, my sleep isn't restful, it is searching. I break the surface briefly many times feeling the momentary assault of sensory overload. Beeps, voices, prodding, disinfectant, and someone clutching my hand. Each time I'm sucked back into the amniotic warmth and I kick on.

I am never in doubt that I will eventually surface for good. It isn't a fight for survival, but it does feel like an effort. Like my body has to expend an extraordinary amount of energy just to propel me back toward consciousness.

The first time I'm awake for a few minutes before I'm sucked back under like quicksand. I realise I am awake when I register the cool air-conditioned temperature and the sensation of a hand in mine, thumb stroking my knuckles.

My eyes are gluey and it takes a moment for me to get them open. Giovanna absentmindedly continues to stroke my hand, her attention taken by the old television mounted in the corner of the room. It appears to be showing reruns of *Judge Judy* and I want to smile at how focused she is on the show, but I'm just emerging from the fog.

I'm still staring at the back of Giovanna's head when she turns and notices my eyes are open.

"Francesca! You're awake! I'm here, baby." She jumps to her feet whispering over me. She kisses my forehead and I want to say something. *Hello. You're here. I love you.* Anything. But the pull is too strong and my eyes roll closed again.

How many more times I move between states of consciousness, I don't know. But I know I am getting sick of it. I want to wake up and stay awake.

"Giovanna?" I rasp, my throat and mouth dry from disuse.

"Hey, you're back," she smiles softly. She looks exhausted. Dark shadows frame her eyes and she is wearing a very rumpled suit. Somehow, despite this, she is still utterly stunning.

"I don't want to go back to sleep," I whinge and she laughs softly. The lights seem brighter this time and the sounds sharper. And I'm able to retrieve memories that were previously out of reach. Painful memories.

"Why are you here?" I ask her and her relieved smile disappears, replaced by an expression riddled with guilt and frustration. Maybe even fear.

She takes a deep breath and cups my cheek in her palm. "That's a fair question, darlin'. I needed to be here when you woke up. To tell you I'm sorry." She sits back down in her chair but leans forward with her arms on my bed.

"I've never been so scared," she whispers, raising her dark brown eyes to mine.

I want to believe that she cares, I do. But this is the same woman who called me 'baby' and held me like I was the most precious thing in her life before ghosting me and saying what we had was "only sex". Twice.

Only an idiot would sign themselves up for a third round of rejection, right?

"Where's Massimo?" I ask.

She inclines her head towards the door. "In the waiting room."

I swallow the lump in my throat and stare straight ahead. "Please can you leave me alone and ask Massimo to come?" My voice is frustratingly shaky.

"Baby, please." Alarm instantly identifiable in her voice. That bloody Marino arrogance had her thinking I would wake up and fall into her arms. I want to. I want nothing more than to be wrapped up in her. But, I can't.

I shake my head aggressively, nose scrunched up as I try to hold back the tears that are threatening to fall. "No! You hurt me!" I cry, my voice breaking. "You made me feel like…like you wanted me…and…and then you broke my heart."

"I know, my darlin'. I'm so sorry. I do want you, baby. So much. Let me explain, please."

"Get. Out." I sob.

Giovanna opens her mouth, perhaps to argue her case, but at that moment a nurse appears.

"You're awake, beautiful!" she exclaims and bustles over to my bedside to check my vitals. She's probably my mum's age, but she oozes maternal care and makes me feel safe immediately.

"Your heart rate is going at a rate of knots, sweetheart," she comments, taking a moment to look at me properly. "What are these tears for? Have you been upsetting my patient," she teases Giovanna, blissfully unaware that she is needling one of the most powerful people in the city.

"She's just leaving anyway," I sniff, and, looking defeated, Giovanna stands.

She presses a firm kiss to my forehead and leans down to whisper in my ear. "I don't want to upset you, baby. But please give me a chance to explain, okay?"

I don't respond, but I do wait for the door to close behind her before I let the tears fall.

"Oh dear," my nurse hands me a couple of tissues and pats my arm sympathetically. "She has barely left your side, you know. You've been out three days and she refused to let anyone else stay with you..."

"Mmmm, pity she wasn't so attentive before I was shot."

She raises her eyebrows and smiles. "These things tend to be wake-up calls."

CHAPTER SIXTY
GIOVANNA

"She's awake and asking for you," I snap at Massi as I reach the waiting room. "She doesn't want to see me."

"That might be because you essentially told her she was nothing to you and ghosted her," he suggests sarcastically.

"Just fuck off and go see her, Massi," I bite back. "I'm going home to shower and change. Let me know if there is any change in her condition and make sure she has one of our guys outside her room at all times."

I can smell myself. I have never wanted a shower so bad in my life.

Stripping off my suit in my bathroom back at the house I step under the water and groan at the relief of washing away three days sitting in that hospital.

The image of Francesca's hurt, as she told me to leave her bedside, is burned into my brain. My stomach is a pit of snakes thinking about how I was able to even speak the lie that she means nothing to me and was just a fuck.

She's perfect. She's perfect for me. I will take Elio's place at the altar in a heartbeat and although the logistics are a bit complicated, I want to see her with a swollen belly, bringing our children into the world. Lots of them.

Clean and in fresh clothes, I jog back downstairs intending to grab something to eat and return to the hospital, but Matty and Elio are sitting at the dining table when I enter the room.

"Hear you got kicked out," Matty's lip curls up into a slight smile.

Staring him down, I walk to the fridge and start pulling out the ingredients for a salad.

"Could be worse," shrugs Elio. "She could've taken a baseball bat to your brand new fuckin' car." He rolls his eyes before busting out a cheeky smile that I can't help but return.

"Little Firecracker might have that lined up for when she gets out of the hospital," Matty chuckles.

I throw chunks of cooked chicken breast onto my hastily chucked-together salad and finish with some balsamic dressing. Grabbing a fork, I begin eating straight out of the mixing bowl I made it in and slide into a chair to sit with my brothers.

"You two look more and more like twins every day," I observe and they do. Buzzed haircuts, deep brown eyes, and famous Marino cheekbones; they are as similar in looks as they are different in personality.

"You lucky bastard," Elio exclaims, grinning at Matty. "Pity you stopped growing early though." He will never willingly relinquish bragging rights for being six foot four while Matty is six foot two.

"Don't worry bro," Matty links his hands behind his head and leans back, "God put those extra two inches elsewhere."

"Alright, enough. Tell me what you've got on the shooting," I interject.

From my seat at Francesca's bedside, I have been running a full fucking investigation into who put a bullet into her and who ordered the hit. With Stefan dead, I have to admit I thought she was safe.

Suddenly serious, it is Matty who speaks first. "Not a lot."

"Did you manage to get Sammy to take you through what she remembers?"

Elio nods. "Yeah, she's pretty shook up though. Did great to remember what she did, but poor girl isn't from our world…she describes four bikies pulling up and entering the gym still wearing their helmets. They drew their weapons and were shooting pretty indiscriminately. Sounds like they wanted to scare everyone. The three guys they took out were all looking to be heroes, RIP. She said Cheska saved her life. Got her away from the front desk and found her a hiding spot, but then had to go find somewhere for herself. The most interesting thing she said was that just before Ches was shot, Sammy saw an older guy in a suit walk past her. He had a gun too. She thinks it was him who pulled the trigger on our girl because she heard him say he 'got her' and he had an Italian-Australian accent…"

"What are the police thinking?" I know that Matty's contacts in the police will be sharing information with him.

"Chasing the bikie angle. They've got no reason to suspect we have internal problems. They're trawling CCTV and they're pretty sure that it is Sons of Satan based on the bikes. Can't imagine the Sydney chapter wanting to burn their relationship with us though."

I'm scraping the last of the chicken salad from the bowl when my phone rings.

"Everything okay?" I answer.

"Francesca knows who shot her," Massimo's voice is low like he is trying not to be overheard.

"What?! Who was it?" My heart races, I should never have left the hospital. I should have stayed with her and made her tell me what she knows.

"It was David."

"He's a fuckin' dead man," an icy, cold calm comes over me and I know I won't feel warm again until that man's life is snuffed out. "I'm on my way back to the hospital now and I'll get your brothers to pick him up. Try and…um get her to talk to me, yeah?"

"I'll do my best," he huffs and hangs up.

Elio and Matty look at me expectantly. "Who?" Elio asks.

"David," I spit.

Matty gets up immediately. "We'll get him to the warehouse for you."

"Keep me posted. Once you've got David, put out the call for all the capos to meet us at *La Fazenda*. I want Dad and Paul Rossi there as well."

The whole drive to the hospital I picture Francesca's conflicted expression when she threw me out. She wanted me there and wanted my affections, but she has such a strong sense of pride and I really fucking hurt her.

She's been telling all of us this whole time that all she feels she has is her self-respect and all of us have stomped all over it. We've kept her in the dark while pushing her around and using her life, her last name, as a tool, a ploy.

I thought I was sacrificing my own feelings for the good of the family by pushing her away, but I just made things worse. I was obsessed with how agonising it was for me not to have her and I took what I wanted at the expense of Francesca's feelings.

She may never want anything to do with me again, but I will do everything in my power to keep her safe and happy.

Including killing her uncle.

I stride into Francesca's room with purpose. My little darlin' will not be throwing me out this time. I'm here to beg, grovel, whatever it takes. The tiny doe-eyed woman has all the power now.

Massimo sits next to her. They're talking quietly and watching videos on his phone. Both of them look up when I enter and panic shoots across Francesca's face. It is like a kick in the guts to know that seeing me does that to her. I can't be worried about that now though. I can't be deterred.

I sweep my suit jacket off my shoulders and drape it over the chair on the other side of her bed. Sitting down, I roll back the sleeves of my dress shirt while Francesca watches my every move. Wary, but also with a spark of hunger in her expression. I lean forwards, elbows on my knees and run my eyes over her drawn, pale face. She is the most beautiful creature I've ever seen.

"Francesca," I murmur, reaching out to hold her hand. She doesn't pull it away, thank fuck. "How are you feeling?"

"I'm okay," she smiles faintly. "You can relax. I won't throw you out again."

My lip curls and she reaches out to poke me in the dimple that forms in my cheek. "That's good to know, baby. Because I'm not going anywhere."

"Right!" Massimo abruptly stands and stretches. "I'll leave you two star-crossed lovers to it."

"Thought you'd never leave. Check-in with your brothers, yeah?" I grin at his retreating back, relaxing now that I know I'm not about to be booted out again.

He disappears and we're left staring at each other. I want to kiss her so badly, but I don't want to push my luck. *Patience.*

"Massi told me you know who shot you, darlin'" I state gently.

She nods, but instead of fear, I'm surprised to see anger flash in her eyes. *Good girl. That's what I like to see.*

"My parents will probably send me back to the UK," she says bitterly.

"Your parents have no say in how David is handled. You're going nowhere," I tell her firmly.

She peers at me through her eyelashes and slides her fingers between mine, sending my heart rate rocketing. *Bring the fuckin' defibrillator in.*

"How will he be handled then?" She whispers.

Standing, I dip down to press a kiss on her cheek. I speak quietly next to her ear. "I'm going to kill him. He will never hurt you again."

Her arms shoot up around my neck holding me close. "I want to be there," she whispers into my neck.

Fuck. I didn't expect that. "Are you sure about that?"

"Yes. I want him to see me and know that I matter enough for him to be punished."

My heart breaks. Of all the fucked up shit my father has done, allowing Paul Rossi to send away his daughter and protect his rapist brother is the most unforgivable.

"You matter, baby. I'm so sorry I ever made you feel like you don't," my hands go to her face, cupping her chin and making her look me in the eyes.

She looks unsure, sceptical, but slowly nods.

"I know we haven't had a chance to discuss you running away…but, I'm so sorry that we put you in that position…" my voice breaks. "Christ. That you felt you had to go to that cunt to escape us…I'm so sorry."

My heart sinks as tears well in her eyes and she looks up to try to stop them from falling. How many of her tears am I responsible for by now?

She looks back down and holds my gaze. It is just for a few seconds and with anyone else would have meant nothing, but with her, the intensity burns a hole in my chest. No words. Just pure connection.

"I'm going to tell you some stuff, okay?" I break our silence with a sigh. "This doesn't leave this room, you hear?"

She nods quickly, readjusting her hand in mine so she can grip it tighter.

"You know that lots of Dad's capos are Rossis? Your family is massive and your Dad being Dad's *consigliere* attracted loads of your relatives in Italy to come to Sydney…"

She knows all of this. It isn't new and her adorable frown shows she is struggling to see where I am going with this.

"…well, with Dad stepping down as boss, the Rossis decided to get together and ensure that your family's power and influence in Sydney is cemented in the

next generation. Sure, they are unhappy with Elio's playboy ways and want him to settle down, but more importantly the marriage was about ensuring that a Rossi is at the top and that her children are the heirs to the *Famiglia*."

"Why did no one tell me?! My Dad knew this?" Francesca splutters. "I should have known!"

"Your Dad is probably the architect of it. Though he pretends not to be and Baz is conveniently the noisiest. But, Ches, the reason we pushed so hard to make it happen is that they said if you didn't marry Elio, they would bring another Rossi in to challenge him...your brother."

Her perfect mouth falls open. "Oh god. That's why he was pretending to care and encouraging me to refuse to get married...Oh my god, I ran to him!"

Her cheeks are growing red and she puts her face in her hands, ashamed.

"Hey, hey, hey," I tug her hands back down to her lap, pressing a kiss to each palm on the way. "None of this is your fault and you sure as fuck don't have anything to be embarrassed by."

Her expression softens a little and I just want to kiss her. Kiss away all of her worries and doubts and all of the goddamn hang-ups that I'm responsible for her having.

Swallowing all the desires I have to show her physical affection, I continue telling her what she deserves to know. "That is why Stefan showed back up in Sydney two years ago."

"And that's why Massimo was sent to break me and Gareth up and babysit me for two years," she adds and I cringe, but nod.

"There were some enticing reasons for capos to consider throwing their support behind your brother. Stefan taking over Sydney would have provided a strong connection to Melbourne. Allegra's brother will be taking over there soon. It has been hard fucking work ensuring loyalty and you marrying Elio...well it felt like it would make it all go away. I thought it was the easy solution, but then you came back...and well, my own feelings complicated things."

The cogs are turning in her brain and I wish I had given her all of this context a long time ago. She is a clever, considered woman and is taking it all in.

"God, Giovanna. Why didn't you tell me all this?" She shakes her head at me in quiet frustration. "We could have worked it out. Come up with a plan.

Or something. I am as much a part of the *Famiglia* as you. You could have had me on your side. I will marry Elio if that is what is needed. We will come up with an arrangement that suits us. I-I won't ever want him like I want you though."

I say her name several times, trying to interrupt her monologue. My angel is willing to go through with the marriage despite all that has happened in order to save the *Famiglia*. But I'm not willing for her to make that sacrifice now. I'm not willing to make it myself.

"Francesca!" I finally get her to stop talking and she looks at me expectantly.

I'm suddenly tongue-tied. I'm so shit at this stuff. I have never been one to declare my feelings. I've had girlfriends and cared about them, but nothing like this. I don't know how to put it into words.

"You won't be marrying Elio, Francesca," I say slowly and she blinks, confused.

"I won't? But you just said that the Rossis…"

"Because I can't watch you marry someone else," I tell her and her mouth makes a little O shape. "You're mine, little darlin'. Ever since you came home, you've tortured me. I can't stop thinking about you. I'm obsessed. I look forward to getting home just so I can see you for a few moments. You're beautiful and sweet and, with the exception of the incident with Elio's car, you're so fucking full of grace, despite what the world has put you through. I have never smiled as much as I have with you. And I think I might die if I never get to taste you again; feel you come apart with my name on your lips."

Standing awkwardly, holding her face in my palms, I watch a slow smile spread across her face and feel the weight of the world lifting from my shoulders.

She reaches up for my face in return and pulls me gently down for a kiss that beats any kiss I've ever had in my life. She sweeps her tongue into my mouth and I feel momentarily lightheaded. It is soft and deepens quickly. It is passionate and loving, not about sex so much about expressing emotion. We express the depth of our feelings without words.

When we finally break apart, I take a deep breath to ready myself for the next part of my pronouncement. I clear my throat and run my hand through my hair.

"Francesca, I know we are in the least romantic setting ever and I wish I could ask you this differently, but trust me when I say I'll make it up to you...but I don't want to cancel the wedding venue and stuff. I still want you to get married this month, but I want you to marry me instead...."

Silence.

I rush to fill it. "I know it's rushed and a bit weird, but I will remarry you in a big fancy ceremony every anniversary if that's what you want. I just want to make you mine...Fuck, say something, Ches. Put me out of my misery."

"I have literally dreamed of marrying you since I was a kid. Even before I knew what love and sex were. You've been my lifelong obsession and I've wished for this moment every time I blew out birthday candles and on every shooting star. I'll go down to the registry office in my hospital gown with you, I don't care. I just want to finally be *your* Francesca Marino. *Sei il mio mondo*, Giovanna," her voice is soft but strong and each word feels like it weakens and strengthens me at the same time.

I dive in and kiss her again. This time it is full of want and a touch of desperation. "Mrs. Marino," I growl. "I love that. I love you, darlin'."

"I love you too," she gasps between kisses. "I'll marry you with two conditions though."

I frown. "What's that?"

"One, I want to change my wedding dress. It isn't what I pictured marrying you in."

Laughing, I agree quickly to the first stipulation. "And number two?"

"Well, I finally got around to listening to the song you mentioned in the club that time; *Iris* by the *Goo Goo Dolls*. Remember? Well, Massimo made me listen to it this morning," she smiles shyly. I remember all right.

"Yeah? What did you think?" I ask nervously.

"I wish I knew that was how you were feeling. I should have listened to it straight away..." her voice trails off wistfully. "My second condition is that our first dance is to *Iris*."

"No arguments here. You're the closest to heaven that I'll ever be."

CHAPTER SIXTY ONE
SANDY

There is a strange energy in the air when I shuffle into the upstairs room at La Fazenda aided by my newly acquired walking stick. Once again it is crammed with capos and I am the last to arrive.

Lowering myself tentatively into my chair and cursing how bloody old I must look, I notice the capos all murmuring to each other. Expressions are puzzled, curious, and suspicious.

What's going on? I thought we were here to discuss the execution of David Rossi.

I get my answer when I turn to look at my children and instead of finding Elio in the boss' chair, he is sitting in the chair to its right. Giovanna sits on the throne looking like she was born to occupy it. She kind of was.

"Before I address the matter of David Rossi," Giovanna booms with ease, "my siblings and I wish to advise you of some changes within the Famiglia."

The air suddenly grows even more tense. Paul looks around anxiously and several men begin to fidget. Even Elio swallows slowly and nervously.

"Tradition is important to our family and we are all committed to protecting our way of life, but… not all change is bad," Giovanna begins confidently.

"My father will have told all of you how I was his right-hand girl growing up. Most of you will have seen it. He has probably told you all that had I been born with a dick between my legs I would be the perfect heir."

A few men nod and chuckle.

I snort loudly and give my daughter a wry smile.

"But, I don't have a dick so the role fell to my younger brother Elio. My brother is brilliant, intelligent, and a legal genius…but he is not the right person to lead the *Famiglia*," a collective sharp intake of breath can be heard, but Elio looks passively on.

"He does not want to be our don. We have discussed this and he has decided to step aside for me to take over… I was born to do this. You all know it. We need stability as we move into this next phase and I bring stability. You are our leaders, our family. I invite you to speak up now if you have any objections."

There is a small pause and then struggling out of my chair to stand, I face Elio, Giovanna, and Matteo.

"You have my support," I say, a slight crack in my voice. "You are right, you have always been the perfect heir. Though that does leave us with the problem of needing a Rossi to be married to you…"

"I'll marry a Rossi, Dad," Giovanna grins, knowing that everyone is trying to figure out how that will work, but there is a slight challenge in her voice. "Francesca has agreed to marry me. We will go ahead with the wedding in three weeks."

There is a hush and then Fat Tony roars with laughter. My heart leaps into my throat, but his laugh doesn't sound menacing.

My eyes dart around each of the faces around the table. Some seem amused, others are pensive, and a couple look angry.

"We are good Catholics, Giovanna…I suspect if God can forgive what you are about to do to David, and the many things like it we have *all* done, he can cope with you having a wife," Fat Tony jokes, breaking the ice and causing several of the capos to join in his laughter.

"Thank fuck for that," bellows Champ Brown, slapping his thigh.

"God love you, son," he says to Elio, "but you had us worried!"

Elio has a grin plastered on his face and it brings a smile to mine. Maybe my boy will shine now that he isn't the square peg in the round hole.

CHAPTER SIXTY TWO
FRANCESCA

I spent just over a week in the hospital after I woke up. Plenty of time for the Marinos to track down Uncle David. They didn't have to do a lot of actual tracking. A few days after the shooting, Elio received a call from Allegra's brother Tommaso. He is taking over more and more of the Melbourne business from Alberto.

Tommaso informed Elio that David had shown up back in Melbourne and was seeking protection from Alberto. He invited the Marinos to come and collect the "piece of shit" because the Romano Famiglia had no place for him.

The Romanos wanted to make it very clear that they had no hand in the actions of either Stefan Rossi or David Rossi. Incidentally, there has still been no sign of Allegra and her children.

It is difficult to know whether Sydney or Melbourne should be accountable for the actions of the two Rossi men. They were after all the brother and son of Paul, *consigliere* of Sydney, despite having worked for the Romano family most recently.

In the end, the Marinos and the Romanos agreed to a handover of David and to call it even.

When I left the hospital today I was given firm instructions to take it easy and give my body a chance to heal. But, for the next few hours, I am more focused on a different kind of healing. The kind that often gets called 'closure,' but I am not afraid to call vengeance.

As promised, after carting him back from Melbourne two days ago, Giovanna held David under the warehouse until I was well enough to leave the hospital.

I thought she would put up more of a fight when I demanded to be there to witness his execution, but I think my explanation convinced her.

I *need* to see him die, but even more, I need *him* to know I am there witnessing his death.

Naturally, my wife-to-be isn't particularly thrilled that I will see her killing…again, but she won't let anyone else do it either. She swore that she would kill him if he harmed me again and she is a woman of her word.

She slept each night at the hospital with me. At first, she attempted to sleep in a chair next to my bed as she had done when I was unconscious, but I eventually convinced her to get up on my narrow bed so I could sleep with my head on her chest. I'm sure she barely got any sleep, but she was stoic about it.

I was anxious about seeing Elio, but when he visited me in the hospital he was relieved as I am that we aren't getting married. He seems genuinely happy for me and thrilled that he can get back to being a Casanova without the unfortunate baggage of having a fiancee.

Giovanna is going to punch Elio soon though. His favourite thing has become cracking jokes about the fact that he has rooted his sister-in-law.

My bubble of happiness has been bolstered by the ease with which the capos and our fathers accepted Giovanna taking over as boss. The anxiety that they would outright reject her was huge, but we underestimated their openness to change.

The next question was whether the Rossi capos would be satisfied with me securing their future by marrying her. Although a couple of old-school homophobes grumbled their displeasure, Giovanna and I won't be becoming a hate-statistic any time soon. We are getting married in a fortnight.

Massimo drives me straight out to the warehouse from the hospital. As we pull into the usually all but deserted gravel car park, I'm surprised to see so many cars I recognise parked outside when we arrive. Including my Dad's ostentatious Ferrari.

"Why are there so many people here? My parents?" I ask.

"This is a big deal, Ches," he says quietly. "It is important that the capos are seen to be supportive of Giovanna's actions."

"Oh, I assumed this would just be us," I whisper as he helps me out of the car.

"David is a Rossi. It's a big deal," he repeats.

We take the lift down to the basement of the warehouse. I've never been here before, but the warehouse itself looks very normal. I know that what we will find underneath it will be anything but.

Nausea caused by pain, medication, and the knowledge of what is about to go down, has me feeling weak and like I need to stay close to a receptacle to vomit in.

The thin layer of sweat coating my forehead and the back of my neck is cold and I shiver as we step out of the elevator. Massi gives me a small grim smile of encouragement and I grimace back at him, hoping that I make it through this without fainting or projectile spewing.

The space we walk into is large and sparse. Everything is concrete and bleak. It is utilitarian and exists to serve a purpose.

The capos are gathered in a cluster of pairs and small groups talking in hushed tones. Elio stands with them, making conversation, a firmly serious expression plastered on his face.

Giovanna is speaking off to the side with my Dad and her Dad, while Matty is in his own world, staring into a huge cabinet full of various tools of torture.

Beyond all of these groups and hanging from the ceiling in the middle of the concrete space is Uncle David. He doesn't look particularly worse for wear seeing as he has been held in the basement for at least two days. He looks dirty, but other than that unharmed.

His eyes bulge when he sees me walk into the vast room, but the cloth gag in his mouth prevents him from speaking. He either didn't know until now that I survived or has gathered that my being present doesn't bode well for him.

Ignoring the increasing difficulty I am having staying upright, I stare right back at the man who thought he could get away with ruining my life, destroying my spirit, and attempting to kill me. He has not succeeded. I may be weakened and in pain, but I will stand and watch him take his last breath.

Giovanna's eyes meet mine and her hard exterior softens for a split second. Given the circumstances, I shouldn't be thinking about how good she looks, but I can't help but appreciate her perfectly fitted suit.

Sandy always taught his kids that performance is very much part of leadership in the mafia. Our history is rich and bloody and now has tentacles all over the globe, and tradition plays a huge role in maintaining our social structures. Dressing the part is about dominance. It is about showing affluence, power, self-respect, and invoking fear.

Today her look is having the desired effect. Killing the brother of her Dad's *consigliere* and laying down a gauntlet should only be done in an Italian suit. Black suit, white shirt, top buttons undone. Her hair is pulled into a top knot, exposing a freshly shaved undercut.

She commands respect even before opening her mouth to speak. She has the energy of a boss and if every man in this room was honest, they know she is the best person to lead them.

She strides over to us and wraps me into a hug, tucking me under her chin. I inhale her delicious fresh scent. It is somehow the most comforting smell on earth and the sexiest. If no one else was here I would melt into her.

"You still want to do this?" She murmurs and I nod against her. "Okay, stay with Massi."

Giovanna moves to stand roughly in front of the gathered men. Her brothers move to stand behind her, Massimo bringing me along with him.

Christ. How long am I going to need to stand here? I should have asked for a bloody seat.

"Killing this man is the first thing I will do as leader of this *Famiglia*," she states calmly pointing to David. "We are a family of honour and respect and I am not afraid to be the one to punish those who dishonour and disrespect us. About eight years ago, David Rossi raped his niece Francesca…"

I hold my head high even though everything in me wants to dip it and stare at the ground. All eyes in the room look at me, but I look straight ahead.

"I found out about his assault on Francesca about two years after it happened and I broke every single one of his fingers, gave him the hiding of his life, and told him to leave. He took off to Melbourne. But, when Stefan Rossi decided to start agitating and thought he was entitled to what our *Famiglia* built,

David saw his opportunity to get some revenge on us and Francesca. He is the one who shot Francesca in the back at the gym. Do we protect rapists? Do we turn a blind eye when one of our own is targeted? Not while I'm in charge. I will give David a chance to speak and then I will kill him for this *Famiglia* and for my Francesca."

The vibe in the room has shifted and there is now a sinister, simmering fury rippling among the men. Some make noises of agreement, others spit furious words at the hanging man.

I watch my father's face. The man who should have been my first defender. He is furious, but it is me he is glaring at. He won't raise an objection because he knows the crowd is not with him. But, I know that given the choice he would again spare his brother at the expense of his daughter.

Giovanna is watching him too with barely veiled disgust. "Paul, can you forgive me for stepping in and doing this for your daughter? I know you must want revenge yourself, but I appreciate you standing aside so I can do this."

My father nods curtly.

Matty approaches David and yanks the fabric from his mouth. The chains holding him up rattle and he groans at the discomfort of the position. A stain that darkens the fabric of his trousers from crotch to calf is evidence that he has pissed himself in fear.

"Got anything to say?" Giovanna looks at him. She's browsing the selection of tools Matty laid out earlier. Loud clinks punctuate her question as the metal of the tools collide in her hands.

"Just get it over and done with!" he barks.

"No denial then? You accept the summary I gave?" she retorts, spinning a small knife in her fingers. "Get him down and sit him at the table," she demands and Matty and Elio obey.

They unchain him and drag his uncooperative body to a square wooden table. It is covered in indentations and cuts, and it is clear that it has been struck by many different types of instruments over the years. The red-brown staining further elaborates on the story it tells.

"I promised you that if you touched a hair on her head I would break all of your fingers again, didn't I?" Giovanna leans across the table, her voice remaining low and calm.

Silence.

"Didn't I?" she shouts suddenly, the tendons in her neck strain, and her jaw ticks.

"Yes!" David exclaims.

Giovanna prowls around the table, never taking her eyes off him. He flinches when she walks behind him anticipating an attack.

She barks out a cold laugh. "I *should* hit you from behind. Seeing as you shot Francesca in the back."

I can't help but take a few little steps forwards as I watch her circle him like prey. I'm mesmerised by her power. Her rage simmers until she is ready to unleash it in bursts of violence.

Thank God no one can read my mind because I'm not horrified or alarmed to see her like this. She looks beautiful. She is my avenging angel and watching her work is energising my soul. I'm feeling stronger, less dizzy, and more like I'm someone who matters.

As Giovanna shatters the bones in each of his fingers with a small hammer, I don't flinch once. She is always in perfect control and every move is calculated and deliberate. Precision. This is exacting revenge in a methodical manner.

Maybe I am more of a mafia princess than I ever realised because David's screams don't affect me. Maybe it is because of what he has done to me and the hatred I hold for him. This is justice and I have been denied it for so long.

On the drive to the warehouse, Massimo told me that David has already given up the names of the bikies he hired to shoot up the gym and they have already been taken care of.

Stefan introduced him to the bikies when he organised for them to visit me at work to intimidate me. That was all my big brother's idea. Stefan was also involved in planning the ambush after Sarah and Tiny's wedding and obviously, when I showed up at his house, he worked with Billy the Kid to get me to the storage unit.

"Times up, David," Giovanna tells him as she pushes away from the table and walks around him again. A lioness shepherding before the kill.

"Look at Francesca," she orders him from over his shoulder and he lifts his head to meet my gaze.

Revulsion fills me and I let it show on my face before raising my eyes to meet Giovanna's.

"Kill him," I order in a voice so cold and flat I don't recognise it as my own.

With a nod, she pulls the knife out of her belt and slashes it across his throat in one fluid movement.

Blood sprays everywhere and then glugs out of the gaping wound in his neck. He is dead in seconds.

CHAPTER SIXTY THREE
FRANCESCA

My hands shake as I unbutton her blood-splattered shirt and sweep it off her shoulders. We're home and in Giovanna's office, finally alone, and I'm nervous all of a sudden. I can't believe she is finally mine. That I don't need to fear that she will be gone in the morning. Though that thought does still niggle away in the background.

She watches me undress her with a dangerous glint in her eye that gives me shivers up my spine. Her body is still in full fight mode after today. For the second time, she killed a man for hurting me.

When she's standing in front of me in just her sports bra and underwear I step closer and suck her bottom lip into my mouth, biting down gently on it. This elicits a low growl from her that turns the pit of my stomach inside out.

I want to make her feel good and submit to the powerful energy of hers that I love so much.

We intensify our kiss, our tongues sliding against each other deeper and more urgently, and then I kiss her along her jaw and neck. I keep peppering a path of kisses further down her body, sliding lower until my knees hit the carpet. I lean over and drag a chair closer to us. She watches me curiously but doesn't ask what I'm doing.

Softly kissing her inner thighs along the seam of her defined muscles, I drag her black boy-leg panties off her body. Tapping the chair I indicate for her to prop one foot up on it and she groans as she realises what I'm trying to do.

I'm nervous and inexperienced, but I scoot closer to her eagerly wanting to taste her again. The way she glowers down at me, her eyes full of dark lust, gives me a thrill and I feel my pussy clench and begin to throb.

Giovanna reaches down and holds my chin firmly in one hand, directing me wordlessly to look her in the eye. "Look at you being a good girl getting straight on your knees for me," she growls.

Good girl. The words do things to me. She could convince me to do almost anything just by calling me a good girl in that low growly voice.

"Take your dress off," she orders. "I want to see your body while your face is buried in my cunt."

I quickly obey. Tugging my dress over my head and unclasping my bra. I leave my fuschia lace g-string on simply because I want her to take it off later.

Not taking my eyes off her hard angular face sporting its brooding frown, I lean forward and softly kiss the mound above her pussy. I like the tidy triangle of black hair she leaves there.

I can smell her arousal and I'm surprised by how much I like that too. Like most girls, I have been kind of conditioned to be self-conscious of my natural smell and I have been anxious that despite my desperation to be with Giovanna, I'll be grossed out when it comes to going down on her.

Now that I'm down here, kneeling at her feet, her glistening pussy open in front of me, all I feel is turned on. My mouth waters knowing I'm about to taste her for the second time and I bury my face in the crease of her hip for a moment to settle myself.

"You okay, baby?" she asks gently and I sit back on my heels abruptly nodding my head.

"I'm just taking my time," I smile what I hope is a sexy smile before I lean forward and slowly swipe my tongue right up through the middle of her folds.

"Ffffffuuuuuuuck," she groans and I fucking love the satisfaction making her feel good brings me. I could get drunk on this power.

Exploring her thoroughly, I lap and suck eagerly between her legs. One of her hands slides into my hair, gripping my head hard. The other hand is behind her neck, her elbow pointing to the ceiling.

Having received enough head in my own life, I know that my exploring will be feeling good, but won't be getting her orgasm building. Time to focus on that plump, hard nub that is just begging to be sucked.

My wet pursed lips slide over her clit sucking lightly on it and Giovanna hisses, twisting her hand in my hair sharply. "That's it, baby," she moans and her voice has me moaning against her in return.

Softening my tongue, I let it flow like water over her clit, forward and back and she presses her hips forward into my face. I hum gently, the vibrations tickling her already sensitive cunt.

"Fuck. Yes. I can't hold back, baby," she warns before both her hands are controlling my head and she's grinding on my mouth.

She fucks my face faster and I can hardly breathe, but I love it. Finally, when she is just about ready to come, she pulls back slightly.

"Suck," she demands in desperation and I quickly pull her clit into my mouth as she comes hard against my face.

Her shudders and groans are almost enough to make me come too. I sit back on my heels and squeeze my thighs together. When she opens her eyes, she runs her thumb over my mouth, smearing her wetness along my bottom lip.

Seeing me squirm, one side of her lip curls up and her dimple deepens. "You all worked up, baby? Tell me what you need."

"Fuck me," I beg and she hauls me to my feet only to shove me onto her desk.

She yanks my g-string off, drags my bum to the edge, and pushes me back to lie flat. "Feet on the edge. Spread those pretty thighs for me."

She stands back watching me, spread wide open for her. "So beautiful," she repeats over and over.

"Please," I beg, my legs quivering with anticipation.

Chuckling she lightly dusts over my clit with her thumb and my hips shoot up off the desk. My cheeks flush, and I'm embarrassed by how needy and desperate I am.

Two of her fingers press into my slick entrance and, after two slow pumps, Giovanna starts to fuck me harder and faster. The bicep on the arm she's fucking me with bulges and her toned shoulders ripple. She is so fucking hot.

Her thumb stretches up to make circles over my clit while her index and middle fingers penetrate me hard and fast. I'm so turned on my wetness is coating her entire hand.

The grand old desk is creaking and my body is rocked by every thrust. She curls her fingers to hit the spot inside me and I begin to fall apart. I'm begging and praying and making all sorts of animalistic noises I've never made before.

"Come for me, darlin'. Come, baby," her voice is soothing and sexy. I want to spend my life on my knees and my back for this woman. She is everything I have ever wanted.

I come hard, crying out her name and she kisses me all over my face until I squirm away giggling. "I love you so much, Gio," I whisper, not used to saying it out loud.

"I love you too, baby," she responds, scooping me up and carrying me through the internal door to her bedroom. Our bedroom, I guess.

"No more fucking for you tonight, my wounded soldier," she teases, dropping me gently onto the bed and climbing in behind me. "I probably shouldn't have been so rough with you just now."

"I didn't mind," I grin. "But I'm happy with cuddles now...So long as you're here when I wake up in the morning."

EPILOGUE
GIOVANNA

"Oh my sweet boy, I do love you, but you're getting under mummy's feet." Walking into our bedroom I hear my wife talking to our toddler in the walk-in wardrobe.

"Xavier Marino!" I call out and immediately hear a little squeal of excitement followed by the unsteady pitter patter of chubby toddler legs in full pelt.

"Mama!" he shouts as he flings himself at me. Knowing exactly what he wants, I throw him in the air, catch him, and twirl him around. He giggles with glee.

"Have you been good today, son?" I ask him and he nods solemnly.

"Did you look after mummy and her big bump?" He nods again.

I look up to see his mummy, my beautiful Francesca, in the doorway to our wardrobe. She wears a deep purple fitted sleeveless dress. It hugs her stunning figure and stretches over her enormous baby belly.

Our twins are due any day now and then we will be blessed and cursed with three babies under the age of two. She always said she wanted lots of kids.

Carrying Xav on my hip, I eagerly make my way over to her, desperate for a kiss after 12 hours apart.

"Hey darlin'," I whisper, kissing her gently. "How are you feeling? We don't have to stay late tonight, Matty will understand."

"I feel like a woman who has spent the day wrangling a chaotic toddler while heavily pregnant with twins," she teases. "Tonight will be fun. I can't wait to celebrate another Marino tying the knot."

She wraps her arms around my neck, kissing me deeply. "We might need to leave Xav with one of his uncles for a little bit though."

"Yeah? Why's that?" I play along.

"Because mummy needs some alone time with mama."

"Oh I see, well Mummy can have Mama whenever she wants," I kiss her again, then pull back, sighing and looking at our little boy.

He is gorgeous and such a Marino. He is dark enough that Elio or Matty is probably his biological father, but all three of my brothers donated while we were trying to get pregnant and we intentionally don't know whose swimmers were successful. Our son is a perfect mix of Marino and Rossi.

Matty's wedding is beautiful and there isn't a dry eye in the house when he tears up as his beautiful bride walks down the aisle to him. They're such an unusual couple in many ways, but I couldn't have picked anyone better for my stoic brother.

As tends to happen at Famiglia events, I get stuck at a table as family member after family member approaches me to show respect or let me know of what is happening in their lives. I watch my wife from afar as she works the room like the queen she is. Never have I ever met someone so graceful and dignified as Francesca Marino. Well, apart from that time she smashed up Elio's car.

Xavier is tired. He has his little head on her shoulder and his arms around her neck. I need to relieve her as soon as possible because the little bugger is getting heavy and for some unfathomable reason Francesca insisted on wearing five-inch heels while full-term with twins.

Francesca smiles so widely when she spots me walking towards her that I'm struck with the evergreen feeling that I am not worthy of her. My angel. My wife.

Massimo beats me over to her and extracts an exhausted Xavier from her arms. He doesn't wake as he is transferred to his youngest uncle's chest nor when Massi plants several kisses on his forehead.

"Massi, can you watch him for a bit? I need Giovanna to help me with something," Francesca asks innocently.

"Sure," he grins. "I hope that G gives you all the help you need." He winks.

The bathrooms at the country estate Matty hired for his big day are bloody over the top. Everything is big and shiny and ostentatious.

Francesca leads me into a spacious full-enclosed bathroom and the minute the door is shut behind us her mouth is on mine.

"Baby please, I'm aching," she whines adorably against my lips.

"What's aching, little darlin'?" I run my hands all over her, savouring every curve.

"What do you need?"

"I need you to fuck me, babe!" She cries desperately and I burst out laughing.

"Ohhhhhh," I can't stop laughing. "You're horny, baby. I thought your back was hurting or something."

"Stop laughing, this is serious, Giovanna! I've been aching for you all day."

"Oh baby, let me look after you." I look around. It isn't the most comfortable of places for fucking when one of you is pregnant with twins. "Do you want me to find somewhere more comfortable?"

"No! Just do it here.' She starts hitching up her tight dress until it is sitting above her bump. "I know this is seriously unattractive, but my body just needs some bloody relief, babe."

There is nothing unattractive about this woman. I sit on the closed toilet lid and have Francesca sit on my knee, her back to my chest. Spreading my legs wide, I hook each of her legs over mine to keep them open.

We share an awkward kiss over her shoulder and I slide a finger into her lacy underwear.

"Jesus Christ. You're soaking wet!"

"I told you," she groans and I get to work making my wife come twice in the bathroom at my brother's wedding.

She leans back into me afterward, her chest heaving and I kiss her behind her ear. We sit for a few minutes and I just listen to her thundering heartbeat returning to a normal beat.

Reluctantly, she stands on shaky legs and rolls her dress back down over her bump with some difficulty. She looks so adorably comical that I can't help laughing again.

"Feeling better?" I tease her.

She gives me a cheeky smile, but it almost immediately drops from her face. "I feel funny," she frowns and rubs her enormous belly.

"Funny how?" I stop laughing.

She freezes, her eyes locked on mine, and her pillowy lips drop open. She flattens a palm at the base of her abdomen and gasps as a small gush of water hits the bathroom floor.

"Best get you to the hospital," I kiss her on the forehead.

Several hours later, I am hit with a case of *deja vu* as I watch Francesca sweat, scream, and squeeze our second and third children out into the world.

She goes into total primal mother mode and I have never in my life seen anything as powerful and as incredible as my fearless wife giving birth. She always wanted this. Motherhood. And I have never seen anyone do it as fucking perfect as she does.

I count each of the fingers and toes on Celeste and Violet Marino's bodies and kiss each of their heads as they greedily latch onto a boob each. With her hair slick with sweat and not a lick of makeup on her face, Francesca's look of pure elation as she feeds our girls is the most exquisite thing I have ever seen.

Naturally, our peaceful moment lasts all of a few minutes as Massimo rushes into the room carrying a wild-eyed Xavier followed by a crying Sammy.

I hold Xavier over the bed so he can see his baby sisters suckling. He is in awe and uncharacteristically quiet. "Mine?" he asks looking from his sisters to me.

"Yes, son. Yours," I murmur to him. Francesca spots the tears rolling down my cheeks and blows me a hands-free kiss.

Matty and his bride arrive next and they have a good cry as they cuddle the girls too. The looks they exchange with each other make me think we should start a family sweepstake on how quickly there'll be another Marino on the way.

The room is packed. As full as my heart. We are all quietly gazing at the newest Marinos and there is a peacefulness despite our chaotic family.

"Look, not that childbirth isn't like a miracle or anything," Massimo breaks the silence. "But an actual miracle happened today…"

We all look at him wondering what on earth he could be about to say.

"Elio said he's fallen in love."

ACKNOWLEDGEMENTS

Thank you, first of all, to every single one of you who have read Giovanna's story. I have been a writer for a long time but you have made me an author. A dream come true.

It is difficult to thank everyone as thoroughly as they deserve when I'm writing under a pseudonym. I am so blessed to have the support system I have and I wish I could shout their names from the rooftops but this humble, cryptic expression of gratitude will have to do.

SSP, you are an angel and I love you. I dedicated this book to her because she is my everything. She has kept me sane through maddening times and been my sounding-board throughout. Without her I would not have had the confidence to see this book published.

Two parents in one, Dad deserves so much more than a mere thank you. He dedicated his life to us kids and has sacrificed more than we even know. Dad, never read this book please!

To my siblings, both. I love and miss you. I'm so proud of you and thank you for all of your inspiration. I hope you won't be too embarrassed that I wrote a smutty mafia romance. Reading your sister's descriptions of explicit sex scenes must be a bit weird.

Thank you also to my sibling-in-law. Thank you for the love and care you show your sister and our three fur babies.

If my Nan and Grandad were still alive they would never know about this book. Good Irish Catholics that they were, they would be saying Hail Marys and Our Fathers for a month of Sundays if they knew what I have written. But they are an ongoing inspiration for me. Grandad for being the exemplar of living for one's family and for his intelligence, wit, and grace. Nan for being a trailblazer for women's rights and never taking shit from anyone. One day I hope to write a female character with even half the drive, fierceness, and style of my grandmother.

To those who read my drafts and gave me invaluable advice, thank you. Georgina, Rowena, Carla, Miriam, Beth, Daphna; thanks for reading a lesbian romance despite being "strictly dickly".

To the women who have been on the frontlines with me in our real life fight. Things feel worse than ever right now. We see more violence and hatred than ever before. But it is always darkest before dawn. These are the death throes and it is scary but we are winning. Keep speaking up. We are worth speaking up for. Our lives and rights are important enough.

ABOUT THE AUTHOR

Victoria Arrow lives on an island in the Pacific Ocean with her beautiful partner and their three animal babies.*Giovanna* is her debut novel and she is currently working on Matteo, Elio, and Massimo's stories.

Printed in Great Britain
by Amazon

56344775R00218